A blue fireball splits the night skies over Ogden, Utah, and then crashes. For three decades the mystery of what fell to earth has been hidden from the American public by its own government. It is rumored to be a vehicle from another world.

For Professor Ted Lawrence the Ogden enigma is an interesting tale told by one of his students. He has no idea it will catapult him into a bizarre run for his life. In the blink of an eye Lawrence has been transformed from teacher to accused killer, from family man to dead man.

THE OGDEN ENIGMA
IS A NOVEL BASED ON INCREDIBLE FACT, AND AUTHOR GENE SNYDER IS AFRAID HE MAY BECOME THE CHARACTER IN HIS OWN BOOK.

THE OGDEN ENIGMA

GENE SNYDER

PLAYBOY PRESS
PAPERBACKS

DEDICATION:

To Sharon Jarvis, whose professionalism and insight helped shape the barest glimmer of an idea into a novel

ACKNOWLEDGMENTS:

To Ed Stouffer, for a number of vital ideas; and to Jacques Vallee, for information and inspiration. Many thanks to Sam Cicchino for needed technical information.

AUTHOR'S NOTE

The novel that follows is just what it purports to be: a work of fiction. To that much I can attest. And while what publishers call the "front matter" of a novel usually consists of an author's dedication and a few rapturous acknowledgments to the people who assisted in the work, *The Ogden Enigma* is a book that demands more. This note will illuminate the genesis of the plot as well as its nonfiction basis.

The discussions of "ley" lines are culled from the actual research of Alfred Watkins, Alexander Thom, Francis Hitching, and others, for whose groundbreaking research I am grateful. While the exact meaning of the lines is still conjectural, many have speculated as Wilhelm Reich did, that they are conduits of power, wellsprings of the raw energy of the planet, which Reich called "Orgone." Likewise, the discussions of ancient megalithic sites are based on the research of antiquarians and scholars too numerous to mention here.

Then, there are the things that are pure fabrication, the grist of the fiction writer's mill. They include Paxton College, the towns of Shore Park and Windlee, and, essentially, all of the characters in the book—except one. He's called by several names in the book, but for the purposes of this note, we'll call him "Charlie." While I can't say where "Charlie" came from or went to, I can assure you he's a real person. And, since November 1977, I've wondered about the strange story he told me.

It was late on a Wednesday night in the fall of 1977; I had just finished a lecture to a college class. The subject had been the unknown, the paranormal, and UFOs, things indigenous to a course that dealt with parapsychology and the occult. In the last hour of the lecture I noticed a man enter the large amphitheater and take a seat in the back. He was not one of my students. Rather, he appeared to be a visitor, perhaps a man whose own class had been dismissed early. I thought nothing of it, as I encourage visitors to drop into my class. I went on with the last part of the lecture, discussing UFOs, the Wheels of Ezekiel, the Great Texas Airship Mystery, the fictionalizations of Spielberg, and the very real research of Jacques Vallee. As I dismissed the class and prepared to leave, "Charlie" approached me.

He told a story of something secreted in the Utah desert for nearly three decades. He said the secret was housed in an airplane hangar at a U.S. Army supply base, near Ogden, Utah. He claimed that on a June night in 1950, five air force personnel had driven a flatbed truck onto the base in the middle of the night. The truck's cargo was covered with a tarpaulin that had been carefully lashed down. He went on to say that after driving the truck into the hangar, the five men hurriedly closed the doors and bent the lock bolts. In the days that followed, a huge security screen was erected around the hangar. It included electrified fences, guard dogs, and a restricted air traffic space above the building. An Air Force Security Service detachment, he maintained, still guarded the hangar, despite the fact that such a detachment would be unusual on an Army base.

The last part of the story was perhaps stranger than

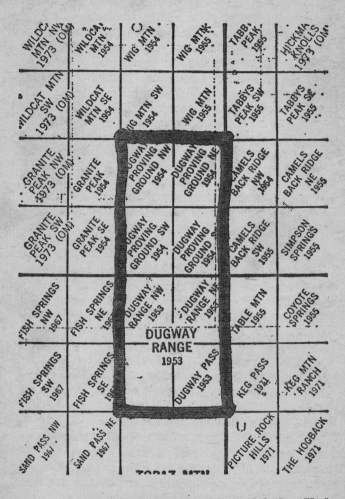

Fig. 1 Section of a topographical map of Ogden, Utah (U.S. Geological Survey), indicating the 1954 expansion of Dugway Proving Grounds.

the rest. He said that all of the five men who secreted
the cargo in the hangar were dead within a year after
the mission was completed. On this remark, he left, with
a vague half commitment to return and tell me more.
He never did. I tried to reach him in the wake of the
story. I never succeeded. I have not seen "Charlie"
since.

In the days that followed, my writer's curiosity was
aroused, and I embarked on a research project to find
whether there was any shred of truth to the story. The
first results were not promising. I could find no record
of a U.S. Army Supply Depot, Ogden, which "Charlie"
had contended lay to the north of the U.S. Army base
at Dugway, Utah. If there was no base, then there was
no mysterious hangar at its desolate, northern end—
and the chances were that there was no secret. The
story was probably a tall tale told by "Charlie." His
protestations of its accuracy, as well as his claim that
he had been part of one of the Air Force security detachments at the base in the early seventies, dwindled
to insignificance. But the story was so intriguing that I
determined to write it as a novel, with the secret in the
hangar as a premise.

In the latter stages of drafting the novel, something
happened that made me think back to the original story
and again ponder its possible validity. Inadvertently I
came across some maps that might partially refute my
original dismissal of the story. The first map (Figure
One) indicates that the U.S. Army base at Dugway
more than doubled its size in 1954. As it expanded, it
would have enveloped the apparently fictitious "Supply
Base" that had been mentioned in the story. The second
map (Figure Two) shows a single triangle, indicating a
part of the Dugway installation set far to the north of
the rest of the base. It is in the exact place that
"Charlie" said the hangar would be found. The third

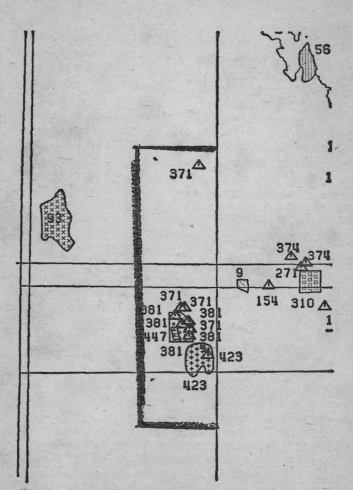

Fig. 2 Installation map of Dugway. The cluster at the bottom represents various structures at Dugway proper. Note the separate lone structure at the northernmost end of the newly acquired land.

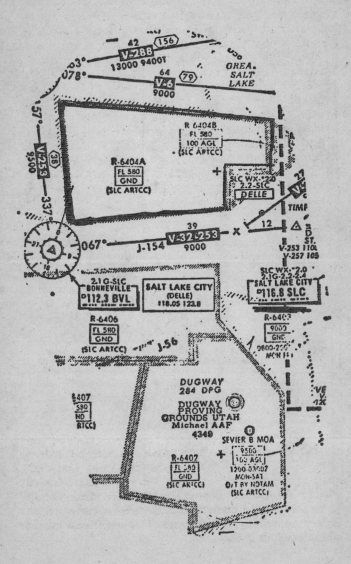

map (Figure Three) is a pilot's map of the area, showing a restricted airspace in exactly the same place that the mysterious "Charlie" said it would be found.

We are left with only questions. Is the hangar there? Was something secreted in it thirty years ago? If so, what? Is it some secret project gone wrong? Is it something mundane? Or is it something exotic, something awesome, something terrifying, as "Charlie's" story seemed to indicate?

And so we are left with a novel and a lingering, haunting question: Just how much of this incredible story is true? The maps shown in the figures are as unclassified as service station roadmaps. They are available from the government for the asking, perhaps with the payment of printing and postage costs. So I leave it to the reader to decide.

For my part, it was the premise for this novel and food for much thought.

Gene Snyder

Fig. 3 Section of a jet navigation map, showing restricted air space over Dugway and its northern extension. (The "R" designation preceding any four-digit number represents restricted air space.) The unrestricted corridor in between is used by planes landing at Salt Lake City airport and for coast-to-coast commercial jet flights; apparently a concession to avoid diversion of commercial air traffic.

CHAPTER ONE

Salisbury 2600 B.C.

The wind was merciless, driving the snow before it like some avenging demon. The great flatlands offered nothing that might stop it, no trees, no hillocks. Nothing. The only shelter lay ahead. And that was the way the lone figure in rags moved, always ahead, as relentlessly as the wind; his tracks across the snowdrifts formed a flawless straight line. Ahead, the snow was smooth, untouched, and less than a mile behind, the wind had erased the blemishes he left. The lone traveler knew that if he fell, or stopped to rest, the snow and wind would turn him into a small, dead, artistically sculptured mound in less than an hour.

Ganth could no longer feel his feet. It had been hours since the crude footwrappings had frozen to his toes. He was tempted to stop and unwrap them so that he could move barefoot. His bare feet would give him more information than the wrappings would give warmth. They told him when the warm spring was coming, and when the first frost blanketed the great stone circle of Avebury which now lay a week's trek behind him. But Ganth knew that he dare not stop, nor even slow.

Suddenly, he paused, raising his head from the protection of the skin robe his mother had lovingly sewn for him. His head popped up and turned from side to side, like a hound sniffing the air for a hare. But the clue he sought was far subtler than a scent, far more elusive. He'd been the only child in the clan who could sense it at all. The Gift was known to his family, but it was rare. They had called it a dozen things: the path of the gods; the moon's road; the sun map. The names had meant nothing to Ganth. He had never seen the sun or the moon, and the only thing his mother had ever said about the gods was that they had touched him. *Touched him!* The phrase made Ganth laugh, despite the blasts of wind-laced snow. *What a thing to call it!*

Ganth had been born blind.

Suddenly, Ganth stopped. There was something there. Yes, something like a tiny voice almost lost in the shrieking, snow-laced wind. His head moved from side to side, half confused, half knowing. His hand reached out from under the skin robe, and his fingers undulated as if he were kneading some bread dough that floated invisibly in front of him in the snowy air. The movement was practiced, methodical. Slowly, his right hand came from the warmth of the cape. With the same practiced, almost agonizing, slowness, he raised it parallel to his right shoulder. *Yes. There. That's one.* He could feel the tingling in his right hand. His left hand, held in front of him, still kneaded the air, searching. He moved it a fraction to the right, then to the left. A little more . . . a little . . . *yes.*

He'd found the crossing point. He turned to his right and started off again, certain that he was nearing his goal. His hand, held before him toward the whiteness he could not see, tingled, leading him unerringly. It was the Gift that let him feel it. The Gift he hated, the Gift he'd have gladly traded for the sight that everyone else in the clan had. But for now, at least, it was something that was keeping him alive and moving him ahead . . . toward the great stone ring. He quickened his pace. The tingling was growing stronger, pulsating up his arm. It was stronger than he had ever felt when he had been in the fields with his mother.

It was less than an hour later when he could start to

feel the warmth on his frozen face. *Yes. There. Just ahead, now.*

What he felt was the heat from a huge beacon fire in the distance. Its flames reached to the sky and were haloed red and orange by the driving wind and snow. Plumes of snow billowed high in the sky, crystals flickering in the heat of a fire that had burned for a full week. It was a tradition, or so Ganth's mother had told him when he was prepared for the pilgrim's journey. She had given him food and drink for seven days only. That was a part of the tradition, too. The acolytes had to make the journey in a week. Ganth had asked why and his mother had simply clucked. It was the way it had always been. That was all she knew. Ganth assumed that if it took more than a week, the acolyte had no business going on the trek in the first place. And with this terrible storm, he thought, only the truly Gifted would get through. There could not be many of them. The gods from the sky were even-handed. They took your sight and gave you the Gift in return. And still, not all the blind received it. A single pilgrimage to the great stone circle was all a blind candidate was allowed in a lifetime. To prove that you had the Gift you had to find the stone circle using the sight of the gods rather than your eyes. If you arrived in the seven-day period, after enduring hunger, thirst, and the perils of crossing rivers, you were a valid candidate for the priesthood.

Ganth could almost shape the pinpricks of energy in his hand. He'd been able to do it since he'd started crawling across the beaten clay floor of his mother's hut to the warmth of what she'd called the fire. That night, Ganth, then a toddler, had stopped short of the fire and turned, moving to explore something more interesting in the cold corner of the hut. His mother had stared at him for a long minute as the child whose blindness she mourned, but stoically accepted, reached out a grimy, pudgy hand and shaped the air before him . . . exploring. She'd held her breath as Ganth had started to giggle. The feeling of the straight line of energy that his hands and his mind touched was pleasant. A toy. It was an hour before she'd dared to form the thought. The Gift. It was that rare.

Suddenly, Ganth started to run ahead, heedless of the obstacles that might lie in his path. He laughed, and his laughter was carried away by the howling wind. He had made it. The priesthood was his!

He stopped. He had forgotten. He had to be accepted by the priests; taken as a member of the order, taught the secrets of the skygods, shown the mystic secrets of the great stone circle and the lines of energy that pulsed from it, keeping Man connected to the gods. A shudder of fear ran through him. What if the priests rejected him?

It was only a few minutes later when the white-robed keepers of the ring trudged out to meet Ganth in the snow.

An old man with a raspy voice took Ganth by the arm and led him to a warm hut with a crackling wood fire and piles of skins that muffled the chill of the clay floor. The old man said little. He unwrapped the skins from Ganth's feet and, with skilled hands, carefully rubbed the circulation back into them. He moved Ganth close to the fire, like a man well practiced in leading the blind. He pressed a bowl of steaming but unrecognizable broth into Ganth's hand, and the boy wolfed it down. After he finished, Ganth listened as the old man started to speak, and he realized that he'd have to fight the drowsiness that had come with the fire and the food. This was not a time to sleep, not when everything had to be done by morning.

"My boy, you are very late for us to consider." There was a stern tone in the old man's voice. Still, it was not one of anger. Rather, it spoke of obligation, a sternness born of faithful performance of duties over decades. The comment seemed to hold Ganth's future in it.

"But—ah . . ." Ganth's protest stopped when he realized that he did not know the name of the old, craggy-voiced priest.

"I am Borag."

Borag! The name struck him like a fist. The high elder himself. It spoke well of the chances of any acolyte to be taken personally to the old man's hut. It also gave the lie to the old man's comment. He could feel the joy his mother would squeal to the other members of the clan when the word was sent back that Ganth of Avebury would remain at the ring and join the priesthood.

But he forced himself to hide his feelings. A strange, tingling sensation was spreading warmth from his stomach upward into his chest and down to his thighs. He had to take care, so that he did not laugh or giggle.

The old man questioned him, forcing him to remain awake to fight the exhaustion that the cold had built and the warm soup had made irresistible.

"When did you first give evidence of the Gift? How is it you feel the flow of the energy? Why do you believe that this makes you worthy? After all, the gods touch many, and very few have the true Gift."

Ganth flushed at the last question. The fatigue was starting to make him reckless. His answers were starting to drift, and he was starting to have trouble separating the past of his childhood from the present of Borag's hut. He was angry at everything: the cold, his mother and the gods . . . and, yes, even mad at the Gift. It all came out in a rage, through the sleepiness and despite the presence of the old man. He raged against being chosen, cursed the gods for what had been more of a curse than a blessing. After a few moments, half spent with the rage of eighteen years vented, he realized to whom he spoke. He could feel a great stone weight settle in his stomach when all he could hear from Borag was silence and the hint of shallow breathing. There would be no returning home, not now. Nor would his mother be able to brag of his triumph to the clan. All of it was lost, gone in the rage of a few minutes. He fell silent, and the silence stood between them for a long minute before Borag spoke.

"You are rash, Ganth." It sounded like a death sentence. There was nothing for it but to accept the pronouncements that Ganth was sure the old man would make.

"Yes, Elder Borag . . . and . . . and . . ." The word came hard to his lips. It was a whisper. ". . . unworthy." He bit his lip when he said the word. If he'd said more there would have been women's tears in his voice.

"Are you always so?"

"No . . . no, Elder Borag."

Ganth paused for a second and swallowed hard. He could still taste the soup.

"But. . . ."

"But?"

"I spoke the truth. It was not something I desired, ever. I'd rather be planting the crop and seeing it, and the colors that I cannot ever see. I mean. . . ." A sob escaped.

"You mean that you never meant to speak as you did, to say that much of the truth, especially to me. This is your only chance to be something more meaningful than a cripple in the clan. And you feel now that you have let all of it go in a moment of anger. It's right. Isn't it?"

Breaking down completely into shudders and sobs, Ganth could only nod spasmodically.

"The fact that you arrived here at all, and in time for the Dawn of the Circle, says that you are right to be tested. The honesty of your rage says it even more strongly. There are many imposters who come . . . many."

"But," he sobbed, "I was disrespectful . . . to you . . . you who decide . . . I . . ."

"It was the soup. It would not let you say anything

but what was in your heart of hearts. You will be tested in the ceremony. Be at rest about that." The man's voice had become a soft whisper. "It does not mean you will be accepted, though. *That* is the choice of the Great Ones we serve. It is the choice of the Gods of the Dawn. Here." Something was placed in Ganth's hand. "You will hold this. You will not let it go until you are told to do so. Presently, priests will come and dress you. There is not much time, and I must prepare."

And he was gone.

Ganth fingered the *thing*. It felt like a twig, smooth and rounded to a fineness that Ganth had never known. He rolled the coolness between his fingers. He had never known a twig to be so cool before . . . like an icicle.

As his sensitive fingers traced their way around the cool stick, he could feel the etched relief of carvings and he tried to read the symbols with his fingertips. After a few moments he realized that there was no chance that he could divine any meaning from them. They were simple decorations, carved with a skill so great that Ganth could not imagine the talent of the sculptor. After a few moments he realized the truth.

The gods themselves had made the carvings!

Only they could work with such precision and such delicacy. He fingered the end of the stick and realized that one part of the thing could move and the other could not. He paused, wondering whether he dare explore further, especially after his earlier rashness had almost angered Borag. But he couldn't resist.

Slowly, he rotated the top of the sticklike thing until he heard a sharp click. The crispness of the sound startled him and he almost dropped the cold, hard stick. Frightened, he tried to turn the top back to its original position, not realizing that he was turning it in the wrong direction. There was another click, and the stick started to vibrate. For a second, Ganth felt at ease. The vibration was the same as in the lines of energy

that he used to find his way in the snow. It was the
same pulsating flow of power that flowed across the
countryside unimpeded by mountains or rivers; the
same tingling, invisible river that came from the skygods and flowed across the earth and then ultimately
back to them.

Suddenly the stick's vibration was more intense, more
powerful. Had he sinned? Had he done something
wrong?

In a few seconds, the raw surge of divine energy was
roaring from the stick, and the thing was starting to
whine and scream. The sound was making a fire in his
head and it was all he could do not to cry out. Forcing
himself to maintain his concentration, Ganth managed
to click the top of the thing back to its original location.
The vibration ceased. The whine stopped with a terrifying suddenness. Outside, two young priests ducked
their heads and entered the hut.

The next two hours flew past, as the priests dressed
Ganth in the white robes of an acolyte and cleansed his
body. They led him to the circle and told him where to
stand. If there were other acolytes, he did not know it.
He did not feel the cold, nor the gale that had pursued
him. There was an eternity of chanting and then a hush.

It was beginning. It. *It!*

The familiar tingling began in his fingertips and
roared through his forearms like a raging fire. His head
seemed to explode with a sound like the wind—but not
the wind. It was a screaming wail that spoke only one
thing, one unutterable thing . . . the gods. They were
making their choice.

The scream ceased abruptly . . . now it was deathly
silent. Ganth tried to think through the terror that
gripped him. How? How would he know? Suddenly,
he could feel the heat.

And then, the light . . . *the great blue light* that
Ganth could see through his tears.

Salisbury June 20, 1950

It was just before midnight, and in five hours the dawn of a summer solstice would rise directly over the heelstone of the great circle, and its dusty rays would trace a flawlessly straight path between the great sarsen blocks and fall on the killing stone of the great altar. Still deserted, the great ring of stones would soon be crowded to overflowing with a cult of Druids, gathering to celebrate the coming of summer. They would come with their white robes and oak boughs and incense and cameras. If there was a real meaning to their ceremony, aside from the frivolous reenactment of what had once been true power, the modern Druids hid it well. They would arrive soon, but for now the plain was empty and quiet, except for the whisper of a breeze from the distant hills.

It was one minute after midnight when the rustle of the breeze was joined by a low, guttural moan that seemed to emanate from the great stones themselves. In seconds, the moan rose in pitch and increased in ominous intensity. The great sarsens and the lesser bluestones started to vibrate, amplifying the sound until it became a scream that echoed back and forth across the Salisbury Plain.

The bluestones started to glow.

In less than a minute, the light was so intense that its raw, blue energy could be seen for miles, had anyone been there to see.

Then . . . there was something else.

Twenty miles above the ancient circle, the pinpoint of light streaked across the sky at a speed too great to calculate. In the split particle of an instant, and with an astounding mathematical precision, its path exactly bisected the altar stone of the circle, which, below, was an almost invisible pinpoint of light. In its wake, the bluestones ceased to glow. The screaming wail diminished, and in a few seconds all that could be heard at Salisbury was the whisper of the summer wind.

The blur of speeding light slashed across the Atlantic in minutes, triggering early warning radar sets in the eastern United States. It followed a dead straight line across the continent, overflying Cleveland, Chicago, Omaha, and Cheyenne. It was over the Great Salt Lake when it seemed to stop suddenly in mid-flight.

It descended quickly, coming to earth in a deserted area, some eight miles north of Interstate 40, halfway between Salt Lake City and the Nevada border, not far from the air force base at Ogden, Utah. . . .

CHAPTER TWO

New Jersey Now

"But the Druids were latecomers. Look at the chart." The tall, dark man fielded the question with a deftness that bespoke a smooth professionalism. The image he presented to the class was cool and casual. They would never know of the gut-wrenching turmoil that was seething inside him.

"Oh, Dr. Lawrence?"

Ted turned to a young face in the back row of the half-filled amphitheater.

"Yes?" His voice was controlled. Ted reminded himself to be patient, that the students' questions were meaningful.

As Ted Lawrence acknowledged the question, the girl seemed suddenly shy, silent for a second.

Ted smiled warmly, brushed back a comma of shaggy brown hair, and flashed through a memory that even his unfriendly colleagues considered phenomenal. "Come on, Alicia. Anyone can disagree. My lectures are always open forums. Just be prepared to defend the point."

The girl flushed at the mention of her name. Lawrence memorized the nearly one hundred names of the class on the first night. After that, he called all of the students by their first names for the rest of the course. He also managed to get readings on their college files and commit them to memory. It made the students think he was indeed psychic. And what else should an instructor be who taught a course called "Consciousness and the Paranormal"? And Ted *was* psychic, at least a little bit, as evidenced by his Rhine card scores. Not all of his skill as a teacher was a product of an eidetic memory.

However, Ted Lawrence did know that Alicia was shy, the product of chauvinistic parenting in a Hispanic home. It was her intellect that had gotten her into Paxton State College, and it was her grades that maintained her scholarship. Saying things in public, coming from a parochial school background, was hard, though. Ted reasoned that the mention of her name and the casual pose would loosen the shyness. He was right.

"But, Dr. Lawrence, Hitching and Gerald Hawkins and all the rest of the researchers say that the Druids were latecomers, too. That's not what the point is. Ponchon says that the carbon dating is off by almost two thousand years. So, I agree that the Druids are latecomers. What I have trouble with is the connection between Stonehenge, at Salisbury, and the network to the other circles. The one you're calling . . . Lee lines?"

Ted smiled again. He moved to the blackboard and took a tiny piece of chalk. He wrote the phrase on the board and announced it, as well: "L-E-Y lines." He looked back up at her and let his eyes scan the class. "Alfred Watkins called them that as a result of his Welsh background. Instead of planting crops, farmers allowed the ground to *leay* or remain fallow. Watkins noticed straight lines in the ground where things didn't grow. They formed . . ." He moved to the overhead projector that shone on the wall above him. It carried the ghostly image of a series of intersecting lines that crisscrossed England and spread eastward through France. ". . . what Watkins called a straight path system. The connection that gives you trouble, Alicia, is that Watkins first noted the lines when he was doing a survey study of Stonehenge. I . . ."

He stopped for a second and realized that Alicia's

confusion must be shared by a number of others in the lecture. *Damn it. I forgot to mention it.* Ted's lightning mind stung itself for a second in self-criticism. It was a key connection, and he'd failed to make it. He'd been going through the lecture in his sleep. He shrugged mentally and forgave himself. It was only fair to allow himself a slip, especially after Lisa, after the final *auto da fe* that had concluded the ten years of marital agony. It had happened only minutes before he'd left the house. He was sure that his wife had planned it that way.

"Yes," she shrieked. *"Yes! You can have them . . . both of them, with my blessing. You've won, Ted. You've won. I'm getting out, and you can have the custody of those precious darlings. I don't really want to see them. I don't want you or your fucking middle-class mediocrity. I don't care how many papers you deliver, or journals you get written up in. You're never going to be more than a churchmouse college professor . . ."*

She was starting to sputter.

"Lisa?" There was a film of restraint over his rage.

"I'm sick of hearing that fucking forced calm, too. You had your chance, Teddy Boy. . . ."

There was a sneering venomous curl to her mouth. Ted was appalled at how sensuous he'd thought her mouth was when they'd met in college. But that was before he'd married Lisa Ryan, married the wealth of the Ryans . . . Ryan Plastics, Ryan Aerospace.

". . . My father gave you every chance in the world to make something of yourself. But no. No. You buried yourself at Paxton. My father—"

"You should have married dear Daddy, Lisa. After all, he is the only one you ever really wanted. I even look like him. Hasn't your analyst ever mentioned that to you? Poor little Electra." He bit off each word, hating himself for saying them. He was letting her get to him, and he knew that was a victory of sorts for her.

Lisa was quivering with fury. Her green eyes flashed,

and she flicked a hand across her long red hair, sweep-
ing it back from her face. "You are a slimy fuck, do
you know that?"

He turned and walked away from her. He moved
across the kitchen and picked up a battered and pain-
fully swollen briefcase. "I'm going to class." The forced
calm had returned to his voice. "See your lawyer after
the weekend, and I'll see mine." He didn't look back
after he closed the door behind him.

He looked up at the dark-eyed girl in the auditorium
seat. The argument had flashed through his mind in a
split second, like a tiny phrase passing through a tape
recorder on fast forward. "I guess I didn't make that
connection earlier. I'm sorry. Thank you for catching
it."

He started to pace and speak, his eyes darting quickly to the clock on the auditorium wall. His explanation
of the connection between Watkins's ley lines and
Stonehenge would be the last thing he'd leave them
with in the lecture. It would wrap things up on the right
note.

". . . so when he looked out from the heelstone at
Stonehenge, Watkins saw that it fell in a straight line
with a standing stone far off in the field. Then he found
that the far stone matched up with a man-made notch
at the top of a distant hill. When he got to the hilltop,
he could form another straight line with a burial mound
and past that the line intersected a church steeple . . ."

He quickly sketched a ley on the board. ". . . on further, the straight line passed through another stone
circle. And then the process started to repeat itself."

He explained to them the subsequent research, the
astro-archaeology of Gerald Hawkins that connected
Stonehenge with the map of the sky as it might have
been seen more than fifty centuries ago. He connected
the sky maps in stone with the straight lines of Watkins
and the dowsing research of Hutching. It all formed a
pattern, he said, one that we've forgotten how to inter-

pret. Carefully, Ted left the last links unforged. The students were starting to stir and pile up books when he heard the question he was waiting to end the evening on. It came from an older woman, seated near the far end of the auditorium. She wore a smart gray suit and her quietly elegant jewelry and clothes spoke of matronly wealth. She was like so many of the others who took the course: monied, older, with grown children, lots of money and time on her hands. And, like the others, she'd taken the course out of curiosity and grown more enthusiastic as the semester wore on.

"Dr. Lawrence?"

"Yes, Mrs. Hull?"

"What is the pattern of all of it? What does it mean?"

Ted shrugged. "I don't know. I have some ideas. What are yours?" His voice rose a bit. "What are all of your ideas? Everyone come in next week with a hypothesis that might explain all of this. Have a happy Thanksgiving. Good night."

They straggled out, starting the long, cold trek to the distant parking lot and the four-day Thanksgiving holiday. Ted took a deep breath and exhaled audibly. It was a holiday he was not looking forward to, but at least he'd gotten through the night's lecture. No one had caught the pain, the anguish. His mask was strong. Ted Lawrence was a professional.

As he tossed his notes into the briefcase and tortured the latches shut, he could feel the fatigue start to slip quietly up the backs of his legs. He had paced through most of the lecture. It was a characteristic that most of his colleagues winked at; they said you could always tell how involved Lawrence was in what he taught by the amount of pacing he did. Ted wondered for a second how many miles he had worn into the auditorium rug in the years that he'd taught the course. How many tonight? Too many. The fight with Lisa came on the heels of a three-day writing jag, designed to break the back of a novel, now a month overdue at the publisher.

Yet he knew a reserve of one day was still there; he had developed an internal barometer of his remaining energy after a year with a line company in Viet Nam. *That* was pushing the reserves to the limit. He was nowhere near it now. He'd get a night's sleep and face Lisa and the "arrangements" in the morning. It was something he did not look forward to, a Pyrrhic victory at best. He pulled on his parka and turned to face three students who came down the aisles in search of answers, clarifications, praise, perhaps even closeness to a man who was rapidly becoming an idol.

"Yes, the paper can research pyramids, but include the research of Pochon. Of course, a paper researching the monoliths of Easter Island could be attempted, but there's not a great deal of data to work from." He rattled off the answers and the students scribbled notes hastily in spiral notebooks emblazoned with the coat of arms of Paxton College. They were something new, hawked by the bookstore. Ted noticed that Mrs. Hull, one of the few who remained, was writing in one.

"That's something new. I don't think we ever printed notebook covers before."

Mrs. Hull smiled. "Not much paper and a thick cover. OK to buy if you're in a rush, but not really worth the money."

Ted smiled back. "I'm surprised Oscar Small didn't have his picture emblazoned on them. They'd sell more of them, then."

Mrs. Hull's eyebrows raised querulously. "They would?"

"Sure. The students and a whole contingent of the faculty could rip off the cover and use it for a dartboard. It's thick enough."

The matron threw back her head and laughed. After a minute she grew serious. "Do you really want a hypothesis for next week?"

He shrugged. "Not really. Just an idea or two. I just

want to pique a student curiosity or two. Something that might carry over the holiday."

She nodded and said she wanted to do a project on the relationships he'd discussed. Ted told her to start with the books mentioned in the lecture, and, when she'd read more, he'd give her some possible theses to pursue. She said good night and moved away a few steps when she suddenly turned, as if she'd forgotten something.

"Dr. Lawrence? About President Small . . ."

Ted smiled, cautiously. The smile covered the distaste he felt for the man.

"He's a neighbor of mine."

"And?" Ted could not be sure what the woman would say next. He imagined gnawing on shoe leather left in his mouth by an intruding foot.

"I agree. He's a prig. A little man. Your clashes with him have won you a lot of 'followers' among my neighbors."

"You mean the neighbors like to play champions of the underdog?"

"No. But he's a petty bureaucrat, and someone has to say it. You've taken on an admirable cause. A thankless one, too, I think."

"Thank you." Ted smiled. It was good to hear that there was support for at least one of the battles he was fighting.

Mrs. Hull was going out the door when Ted saw the man in the last row. He had been sitting quietly in the dim light, waiting. Ted groaned inwardly. The last thing he needed was another student asking about a project. The shank of the evening was starting to wear through his patience, though Mrs. Hull's comment had given it a bit more cheer. Perhaps he could put the man's questions off, at least until next week.

As Ted moved up the carpeted stairs, the small slight man in his mid-thirties got to his feet and moved to intercept him. Ted recognized the man and quickly flipped through his mental file for the name. Howard . . . Charles Howard. The man was quiet, associating with none of the other students in the class. Ted had read the man as a loner, concerned with completing the course as anonymously as possible. Howard, as far as Ted remembered, did not make a single contribution, nor ask a single question, throughout the course. Why now? Why a question or a conference now, Ted wondered, feeling the aggravation starting to swell inside of him. As Charles Howard neared him at the top of the steps, Ted could begin to read why, before the man spoke. Howard's slender hands moved like birds. His forehead was dotted with tiny beads of perspiration and his eyes carried a look that Ted had seen more than a decade before, in Viet Nam. It was the look of men in the middle of an ambush. It was a look of fear.

"Dr. Lawrence?"

"Yes? It's Mr. Howard, right?"

Howard smiled a tight, frightened smile. "Yes. I'm surprised you remembered. I know I haven't said much in class."

"I try to remember all my students' names." The response was terse, cool, efficient. There was no sense in getting chummy. Still, the look of fear in Howard's eyes seemed to beckon to Ted. There was something of a plea in it.

"What is it that you wanted, Mr. Howard?"

The man's hands wrung for a second before they started their bird-like nervousness again.

"Well . . . it's . . . I don't know how to start."

Ted groaned inwardly. This was the last thing he needed. "Start anywhere, Mr. Howard. But please start. I want to get home."

Howard nodded with a slight twitch. The man's eyes darted across the auditorium, now quite empty. After a few seconds his eyes returned to Ted's. They were cold, blue, and still frightened.

"You were in the service, Dr. Lawrence."

Ted blinked. "Is that a question or a statement?" Ted could feel that there was a slight trace of an edge starting to creep into his voice. Fatigue, pressures, Lisa, Oscar Small, an overdue book contract. All of them were coming together, and he didn't want them to.

"I . . . I gathered that from the lectures. You mentioned the service once or twice. You also mentioned Viet Nam, and something about Psy-Ops."

Ted could feel the hackles rise on the back of his neck. *He had never mentioned Psy-Ops.* It was not something he was proud of, nor did he often speak about it.

"I never said anything about Psy-Ops, Mr. Howard. I did mention being in the service. All I said was that I was a captain in the army in Viet Nam."

"Oh. Well, maybe it was something I wanted to hear, something that would let you help me to make sense of all of this. You weren't in Psy-Ops, then?"

The question, placed in the form of a clarification, was either innocent and disarmingly blunt, or clever and well put. And it was dredging up a part of Ted's service years that he'd rather have forgotten.

It had been in the last three months of his tour. He could smell going home as he could feel the fear of not staying alive to see that day. One could only lead a rifle company on search missions for so long. After a time, the law of averages caught up. Three quarters of the original company were either killed or medevac cases. Though he wore no symbol of rank on patrol, it was only a matter of time before a Cong would pop him, if not because he was an officer, simply because he was a target.

Then he'd taken up an offer from another captain. The man had needed combat time to round out his tour; it was something valuable to an army regular. Combat duty with a line company weighed more heavily on promotion boards than desk time with a Psychological Operations unit did. They'd managed to arrange a transfer, thanks to a case of scotch presented to Ted's adjutant and another presented to the Psy-Ops captain's superior in Saigon. Ironically, it was only days after he reported to his new unit and saw his new quarters, complete with hot water and flush toilets, that Ted had learned of the other captain's death on his first patrol.

For Ted, the last three months of the tour, the time spent in Psy-Ops, was nearly as grueling and grisly as combat. He learned about the political corruption, the black market, the assassinations. kidnappings, wholesale slaughter of villages in the "Phung Wong" program. It all represented the detestable underside of a guerilla war. It was not something to be proud of, nor was it ever intended to be so. It was survival, pure and simple. Still, it was something that Ted rarely mentioned. And now, Howard's circuitous questions reminded him of the circular rhetoric of the interrogator. He had learned that. too. in those last three months.

"Mr. Howard. Whether I was or was not in Psy-Ops is no real concern of yours. Now, just what do we have to discuss?"

"I'm sorry, Doctor. All I wanted to do was to make sure that you'd carried some security clearances. It would allow you to see some truth in what I was saying. You see, if I told you that my security clearances were T.S., COSMIC. CRYPTO, ALPHA-RED, DARPA-RED and several others, would that mean that I might be telling the truth?"

Ted nodded. "It might " Inside, Ted whistled to himself. He'd named some of the most elite security clearances that the armed forces had. Ted himself had carried the first two mentioned. and had been cleared for the last one, though he'd turned down the Defense Department job that had required it. As far as Ted could remember, even the names of DARPA-RED and other such clearances were classified. What was this man getting to? What was ALPHA-RED? No. Ted pushed the curiosity aside. "OK. I have some familiarity with those kinds of clearances. You have credibility. What do you want to talk to me about?"

Howard's hands stopped moving. He riveted Ted with his eyes. They held the intense look of a man who thought his very life might rest on the believability of what he was about to say. It was not a look that could be faked, and Ted knew it.

"There are three parts to it. I'll take them in order and then I'm going to ask for a reaction . . . not a put-on or a polite smile. Just a reaction."

He cleared his throat but his eyes did not move from Ted's. "The first part of it happened in 1950. I'd give this part a B-two rating. I'm sure you'll know what that means, no matter how cagily you fielded my earlier questions."

Ted nodded, though Charles Howard did not really seem to stop for any acknowledgment. Howard began his incredible story . . .

It was a warm June night in 1950. At the U.S. Army Supply Depot in Ogden, Utah, warm westerly winds swept in from the Great Salt Lake, blowing plumes of dust across the midnight to two A.M. guard shift as they rode back to their barracks. In minutes, other sleepy GIs would take their places, peering through the dust, squinting into miles of pancake-flat desert. The mounting of the guard at the depot was more of an army tradition than a function of real security. Though the Korean War raged more than eight thousand miles to the west, no one really believed that "gooks" would attack a sleepy supply depot in the American desert. After all, what was there to steal? Paint? Mess trays? Sacks of cement? No. Ogden was a tomb; the post where career officers and enlisted men were sent to serve their last tours before retirement. Nothing exciting ever happened there . . . until two A.M.

Taking the most secluded route possible through the stacks of supplies, a U.S. Air Force flatbed truck moved slowly across the base through the swirling clouds of windblown dust. On the trailer, the cargo lay carefully lashed down and shrouded by a heavy tarp. Surrounding the cargo were three Air Force officers, armed with rifles and sidearms. In the cab, two airmen moved the huge driving rig ahead on a predetermined path. The sentries squinted for a second at the truck, then waved it past. It was the only thing that broke the monotony of their two-hour watch.

Lumbering eastward, the truck left the supply area of the post and moved out into the miles of surreal desert at the east end of the post. It had been the army's goal to expand the post in that direction when they bought the land in 1945. But, with the end of the war, there seemed no need to build any more than the single structure that stood out on the horizon: a large old aircraft hangar.

With the hiss of airbrakes, the truck slid to a stop in front of the hangar's huge sliding doors. With the headlights to illuminate their work, the two airmen in the cab got out and unlatched the bolts, then, with difficulty, dragged the creaking, rusty doors open. The officers unslung their rifles, ready for anything.

With the doors open just enough to admit the truck, the two airmen jumped back in the cab, and gunned the truck ahead into the gloomy, dark interior. With the lights and the motor still running, the five men scurried away from the truck and out through the doors. The five of them swung the huge door shut and methodically slammed the bolts home. Then they bent the bolts with pinchbars, and assembled in a small group a few yards from the hangar doors.

The senior officer, bearing a nametag that identified him as Major Thayer, slipped a few sheets of paper from inside his starched fatigue shirt and started to read several paragraphs to the assembled group.

"Now listen to this. It comes from Chapter Eighteen, Section Three of the National Security Act. When I finish, each of you will be required to sign a statement indicating that you have heard the provisions of the act, and that you swear to abide by them. Is that clear?"

The two other officers nodded immediately, while the two enlisted men glanced furtively at one another for a long second before also nodding.

He looked to each of the four men for a long minute, then started to read.

"An act of treason against the United States of America is defined as follows . . ."

As he read the long statement, the four men shifted restlessly from foot to foot. It was the second time in less than twenty-four hours that they had been read the same statement. The first time had been when they had been assembled in the middle of the night and been assigned to the mission. They had signed then and they would sign now. It was all a formality.

". . . any of the abovementioned actions," the youngish major droned, ". . . will, if carried out in time of war or national emergency, be considered an act of treason against the United States of America. The punishment for such actions will be death or life imprisonment." Again, he looked up, fixing his dark eyes on each of the others in turn. "Is all of that clear?"

They again nodded, and he gave them each a copy of the document. They signed.

Seconds after the major tucked the documents back into his shirt, the five men fanned out to form a primitive defense perimeter around the hangar.

It was less than an hour later when a large army truck full of guards arrived at the hangar. It was followed by a flatbed similar to the one inside. Quickly and efficiently, troops fanned out and relieved the five who had set up the security cordon for the hangar.

Then oxyacetylene torches were rolled to the doors, where huge, six-inch-thick slabs of armor plate were welded across the doors. Meanwhile, other GIs painted over the windows to hide the enclosed flatbed from the eyes of the curious. It was nearly dawn when an Air Force sedan arrived to take away the three officers and two airmen that had manned the flatbed.

In the weeks that followed, details of carefully screened airmen and soldiers erected a series of three fences around the hangar. The middle fence was charged with forty thousand volts.

In the years that followed, the United States Air Force Security Service was assigned the responsibility for the security of the hangar. A crew of six hand-picked and carefully cleared men was assigned to hangar security for a full two-year tour. When they completed their tour, they were relieved and another crew was assigned. Their orders were to turn back anyone attempting to penetrate the outer fence, and, should the fence be penetrated, they were ordered to kill any interloper, without warning. If such a penetration should occur, the detachment was warned that they all would be court martialed for criminal neglect of duty.

Among themselves, the detachments of airmen joked about what might be hidden at what had come to be called "the site." Was it a secret weapon? A dreaded germ bomb? How about a nuclear warhead of immense proportions?

As the years passed, their curiosity turned to humor. What forgotten secret was there? A general's lunch? Letters from a president to his mistress? In the three decades that the hangar remained secure, the most interesting, the funniest, and the most frightening rumor came from an airman who'd helped seal the hangar in the very beginning.

He claimed it contained a flying saucer . . .

*   *   *

"Then, in the middle of a winter snowstorm, word was flashed from the Defense Department to the security perimeter. Leaving one man in the underground command post, the five remaining men left to meet a car approaching the gate."

Ted's eyes leveled on Charlie's. "And you were one of the airmen?"

Charlie nodded nervously. "Yes. I had been stationed at the site for about fourteen months when it happened. It was nearly midnight when a rented sedan arrived. Inside, there were five civilians. At least I think they were. Five of us greeted them, while one man, his name was Andy Rodgers, stayed on duty below, watching the security console. We shut down power on the electrified fence and the ten of us drove inside, toward it."

Charlie Howard held up both hands, spreading five fingers on each. The right hand represented the airmen, and the left stood for the visitors.

"We got out of the car and moved in that formation, because the five of us at the site had explicit orders to kill any of the five of them who might attempt to penetrate the third fence. I'm sure they had the same orders about us. They set up some infra-red 'sniffer' apparatus, and we radioed the calibrations to Rodgers in the control room. The whole operation took less than an hour, and I don't think more than ten words of extraneous conversation passed between the ten men in that time. Nobody even looked in the direction of the third fence. By the time they finished, the sniffers had increased our security capability by about thirty percent, though I can't really say we needed it; we already had damn near the best security in the country. The plan included a dead air bubble on all of the FAA maps. I'd heard, though I can't verify it, the bubble included the routine rerouting of Air Force One as well as all commercial traffic."

Charlie looked to Ted and took a deep breath before he spoke again.

"That's the second item. I can vouch for all of that, as I was personally involved. The third part is something that . . . well, it forms the reason I'm here talking to you at all."

Charlie paused for a fraction of a second and drew a battered pack of filtered cigarettes from his jacket pocket. He lit one after offering one to Ted.

"I guess I'm stalling a bit about the third part, Doctor. Do you want to hear it?"

Ted stared at the man, looking for a hint of the fear he'd earlier perceived. Yes, it was still there, or Howard would not have offered the cigarette. Nor would he, if he'd been a jokester, assigned anything less than A-one credibility to all of the information he had given thus far. The assignment of ranking that the Armed Forces gave to gathered intelligence was split into two parts. The first digit indicated the reliability of the source of the information. The second digit ranked the credibility of the information itself. A-one was flat-assed, ironclad right. D-four was something out of the Brothers Grimm. Howard had assigned everything so far a B-two. It was appropriate, or so it seemed. It was also possible that the man had some experience in intelligence and was spinning the tale of his life. Ted was almost too fogged with stress and fatigue to make an accurate judgment. He was being given an escape clause and he knew it. He could turn and go and not hear another word. To stay and listen was to make a commitment of sorts. Perhaps a dangerous one. He tried to ponder it logically for a few seconds, but he could feel the insatiable pull of his curiosity, that same curiosity that had led him to complete degrees in fields as diverse as psychology, physics and literature. Did Howard know it? Was it all bait of some sort?

"Why the choice?"

"First, because there might be a very real risk in

your knowing this, and second, because it's part of what you can do to help me, if you're willing to hear it, that is."

The decision had to be made. The approach was, it seemed to Ted, loaded with the kind of subliminal cues that were designed to attack his resistance on two fronts at once: professional and personal. The hint of a plea for help would nudge the former, while the curiosity would attack the latter. It was well known that Ted Lawrence's fiction plots were sweeping and terribly clever in their development of mystery. The writer who wrote them had to be curious. There was nothing else that he could be. In the final analysis, the curiosity of the writer and Ted's fuzzy mental state won out over prudence. Even if he was being had, the rest of the story was a must.

He nodded.

Howard smiled a tight half smile. There was no joy in it. "The third part starts about a year ago, when Andy Rodgers called me from his home in Boston. He was a close friend. . . ."

"And the man on the console that night in the snow?"

"Yes, he was." Howard's voice was, for a second, a whisper.

"He called and mentioned that he was going to try to set up a reunion with the other four of us who lived in that hole in the ground for more than two years. I thought it was a great idea . . . then. Now . . ." The man paused and breathed deeply. The breath seemed not to lighten his mood a whit.

Ted watched the man closely, searching for a slight hint of body language, a twitch, a blink—all of the signs his training at Psy-Ops had taught him to look for— anything that would have told him Howard was insincere. There was nothing, but then Ted realized that he was almost a decade out of practice. The man was either well trained or totally sincere.

"Well, let me finish. Andy was working at Boston U.

He was getting a master's in something, and so he had access to a great many research materials. It didn't take him long to get the addresses of the other four. Two weeks or so, I think. He called me only after he'd checked and double checked. I'll never forget the way his voice sounded." Howard shook his head for a second. "The first man he'd managed to get in touch with was Tony Patrino. Turns out Tony was living in Springfield, not far from Boston, writing for a local paper there. I don't remember the name. Tony told Andy that he was in the middle of writing a story about the base, something to do with the Freedom of Information Act. It was designed to put some pressure on the government to release information about what might be in the hangar. Tony told Andy he'd unearthed something stupendous. To make a long story short, do you remember the five men who drove the flatbed to the hangar back in 1950?"

Ted nodded.

"All five of them were dead within a year of the event. Two of them died in a plane crash together. They were a captain and a lieutenant, I think. A third, the truck driver, died in a car crash. One of the last two committed suicide. Hanged himself with his necktie. The fifth, a major, simply disappeared. He drove off to work one morning and never got there. No trace was ever found."

"How does all this relate? People die that way all the time. If the two officers were stationed together, there was a good chance that they flew a lot of hours together. That would increase the odds on both of them dying in the same crash. For the others, car crashes and suicides happen every day. As for the one that disappeared on the way to work, well, that could be anything. A bad marriage, debts, loan sharks, maybe just neurosis."

Charlie Howard shook his head.

"There's more. Andy got caught up in the mystery

of all of it and started helping Tony with the research. He also tried to locate the other three men in our outfit." Howard paused and took a deep breath, exhaling audibly. "The three of them, Walter Haskin, Mort Collins, and José Perez . . . they were all dead."

Ted blinked. "How?"

"Several ways. A boating accident, that's how Collins died. Perez burned in a tenement fire, in L.A. Haskin got shot in a deer-hunting accident in Maine. Andy told me all of that on the phone about six weeks ago. He said that he was writing letters to their families, trying to find more information. But it didn't seem like there was any real reason for a three-man reunion."

"So that makes it eight men dead, all connected to the hangar?"

"No. Tony and Andy managed to dig up records, God knows from where, on five more airmen who'd been at the same duty station before us. All of them were dead. Again, it was in a variety of ways. He sent letters to their next of kin and he must have started getting responses, because when he called me a couple of weeks ago, he was excited about something a relative was sending to Tony in the mail."

"What was it?" Ted's curiosity was getting the better of him.

"I don't know."

"Your friend Andy never said? Or it never arrived?"

"It arrived. It was mailed to the newspaper in Springfield. Tony and Andy were both there late that night, working on whatever arrived along with all of the other materials they had gathered. They were in the back when the fire started."

Ted could feel the sudden sweep of a chill. His neck was gooseflesh.

"Were they . . . ?"

"No. Just Tony. There was not enough left to identify. They managed to confirm the identity through a dental record. But there was only one body in the building. It had been totally gutted. Everything was gone, all of the records they'd been gathering, everything."

"And Andy?"

"He never went home. No one's seen him, since. The Springfield fire inspector said that the case was probable arson, but there are no leads."

"Where does all of this leave you?"

"Terrified."

"Why?"

"I got a call from Andy two nights ago. It was in the middle of the night and I'd been out with a couple of friends the night before. We'd had a lot to drink."

"Where was he?"

"He didn't say. Said there was no reason for me to know. He sounded, well . . . scared shitless. Carried on about being followed. He said he needed my help and that he was sending me something. He talked about his sister, in Boston, and his lawyer, but he didn't mention the name. I called his sister the next afternoon. Someone else answered, a man who claimed he was her husband. He told me she couldn't come to the phone. She was taking the death badly."

"Death?" The gooseflesh again swept up Ted's neck.

"Yes. Andy. He'd been in a Scollay Square flophouse and he'd gotten into a fight with some wino. Andy'd gotten smashed in the head with something heavy. It had killed him. The family had just found out a little while before I'd called."

"What about the wino?"

"Gone. At least when I'd spoken to them, there'd been no leads and no arrests."

"Did the something ever arrive, the thing that Andy was sending?"

Howard shook his head, then reached up and ran his fingers through his long hair.

"No. Maybe he never got to send it. Maybe he

threw it away. It could be that it just hasn't arrived yet."

Ted folded his arms against the chill that threatened to shudder its way through him. *Madness,* he told himself. *It's all madness!*

"Well, Howard? I guess we have to wonder what's in the hangar. Or at least you do."

Charlie Howard shook his head. "I *have* wondered, Professor. Believe me, I have. First I thought it was a new bomb. When the flatbed was put in the hangar, the atom bomb was pretty new. Maybe this was a super bomb, a first experiment working in the direction of a hydrogen bomb or a watchacallit . . . a neutron bomb. Then that didn't make any sense, because one of those things gone wrong would have leaked radiation all over the place. They'd have dropped it in the sea or buried it somewhere in a mountain. Then, I thought it might have been a biological warfare weapon. You know, something lethal with no antidote. Past that, my speculations just got weirder and weirder. Christ, I don't know . . . some Frankenstein monster that the Defense Department created and then didn't know what to do with. Then, with all this stuff about Andy and Tony and all those other guys dying, I stopped worrying about what was in there and started worrying about staying alive."

"Why have you told me all of this, Mr. Howard?"

"You're a writer. Right?"

Ted nodded. God, he could see it coming.

"The way I see it, if the package, or whatever it is, ever comes in . . ."

"No. I don't want it. I don't need to write a story about it."

The words stood between them for a long minute. Charlie broke the silence. "I see. Well, it was stupid to mention it, wasn't it?"

"If anything does arrive, I suggest you ditch it some-

where. Throw it in the ocean. Forget you ever knew
Andy or Tony. Are you married?"

"No."

"Move away. Change your name if you can."

"I can't. They'd find me anywhere I went."

"Who's they?"

"The government, the Mafia, the fucking bogeyman.
I don't know. Whoever killed all of those other guys."

"Are any of them still alive? I mean from the time
that the hangar was closed until now?"

"That's one of the things my two friends were trying
to find out before the fire. I'm not about to try to
follow up on that. No, Professor. The only thing I
can do is manage to get all of this publicized as soon as
possible. Too many people are dead. I came to you because you're a writer. I thought, with publishing connections in New York, there was a chance that the
thing could be gotten in print fast. You could have all
of the proceeds. All I would want would be my name
plastered across everything. Enough publicity might
make me immune. Maybe they would think that I
would be too awkward to kill?"

Ted shook his head. "That's unrealistic. First, I don't
have the kind of name or contacts in the business, *yet*,
to get this story in print. Not, at least, without the kind
of documentation that was burned in that fire. Even
if there were carloads of information, including lie
detector tests on you and everyone else connected with
all of this, the chances are very good that not a
publisher in the city would touch it. They'd all be too
frightened about litigation with the Justice Department.
No. I don't see that there's a chance to get all of this
published, especially with all of the real information
burned in that fire you mentioned. If there is anything
to all of this. . . ."

"What do you mean?" There was a shrill tone in
Howard's voice. It was clear that he thought Ted was
calling him a liar.

Ted started to protest when the auditorium door opened, startling both men. Malcolm Withers peered in and caught Ted's eye. He was the senior security patrolman on the college force. Ted glanced at his watch. Withers would be checking classrooms and outside doors. It was close to ten-thirty. "Hi, Malcolm."

"Oh, hi, Dr. Lawrence. Workin' late?"

"A little bit, Malcolm. We'll be out in a minute."

The broad, black face smiled, revealing a single gold tooth fitted in line with his incisors. Ted had always thought that the smile would have made Withers the perfect nineteenth century pirate.

"No hurry, Professor. Just slam the door hard when you leave." He fitted a key into the lock on the panic bar door and tested it. "It'll lock itself, now." The goldtoothed smile broadened. "Happy Thanksgiving, Doctor."

"You too, Malcolm."

The security man smiled, as if to extend the remark to Charlie Howard. Charlie smiled a thin-lipped smile in return.

It was a few seconds later when Ted's eyes met Charlie's again.

"There's not much else I can tell you, Mr. Howard. It's not that I don't want to help. I just don't think it would do any good. I'm sorry."

Charlie nodded. "I see. Well, it was a chance, anyway. G'night, Doc."

The man was gone before Ted could respond.

Ted Lawrence stood at the top of the auditorium steps for a moment, thinking. His curiosity wrestled with his sense of self-preservation. The latter won. Either Charlie Howard was out of his mind, and there was precedent for that among some of the lunatic fringe that took Ted's course, or the story was true, in which case there was nothing that Ted could do for the man.

Ted buttoned his coat and started off to the parking lot.

A cold November wind hit Ted from the side, and he speeded up his pace. The full moon he'd remembered seeing when he'd entered the building was long since shrouded by a bank of thick clouds, and there was a smell of snow in the autumn sky. Something akin to a ground fog had slipped across the parking lot of the huge campus. It haloed the lights and softened them into a cocoon. It was not uncommon for autumn nights at Paxton to have that kind of misty atmosphere; the campus was less than five miles from the Atlantic. The fast-cooling land breezes often clashed with the warmer sea winds, creating a barrier of foggy drizzle that shrouded the coast for weeks in November. Ted always thought it was something out of Poe; quite appropriate accompaniment for Howard's story tonight. He could hear the click of his footfalls against the asphalt as he crossed the parking lot. Suddenly, he stopped. The lights had winked out.

Some thirty yards behind him, a lone figure crouched down in the shadows near the corner of the building. He had watched Ted and Charlie Howard leave the lecture hall within seconds of one another, and he suspected that they had been talking. He pressed the talk switch on a small radio and spoke softly into it. Ted's description and the location of his car, the last one in the parking lot, were efficiently passed on.

Ted stood for a second, trying to get his night vision. Howard had held him long enough that the ten-thirty "lights out and let's save money on the utilities" policy of President Oscar Small had come into effect. Small had endeared himself to the economy-minded board of trustees with a policy that cut the night lights early, skimped on security patrols, and dropped the thermostats to fifty in spring and fall. Ted remembered characterizing the policy in the ever-controversial student newspaper, *The Paxton Guardian,* as Small's "miner's lamp and overcoat" policy. He'd gained stern looks from the administration for that one. Now, Ted's clashes with Small over finances, tenure, and labor negotiating had, after eight years, become a sort of local entertainment.

All of the attendant turmoil had done a great deal to aggravate his wife, Lisa, who had long since abandoned hope for Ted's career when he'd refused a management position with her father's company. Companies, Ted reminded himself; there were eight of them now, ranging from airborne electronic systems to pharmaceuticals. The Ryan conglomerate seemed to own a piece of everything . . . except Ted. How had it all gone so bad? How much had been him and how much her? He shrugged the questions away. It was all academic. It was over. They'd divorce and he'd get custody of Michael and Dawn. And so be it.

He could see the dark shape of his Chevy sitting alone in the fog-bound lot. He moved toward it cautiously, his memory fleeting back to night-search missions in Viet Nam. Quiet terror on moonlit jungle nights when a cough or sneeze would give away a position and summon a rain of death from mortars in the distance. There was no fear now. Only emptiness. There was no joy in winning a custody fight with Lisa.

It was nearly ten-forty-five when he got the car fired up and moving in the direction of the college's front gate, which he prayed was not locked. It wasn't. He waited at the gate for a break in the light traffic, then moved out onto the small two-lane road that fed traffic past and into the college. He pushed the feud with President Small away, and the wearying class, and that strange man, Howard. He was bleary-eyed and all he wanted to do was get home through the fog.

The dark sedan was in perfect position forty yards down the road, waiting. It sat darkly in a blind driveway, invisible from the road, but still with a full view of the college's front gate. In the right seat a man, dressed in a dark suit and a light topcoat, resembling any local businessman, held small binoculars to his eyes in a most unbusinesslike way. Through them the fog evaporated, and everything in the gloomy November night stood out in the glowing hues of green and white. The device was a starlight scope, a far more advanced version than Ted Lawrence might ever have used in Viet Nam. To the man's left, the driver held a hand mike close to his mouth. He spoke in soft though precise tones.

"Ghost One from Ghost Two."

"Ghost One, roger."

"Subject has driven past our station and is moving out the back gate. We'll stay with him. Have you seen the man that Ghost Three reported on?"

There was a pause, followed by a burst of static. "Ah . . . roger, Two. We have him. He's turned in our direction, and will be passing in less than a minute. Stand by."

The man in the right seat swept the starlight scope along with Ted's car as it passed. The driver nodded and then pressed the button on the hand mike.

"Two?"

"Yes?"

"We'll follow and get a routine workup on the car. We'll meet you at position six at say . . . oh three hundred. Confirm? Over."

"Confirm."

The man in the right seat lowered the scope and grunted. Position six was an all-night diner some ten miles distant and oh three hundred was four hours in the future. It would be four hours before any of them could even get a cup of coffee. Shit, he thought. He started to wonder why he didn't find another job. The amount of night work on this job was excessive. Night work on Thanksgiving Eve was unforgivable.

He started the car and released the hand brake, then slowly pulled out onto the dimly lit road. They came up behind Ted's car less than a mile down the road, where he waited patiently for a long traffic signal. The two men in the chase car considered that the operation was routine and simple. They simply noted the make and model of the car and the license number. In a matter of hours the data would be available from the registration computer files in Trenton. A dossier would be started on the owner, then married up with any cross-check information in other files . . . government files.

Ted looked only once in the rear view mirror. There was nothing unusual about another car waiting for a light.

The light changed. Ted eased the Chevy up through the gears and started home. The sedan turned off onto a side street. They had what they needed.

It was an hour later when the Motor Vehicle computers spit out the driving record of the owner. In another hour a file was started on LAWRENCE, THEODORE MARTIN. In the morning it would be cross-matched with other files, other records. The dossier was being built.

The nightmare had begun.

CHAPTER THREE

The Lawrence home was a large, white colonial, well situated on two wooded acres in Weston, a tiny suburb of Shore Park, the once famous seacoast resort center. Weston had been settled in the early seventeen hundreds, the colonial farmers finding the location perfect for several corn and potato crops a year. In the early years of the twentieth century, the farms started to break up into small farmlets that ultimately surrendered to the land developers in the post–World War II housing boom. Seven years earlier, Ted had managed to catch one of the last farmers before he caved in to the developers. He bought a two-acre parcel from the man, and built his home on it. A small dirt side road led to the long driveway, which in turn sloped upward on a rise to the house. On a clear summer day, Ted could see the ocean from his picture window.

Outside, the first day of December announced its arrival with a cold, hard downpour. It beat against the side of the house and pelted a tattoo against the large picture window in the living room. It was the kind of day that called for a roaring fire in the den fireplace, the room where Ted liked to work best. But Ted could not muster the ambition to lay one in the firebox. The wood would be rain-soaked, since he'd forgotten to bring some in to the garage. He looked out the living room window to the road beyond the sloping front lawn. He sipped black coffee and realized that he didn't have the ambition to do much of anything. He had spent the first hour of his day off shambling in a terry robe and moccasin slippers, staring at the cartons and stacked crates that formed the monument of a dead marriage. He hadn't realized just how much Lisa was going to take with her. It had taken them the better part of two days to inventory everything. They worked over lists of possessions categorized as "His," "Hers," and "Ours." The latter category was carefully divided with both him and Lisa acting as bloodlessly as coroners conducting an autopsy. It was too depressing. A vision of graves registration at Tan Son Hut Air Base flashed into his mind for a split second. Aluminum caskets homeward bound, green tags reading "Remains Not Viewable."

He shrugged it away and headed for the shower.

He let the steamy water beat on his shoulders for a long time, trying to erase the strange chill that echoed the clammy feeling of guilt and sadness. How would Michael take it? His son was easygoing, unflappable. Ted was sure that Mike was going to be all right. But more important, what about Dawn? She was very bright, very sensitive, and tried very hard to be self-reliant. There had been no reason for it, at least that was what the doctors had said. It was a birth defect, pure and simple. The medical staff wrung their hands but could do little more. Dawn Lawrence had been born blind.

He climbed out of the shower and toweled briskly in the steamy bathroom. The memory of all of it was bitterly clear. He had blamed Lisa. And she had blamed him. It was his genes . . . hers . . . his . . . hers. Their blind infant daughter had, for a time, dwindled to insignificance as they shuffled the guilt back and forth between them. It went on for almost a year, and finally stopped. But the marriage was irreparably scarred by it; a slash that would never heal.

When Dawn had been a year old, the tactics shifted. Lisa attacked Ted's career, his being "buried" at Paxton. In response, Ted dove into the task of training

Dawn. He couldn't count the times he'd looked down at her in her playpen; her exquisite, blue sightless eyes tore him apart. He started a crash program. He read everything he could find on Braille and on the training of the blind, on "The Family and Its Treatment of a Blind Child." It did have an impact.

And then, as if by some ironic, left-handed gift of the gods, the other shoe fell. Dawn had a gift that matched the impairment. She was brilliant. Ted had seen her intuitive grasp of mathematics emerge early. She'd been four on the day he'd brought home a small abacus for her to play with. He reasoned that she'd be able to feel the beads and the tactility of the device would allow her to relate to numbers clearly. He'd underestimated her. In an hour she'd mastered the simpler concepts of multiplication which Ted had seen orientals carry out with lightning speed in Southeast Asia. Then she'd suddenly started to substitute number values, as if the ones on the small wire frame were not challenging enough. It took Ted a few more minutes to realize that she was starting to raise numbers to powers, intuiting that she could then work backward to get the original number. Dear God, he thought. She's intuiting logarithms. It was then that he started to see her awesome potential. As time passed, she grew more able to grasp and integrate two abstracts at once. Perhaps it had something to do with her blindness, perhaps it didn't. All Ted knew was that it had redoubled his commitment to provide the best education he could for Dawn. Lisa, conversely, seemed to pull back from Dawn and Michael both. It left Ted to act as father and mother to both of his children. So when the constant arguments about custody started to erupt between them, there was no chance that he would give up Dawn and Michael to his wife.

Ted moved into the bedroom and pulled on a pair of jeans and a sweater, then thrashed around his closet floor and came up with a pair of sneakers. He was going to have to get to work. There were three chapters of a novel still scattered in the den, and there were two or three days' work left on the project before he could get it into the mail to Cathy Seward at Halleck Publishers. The finished manuscript represented money, the second half of the book advance that Ted was going to need financially to survive the divorce proceedings.

He was late on the manuscript for *Sander's Bay*, by about five weeks, and Cathy had tactfully not called about it. Ted dropped her a note saying that he was trying to work out the last of the conclusion so that there'd be little need for revision. It was a lame excuse. Cathy could read between the lines. She'd known about Ted's marital problems. Ted had been frank about all of it.

He moved from the bedroom to the den, pausing to refill his coffee cup in the carton-littered kitchen. His den office was strewn with files, student papers, manuscripts in various stages of development, and, above all, books. They ranged from physics to psychology to the great works of western literature. He sat down at the typewriter and started to peck away at the last chapters of *Sander's Bay*. Not a bad mystery, he thought, and a simple way to supplement his income. He'd managed to write three books in four years. All three had gotten published, thanks to Cathy. Essentially, they were mysteries, with a touch of politics here and there. The plots came easily to Ted as had the writing itself, until life with Lisa had become unbearable.

He had been working for just over an hour when he realized that he'd managed to get ten good pages out of the typewriter. At that rate, working for the rest of the day, he thought he might get the thing done by late afternoon, when Dawn and Michael got home from school. He looked up from the keys (he'd never really mastered touch typing) to see that he'd typed the last three sentences on orange mylar. There was no impression on the paper. Cursing, he realized this was his last ribbon, and he was not about to go out in the rainstorm to buy another. He'd have to finish writing the book in longhand, even though his handwriting left a lot to be desired.

He thrashed for some paper on the desk and fished a yellow pad out from some student papers from school. He was about to tear off the top sheet and discard it when he read what was written on it.

HOWARD . . . OGDEN . . . BOSTON . . .
NEXT WEEK????

It was only meant to be a reminder, a jog to the file-card memory; something that would trigger the incident like a video tape replay. It did.

Howard had not come back. At least, he had not appeared in Ted's class. Had he gone underground? Changed his name? Left the area? And how much of all of it was true? In the week of agonizing inventory spent with Lisa and the hours orienting Dawn to the locations of the boxes, cartons and assorted junk that now filled the house, he'd let the incident slip into a mental holding pattern. Even when Howard had not come to class last night, Ted did not allow himself time to muse over it. He made a note to check the man's files tomorrow, then ripped the sheet from the pad and started to write. He'd filled more than eight pages with the last chapter of the book, and was perhaps just a page short of wrapping the damn thing up when the phone rang.

"Hi, Ted. It's Cathy."

"Hi. This is where I beg for mercy, right?"

There was a slight, nervous laugh at the other end. In her office, Cathy Seward sat staring at a sheet of memo paper from her editorial director. The message was brief. *What's with Lawrence and SANDER'S BAY? Nail that down.* It was signed simply: *Walt*. Walt Vertagglia was a demon of an editorial director, a man not terribly excited about the manuscript in the first place. In the chain of command he sat just above

Cathy, like a general manager, and demanded that things be done on time and neatly. While Cathy was known for both timeliness and neatness, her up and coming prize author, Ted Lawrence, was neither. She had shuffled things around Walt since she got the note from Ted about needing an extension. Walt was just as apt to say that Ted had *officially* missed a deadline and ". . . how can we start to exact penalties and after all, he's *your* author, Cathy."

There was nothing she could do, except call Ted and check where things were. It was hard in a number of ways. She hated in general to be pushy. Especially with Ted. An occasional call to "see how things are going" and a several-times-a-year editorial lunch were all that she could allow herself. Otherwise, she spent the rest of the day depressed. Despite the fact that they'd known each other for five years, it had taken Cathy the better part of a year to realize that the depression after calls and lunches was the symptom of something she recognized. Slender, attractive, stunningly witty Cathy Seward, Columbia graduate, rising senior editor, career girl, and slightly lonely single woman, was in love with Ted Lawrence . . . a married man and father of two children.

It had been all too easy for Ted to start to see her as confidante, as close friend. But love, that was something else. Cathy did not "poach" married men, not ever. It was a promise she'd made to herself while she was in college, after having a disastrous affair with a married instructor. It had been misery for her, and, she suspected, for him. The meetings on stolen weekday nights, the secretiveness that at first was exciting and romantic and later grew to be an exercise in frustration and exasperation. The lonely weekends, when he could not call. No! She had ended it and vowed never to get involved with a married man again. She'd settle to be confidante, sister, editorial helpmate, and that was *all*.

She had taken a deep breath and looked again at Walt's note before she dialed the number.

"Cathy Seward, girl editorial genius, I am scribbling the last page of *Bay* as we speak. How's that for irony?"

"Fantastic." Cathy sighed in relief. How much did he know? Suspect? Nothing? Everything? She hoped both at once. "And now the big question. When? Walt's starting to write snippy notes. Did you say scribbling? I thought you typed your drafts."

"Yeah. But I'm out of ribbon and I want to get this done before I lose the threads."

"I've never known you to lose a thread before."

He groaned. What the hell. "I lost a few this week, Cath. Maybe more than a few."

It was a lead line and she knew it. Cathy didn't have to search her intuition far to uncover what it was. "Lisa?"

"Yes." There was a pause, while the phone seemed distantly to beep and whir. Noise on the line? The storm? Neither of them paid any attention to it. Though Ted really didn't want to speak of it, he sensed that he had to. It would be better. It was the reason that the entire project was late and there was no sense in asking Cathy to extend herself and get in hot water with Walt Vertagglia without a reason.

"We're getting a divorce, Cathy. I'm getting custody of Dawn and Michael. And that's why I haven't . . ."

"I kind of thought so. At least that's the feel I got from talking to you last month. I'm sorry for you and the kids."

It was the only thing Cathy could think of to say. When he had said the words, she had felt her stomach knot. She could feel Ted's pain in all of it. And there was something else, something more intense. Was it hope? She grew instantly angry at herself, feeling like a vulture waiting for the last death throes of the wounded marriage to end. She pushed it all aside.

"Thanks." Ted pulled a cigarette from a battered

pack and lit it, inhaling deeply before he spoke. "I . . . know this is a bit crass, but as soon as I turn in this novel, I want to discuss my next project. I know I've got to get on something, fast."

"Money?"

"Right. The divorce will cost money, especially with the Ryans across the table with Lisa."

"They're not going to contest custody? That was Lisa's and their objection for the longest time, wasn't it?"

"Yeah. But Lisa threw in the towel. I think she convinced them that she disliked the kids almost as much as me. There would be no purpose in it, just for the Ryans to raise grandchildren. None at all. Besides, Lisa would never see them. She's too ready to renew her passport in the jet set. She drools when she thinks about all of those horny Riviera Frenchmen."

"How's Dawn taking all of it? From the time you had them both in at that lunch last year, I remember that she's bright, but she seems pretty vulnerable. Is she holding up?"

"She thinks it's her fault. Michael does too, but he isn't saddled with a handicap. She thinks her blindness did it."

"Is she right, Ted?"

"Partially, God knows. There was a lot of guilt, especially in that first year after she was born. Michael's birth kind of removed the onus for both of us, but Dawn harbors a lot. The trouble is she's so damn bright, you'd think she's older. I have to remember she's only ten; emotionally, I mean."

"She's going to need a lot of love when this thing is all over. Michael, too."

"I know."

Ted saw that the ash was about to fall. He cradled the phone against his neck and flailed at the cluttered coffee table in search of an ashtray. Instead the ashes fell on the top sheet of yellow paper with the reminder about Charlie Howard.

"Ogden," he absently mumbled.

"What?" Cathy said.

"Oh, just a note on a paper. Ogden . . . Ogden, Utah."

"A land deal, a plot, or a new place to move to?"

"None of the three. Just a crazy story a student told me."

Cathy recognized Ted's tone. It was one she'd heard before, musing, pondering, the beginning of something in his writer's mind.

"What story? I'm curious."

Ted paused for a second. He supposed there was no harm, not in just the telling. The chances were he'd never see Charlie Howard again, in any event.

He told it to her, just the way it was told to him. He was three quarters of the way through the incident when Cathy interrupted.

"He wanted you to write something about it."

"That's what he asked, but I turned it down. I mentioned possible government litigation. There's no percentage in writing something about the government and having them get royalties, fines, and all of the other profits. Besides, if anything Howard said was believable, the writing of it could mean your life."

"But Ted, that wouldn't apply."

"Why?"

"Because those suits usually involve factual incidents in a nonfiction book."

"And?"

"And if the writer is smart—or if his editor is smarter—they massage the thing into a novel. Thinly disguise everything in a fiction plot and cover themselves with an 'any resemblance to persons living or dead . . .' disclaimer. Then there would have been little for the government to pin a suit on."

Ted caught the drift. "Cath, I've heard you talk this way before, remember?"

"Of course you have; at the beginning of *Sander's Bay*. You asked how you could get away with fictionalizing that rat's nest college you work at and still avoid getting into a lawsuit with President whatsisname . . . Small? Short?"

"So Howard's story could be a novel, as far as you see it?"

"It's possible. It sounds exciting and it's timely. Fiction exposés are in."

"How. . . ?"

"Start it the way it happened. Make yourself a character in it. Take off from there."

Still remembering the fear he saw in Charlie Howard's eyes, Ted balked.

"I don't know, Cath. Can I think about it?"

"No."

"What?"

"Talk about it, instead. When will the scribbles end on *Sander's Bay?*"

Ted looked at the typed and handwritten pages. "Tonight. Then allow a few hours for it to get cleanly typed. It'll take a couple of days to pull together. That includes Xeroxing. I could mail it out, say, Friday."

There was a pause for a second as Cathy flashed through her calendar.

"Why not come in Monday with it? We'll lunch."

"On the company?"

"Is there any other way? And I'm serious about the new novel. I'll think up some twisty-turny things for the plot. OK?"

"OK. But I'm not a hundred percent sure of it. I mean, there's always the chance that the guy, Howard, was a fruitcake."

"Ted, the credibility of the thing has nothing to do with it. Who really cares what's in that hangar, and if all those men were killed by something . . . well . . . sinister. You know as well as I do that there's nothing either of us could really do about it. But a novel. That's something else. It can imitate reality, and they, whoever *they* might be, couldn't sue or anything, for fear of publicity. We'll set it somewhere, perhaps in the Midwest. Change the whole setting. But the gimmick of something out there in the desert that perhaps men have been murdered to protect, that's a great plot hook. Are we firm for Monday?"

She was excited in a way Ted had not heard before. Bubbly. She sounded like a woman . . . in love? He wondered. Though he didn't have an inkling that he, and not some boyfriend, or the excitement of the potential of a new novel project, was the cause of all the excitement. They set the time at noon, in her office. Ted made a mental note to get a sitter who could meet Dawn's bus and then Michael's.

He peered out the window to see that the rain had abated. There were even a few bright spots in the low undercast that had sped in from the sea. He was committed now. The final fussed-over version of the book would have to go with him to the city on Monday. There was something clean about it. No maybes, no perhaps. It was like a Hemingway kill. He liked that kind of pressure. It made him produce. Indeed, the three previous novels were produced under exactly the same kind of pressure. He got up and, feeling somewhat renewed by the conversation, loped to the other end of the sprawling ranch to get a windbreaker, his wallet, and car keys. Now he absolutely had to have typewriter ribbon.

The round trip took nearly an hour, and the rain seemed to start again as soon as he got in the car. The roads of Weston, the small seashore town, were slick and rainswept, though blessedly empty of traffic. The tourist season had been over for several months. If he'd tried to make the trip in the middle of July, rather than in the first week of December, the round trip would have taken twice that. He got a whole box of ribbon cartridges; enough to get another novel in draft if the conversation with Cathy yielded anything. He could feel his stomach start to tighten as he turned into the long, wooded driveway that led to the secluded Lawrence house. Lisa's black Mercedes coupe was in the driveway. He hadn't known where she was all day. He'd simply gone through the routine of getting Dawn and Michael off to the school buses without questioning the fact that she'd been gone before he awoke.

Lisa was in the kitchen, and she was two martinis into being nasty.

He shucked the windbreaker and tossed it over the back of a chair. She turned and looked at him. She was a beautiful woman. It was something that Ted would always have to admit. Her ruddy hair was pulled tightly back against the sides of her head, and her deep green eyes glittered.

"I'll be moving out a week from today. I found a place. Teddy Lawson, the tennis coach at the club, put me onto it."

"Where?"

"What difference does it make, Ted?"

"Only to Dawn and Michael. They might like to know where their mother is living."

"Ex-mother. That's what you mean, isn't it?"

"Very well. Ex-mother. Perhaps biological parent would be more appropriate."

He moved to the small liquor cabinet that they had housed in the kitchen. If she had gotten anaesthetized for the evening there wasn't any reason that he couldn't. But it would just be one. He didn't want to get ugly.

She stood, arms folded across her breasts, defensively. He could have told her a great deal about body language and non-verbal signals. He'd taught a course in them once. But again, there was no sense.

He poured a healthy shot of bourbon into an ice-filled glass. Over the top he dashed a bit of vermouth. Lisa had always said manhattans were a woman's drink. It was part of her assault on his virility. He pulled deeply at the drink and looked at the clock. Both children would be home in less than fifteen minutes. If there was any jawboning to be done, he wanted to get it out of the way before it erupted into an ugly scene that Michael and Dawn could witness. He knew that there was something in Lisa that would have liked that. He didn't quite know how to define it. Resentment. Insecurity. The manifestation of psychoneurotic pressures. He didn't really care about definitions anymore.

"Well, where's the place?"

"Up on the heights. It's the closest place to the city."

"And the club?"

"And the club. I'd be going sooner, but the apartment won't be ready until then."

The Atlantic Heights were the Pacific Palisades of New Jersey. High rise condominiums crowded together, affording a breathtaking view of the New York skyline after dark. It was suited to Lisa's tastes, or, perhaps more accurately, to her father's money. Ted doubted that she'd be there much of the time. She was itching for Europe, and he knew it.

"Lisa, is there anything else that we have to . . . negotiate? Anything vital?"

She looked at him, appeared to start to say something, then stopped. After another second of perusal, she spoke. "Just the revision of all of the credit cards. I called to cancel them. I'll be getting my own in a matter of a week." She paused again and spoke, as if unable to resist the opportunity. Ted could see what was coming before she spoke. It was obsessive-compulsive behavior, and there wasn't a thing in the world he could do to change it. It was just that kind of compulsiveness that had made Ted frightened over the last few years about her relationship with the children, especially Dawn. If there was a flareup in Lisa's personality, Dawn would be, as the symbol of guilt and of the breaking of the marriage itself, the most likely victim. It was the kind of thought that woke Ted up occasionally in the middle of the night.

"Besides, I'll be able to get more of the cards and things I want, now."

"Don't you mean Daddy will?" His answering retort came before she had the words out. It was the same kind of verbal quickness that Ted had used to devastate Oscar Small when the two crossed swords over the negotiating table. It may have been the same lightning ability that helped to destroy his marriage. But ever since Ted had been a child, growing up in the steaming, filthy jungle of a South Bronx ghetto, the only child of an itinerant gambler and an all-suffering drudge of a mother, he'd followed the cardinal rule. Hit hard! There was no respect without that. Sometimes, there was no survival. The motto of the street had been "do unto others before they do unto you." It was something that he had never lost. As he grew, and moved to gentler settings, the "hit hard" philosophy became a facility for verbal exchange. As immediate and reflexive as it was, Ted wondered how much of a role it played in getting him and Lisa to where they stood at the moment. It formed part of the pressing sensation of guilt that was only just starting to dissipate as the first pull of the manhattan started to have an effect.

There was a sardonic curl to Lisa's smile. Ted raised a hand before she could speak. He was starting what he'd wanted to avoid with the kids due home.

"I'm sorry, Lisa. That was uncalled for."

"True."

A horn honked in the driveway. It was Dawn's bus.

Dawn Lawrence was a beautiful girl. There was an easy looseness to her movements that would never hint to the casual observer that she was blind, especially as she moved through the house. She had memorized the positions of all of the furniture, and the relative distances, so well that she moved uncannily. Many of the locations that she frequented outside the house she had also committed to memory. Sometimes Michael helped her. It made him feel more like a big rather than little brother.

Dawn came slowly toward the kitchen. She was tall and lean and fair, with an almost nordically blond head of hair. Her beautiful blue eyes were covered by Snoopy sunglasses, and she carried a small fold-up cane which she unlimbered as she came into the kitchen.

Dawn stopped the second she closed the door behind her.

"Dad? Mom? You're both here?"

Lisa nodded then shook off the nod. "Yes. How could you tell?"

Dawn smiled broadly, revealing a mouthful of braces. "I can smell gin and bourbon. Martini and manhattan. You both have to be here."

"Dawn, you win the prize." Lisa's voice was tentative.

She swept the cane in front of her. "Any more surprises floating around?"

Ted tossed down the last of the drink. "Just the cartons in the living room. But watch out for the den, sweetheart."

"It's a rat's nest?"

"Yeah. As usual."

"Did you finish the book?"

"Close. Probably tonight."

"Oil up the Braille printer. In a couple of weeks we'll have a copy of your latest novel. And you'll dictate it?"

"Why break tradition?"

Again, she smiled a broad, brace-filled smile. There was something else behind it than the prospect of reading one of Daddy's books. "Mrs. Direggi said that if I kept working hard, I could finish that math book by Christmas. She asked if you could get the next one arranged in Braille."

Lisa looked across at her daughter after pouring herself another martini, one she clearly didn't need. "A twelfth-grade one?"

Dawn beamed. "Yup."

Ted came across the kitchen and hugged her. "That's great, honey. I'll get it arranged."

"Oh, and Daddy?"

"Yes?"

"She mentioned you might get the physics and the chemistry ones, too. Could you?"

"Of course." Dawn's academic precociousness was something that Ted had managed to integrate into his expectations, though they gave Lisa some problems. She always felt that Dawn was some sort of a freak, more for being brilliant than for being blind. Ted was sure that Lisa felt the intelligence was a reflection of Ted, rather than of her, and that galled her. She had spent a great deal of time trying to talk Ted out of letting Lisa out of the small school for the blind that was, blessedly, only a few miles away. As it was, Dawn was running out of courses there. She would have to be mainstreamed in the following year, though Ted was not sure where or in what grade. As it was, she was ready for high school work, at least in the sciences and in math, though her linguistic development was back in something like the seventh or eighth grade.

There had also been a dispute over letting Dawn commute daily to the school for the blind rather than living on the campus and seeing her parents on the weekends. The latter is what Lisa wanted, but Ted outlasted her. He rearranged the house so that it would not contain all the common things that could be death-traps for someone not sighted. Then he started to get Dawn home on weekends, to orient her to the house. She had to learn the position of everything in the house, something taken for granted by the sighted. Also, housecleaning could not move normal things that might get moved in a sighted home: toothpaste, occasional chairs, water glasses, and Michael's roller skates. Once everything was in order, Ted managed to get the school to agree for her to commute. A school bus on the regular town system, specially equipped for transporting the handicapped, picked her up and dropped her off, as the stop was on its normal route. Dawn had adjusted excellently. Even her teachers at the special school admitted it. The great danger of allowing a blind child to live at home was not as much physical as psychological. The temptation was for the parents to do too much for the child, thus increasing the self-pity she might feel, and stifling any initiative. Clearly that was not the case with Lisa. Ted also had determined to give Dawn all the elbow room he could. The process of letting her make her own mistakes, including smashing into things and misplacing things, was agonizing. But it was successful. Even small, slender, dark-eyed Michael, who at five and six years old had resented the privileges that he sensed Dawn was getting (*Why can't she do it for herself? Why can't Daddy read the homework books to me?*), had suddenly grown from her being home. In his eyes, he wasn't a runt kid brother anymore. Rather he was something like a big brother, reading to her, helping her. He'd grown so overprotective there were times Ted felt he had to double back and give extra things and time and love to Michael. He did. The time and energy drain was enormous, and if it weren't for his ability to do routine lectures, interspersing set patterns of information with "winging it," the chances were that teaching would have been a flop.

As he watched Dawn move off down the hall toward her room, briefcase in one hand and white fold-up cane in the other, he could feel a blend of love and fear. Would there be enough of everything? Money? Time? Even with Lisa's surliness, she had been another person to help assume responsibility. He started to pour himself another drink and stopped when he heard Michael's bus arrive at the street entrance to the long driveway.

Michael was as dark as his sister was fair, and he

was every inch an eight-year-old boy. He shucked off his yellow slicker and flew through the kitchen, speaking perfunctorily as he went.

"Hi, Dad." He paused for a second when he saw his mother. "Hello, Mom." There was a different tone in the greeting, and Ted knew that Lisa could hear it. "What's for supper?"

It was a ritual. Michael, Ted had long ago concluded, was a walking stomach with minor attachments of arms, legs, and head. The question was one asked daily for more than a year.

Lisa looked at Ted with a vaguely challenging air. The look spoke of a release of responsibility. It said, *Get used to it, Mister smart-ass Doctor Lawrence. They're all yours now, not mine.* Ted caught the look but chose not to respond.

"Chicken, Mike. But it'll be a while."

"Great. I want two drumsticks and no yucky sauce. OK?"

"OK." Ted smiled. It was a victory. The question had been directed to him, not Lisa.

"I got my homework done on the bus, so I'm gonna watch Spiderman on TV." The voice was a receding yell, as Mike ran down the hall in the direction of the living room and the TV. Ted didn't bother to answer. Instead, he turned to Lisa.

"Are you staying for dinner, or did you make another arrangement?" The question was factual enough, without a strain of arrogance about it. But it seemed from her eyes that the last martini had created more fog and more anger. "Is that a challenge?"

"Christ, no. Just a simple question."

"Yes. I'll stay. But I've got to go out tonight and see that apartment agent."

"OK. I'll . . ."

The phone rang just next to his ear, and Ted jumped. He grabbed it only a second into the ring. The caller was Lonnie Carlton, a chemistry professor at Paxton.

Lonnie was a colleague, but not someone used to calling Ted at home. They were a minute into the conversation when Ted realized that Lonnie was stalling, trying to find the right words to break the news. It appeared that he was calling in an official capacity, that of the president of Paxton's faculty union.

"There's no other way to put it, Ted. There's been a rif." It was a phrase all too common and frightening in college faculties since the declining birth rate had resulted in falling enrollments. A reduction in force was an unplanned and uncompensated layoff, the kind that management, whether industrial or educational, reserved to itself in every contract. There was nothing that the unions could do about it except to demand that the enrollment statistics warrant such a layoff and that it be carried out in a clear "last in, first out" manner.

"How extensive, Lonnie?"

"Very, Ted." Ted was getting the drift about the unusual call. But it was crazy. Ted was too senior, too far up the list. He looked across to Lisa, who looked back with mild disinterest. She had not been able to catch the meaning of the call from his side of the conversation, and that was the way it would have to stay.

"Be specific, Lonnie."

"It went to you, Ted; you were the last one on the list. Looks like Small had the last laugh after all. I'm really sorry. We're trying to set up a mediation meeting for the thirty . . . ah . . . two people involved. The state rep from the union will be there."

Ted couldn't believe it. It was a tactic he never would have suspected. Moreover, he was far too senior. He had spent more than eight full years at Paxton, getting tenure after the fifth. It was all wrong. He fought back the anger and the outrage, constantly aware of Lisa's presence. If there was one time he didn't need her around, it was now. "Ah, Lonnie?

How was all that, ah, managed, if you know what I mean, given all of the seniority involved?"

"You mean yours?" Lonnie paused on the other end of the phone. He knew that Ted was never this indirect about questions, especially of this nature. "Ted? Can't you talk?"

"Well, not really."

"Oh. I see. Well, I'll make it short. We can discuss it in more detail tomorrow. What he did was use your position in the Psychology Department. There's a stipulation in the rif part of the contract that seniority can be computed by longevity in a given department, and despite the time you have with the college, you had three years in Literature and then three more in Physics. The last two have been in Psychology. Have I got that right?"

"Yes."

"Well, he's riffing you on the basis of the psych team seniority, where you're low man on the list. The worst is . . . it's a mid-year rif. Starts January first."

"What about a 'bump' back to any of the others?" Ted's eyes darted to Lisa. Educational jargon never interested her. It was like a foreign language. She had not yet caught on that the call was dire. She had not deduced that her about-to-be-ex-husband was going to be out of a job. It was a small blessing. A "bump" meant removing someone more junior to yourself back in another department in which you were qualified to teach. The whole business could become rapidly cutthroat and create ugly scars that might divide a faculty forever. Still, union allegiance was one thing, and losing a lucrative teaching job in a declining market was quite something else.

"Can't work, Ted. The rif cuts across all the departments and divisions. Small is gutting the place. With three years in Lit and three in Physics, you'd still be ranked by the last man riffed. Both of those are small departments, remember? No, this one's wired together.

All we have to go on appears to be procedure, relative to the enrollment statistics. We'll meet tomorrow; I've called a membership meeting for twelve-thirty. Ted, like I say, I'm really sorry about this. You've always been out front with helping the union. We're going to do everything possible. I mean . . ."

"You mean it looks like it's ironclad and now you have the dubious pleasure of calling the rest of them . . . or us. Right?"

"Right. Tomorrow?"

"Right, Lonnie."

He hung up, and Lisa cocked her head to the side the way she always did when she had grown curious.

"What was that all about? Another one of the internecine battles with Small?"

"Yeah. Something like that. Lonnie and I have to work out some tactics."

He crossed to the small bar and with an air of perhaps too much casualness poured and took a long pull at another manhattan. Lisa did not pursue the call any further; the chances that the explanation was accepted were good. If she found out that Ted Lawrence was going to be out of work in five weeks, she might monkeywrench the divorce or custody of the kids. Ted could feel the sour taste of fear deep inside.

Outside, in the teeth of the cold rain, a dark sedan plowed through the watery roadway and passed the Lawrence home. It was the second pass of the day. The first had been made just after Lisa had left in the morning, and it had been unobserved. In the right seat, the passenger thumbed a mike switch as he peered through the rain-spattered window at Ted's Chevy standing at the far end of the driveway.

"Ghost One, this is Ghost Two."

"Roger, two."

"Subject remains on location. That midday jaunt was the only outing."

"Very well, Ghost One. Take a dinner break. We'll cover until your return at twenty hundred. Confirm."

"Confirmed, One. Out." He released the switch and turned to the driver.

"Dinner break and right back. I think someone's got his head up his ass on this operation."

"Yeah." The driver commiserated. "They call that retrocranial insertion."

The men laughed and drove away in the rain.

CHAPTER FOUR

It was close to midnight on Saturday and Shore Park was like a tomb. The small resort town on the Jersey coast was long since down to its winter population of something over four thousand. It would swell to six times that much in the height of midsummer tourism, and then plummet in the fall. During the midwinter months businesses hung on, generally relying on the profits made during the previous summer. Restaurants, jammed by seafood enthusiasts in the summer, now sold dinners for a quarter of their usual price. Motels and old beachfront residence hotels, many of them decrepit and more than a century old, rented efficiencies, rooms, and small apartments on the basis of winter leases, spanning from October to May. In the summer, the prices of the accommodations were known to go up by six to eight hundred percent; in the winter, the cheap lodging and food attracted students, artists looking for scenes to paint on the winter beach, and writers who sought for solitude. In the midst of a bitter mid-December, then, it was common for Shore Park to drag in its streets near midnight, even on a Saturday night in the Christmas season.

Charlie had figured it out when he was in the diner, two blocks from home. He'd thought that the last of the swiss steak and french fries special was going to come back up when he accidentally spied the man coming in for a pack of cigarettes. Their eyes had met for only a second before the man had looked away. But

Charlie had made the connection. It was the same man he'd seen on the Paxton campus almost two weeks ago. It was the same fur-collared topcoat and dark suit. He'd have bet his life on it. The churning in his stomach told him that there was a chance that he already had done just that . . . bet his life.

How could they know . . . HOW? And so fast. It only arrived yesterday!

He fought away the urge to run, to hide. What was it Lawrence had said? Move away? Change your name? Perhaps he could. There was just a chance. Get rid of it, mail it out. Leave no trace. Security Service had taught him at least how to do that. They didn't have him, not yet. He'd made the tail. He'd seen them, and the chances were good they didn't know it. It gave him an edge; not a big one, but perhaps there was a chance it was big enough to survive on.

He finished the coffee slowly after the man left. He planned things out. It was a few more minutes before the food settled and he knew it was not going to come up. But then the plan of action started to form. The chances were that he would go back to the car and then on to the small apartment for the night. The tail car was probably in the far, dark end of the large diner parking lot. If they were being ultracool, they'd be a bit down the block at the first intersection leading to the apartment house that had once been an ancient residence hotel. They'd pick up his small blue VW as it passed, and then shadow it to the apartment. Or they might simply radio to another unit on site. The thought chilled him. How many of them were waiting for him? How long did he have to live? He found himself again amazed at the speed with which they had managed to pick up the trail. The package had only arrived in the mail *today. Only hours ago!*

No, they had to have known before, well before. They might have even been shadowing last week when he'd talked to Lawrence and had gotten the advice to run. It was ironic that it was probably too late when the warning was given. In any event, it was too late to try to run now. And he was too outnumbered to fight. He ran his hands through his dark hair and stared at his image in the marbled mirror that decorated the counter wall across from him. The beginnings of a plan started to form in his mind. It was a plan that, as yet, had no conclusion. It was simply an expedient. No matter what, he was going to have to slip them for a few hours, send them in circles, at least long enough to get back to the apartment. Everything he owned was there: bank book, savings passbook, cash, and a few uncashed VA checks. He'd have to get to them undetected before he could manage to get anything else planned.

He asked the waitress, a weary, slender woman in her fifties who called everyone "dearie," to total out the check for him and looked at his watch. He'd been in the diner for just over twenty minutes. The average meal might take forty-five minutes. He knew that he could make it back to the apartment undetected in perhaps eight or nine minutes, even on foot through the maze of alleys and service areas downtown. How long would they wait before they sent in a second man for a pack of cigarettes or a trip to the john or coffee to go? Another half an hour, if they were real professionals. So he had just over half an hour of loose time if everything went right. Just over half an hour . . . to do what? He didn't know. But it was half an hour free of the tail, half an hour's breathing space. He'd figure the rest as he went.

The waitress handed him the check and cocked her head to the side curiously. "No dessert tonight, dearie?"

He shook his head. "No time. Got some more studying to do."

She smiled thinly. "Why don't ya pay up front?"

He shook his head and handed her a five and the check. "Do it for me. Keep the change. Is that worth the walk?" He smiled broadly.

She nodded as she looked at the five, and calculated the amount of the tip, which was considerable. " 'S worth the walk."

As she moved away in the direction of the register, Charlie headed for the rear of the building.

As he moved toward the men's room, he mentally visualized the position of the kitchen and the rest rooms vis-a-vis the rear parking lot and the spot down the street, which formed the two most likely intercept areas. Yes. It was right. The men's room window was hidden from both.

The window was partially blocked by the wall of one of the stalls. It was also, Charlie soon found, one son of a bitch to open. The top pane of the frosted and wire-lined window had been fitted with an exhaust fan. The lower part was deadbolted to secure it against forced entry. Luckily, there seemed to be nothing resembling a burglar alarm or detection system. He fished through his pockets and in a few seconds came up with a small fingernail clipper, the kind designed to fit on a keychain. It offered little leverage, but it was all that he had. There was no way he could go out front and ask "dearie" for a screwdriver so he could force the men's room window.

It took precious minutes for him to torture out the greasy, screw-headed bolts. The last bolt refused to budge. Frustrated and sweating, more from fear than from the work, he bent the fan frame back and forth until the cheap pressed steel snapped. He set it on the sill, moved the upper pane to its position, then raised the lower one as far as it would go. It allowed him just enough room to squeeze out.

The drop to the asphalt was only a matter of feet, and Charlie landed in a wary crouch. He peered around for a second, trying to get his night vision. He'd succeeded. There wasn't a car in sight. He took the bent fan from the sill and placed it on the ground, then raised and lowered the upper and lower frames into a closed position. There was no sense in filling the room with blasts of cold air; that would attract attention. As it was, "dearie" would not notice his coming or going. She never did. Buttoning up his Air Force parka against the biting wind, Charlie looked up. The sky was filled with fast-moving scud clouds. There was a storm coming, a snowstorm by the look of it. There was no moon, in any event. A storm could only help conceal him, slow chase cars, and generally give him more breathing space. He still did not know what for. What was he going to do?

He pushed the question aside, along with the fear, and moved quickly across the dark open space of the diner's delivery area into the cover of a warehouse wall that ran adjacent to it. There was a row of stores just a hundred yards past the end of the warehouse, and there were lights on on some of the second floors. Charlie remembered that many of them were rented lofts, occupied by black and Hispanic families. As he passed by them, he could hear music. Christmas carols. *Noche de paz, Noche de amor. . .* The tune was familiar. "Silent Night."

It was only two or three minutes more before he got to the back entrance of the Victorian building that had seen God only knew how many owners and tenants. Like most vintage buildings, it had the remains of a servants' and tradesmen's entrance, though clearly there were no servants nor any tradesmen to speak of in recent history. The lock was a simple door-handle type, and Charlie made short work of it with a credit card that he had fished out of his wallet. He made it upstairs to his apartment some twelve minutes after telling the waitress to keep the change.

He slipped into the darkened apartment and moved carefully through the darkness toward the window that was flooded with the eerie glow of a mercury vapor streetlight only a few yards away. Luckily, the blinds were down and there was just enough space between them to afford a view of the street. He took a long time looking for any unusual cars. They weren't there. Nothing was there. But Charlie knew that the chances were that shadow cars would never put themselves in a position where they could be observed.

He moved to the chair that stood in view of the door and tried to think. Were they the ones who killed Rodgers? Patrino? All the rest? If they were, and they'd trailed him for more than a week, there had been ample time for a hit, if that was their mission. Why tie up a shadow force for a week or so in surveillance if all that was wanted was a hit? For that matter, they could have easily hired someone local and then killed the hit man after the job was done. No, it wasn't just a hit. They wanted . . . *the package. Dear God, they want the package!*

He couldn't figure out how they'd known about the package. Hell, he didn't even know himself what the thing inside was. But getting rid of the package was vital. Short of sending it back to a dead man in Boston, there was only one place he could mail it.

Hunkering down in the darkness, like a soldier on night patrol, Charlie moved across the large high-ceilinged room to the bathroom. Feeling his way along the tiles, he reached the sink and fingered the large mailing envelope. He peeled away the tape that held it fast to the underside of the sink and retreated to the living room.

He froze.

A noise? In the hall?

He strained to hear anything else. A creak, a shuffle. There was nothing save the wind and the distant sound of flood-tide waves pounding relentlessly on a distant jetty.

He breathed deeply and felt his way to the desk in the corner of the room. It was an old oak affair with a roll top and a dozen drawers, junk collectors for everything from bills to stamps. It was the latter he was after. He fished in a drawer silently, agonizingly, trying to *feel* stamps. He was in the next to the last drawer when his sweating fingers stuck to a page of stamps. He slipped the sheet from the drawer and detached ten, reasoning that they'd be enough to get the package there. Even if they weren't, it would be delivered and the addressee would pay postage due, he hoped. He started to look for a manila folder he'd left on top of the desk. Yes, there it was. He pulled two Xeroxed sheets from the folder and inserted one into the envelope. The other he folded into fours and slipped into his shirt pocket. He'd found a tape dispenser in one of the drawers and set it aside. Now he pulled several strips of masking tape from it and sealed up the package.

He crawled to the window and used the light from the streetlamp to scribble over the previous mailing address and return address. Below the former he printed the name and address he wanted. He would put no return address on it. The last thing he wanted was to see the package again. Satisfied, he sat quietly for a moment beneath the window. His hands were shaking and his stomach was churning. He was frightened, but so far he was pleased with himself. And more than that, the rest of the plan was clear.

He'd retrace his steps, drop the package in a mailbox on the side street he had to cross on the way back to the diner. He buttoned up the parka and got to his feet, tucking the package under his arm. Suddenly he froze rock still. He could feel a cold terror wash over him. Something was wrong. Wrong. He forced himself to stay calm. What was it? Something was different . . . changed. The streetlight. *It had gone out.*

The room was now in utter darkness. He turned and peeked out between the blind and the window frame. All of the lights on the street had gone out. After a few seconds he smiled to himself. A power failure.

It had come as if on order. Darkness was a friend, especially now. Charlie moved slowly toward the door and suddenly remembered the folded sheet he'd put in the shirt pocket. He set the package at his feet and, removing the paper from his pocket, slid his hands along the wall until he felt the picture frame. It was a cheap print, a seascape that Mrs. Walchek had described as "elegant decoration" when she'd advertised the efficiency in the local paper. The frame was plastic, and the print itself had been laminated to a sheet of cardboard, backed by another, heavier, cardboard sheet. Charlie took the folded sheet and slipped it between the two pieces of board, pushing it in as far as his fingers could reach.

He picked up the package and slowly opened the door. Behind him, the streetlight flickered to life for a second, as if it had been given a reprieve. But it was shortlived. In another second, the light and all of the others on the street went black again. *Engineers tryin' to get secondary generators on line,* he thought. They'd failed, and that was going to be helpful.

It took him seven or eight minutes to work his way to the side street a block from the diner. He slipped the package in the mailbox and moved quickly to the back of the diner parking lot, which was pitch black. Oddly, he had just slipped behind the wheel of the VW when the streetlights came on again. He started the car and moved off through the parking lot, then turned right on the main access road.

The men in Ghost Two sat just out of range of the fickle streetlight. Both of them had seen their night vision shattered and redeveloped several times in the past half hour.

With a suddenness that startled the man on his right, the driver leaned forward and jabbed an index finger toward the windshield.

"There! What's that?"

The man on the right lunged forward, his nose only inches from the windshield. Both men looked as though the car were in the middle of a panic stop.

"Where?"

The driver shook his head in exasperation. "At the side door, but . . . I'm not sure if it was a shadow or me."

"Our boy?"

"There are other boarders in the house. Two, I think."

"Wait." The man on the right grabbed the mike from the radio set in the dash between them. "Ghost One? This is Ghost Two."

"Roger, Two." The voice answered instantly. "I was just about to contact you. Subject will arrive your location in about one minute. He's in the blue bug. Remain on station. What did you want?"

The man in the right seat looked at the driver. For a split second their eyes questioned one another before they nodded in an unspoken agreement. "It was nothing, One. We'll remain on station. What time's the relief?"

"The usual. Zero three hundred. Out."

The man on the right seat folded his arms against the cold. Without the motor running, the car had become clammy as a tomb from the chill, damp sea air. "Are you sure you saw something?"

The driver shook his head. "No. Just a shadow, or maybe another tenant. It couldn't have been our boy. He's just pulling up now. Look."

Across the street and a distance down the block, the blue VW was parallel parking in front of the old Victorian building.

The driver leaned back and pulled his overcoat collar up. "Yeah. At least *he'll* sleep tonight. We sure as shit won't. Remind me to bring a thermos tomorrow.

We could both . . ." He stifled a yawn. ". . . some coffee."

Charlie moved up the creaky stairs as quietly as possible. His fear had calmed a bit. If they came now, he could plead ignorance. He'd never seen a package. He didn't know a soul in Boston. It would be the best acting job of his life.

As he moved down the hall his confidence grew. He'd reacted well. It was something that he could be pleased with. He was a survivor. Now he'd have to perfect every nuance and gesture for the visit, when it came. He unlocked the door and opened it. He closed the door and reached for the switch.

He stopped. His eyes widened. His jaw sagged. The terror gripped him like a vise, cutting off his breath and his ability to move.

Across the room, silhouetted by the light from the streetlamp, stood a man.

"Good evening, Lucas."

CHAPTER FIVE

Ted peered absently out the grimy train window toward the Jersey meadowlands. It was perhaps the worst way to approach New York City. Everywhere there was clear evidence of blight, pollution, and general ugliness. He could smell the stench of the Bayway refineries through the closed windows of the rattletrap Jersey Central commuter train. In the distance were marshes Ted knew no self-respecting fish or bird could live in for more than a few days before it threw in the towel and died of something.

Close to the tracks, billboards flashed past. Some advertised hotels, some Broadway shows. One heralded fun city with an "I (Heart) New York" slogan. Over it a graffitist had spray-painted "support your local mugger." Ted chuckled and the laugh almost broke the depression he'd felt since he'd gotten on the train an hour earlier. Lisa had been forced by her new lease to put off moving for at least another week. Dawn was tripping over boxes and Michael was complaining that he couldn't find anything in the house. The boy was always looking for something vital, like a pet hamster or a stamp collection.

On top of all of it was the loss of the job at Paxton. The day after the phone call Ted had met Lonnie Carlton over coffee in the college faculty dining room. Carlton was tall and thin with a great rooster comb of graying hair that rose majestically over thick, bushy eyebrows. His voice carried a slight hint of Georgia in it, though the hint was more affectation than regionalism. Lonnie hadn't been to Atlanta in more than four decades.

"Ah don't think there's a way in hell around it, Ted. Ah'm straight on this. Ah talked to Art Berger, ya know, the union attorney. He says it's something like an oversight in the contract. It was something that we could not realistically have anticipated."

"What you're saying, Lonnie, is that the whole thing was a screw-up in the negotiations operation, right?"

Lonnie peered into the bottom of a styrofoam coffee cup, as if to find some oracular revelation there. "Ah . . . yeah. I guess so, Ted."

The two men shared each other's eyes for a second. "Poetic justice, Ted? We might have traded it away in all the fuss and feathers with you and Small. And, in the heat of the moment, we let it get past us."

Ted nodded. It was defeat, and he knew it. More than that, it was indeed poetic justice. Ted had been the prime opponent to Oscar Small in the negotiations. The two had created avalanches of press coverage, with Ted winning most of the clashes. Somehow, the notion of departmental seniority had slipped through the cracks and been placed in the contract in the words Oscar Small wanted. The college president had gladly played the fool. He knew it would be less than eight months before he had the ultimate laugh. Along with Ted, five of the seven negotiators had been quietly let go in the same way. As the chairman of the committee, or rather the co-chairman with Lonnie, Ted had little to complain about. He had seen the document, read it, initialed it, and taken it to the membership for approval. He had been hoisted on his own petard.

Ted's attention returned to the present, where his train was just pulling into Penn Station over fifteen minutes late. Ted slipped through the crowd and hurried up the stairs to the main level. He moved like a seasoned commuter, briefcase leading, knifing through clusters of people until he managed to get to the cab stand. He ducked into the back seat just ahead of a portly man who sputtered at having been beaten to the cab.

"Four-fifty-two Park."

The driver nodded and sped west on Thirty-second Street.

Ted leaned forward. "Were you going to go through the Grand Central bypass?"

The driver nodded and half flicked his head back toward the bulletproof glass that separated him from Ted. "Yeah. Why?"

"Don't. Turn north on Sixth and then take a right through Radio City. It's a little faster that way."

"Any way you want it, buddy." The driver settled back and concentrated on his driving.

Ted could have told the man that the trip he'd outlined was actually longer on the meter, but the crosstown traffic through Radio City was light compared to the logjam of delivery trucks in the blocks south of it. He had spent the summer between high school and college driving a cab in Manhattan. There was little about the city Ted did not know, especially the roads. "Faster but longer" had been his specialty. The meters were set for mileages more than time.

His estimate of traffic proved right. Soon the driver let him off in the midst of the massive black glass and steel Park Avenue monoliths. He tipped the cabbie an extra dollar and moved through the lobby with the same ease that he had through Penn Station.

He waved to Judy, Cathy's secretary, and moved down the labyrinth of offices that housed the editorial department of Halleck Publishers. He turned the corner in time to see Cathy standing at her desk, registering surprise. She was just reaching for a buzzing intercom phone.

"Even money it's Judy telling you I'm here."

She picked up the phone. "Yes?"

She smiled up at Ted and nodded. "Thanks, Judy."

She looked across at him as she hung up the phone. She was stunning, but there was something different about her, something that, in the rush to get in, Ted could not immediately place. "You cut your hair."

Her light blonde hair had been shoulder length the last time Ted had seen her. Now, it was shaggy, pixie-like. It lent a certain sensuousness to her sharp nose, and her eyes, always large, blue, and expressive, seemed even larger.

"Weeks ago. Like it?"

"I love it. I know why you cut it, too."

She blinked, surprised for a second. "W—Why?"

"To lure unsuspecting writers into taking smaller advances."

"Oh. Naturally." The remark was a recovery and Ted knew it. Cathy was quick enough to come up on her feet after being taken aback. But what had done the "taking aback"? It was the usual banter for the two of them. He assigned a small area in the back of his mind to be concerned about it later.

Cathy looked at her watch. "You're actually early."

"Is it *that* rare?"

"No. It's just that the railroad always manages twenty minutes in delays. I think it's part of their union agreement."

"Cathy, me girl, I could tell you a thing or two about union agreements."

She cocked her head to the side and stared at him analytically for a second.

"Like what?"

"Later. Over lunch. And where is that, the starving writer asked hungrily."

"The Jefferson. It's close and it's pretty cold out. OK?"

Ted smiled. "Halleck's paying, so we'll go anywhere you like."

The Jefferson was small but comfortable. It was on

Fiftieth, between Madison and Park, not too far from Publishers' Row, and close enough for the waiters to be used to writers and editors sitting for hours jabbering about money, contracts, and revisions. Befitting its name, the restaurant was early American, with ersatz musty booths and dim lighting. Everything in the place seemed to be oak, or something that would pass for oak. Red checkered tablecloths and red accessories made the place a cross between an Italian luncheonette and a colonial brothel. Ted and Cathy had often joked about it in the dozen or so lunches they'd had there. Two books earlier in their professional relationship, Cathy had been in an exotic lunch mood for something over half a year. Ted suspected that it was something stemming from her free-wheeling company credit card and title of senior editor. At twenty-eight, she had been one of the youngest in Publishers' Row to achieve that kind of status. And, though Halleck wasn't huge, like a Harper and Row or a Macmillan in nonfiction, the size of the company did nothing to diminish the status derived from her position versus her age.

At the end of the six-month spree, Ted had been through Indian, German, Japanese, and Greek restaurants in four consecutive lunches. The fifth lunch, as Ted remembered it, had been a discussion about *The Morresy Quest,* a Holmes-like mystery that had netted Ted a good sales record and springboarded him into a higher market value. Cathy had also bought and edited *The New Savages,* a skyjack thriller that had gotten optioned out for a film, and *Sander's Bay,* a quarter-of-a-million-word opus about a New England family. Ted had managed to go after three different markets in three different books, with some success. By her own admission, Cathy had made it clear that *Sander's Bay* been her least favorite of the three. Still, she had been there to do editorial wizardry when it was needed. The shaping of some of the fuzzier characters, the compounding of a number of the plotlines, all of those things were far more hers than his, and Ted knew it. He had, in return, dedicated *The New Savages* to her and given her glowing acknowledgments in all three books.

Despite the way Cathy often wrinkled her nose at the period of *Sander's Bay* and the historical style of the book, she had managed to marshal enough support through Walt Vertagglia and the rest of the higher echelons of Halleck to have the epic listed as a special edition. That meant that the house would print a quarter of a million copies and give Ira Kelton, Ted's film and television agent, a little clout to hit the networks. Ira had been an addition to Ted's career in the two years that Ted had known him. They had met through a mutual friend at a time when Ted had not ever considered television as a market. The smallish, balding man, who always reminded Ted of Swifty Lazar, had gone right out and gotten an option on the earlier skyjack thriller. The deal was still "pending," and had been for more than a year. Would they commit to screenplay money? Ted and Ira had batted it around twenty times on the phone.

"It's like Machiavellian politics," Ira had said in their most recent phone exchange. "The vice president supporting the property is trying to dog paddle through the tidal waves created by the ones getting the axe around him. They're putting their names on the doors at NBC with masking tape these days. We have to sit it out."

It was only a matter of a week or two before the year option ran out, and Ira informed Ted that the crisis of renegotiation was starting. Ted couldn't be sure that all of the Machiavelli talk was nothing more than Ira trying to look good at his job. But it didn't really matter much. The network had already paid eight thousand for a condensed and dehydrated "treatment." Being that much to the good, Ted was not about to collapse if they dropped the idea. Still, the kind of treatment that *Sander's Bay* got at the hands of Halleck's promotion budget could mean a lot to the delicate negotiations at NBC. There was no attempt in any way to exclude Cathy from their plans, and Ted and Ira discussed strategies often in three-way lunches at the Jefferson. It was in those that Ted realized how tough a businesswoman Cathy could be when she had to fight out a point. It made him realize that Cathy Seward was someone that no one wanted for an enemy.

The maître 'd led them to an oak booth at the back of the restaurant. Ted sat down and put his briefcase on his lap, snapping open the lock.

"I brought in those revisions of *Sander's Bay* you wanted. Do you care to look at them before we eat?"

"Just a quick look," said Cathy. "I don't want gravy stains on the manuscript."

She took the loose sheets and started to read, taking time out to order drinks. She was a speed reader and raced through the pages, handing them back to Ted at the precise moment the waiter returned with their drinks.

She looked up at him from the last pages of the typed manuscript.

"She's Amy, isn't she?"

"Who?"

"Lisa."

"Lisa's Amy?" It was half a question and half a statement, though as he said the words, Ted realized that it was more the latter. *Sander's Bay*'s shrewish matriarch, a cross between Daphne du Maurier's darkly sinister housekeeper in *Rebecca* and Albee's Martha in *Virginia Woolf,* was rooted in Lisa in ways Ted had perhaps not himself seen in the earlier years of their marriage. But she grew into the role, and perhaps writing her out of his system was a safety valve for his psyche. It didn't matter much, Ted thought. Lisa never read the books, anyway.

"That's three, now." Cathy smiled benignly, but with sincerity, as she brushed a wisp of the shag haircut away from her forehead.

"Three what?" Ted half knew what she was going to say.

"Three Lisas."

He nodded and took a sip of Cointreau. "Guilty."

He was aware as well that he had done Lisa in other books. But letting her burn to death in the last-chapter immolation of the Sander's ancestral home on Cape Cod was perhaps taking things too far.

"Too much?"

"Blessedly, not to the readers."

"That's a relief." They laughed.

She looked thoughtfully at him over the rim of her glass.

"Now, you'll have no more need of female heavies. You can christen a few males in the next book. Unless . . ."

"Unless the book is something that we decide we can't write."

She cocked her head to the side a fraction and raised an eyebrow.

"I was going to say, unless you decided to start dissecting your slave-driving editor. Why wouldn't we have a book?" She was reacting more to the tone of the statement than to the content. Caution, especially literary caution, was something she had not heard from Ted before.

He laid the whole thing out again, the conversation, the kinds of things that had been left unsaid between Charlie Howard and him. The most important factor was that Ted was sure that Charlie Howard's fear was real.

"I'm almost not sure what to write. If Charlie's story was lunacy, then I suppose we could make the thing a novel. If he was telling the truth, well . . ."

Cathy looked at him intensely. "You're frightened,

aren't you." Her tone said that her statement was a conclusion and not a question.

Ted shrugged. "I don't know, Cath. I just don't know." The fear he had seen in Charlie's eyes tightened around his throat like a noose. There were things that it was hard to communicate, like Ted's working in Psychological Operations in Viet Nam. The machinations of the field operatives were more Machiavellian than Cathy, or even Ira, could have ever imagined. Life was cheap there. Ted was starting to think that perhaps life might be cheap here, too.

"Ted? I'm not talking about an exposé. I don't think we have the research clout for that, although I wish we did. Let's assume that this man who came to you was crazy, or that the whole thing was a joke. We could still make a novel from it. The possibilities are fantastic. It doesn't matter what is in that hangar, if there really is a hangar, I mean. Think of what we could invent to put in there."

Ted nodded. He could see that Cathy was working up a head of steam. She was on the trail of a novel plot and he knew it. He watched as she got her notebook from her purse. Despite the fact that his better judgment was against it, Ted was starting to see the possibilities of a novel in the bizarre affair.

"Maybe we could take the line that the government was doing some research on, say, germ warfare, and it got out of hand. Maybe they managed to secrete some of the stuff in the hangar and they were killing off people who got too close to . . ."

As she spoke, Ted started to catch her excitement. He interrupted. They did that to each other constantly. "Wait. Germs or gas are out. If that were the case, the government would have put the flatbed into Dugway. It's far more secure, and besides, germs and gas would have been stored underground. If there were really battleship plate welded over the hangar doors, it wouldn't have had any impact on the containment of those substances. It has to be something else. We can make it something that the government simply *had* to lose somewhere, and something that human lives were small cost to hide. See, if it was gas or germs, they'd probably come in a canister container, and not on a flatbed. No. It would have to be something heavy, or bulky . . . something that simply couldn't be gotten rid of any other way."

"Ted?"

"What?"

"I've got a wild idea."

He leaned forward, his face curled into a mock grimace, his strong hands gripping the edge of the table. "Okay. Fire. I'm ready."

"There's a UFO in the hangar. How about that for a plot?"

Ted started to laugh. "You're incredible," he said through the laughter.

She stared at him querulously. "Too far out? You know, green men and all that?"

He shook his head. "No. Not too far out at all." He reached down and opened his briefcase, fishing for his too expensive and too thin Paxton College notebook. Cathy had started to roll out ideas and they sounded good. He was going to have to make notes. He noticed that the newspaper he'd brought to read on the train was still folded in the bottom. He opened the notebook to the last written page, then tried to smooth out the wrinkled newspaper. "Interested in *The Sentinel,* the hottest little daily in the state of New Jersey?"

Cathy shrugged. "Only if it publicizes your latest book."

Ted opened the paper with a flourish. "Only if my publisher sees fit to advertise my latest book."

He and Cathy laughed together. Book publishers were notoriously tight-fisted with advertising budgets. The laughs died as Ted's eye caught a headline.

VET, EX-MENTAL PATIENT, TAKES OWN LIFE

His stomach lurched for a second. He could feel the fear wash across him, as on his first mission in the jungle. It was there . . . there on page three. He hadn't looked at the page on the train. He'd simply gone from page one to the crossword. The face that stared at him placidly from the halftone print of the paper was that of Charlie Howard. The name in the caption was different, Lucas Morgan, they called him. But there was no mistaking the face. It was one that Ted had seen sitting in the back row of the amphitheater for nine or ten weeks.

He forced himself to skim over the story, while, frightened by a look she'd never seen on Ted's face, Cathy waited. The reading did nothing to help him regain his composure. The man in the picture, an ex-mental patient recently released from a VA hospital in the northern part of the state, had committed suicide by hanging himself with his necktie.

The five men who'd been on the truck when it rumbled onto the base; all of them had died within a year. One had hanged himself with his necktie.

Ted turned the paper around to face Cathy. She looked at the face in the picture and then her eyes met Ted's. "The man from the class?"

Ted nodded.

Cathy cocked her head to the side. "Are you sure, Ted? The name's different."

Ted nodded again, with assurance. "It is, Cath."

They sat in silence for a minute, with all the enthusiasm of the new novel suddenly drained. They were sobered.

"Ted?" she asked with a delicacy in her voice.

"Hmmm?" he said, lost in thought and still looking at the picture.

"We have to write it now, I think."

"You mean as an insurance policy?"

"Yes. Perhaps."

Ted folded his arms and looked at her. "Funny, that was what Charlie wanted me to do to help him survive."

There was a caution in Cathy's face, and Ted was happy to see it there. If there was one thing that he was pleased about, it was the fact that he had not mentioned to her the manners of the deaths of all of the airmen. He tinkered mentally with the idea of revealing that to her, too. But he decided against it. He thought it unfair, in a way, to ask her to support him without all the facts at her disposal, yet, since he'd read the story, a new dimension had been added: his safety, and perhaps hers. He would have to go on with the investigation, but there were things that he could not tell her . . . for her own good. Still feeling ambivalent about his decision, he went back to her office with her and they Xeroxed the *Sentinel* article. They started a file with it, ostensibly to become part of the "novel."

Charlie Howard? Or Lucas Morgan? As Ted joined the commuter rush, he decided to visit the offices of the *Sentinel* in the morning.

CHAPTER SIX

Hank MacKenzie groaned as he looked at the stack of mail on the sorting table. It was the beginning of the Christmas onslaught. The peak would be in three to four weeks, when the windows of the Shore Park Post Office would be jammed with damn fools who didn't heed the warning to mail early. They'd be screaming about packages that *absolutely had to* get to Podunk or Polynesia before Christmas. They'd ask about sending them registered or certified and Hank would have to patiently explain that registration and the chain of postal hand receipts required on each of them slowed the movement process by as much as a week in the Christmas season. It was the time of year that he counted the years and days left until retirement and quietly cursed the whole holiday season. He put down the coffee cup and crossed the sorting room to speak to the two part-timers who'd been hired to deal with the Christmas surge. One was a young man, about twenty, named Cliff something or other. The other was a heavy-set woman in her fifties whose name escaped him totally.

"Both of you come with me." He led them across to the sorting table and they dutifully followed.

"This is the input table. The initial sort happens here and it's the part of the flow that you have to keep up with. In another week we'll have to add another table and after that we'll be piling the stuff on the floor. Here we'll separate by class according to the postage and the requirements on the chart." He pointed absently to a rate chart that was tacked to the wall above the table.

"Separate the first from the third and the fourth class circular material." He pointed to the bins for each. "Then, pull the packages out and pile them over here." He pointed to the separate long table that led to the canceler. "At least for today, you'll have to finish the pile, then move to the sorter and cancel the packages, then organize them by town. By next week we'll have another part-timer on staff to handle the packages. For now, we'll have to double up."

Cliff asked a few questions, and Hank answered them before retiring to the front window and letting the two of them start on their own.

Cliff and the woman, who introduced herself as Grace Saunders, spoke nervously as they started to sort the mound of mail on the table. They were having a hard time trying to envision the kind of massive crush of Christmas cards, packages, and parcels that Hank had said would flood the office. It was clear that both of them were intimidated by MacKenzie's attitude.

They were an hour or so into the sorting when Cliff came on a soggy packing envelope with a fragmentary, rain-smeared address. He peered at it to try to make out the numbers. He managed to get them, but the name of the street was almost totally washed off. He grumbled to himself that the addresser must have been drunk. The writing was a wild scrawl. He took a felt-tipped pen from his shirt pocket and started to try to trace the name of the street on the package. He got a few letters but could not find any street name close to what was on the envelope when he looked in the street ZIP directory. He turned to Grace.

"Is there anything that you can make out from this?" he asked in a quiet voice. Neither he nor Grace wanted to attract MacKenzie's attention.

She peered at the package for a long minute. Cliff

could see a sparkle of recognition in her eyes. She smiled. "I know the name. He's one of my teachers at Paxton State College. It's Dr. Lawrence. Wait."

She moved across to the phone directory near the end of the long counter and swiftly looked up Ted's address. She came back and wrote in the correct address on the package. Then, satisfied that she'd done a good turn for Ted Lawrence, she passed the envelope to Cliff, who started to line it up in the sorter.

Cliff set the battered package in the feeder tray of the automatic canceler. It was too big, and Cliff was stumped. MacKenzie had never explained what to do in such a circumstance. His briefing had been terse and cryptic at best. He turned the package on its side and found that he could manage to get it into the tray. The problem now was that the package, if passed through the canceler, would have the cancellation marks in the wrong place. It didn't matter, Cliff thought. There had to be thousands of packages like it with cancel marks on the wrong spot. The letter carrier would deliver it, no matter what, now that the address was clearly written by Grace. He slammed the package on both sides, insuring that it would fit smoothly in the machine, and nudged it in the direction of the funnel-like feeder. It moved ahead smoothly until it was next to the electronic sensors. Then all hell broke loose.

The automatic canceler started to hum, then sputter, then it seemed to erupt into a shower of sparks. The machine started to go crazy. Smoke billowed from the top, and packages and letters swirled up toward the ceiling, falling like snow in the direction of Cliff.

MacKenzie yelled from the front window and started for the sorting table on a dead run. Grace screamed, afraid that the smoking machine, which was threatening to break loose from its mountings, was going to explode and kill all of them.

Cliff backed away, his eyes wide in terror. All he

could think of was that he was going to lose his Christmas job. As he backed up, he tripped over a sorting table and fell heavily into Grace. They tumbled to the floor in a heap, with letters and packages falling all around them. The sorting machine was emitting a noise like a soul screaming in agony when MacKenzie skidded to a halt in front of Grace and Cliff.

"What the hell . . . ?" He bellowed over the scream of the machine. They didn't answer him. It was all they could do to manage to avoid getting hit by a rain of falling packages.

MacKenzie turned in the direction of the berserk machine. He dashed to the adjacent wall and yanked the fire extinguisher from its rack, then headed to the machine. He reached the table, almost losing his footing on envelopes and skewed packages. But MacKenzie was not a man to panic. He reached for the emergency switch below the table. What happened then horrified Cliff and Grace.

A tongue of blue flame licked outward from the bottom of the machine and stabbed at MacKenzie's hand. The shock picked him up and threw him backward some five feet. The fire extinguisher, triggered into life by the same bolt of energy, spewed carbon dioxide gas across the sorting room. Cliff pushed himself to his feet and staggered in the direction of the inert form of MacKenzie. As he leaned down, he could see that the man's eyes were moving and he was making gestures in the direction of the machine. His lips moved but there was no sound. Sure that MacKenzie was not dead, Cliff corralled the errant fire extinguisher and, aiming it in front of him, he advanced on the machine. The fog of CO_2 extinguished the flames, and when he was sure they were out, Cliff threw the cylinder at the plug that attached the machine into the wall. The impact managed to dislodge it.

The machine fell silent.

MacKenzie was taken to the hospital for observation,

though it was the opinion of the doctor who arrived with the ambulance that he had suffered a mild electrical shock plus cuts and bruises. A second shift supervisor, whom neither Grace nor Cliff knew, arrived and helped the rest of the shift clean up the mess.

Among the things swept up and hand sorted was the package destined for Ted Lawrence. In the confusion it was tossed into the wrong bin. It would be a day before the route man discovered the error in sorting, and it would take another three days before the battered package would be delivered to the proper address.

The madness in the sorting room was explained as faulty equipment, and MacKenzie was directed to reinspect all of the sorting equipment as soon as he came back to work.

CHAPTER SEVEN

The *Sentinel* staffers had been enthusiastic, but the visit had yielded little in real information. They had gotten the story of the death from the local police, who had been summoned by a hysterical landlady. Charlie Howard's body had been moved to the morgue, and the information about his name and background had, according to a *Sentinel* editor, been gathered from a check of the man's VA records. Why the name change? Why Lucas Morgan rather than Charlie Howard? Were they the same man or just look-alikes? Ted had pondered the idea as he walked from the century-old newspaper building and into the parking lot. With the exception of time spent in a state psychiatric ward of a VA hospital, the backgrounds matched, as did the addresses.

Ted settled himself behind the wheel and fished out his note pad. The actual interment would be late this afternoon. No one had claimed the body, and the American Legion had assumed the responsibility for a small memorial service. The fees would be paid by the government, and a local clergyman would be in attendance. The cemetery would be only half an hour's drive from Ted's home. Ted started the car and drove home through the light sleet. There were a lot of things to think about.

He had been sitting on the couch in the den for about fifteen minutes when the idea struck him. He reached for the phone and dialed Paxton's number.

"Paxton State College."

"Registration, please." The college had spent millions for an on-line computer system that allowed students to register for courses by having a clerk simply enter the data on a computer terminal. All he'd have to do was . . .

"Registration, June Murphy."

"June? This is Ted Lawrence. I've got a favor to ask."

Ted looked down to the computer roster of the students in his parapsychology class and the underlined name of Charles Howard. It only took a minute for June to punch in the student's number and for the computer to display the record on the screen.

"Dr. Lawrence, I'm sorry."

"About what?"

"About the record. We don't list a student by that name. Are you sure you have the right roster entry? Is there a chance that the roster is from the beginning of the semester and he might have been dropped from the course?"

"I didn't drop him, June, and there's no notation indicating that he dropped. He was a student in good standing in the course until just over two weeks ago. Can you pull the file copy on him?"

June sighed. Ted could tell she was aggravated. A million-dollar computer was supposed to eliminate the need to go through file drawers for manila folders.

"Doctor, it'll take a few minutes."

"I'll hold."

It took more than a few minutes, and when June came back on the phone there was even more aggravation in her voice.

"Dr. Lawrence, the roster you have has to be erroneous. We don't have a file on Charles Howard. We have another Howard, Angela Howard, but she has never been in one of the sections you teach."

Ted thought for a second. "Can you punch in the same number and check the name Lucas Morgan?"

"Of course." There was a slight pause. "No record there, either. I'm sorry. It looks like your student slipped through the cracks. I don't really know how it could have happened. There's a chance that he might have been a student at one time, say several semesters ago, and we might have slipped up on an initial computer entry."

"But you'd have a file copy on paper, no?"

"We would."

"And you don't?"

"We don't. And darned if I know why. Do you want me to dig a little more?"

"No, June. Thanks—and can you switch me to Alan in the VA office?"

"Sure, Professor."

There were no VA records under either name. Charles Howard, Lucas Morgan—neither man existed. Everything had been neatly erased. Ted hung up the phone and started out the glass doors to the chill December day. The sun had slid behind a wall of gray clouds, and the wind from the sea had picked up. The odds were that there would be more sleet by sundown, perhaps even snow. It would be a cold, bleak afternoon for a funeral. Ted chuckled blackly. A funeral of a man who seemed never to have really existed. Would the ghost of Charlie Howard laugh at that? He wondered. He remembered the fear he'd seen in the man's eyes. He thought not.

Shore Park Memorial Cemetery was set on a small hillock of land that overlooked the curving coastline. The sea wind was whipping drizzle and fog in from the water, and the scene reminded Ted eerily of a surreal World War One battlefield.

The flag-draped casket sat barren above the fresh grave, while four American Legion members, complete with small overseas caps, straddled each side of the site. At the head of the casket an overcoated minister rubbed his hands against the cold and pulled a small, black prayer book from his pocket. Aside from the Legionnaires and the minister, a bugler from the local Boy Scout troop stood at rigid, frozen attention, awaiting his cue to play Taps. The cue was to come from the head of the Legion detachment, who stood a few feet back from the scene.

The American Legion Commander.

Dear God!

With everything that had been going on, Ted had totally forgotten. The tiny, spectacled eyes, the tight lips, and the pale complexion.

Oscar Small!

The college president had been the commander of the post for more than a year and, now that he stood in the drizzle, Ted realized that he'd known it and forgotten. It was noteworthy as well as awkward. But at least, he reasoned, his presence might just be making Small more uncomfortable than Small's was making him.

The minister finished the last words of the service with the speed of a man who had a number of other appointments to keep. The two ranks of four Legionnaires saluted on Small's thin, high-voiced command, and the lone Boy Scout played a tinny taps, most of which was blown away by the stiffening wind.

There were no other mourners. No one to seek out for information. No leads to ferret . . . nothing.

The detachment and the minister moved in the direction of their cars, leaving Ted and Small standing across the still-open grave from one another. Small did not make an attempt to avoid Ted. He knew that he was dealing with a master of confrontation. Ted waited for the college president to speak.

"Was the man a friend, ah, Dr. Lawrence?" Small asked, tentatively.

Ted shook his head. "No, Doctor. Just a student. It's

just something I felt I owed one of my students, especially another Viet Nam vet. You understand, I'm sure." Ted smiled thinly and his eyes bore into Small's, who looked away. He wondered if the president was going to mention his being laid off. Or was Small worrying that Ted would?

"That's laudable of you. Now, if you'll excuse me, I have to get back to work."

Small moved past Ted, his pace quickening. He was a man tactfully fleeing. Ted wondered if it was simply the awkward unexpectedness of the meeting or something else. Small seemed truly frightened. He made a mental note to ponder Small's reactions further, when he had the time.

He looked from the retreating form of Small down to the casket. Stripped of its flag, it was clearly the cheapest that could have been bought. He felt silent rage build inside him at the man or men who had killed Charlie and the men in Boston and all the others. The frustration and resentment boiled up in his stomach like a stew in an overheated pot. For a second he wished he could write a real nonfiction exposé that would knock the sons of bitches flat on their asses. But the rational side of him said there was no chance of that. All Charlie had wanted to do was to get away from them alive. The writing of an exposé was something that could get Ted killed ten times over. No, Cathy had been right. A novel was something different, something safer. Hadn't Simpson and Burger managed to do that with the clandestine Philadelphia Experiment? And Jackie Susann and all the others. Hadn't they all managed to stay out of the range of lawsuits by writing their works as thinly disguised fiction? He pondered the possibilities of writing the novel that he and Cathy had discussed, as he walked down the hill with a frigid wind blowing at his back. Yes, the only thing to do was to put all of it in novel form. But first he absolutely had to have more information on Charlie. He owed the man that, at least.

The old Victorian house was shabby. It was several years overdue for painting. In the eaves, several shingles had slipped, and there were a few upper-floor windows where boards had replaced glass. It was a hell of a place to have to die.

Mrs. Walchek was helpful in a hand-wringing sort of way. She was short, plump, nearing sixty, and widowed for more than fifteen years. Ted remembered seeing women like her when he was a child, in the ghetto of the South Bronx. They always wore black, as Mrs. Walchek did. They constantly prayed their beads and lit candles in the local Catholic church. An almost compulsive religiosity gripped them. Somehow it seemed that Mrs. Walchek had grown from the generation he had seen as a boy. The inner hall of the old house had its Madonna and a small, brittle shred of palm from the previous Easter. But Mrs. Walchek, no matter how devout in matters of the soul, still had managed to become something of a businesswoman.

She lumbered up the stairs to the second floor, which smelled of cabbage. She puffed and spoke as she moved, and Ted followed.

"Well, Doctah, I tell ya, it's terrible for my business, if ya take my meaning. With the story and the paper and all the police, I was sure I wouldn't get another renter for the rest of the winter. Ya know, the summer takes care of itself, what with all the families coming from the city and all. But between now and then, well, I was really worried."

"I understand," Ted said sympathetically.

She was still talking as they reached the door to the "studio" apartment.

"I was really surprised. I mean the way they done it and all . . ."

"Who? And what did they do?"

"The men from the VA. They was here right after it happened. Really nice, ya know, sorta clean-cut an' all. They was here the same afternoon I found poor Mr. Morgan. I mean I found him in the morning, but they was here in the late afternoon."

"What did they want?"

"Well, they said I wasn't supposed to mention it, but seein' as you was one of his professors an' all . . ." She paused for a second before she went on. Ted looked around the room. It had been thoroughly cleaned, or else Charlie, or Lucas, had been compulsively neat. The room was in the front of the house, and the windows looked out on the windblown and semi-deserted street. The convertible couch-bed was neatly folded away, and the coffee table in front of it had been polished to a glassy finish. In fact, the whole studio smelled of polish and disinfectant. To remove fingerprints? Ted wondered. In the corner of the room an old desk had also been put in order. The place looked like a barracks.

"Oh . . ."

"What?" Ted turned to her.

"I thought that book was here, the one poor Mr. Morgan got from you. Musta left it downstairs. I'll get it for ya."

She turned and lumbered down the hall and the stairs, leaving Ted alone in the room. The book had been a ploy, the method Ted used to gain entry. He'd mentioned a book that he'd loaned to "Lucas" and hoped to find in his personal possessions. But it looked as if the "men from the VA" had cleared away everything. Still, he'd been lucky. There apparently had been a book left. He listened for Mrs. Walchek's footsteps to get some distance below before he started to look through the apartment. He didn't know what he was looking for, or even why he came. Perhaps it was his words at the grave. He moved to the desk and opened the drawers. They were empty and wiped clean. They smelled of Lysol and polish, as the rest of the apartment did. The huge old oak bureau was the same. All traces of the previous renter were gone. The room was certainly cleaner than the rest of the rooming house seemed to be. Mrs. Walchek did not seem to be much of a housekeeper, while the men from the VA seemed to have been unbelievably meticulous.

The kitchenette, which was little more than a converted closet, and the bathroom, where Mrs. Walchek had found the body, had been essentially scoured in the same way. How had the paper mentioned he'd done it? Looped his tie around the overhead waterline that fed the old-fashioned high tank toilet, tied the other end around his neck and jumped from the top of the john. Ted shuddered. It was a ghastly way to die. And there was no note . . . nothing. And the VA comes in and collects everything in a matter of hours. Unbelievably efficient of them, Ted thought.

He moved back into the living room and stark brown walls. A single print, a seascape, sat perched on a nail a few feet from the door. Ted peered at it for a minute. There was something wrong about it. It was crooked . . . ever so slightly crooked. Odd, how a crooked picture could be left uncorrected in an apartment that had been so totally cleaned and organized. He walked over and reached up to straighten it a fraction. Had he moved the picture in any other way or at any other place on the frame he would not have felt the double thickness of paper. He could hear Mrs. Walchek starting up the stairs as he ran his hand over the back of the print. Yes. It was a lump. Working quickly, he pried apart the backing and slipped the paper from between the two pieces of cardboard. Mrs. Walchek was just a few steps from the door when Ted corrected the angle of the picture and stuffed the paper in his topcoat pocket.

"Here it is, Doctor. The men who came left it with some school papers that they said didn't belong to poor Mr. Morgan."

"Thank you." Ted took the book, seeing that it was a library book from the Paxton collection. Oddly, it was a book Ted had on reserve for his parapsychology course. The trip to the rooming house was suddenly, luckily legitimized. The text was a compilation of essays on Stonehenge, ley lines, and astro-archaeology. The chances were that Lucas was going to set up a research paper using the book.

"Mrs. Walchek?"

"Yeah, Doctor?"

"You were talking about the men from the VA? Why they came?"

"Well, they said they were from that VA hospital upstate, the one at Dobbs? They said he was an out . . . outlet patient? Something like that."

"An outpatient?"

"Yeah, that was it. Anyway, I told them he had a lease until June, and now it looked like I was going to be out the money for the rest of the year. Winter renters are hard to find, especially this late in the season. They said not to worry, and that the government would take care of everything, and that there was a fund for things like this. Then they paid me for the rest of the lease. Odd, though."

"What?"

"When they paid me, they took the lease with them. I never seen anything like that before. But the check cleared the bank, so I didn't worry about it. It was awful nice of them. Ah . . . Doctor?"

"Yes?"

"You wouldn't happen to know of any of your students that might like a nice, clean place to stay real cheap for the rest of the year, wouldja?"

Ted smiled his best smile as he fingered the folded piece of paper in his pocket.

"If I do find any, Mrs. Walchek, I'll send them right over."

"Thanks. I don't want none of them hippies or marijuana smokers. But somebody nice, clean-cut . . . ya know?"

"I know."

Ted walked to the car both frightened and excited. He unlocked the door and slipped behind the wheel. The rain spattering on the windows and windshield obscured him from the outside. He pulled the paper from his pocket and unfolded it.

Orders! A single Xeroxed copy of a set of orders that assigned A/1/C Morgan, Lucas J. to something called Project Unicorn. Ted looked down the cryptic codings on the rest of the page. The security clearances carried were near the bottom.

TOP SECRET . . . COSMIC . . . CRYPTO . . .
ALPHA-RED . . . DARPA-RED

They were the ones Charlie had mentioned in their conversation the night before Thanksgiving vacation. He looked back up the page. The assignment orders covered a number of names, listed in alphabetical order. Among them were PATRINO, ANTHONY and RODGERS, ANDREW. They were the names of the dead men in Massachusetts. Everything was true . . . everything.

He started the car and drove toward home.

Half a block behind, another car pulled from the curb and followed at a discreet distance.

CHAPTER EIGHT

It was Saturday morning, and Ted was happy to see the sun after more than a week of leaden skies and chill rain. Outside, the temperature promised to creep into the forties and Ted had already told Michael and Dawn that he would drive them to the county museum, which had a new "hands on" set of exhibits Dawn would enjoy. Michael would like the exhibits about American Indians and the local tribes. He'd been collecting arrowheads for as long as Ted could remember.

The real reason he was going to take them out was nothing more than an open secret. They'd all spent a tense week with Lisa still in the house. There had been sniping back and forth, and Dawn was being upset with the clutter that impeded her progress through the house. But thank God the divorce and the delay in Lisa's moving out had not erupted into full-scale conflict.

On top of all of it was the copy of the orders he'd gotten from the rooming house. He had gone over them a hundred times, and each time they seemed to confirm more tangibly what Charlie had said about the strange assignment in Utah and the dead airmen.

He had called Cathy about the find, and she'd asked for a copy for safekeeping. Ted already had the copy sealed in an addressed envelope next to him on the den couch. Another set had been placed in a hastily rented safe deposit box, the key to which jingled in Ted's pocket. He had gone through the library book a page at a time to look for any marginal notes that Charlie might have made. All he had found was a small arrow that pointed to Ogden on a fold-out map. The map itself was a projection of ley lines, done by the devotees of the theories of Alfred Watkins. According to one theory, the world was connected by an intricate series of straight lines set up by the ancients to mark subterranean lines of power, planetary power. Supposedly, it was a power that the ancients knew how to tap, and modern man had forgotten. The only mark made on the map was the small arrow in black ink. Ted had to assume Charlie had made the marking. It was too much of a coincidence that it had pointed to Ogden. What was unusual about the arrow was not only did it point to Ogden, but also to an intersection of lines that quartered Ogden like cross hairs on a telescopic sight. It seemed that in addition to the clandestine activity that had transpired at the small Army supply base, the place, or at least the nearby city, was at an intersection point of two ley lines. He made a mental note to mention it to Cathy. Perhaps she could find a book plot in that, too. He smiled to himself for a second as he thought about her.

"Daddy?" It was Dawn, standing at the door to the den, seemingly afraid to come further for fear of stumbling into something.

"Yes, honey?"

"Are we going soon?"

"Yeah. As soon as I get back from the post office. I have to mail something."

"Why don't you just give it to the postman? He'll be by any time now."

"It's kind of important, honey. I want to send it direct. We'll leave as soon as I get back. See if you can get that little brother of yours organized for the trip. Where's your mother?"

Dawn frowned. "She's up in the kitchen, drinking coffee. I haven't been up there. Every time I get to know where everything is, she moves things. Daddy, when's she going?"

"Day after tomorrow, hon. That's firm. The moving men will be in to get her things right after I get you and Michael off to school. By the time you get home in the afternoon the minefield will be all cleared away. Things should get easier after that."

As Dawn tapped her cane along the hall that led to her room, Ted grabbed his parka and headed up to the kitchen. Lisa stood in the center of the chaos that the kitchen had become in the moving process. She wore a green dress to match her eyes, and the color contrasted startlingly with her hair.

She sipped the coffee and looked at him. "I thought you were taking the children."

"I am. I have to mail something first. I should be back in half an hour. I'll take them then, and you can have time to get the rest of the things together."

"Oh." She nodded and sipped her coffee. It was a strange exchange, quiet, terse. Ted nodded and headed out to the garage. What a hell of an ending to a marriage, he thought. We stand there saying as little as possible to one another and being civil. Jesus!

As he headed out the driveway he saw the mail truck stop at the pillar box and stuff it with things. They'd be Christmas cards and junk mail, Ted thought. He'd pick them up on the way back. He turned left onto the side street and headed for the corner.

A hundred yards down the street, another driver started the motor of Ghost One. In the right seat, a man downed the last of a cup of coffee. He jammed the styrofoam cup in a small paper bag on the floor and grabbed for the radio microphone.

"Ghost Two from Ghost One. We'll stay with subject. You stay on the house. Acknowledge?"

He released the talk button and waited. All he could hear was static.

"Ghost Two? Do you acknowledge?"

More static.

The driver eased the car out onto the side street and his eyes darted to those of his partner.

"Hurry it up. I don't want to lose him."

"Ghost Two? Do you read?"

Nothing. Just static.

The man in the right seat slammed the mike back into its cradle.

"Those assholes. I told them to inspect their equipment yesterday."

The driver shook his head in nervous agreement. "We can't wait," he said. He accelerated to maintain contact with Ted's car as it rounded a distant corner.

Seventy-five yards down the road, Ghost Two sat parked just off the side of the road. On the transmission hump, the radio hissed with static. The set was in perfect working order, and the message from Ghost One had come through flawlessly. But the driver and his companion had not heard it. They had not even had time to hear the hissing spits of the two silenced pistol shots that had slammed through the passenger side window. The first shot caught the man in the passenger seat just to the rear of the right eye. In the split second that it took for the bullet to mushroom against the soft tissues of the frontal lobe, the left side of his head exploded outward from the hydrostatic shock of the impact. The driver barely had time to turn into the shower of blood, skull fragments, and brain tissue before he was hit above the right eye by the second shot. Both were dead before their bodies had time to slump to the blood-drenched seat.

Dawn was standing in the kitchen, zipping up her parka and pulling on a pair of warm ski mittens, when Lisa came in with the mail. There were five Christmas cards, all addressed to Mr. and Mrs. Lawrence. She slapped them down on the kitchen table like a poker player slamming down a winning hand. Perhaps they could split those up as they'd split up everything else in the house, she thought. There was a battered package addressed to Ted, which she also slammed down on the table. The rest, eight or ten pieces of junk mail pushing sales, retirement packages, and subscriptions, she started to tear into pieces and toss into the plastic garbage can that stood in the corner. She took no notice of Dawn until the little girl spoke.

"What are you tearing up?"

Lisa turned quickly, and when she spoke there was an edge in her voice.

"I'm not ripping up dear Daddy's mail, Dawn."

"I didn't say you were, Mother." The child's voice was shrill, and there was a slight quiver to it. "All I said was . . ."

"I know what you said and what you meant."

"No, you don't."

"What?"

The small exchange was building and both of them knew it. It also became rapidly clear that neither one could stop it.

"All right, little Miss Smart Ass, what did you mean?"

Dawn was on the edge of tears, that rimmed full in her sightless blue eyes.

"You never loved him, d-did you?"

"*That* is none of your business. Do you hear me?"

"I . . . I just can't wait till you leave here."

Lisa was livid . . . speechless. She stormed across the kitchen and grabbed the lone, soggy package that had been addressed to Ted. She slammed it into the front of Dawn's blue and white parka. "Here! Here's your father's precious goddamn mail. You can stand guard over it until he gets back, and do me the favor of not speaking to me again."

Dawn was shaking with anger and fighting tears. She

snapped open the fold-up white cane and tucked the package under her left arm. She gave her mother a wide berth and went to the kitchen door.

She moved down the steps and into the backyard acreage that she knew and felt comfortable in. She had learned the position of every bush, tree and shrub over the years. The plot was more than two acres deep, and the back acre Ted had let grow wild. He'd often taken her and her brother there to tell them stories, and, Dawn had recently suspected, when the bickering with Lisa had become too intense.

She turned her head to the sky and allowed the fleeting warmth of the December sun to play on her face. Daddy had said that the sun was yellow, though all of the Braille science books had said that while a G-type star was indeed yellow, the light emitted was white. When she'd confronted him about it, he'd said that actually the colors of sunlight depended on atmospherics and that the sunlight could appear to be many colors. Though, he'd admitted, scientifically she'd been right. Her father never made her feel different, never made her feel like a freak as the children at school sometimes did.

She moved her head down and sniffed the chill air. Her feet shuffled through the crunching leaves like the sound of milk rolling over her Rice Crispies. She threaded her way back through the path that they had worn thin in the summer. It was a few minutes later when she got to the small clearing. She tapped the cane to the right and it hit the log she remembered was there. She squared herself in front of it and sat down, shifting the envelope in front of her as she moved. She reached around and gripped the envelope with two hands as though it were some sort of life preserver. The pain of all the anger and frustration seemed to descend on her like a cold veil of ice. She hugged the envelope and started to cry.

She wasn't sure just how long she'd been there when

she heard the car pull into the driveway. She fished for a handkerchief in the parka pocket and blew her nose, then wiped the warm, jagged lines of salty tears from her face. It took a few minutes for her to manage a deep breath without a sob. She took her time. There was no sense in letting Mother see her this way. She started back to the house, using the cane more from habit than for a guide over the familiar path.

She was still some distance from the house when she stopped suddenly. She thought she heard a sound. Another car in the driveway? No. The same car . . . leaving. She started moving more quickly. He wouldn't have taken Michael and left without her. He simply wouldn't. Maybe Mother had left. Dawn thought that might be a small blessing.

She came in through the kitchen door and promptly skidded and lost her footing.

Her shoulder and hip hit the tile heavily, though luckily she managed to protect her head from the impact of the fall. As she tried to get up, she slipped again on something wet and warm. Had her mother dropped something? Something warm, sticky . . .

It was some ten minutes later when Ted pulled into the driveway. He turned off the motor and trotted up the steps toward the kitchen door. As he opened it and stepped into the kitchen, he stopped, frozen, horrified. *Jesus . . . sweet Jesus!*

The mortal remains of Lisa Lawrence lay on the floor of the kitchen, her back half propped against the door of the refrigerator. The right side of her head was . . . gone. Blood and fragments of gore were spattered across the tile floor, and there were skid marks in the blood that led out of the kitchen and into the hall.

He stared at her for a long minute before he dared to move. When he was sure he wasn't going to be sick, he moved toward her, avoiding the bloody smear on the floor. He reached down and gingerly fingered the side of her head that wasn't shattered.

Still warm. Minutes ago. Minutes!

His eyes darted back to the blood.

My God. The children!

"Michael? Dawn?"

Nothing.

"MICHAEL! DAWN?"

Nothing.

He ran to the hall, this time heedless of the pools and smears of blood.

He tripped over the huddled form of Michael in the hall. The child had been shot once behind the left ear. It was professionally done, as with Lisa.

Suddenly Ted was afraid to look further, irrational. He dropped to his knees and looked at the limp form of Michael. The boy had on a coat. He'd been waiting for his father to come back so he could go to the museum and see the arrowheads. Jesus.

He started to lift Michael's body and then stopped when he realized that half the head was gone. It wasn't Michael anymore. Just as Lisa wasn't Lisa. Just corpses. The memory of Viet Nam sprung to him from a fog of forgetfulness. The ambushes in the Mang Giang Pass. The dead troops shoved from their machine guns like rag dolls. Dead, just corpses, no longer soldiers. But this was not war, not now, not in New Jersey. It was something more insidious than that.

A sound.

Ted froze.

Another.

He strained to hear it. A sob . . . from the living room.

"Dawn."

Ted pushed the body of Michael aside as he might have moved one of the dead in an ambush.

Dawn was sitting in the middle of the living room. Her cane was on the floor next to her, and her parka and dress were covered with blood. Her arms were tightly folded across her chest. They clutched a package.

"Are you going to kill me . . . too?" she said in a tight, thin voice.

"Dawn. It's Daddy."

He started toward her.

"Please don't kill me, too. Please?"

He scooped her up and held her. "It's Daddy. Daddy, honey."

D—Da—?" She collapsed against his shoulder, sobbing hysterically.

It was ten minutes or so before he managed to calm her down. She told him she had slipped on the blood in the kitchen and then discovered Lisa. Terrified, she had gone into the hall and tripped over the body of her brother. She had stumbled into the living room and stayed there when she heard the car in the driveway and the kitchen door open. She told him about the sound of the car she'd heard from the backyard, through the last of her sobs and shakes.

Ted started to pry the envelope away from her but she held it tightly.

"No. It was the mail. It was for you. I took it with me."

He started to answer when something caught his eye. It was the lamp in the far corner of the room, the lamp Lisa had paid over a hundred dollars for, almost seven years ago. It had been overturned and shattered. As he scanned the room, he realized that all of it was a shambles. He had not noticed it before. The living room had been hurriedly ransacked. Robbers? He shook his head. Why murder a woman and a child just for a robbery? Could they have been junkies? Strung out? Crazy?

He looked back to the terrified, blood-smeared form of his daughter. Luck.

It had been sheer luck that she had not been in the house. For that matter, it had been sheer luck that he had not been there, also.

He reached down and slipped the package away from her. He was about to toss it away when he noticed the odd, almost indecipherable address and the crooked stamps. The package had been mailed in a hurry, he thought. Next to the stamps was what looked like a cancellation mark, though most of it was under the stamps. Odd. Someone had used the envelope a second time. The semicircle of black print half ringed the fragments of a word. The point of origin of the first mailing. It said BOS.

The thought struck him like a hammerblow. Boston. The man in Boston.

He turned the package over. The second cancellation was on the wrong side, but the more recent printing was more than clear. SHORE PARK. Charlie?

"My God."

"W—what, Daddy?"

"Nothing, honey. Just rest for a minute." The Shore Park cancellation was dated the same day Charlie was found by Mrs. Walchek . . . and the men from the "VA."

"It was my fault," the little girl said. "Mine."

"What?"

"My fault. It was mine, Daddy. Mommy and Michael. They—I—if I hadn't had the fight with Mommy, and I hadn't gone out to the back, maybe they wouldn't . . ."

"Dawn." It was a tone that she had not heard from her father before. "I want you to listen to me. If you had been here, you would have been killed too. There was nothing you could have done about it. There would have been nothing that I could have done about it. If I had been here, the chances are that I would have been killed too. Do you understand me?"

She thought for a second and shuddered her way through a deep breath.

"Yes, Daddy."

"And there is no blame. Understand?"

Inside him a rage was starting to build. Against Charlie, against everything to do with the story he'd been told that night before Thanksgiving.

"Just sit here a second." He got to his feet and started to the phone. The police would . . . He stopped in mid-thought. The police would what? They were going through an ugly divorce. All of Ted's co-workers knew a thread or two of the marriage difficulties. Then there was the loss of the teaching post. The lines of the newspaper story started to form in his mind. *"Despondent college professor, out of work, kills estranged wife and son in marital dispute."* No. Not the police.

He thought for a second. They had wanted the package. Perhaps they had been waiting for the mailman so that they could move on the house. If the men from the "VA" had done such a tidy job with Charlie, they would not leave the Ted Lawrence case sloppily half done. No. They'd . . .

The phone rang. Ted jumped, and his adrenaline surged, making him shake.

His car was in the driveway, and they'd know he was here. They were making sure. But who were "they"? Who were the men from the VA?

He let the phone ring and started back to Dawn. He scooped her up and headed for her bedroom. He grabbed two or three dresses, a couple of pairs of jeans, underwear, tops; the things she would need on a trip. He piled them on the floor and placed an open suitcase retrieved from the top shelf of her closet on the floor next to them. He told her to pack them and wait. Nimbly, she nodded and started to do what she was told.

Ted threw some things in a bag in his bedroom and tucked the still-unopened envelope in the same suitcase. He ran to the den, which had also been demolished in the search for something, and leafed through some of the bonds and savings books that he had stored there. He didn't know where they would run or how far, but he knew that they would need money, and he'd have to close out the accounts and convert the bonds as soon as possible. In the process, he slipped the passport into his pocket. It was a family one, with a picture of him and Lisa when the two children were much younger. He stared at it for a second before pocketing it.

He moved up to the kitchen and peered out the window. Except for his car parked in the gravel driveway, there was nothing in sight. It took him only a few minutes to load the bags in the car and get Dawn firmly planted in the front seat.

Ted moved the car carefully out of the driveway. Fighting the urge to floor the accelerator, he moved at normal speed down the side street and took a left at the intersection, then headed toward the Garden State Parkway. Several glances in the rear view mirror told him that there was no one following him, though he could not really be sure. There were the normal number of cars on the road for a December weekend, and none of them carried huge banners saying "VETERANS ADMINISTRATION," or "GOVERNMENT KILLERS." He had turned onto the Parkway's northbound entrance and was well on the way to the Shore Park tollbooth when he realized that he had no idea where he was going. Away. Just away, was all he could think about back at the house. Now, the destination started to form in his mind. New York first. It would give them breathing space; a hole to hide in for a few days until he could get things straight. All of the savings books and negotiable securities that he carried could be converted there. He reasoned that he'd have to do that soon, before they found Lisa and Michael. He watched the road and the mirror, and glanced occasionally across at Dawn, who sat quietly next to him. It took him a few minutes to realize that he had started to cry. How could it all have happened? How?

The tears stopped by the time he had crossed the

Raritan River bridge and shifted from the Parkway to the New Jersey Turnpike. He was five miles north of the interchange when he pulled into the rest area to take Dawn to the bathroom. She'd been squirming for a few miles but was apparently afraid to ask if they could stop. Finally, her urgency had overcome her caution. Ted corralled a woman traveler in her thirties to help Dawn into the unfamiliar ladies' room and waited in the round foyer. It was filled with soda machines, a souvenir shop, a bank of phone booths . . . the normal paraphernalia of rest stops all over the country.

When Dawn reemerged from the ladies' room, Ted bought some packages of cupcakes and peanut-buttered crackers, a couple of cartons of milk and a package of antacid pills for his stomach, which had been churning for the better part of an hour. He put them in a fold-up box and sat Dawn with them on one of the benches. He headed for one of the phones. There was no sense fighting it. He couldn't do this by himself. He had considered the idea fleetingly, while Dawn was in the bathroom, and had decided on it. If he had been on the run alone, the chances were that no one would ever find him. But, with Dawn, it was an entirely different matter.

He dialed the number.

"Hello?" There was surprise in the voice. It said that calls rarely came at home, especially with the phone number being unlisted.

"Hello, Cathy. It's Ted."

"Ted! What a surprise. You—" She sensed it. "Is there something wrong?"

"Yeah. Very wrong. Could you handle a couple of visitors?"

"Ah . . . sure. Who's with you?"

"Dawn."

"Not Michael, huh?"

"N—no. I can explain when I get there."

"Where are you? I mean, how long before you get here? I'm sitting here with my hair in a towel and half dressed."

"An hour, an hour and a half at the most."

"No problem. You remember how to get here?"

Ted mentally worked his way through the narrow SoHo streets to the loft that he had been to once before. It had been three years earlier, when Cathy had given a housewarming for the loft she'd been wanting to buy for years. Ted had liked the place and the people. Lisa had not. He remembered that they had bickered on the way home.

"I remember."

"Good. Well, I'll see you in an hour or so."

As he hung up, he realized that the questions she might have asked had simply been skipped over. She knew something was wrong and that it could not be discussed on the phone. He thought for a second about her reactions. She hadn't hesitated for a second. It pleased him, he thought. As if anything could please him after the horror he had found at home. He knew that he hadn't let it in yet, merely shielded it. The terror of the deaths was in a mental Pandora's box, and he would open it only after things had settled down. Dawn was still numb, armored. And it was her that he allowed himself to consider: her reactions, her angst, the impact that finding the bodies of her mother and brother might have in years to come. Dawn's intelligence was a double-edged sword. Her mind was years ahead of her emotions. She'd have to be treated carefully.

He opened the door of the booth and started toward the bench.

She was gone.

Ted's stomach tortured its way into a knot. He walked quickly across the lobby and through the glass doors. Dawn was standing at the top of the steps. He came over and put an arm around her, still tense and shaking slightly.

"Dawn?"

"Oh. Hi, Dad." She turned her head toward his voice and wrinkled her nose. "It was hot and smoky in there, so I came out here. I thought you wouldn't mind."

"That's OK."

He took the box of food from her and they went back to the car.

It was less than twenty minutes later. They were abreast of Newark Airport, and Ted had just signaled a lane change, intending to take the Turnpike extension to the Holland Tunnel. It was then that he took notice of the car. He had seen the dark gray Chrysler before in the mirror. It had remained a few cars behind, he thought, from just after the time that he'd pulled out of the rest stop. But there was always the chance that the car had been shadowing him all the way from Shore Park. He wasn't great at trying to spot surveillance, in any event.

He eased his speed down to forty and started up the right cutoff for the exit ramp. He could see that the Chrysler was doing the same. Suddenly he snapped the blinker the other way and moved back into traffic, cutting off a small VW in the process. The angered driver leaned on his horn and shook a fist at Ted, who ignored him and started to get speed back up in the right-hand lane. His eyes darted to the mirror.

The Chrysler was still there. It also had shifted back to the main portion of the three-lane road. It still kept its distance, but the Chrysler's driver now had to know that Ted knew. So Ted reasoned that they would pretend for a while. The first chance he would have to lose them would come at the Lincoln Tunnel.

"Dad?"

"Yes, honey?"

"Why did you do that?"

"Do what?"

"Swerve. It felt like you were going to turn off and changed your mind."

Ted shrugged, though his hands were white-knuckled on the wheel.

"Thought that the Lincoln would have less traffic than the Holland."

"Oh." She went back to her donut and milk, pensively.

The Lincoln Tunnel was jammed. It took Ted twenty minutes to negotiate the wide, sweeping curve of the approach ramp. Two of the three tunnel accesses were inbound, and one was outbound. Ted thought that later in the day they would shift to accommodate the hordes of Christmas shoppers who would be fighting their way back to New Jersey, with presents locked safely in their trunks. At any rate, the two tubes going to the city were a blessing. Cars were lined up eight abreast, waiting to pay the toll to enter the tunnel.

He looked in the mirror. The Chrysler was tucked seven or eight cars back in a lane to his left. It was right where he wanted it.

He fished in his pocket for the toll and came up with a wadded dollar and two quarters. The exact change would give him the extra seconds he would need when he pulled from the booth to the tunnel entrance.

He rolled down the window and stuffed the toll into the hand of a bored-looking black woman wearing a green winter uniform. He took off in the direction of the left tube entrance. The Chrysler's driver, apparently alert to the possibility of losing Ted, had skipped ahead, cutting off a line of cars approaching a tollbooth. Ted could hear horns and shouts from the angry motorists. Ted moved forward slowly enough for the Chrysler to nearly parallel him in a left lane. He would have to move quickly, before the driver of the Chrysler could react. He prayed he didn't get stopped by one of the half-dozen transit police who were waving traffic into the lanes.

It was less than ten feet from the tunnel entrance, just before the pylons prevented lane change, when Ted spun the wheel to the right and sped into the right tunnel rather than the left. Locked into its lane by several cars in line, the Chrysler was not able to make the shift. They would have to move through one tunnel while Ted moved through the other.

By the time he passed the New York–New Jersey marker, Ted had accelerated to fifty and was moving with the flow. He had been lucky. The tube he had chosen had been lighter in traffic than the one that the chase car was in.

He came up the exit ramp and still could not see the Chrysler.

He downshifted and swung right, curving south to the Forty-first Street exit.

Luckily, there was no car in sight when he eased into the westbound traffic on Fortieth Street. He slipped to the right-hand lane and signaled a turn that would take him south on Seventh Avenue, and he was just starting to breathe easily when he saw that the Chrysler had appeared in his mirror and had turned with him. He accelerated and slipped through lanes to the left side of the broad street with all of the skill of a man who'd spent time as a New York cabbie. Ted shook his head, realizing that he would never have considered that the time he'd spent driving a cab back then would have paid off so well now. But a glance in the mirror told him that the driver of the Chrysler was no slouch, either. He managed to make up the distance with alarming speed, and took up a position three cars behind Ted. With driving skill apparently equal, all Ted could do was to count on the size difference between the two cars. The Chrysler just could not go with ease into the holes in traffic that Ted's small Chevy could.

He swung left on Twenty-third and moved through the Gramercy area, weaving through the narrow side streets that interlaced Park Avenue. He drove all the way south to Houston and into the tangled weave of paved alleys that made up Little Italy. Somewhere after the move through Gramercy he lost the Chrysler. He swung east to Bowery and then north and west to SoHo. He parked in a small lot near Cathy's, breathed deeply, and got Dawn and the bags out of the car.

CHAPTER NINE

"They're dead, Cathy. Both of them, shot in the head."

Cathy sat across from Ted and Dawn on a huge, U-shaped, conversation pit couch. She was dressed casually in a pair of jeans and a blue work shirt.

As Ted spoke, she looked down at her bare feet for a second. When she looked up, her face was paler than Ted had ever remembered seeing it. The blue of the shirt seemed to deepen her eyes.

"Dear God, Ted. And Dawn found them?"

He nodded.

"How? What?"

He told her.

"And you think it all goes back to the man who told you the story. The one who . . . She looked quickly to Dawn. "The one who committed suicide?"

Ted nodded and took the envelope from his lap. He placed it on the table in front of them. "It has to be the connection. He said he was expecting things from the man who died in Boston. The first postmark is from there. The second one is from Shore Park. It would have been mailed the night that Charlie died. He must have been trying to get rid of it. It makes sense. There was no one else he said he could send it to. It ties to the set of orders I sent to you, this morning. If I hadn't been at the post office, and if Dawn hadn't been in the back . . . I . . . we . . ."

"Hang on." Cathy got to her feet and headed off

across the wide loft in the direction of her kitchen. The Pandora's box was prying its way open. Ted didn't want it to, but there was no stopping it.

In a few minutes, she came back with a bottle of Jack Daniel's and a glass filled with ice. She poured several ounces over the ice and handed the glass to Ted. His hand shook noticeably as he took it.

"Drink that."

He bolted the bourbon down and placed the glass on the table. There was something strange about it.

"Cathy, you never mentioned that you drank bourbon."

"I don't. But you did."

"Thanks." The gesture didn't escape him. It had been something mentioned literally years before, in passing. Ted wondered how long the bottle had waited on the shelf for him. The wondering stopped when he looked back to the envelope.

"Cathy, they had to be after this. They tore the place apart, I think, looking for what Dawn had with her in the backyard. And they are still after it."

"How do you know?"

He told her about the Chrysler and how he lost the tail in traffic.

She frowned and looked around the chic and well-decorated loft. "Can they, whoever they are, connect us up, do you think?"

"I don't know, really. They had to know that the mailman was carrying the package to my house. There's no telling how much more they know. Dawn and I can leave in a little bit. There's no sense getting you further in all of this."

"I'm already in it, Ted. The package you mailed to me will get here Monday. We have no way of knowing that with the postman won't be your friends in the Chrysler."

"I don't think so. Otherwise, they wouldn't have been so desperate to keep the tail on me."

Cathy got to her feet and moved to the large studio windows in the front of the loft. A dour midday sun cast a pale yellow light into the loft.

She looked to the street, three floors below. "There's nothing unusual. At least there doesn't seem to be anything." She shook her head as she came back to the couch. "Then again, I'm sure that our friends in the Chrysler wouldn't be parked out front staring up at the windows."

She looked to the envelope and then to Ted, who had downed another, though smaller, bourbon. She looked like someone about to jump from a plane without a parachute.

"I guess we'd better open it and see what Charlie— or Lucas—died for."

"I guess," Ted said.

He tore off the strip of tape that sealed the envelope together. Ted gingerly reached in and pulled out a folded Xeroxed sheet. He unfolded it and discovered that the sheet was a duplicate of the one that he had put into the mail that very morning. He handed it to Cathy.

"I was right. It was from him. This is the same one I found in his apartment."

As Cathy looked quizzically at the orders, Ted reached in and took a smaller envelope from the larger one. It was blank white manila, and it had been sealed with a strip of tape. He felt the object inside before he opened it. It had the feel of a ball-point pen. He ripped open the top of the envelope and removed the pen.

It wasn't a pen.

Rather, it was a slender cylinder of highly polished metal. Ted thought immediately that it was stainless steel. It was some four inches long, segmented in the middle as a pen might be, and it came to a tapering, rounded point at one end. Oddly, there was no ball at the tip, only the rounded end. The other end, which Ted started to think of as the top, was not tapered and appeared to be flat, though the turns of metal that led to the top were burnished and smooth. There was no pocket clip.

He shook his head and passed it over to Cathy, who had stopped reading the orders while he opened the envelope.

She fingered it for a second, curiously. "It's like a pen."

Ted nodded. "That's what I thought. But there's no aperture for the ball."

"There were fountain pens before there were ballpoints. The top might just be the cap." She turned the top; it rotated easily in her hands. It did not, however, seem to unscrew. Cathy tugged gently, trying to pull the top from the body. With an audible click, it moved apart from the body, some quarter of an inch. But even a strong pull did not dislodge it further. Cathy pushed the separated pieces back together and they responded, again with a click. She fingered the middle gently, then peered closely at the strange object.

"Ted? Are these decorations?" She passed the pen back to him.

He squinted at them. They appeared to be an intricate pattern of curved and straight lines, minutely and exquisitely etched.

"They look almost Moorish. But I can't say whether they're decorative or functional." He tugged the pen open and it responded as it had for Cathy. Applying all the pressure he could, he could quickly see that it would not come apart. He pressed it back together and looked up at her. "Have you got a magnifying glass?"

She thought for a second and her brow wrinkled ever so slightly.

"I think so."

As Cathy rummaged through kitchen drawers for a long-forgotten magnifying glass, Ted turned the "pen" over in his hands slowly, as if to gain something by osmosis. All of the men, was this what they died for? A ball-point pen with some scratches? He looked at the photocopy of the assignment orders. Was the pen a part of Project Unicorn? Had the pen been in the hangar? How did it all connect?

"Daddy?" Dawn had moved closer to him on the couch. Ted reached across and slipped his hand around her shoulder. She seemed to burrow into him for a moment before she looked up. "What is it you've been looking at?"

"This, honey." He placed the pen in her hands and watched as her delicate fingers flew across the surface like birds. She wrinkled her nose and kept examining it. It took her a minute to find the marks on the barrel. She held them delicately between her thumb and index finger as she slowly rotated the barrel. "These marks?"

"Yeah. That's what Cathy's getting a magnifying glass for."

Dawn shook her head. It was a gesture Ted recognized as meaning that something either was challenging or perplexing her. "They're . . . funny."

"How do you mean?"

"I don't know yet." She went back to examining the pen with her fingers.

"Ted?" Cathy called from the kitchen. It was tinged with urgency, perhaps fear.

Ted moved quickly to the kitchen. He was about to speak when Cathy placed a finger to her lips, then pointed to the small transistor radio on the table.

". . . so, to recap, Weston, New Jersey, police report that the bodies of Mrs. Lisa Lawrence and her eight-year-old son, Michael, were found about an hour and a half ago. Our reporter on the scene, Hal Michaels, indicates that the preliminary report is that the thirty-two-year-old housewife and daughter of the prestigious Ryan industrial family was killed by a single gunshot to the head. It's reported that her son was killed in the same manner. Hal Michaels says that the police consider *that the killings were 'execution style,' and they have shaken the residents of Shore Park.*

"A search is currently under way for ten-year-old Dawn Lawrence, who, Shore Park school officials report, is blind. The concern is that the child might have wandered away from the scene and gotten lost in the nearby woods. Dogs will be used in the search.

"Of even more importance in the search is Dr. Theodore Lawrence, husband of Lisa and father of the two Lawrence children. Police are searching for him in connection with both killings and the missing blind child. Preliminary reports from Paxton State College, where Dr. Lawrence was an Associate Professor of Psychology, indicate that he was recently laid off from his teaching post in a general faculty cutback. In addition, a representative of the Ryan family issued a statement only moments ago, indicating that the Lawrences were estranged and in the midst of a divorce proceeding. In sports . . ."

Cathy snapped the radio off. "My God, Ted. It looks like they . . ."

"I know. That's why I got out so fast. Also, I thought that they might come back and get Dawn and me and anyone else that gets between them and that . . . thing . . . in the living room. God, what a classic setup. And the Ryans will get all the mileage they can from it, too. There was never any love lost between them and me. They wanted Lisa to hang on for custody so that Dawn and Michael would be grandchildren. Lisa was their only child, you see. She had just given in on that point. I was going to keep the children. Lisa—God, I don't mean to speak of her this way—Lisa wasn't much of a mother."

Cathy nodded and looked at him intently. "I know," she whispered.

"From *Sander's Bay.* Right?"

"From all the books, Ted. There was an unhappy marriage and a rotten mother in all of them. An editor who . . . cared couldn't miss it. Ted, what do you want to do? By tonight, they'll be widening the search for you. By tomorrow, they'll be calling you a killer. That's the way media sells air time. Is there a way to get leverage? I mean, I could take it to Walt Vertagglia and we could punch it through the editorial committee. If you worked here, you could get enough together for a 'six-day miracle' book, pretty fast. If we went all out we could manage to get it into print in a few weeks. Then, with the book on the streets, you could give yourself up, and we'd have something to fight with."

There was a penetrating blue to her eyes and a determined set to her chin that told Ted she was in it, all the way and no matter what.

"Whoever's after the 'pen' in there," he gestured in the direction of the living room, "won't hesitate to kill you, Dawn, and me as long as they get back what they lost. Are you positive?"

She nodded with a finality that Ted thought must have resembled the fatalistic nods of the Zealots of Masada besieged by Roman legions. "I'm sure."

"I just wanted to make certain you were, I don't know . . . warned. After this morning I . . ."

He couldn't stop it. Not now. And he didn't want it to happen.

He started to shake.

Cathy came across the few feet of kitchen to him. She reached up and held him for a long moment until the shaking started to subside. Ted could feel it in her; that intangible something; the angle of her body; the pressure of her fingertips on the back of his neck; the feel of her breath on his shoulder. There was so much more there than just consolation. So much. And the timing was so terrible.

"Daddy?"

They timidly backed away from one another and went into the living room.

Dawn was still examining the pen. Ted sat next to her, and Cathy sat on the floor.

"What is it, honey?"

"It's mathematics. I'm sure it is. There are two sets of marks. They seem to mean two different things. The top one, up here?" She pointed to the minute ring of engravings. Ted had not even been able to determine that there were two sets of markings. Apparently Dawn's fingers were more sensitive than Ted's eyes. "The top one establishes some kind of symbol. Then it seems to add some factors, like algebra. Then they seem to move to other symbols through . . . well, I don't know how. But it seems like the numbers get bigger."

Cathy handed Ted the magnifying glass and he took the cylinder from Dawn.

It was incredibly complex. He wondered at how her tiny fingers had even managed to separate one symbol from another. And, at first glance, Ted couldn't see a pattern. After a few minutes, he could start to see one.

The first symbol, a sort of curvy, backward seven, was some sort of X, an unknown which the following equation might solve.

They gathered pads and pens. Dawn pulled her Braille writer from her suitcase and, with the help of a calculator that Cathy supplied, they started to try to make sense of the engravings. An hour later, they stopped for sandwiches and a listen to the news, where the "Weston killings" received further radio coverage. This time the Ryans had made another statement, to the effect that Ted's psychological condition at the time might have led him to any action, even violence. Ted silently cursed them and went back to work.

It was the middle of the afternoon and a dusty, cold sunlight was slipping through the windows at the back of the loft, when Ted stopped and stretched.

"I don't know," he said. "I think it has something to do with calibration. The math connects with physics, but it's past me. All I can think is that it's part of

THE OGDEN ENIGMA 139

something larger. It might be something to do with a weapons system. But the mathematics of that sort of thing should be clearer. I mean, there are symbols there that I've never really seen before, in or out of physics. It's the unicorn's horn."

Dawn giggled. It was the first thing resembling humor he had seen from her since the murders. The horror of the morning had been replaced by the intensity of the problem of the pen. This was a sort of breakthrough, this giggle. She was still ten, and resilient.

"Unicorns only live in books, Daddy." There was a terribly grown-up tone to her voice, that formed a strange counterpoint to the giggle seconds earlier.

"I know, honey. But this one lives in a hangar, I think. And I can't figure out what it is."

She shook her head. "You always told me that *anything* in mathematics could be figured out, Daddy?" Her tone was querulous, confused, as if a trust had been broken.

"Anything can, Dawn. All I said was that it was past my ability. Some of the equation symbols are unknowns. If you don't know what the symbol means, you can't solve the equation."

"Let's get some books, then. I mean, then we can figure out what the symbols mean. If we can do that, we can solve the problem."

It was so simple he hadn't thought of it. Or perhaps he had thought of it and discarded it, because it meant going back out in the streets. He reassured himself that the car that had been following them had been baffled by the route he had taken.

"Ted?" Cathy said. "The Forty-second Street Library is open for another two hours. Maybe I . . ."

He shook his head. "No. It would have to be me. I think I know more of where to look and what to look for. I could do it faster. We academics are good in research libraries." He got to his feet and grabbed his jacket. "I'll need some references on tensor calculus, and some on differential. Oh, and something on quantum mechanics. Whew. Been a long time since I even thought about all of that." He reached into his pocket and came up with two of the savings books he had hurriedly grabbed when he and Dawn had fled. There would be no way he could manage to get to either of the banks, not now. They might be watched. The bonds were not easily convertible either. Suddenly, money was going to be a problem.

Cathy fished through her purse as she crossed the room. She came up with a buff-colored card. "Here." She handed it to him. "This is my card. Take out what you need on that." She eyed the savings books. "You're not going to try a bank, are you?"

"No. But I was just thinking that I have to pay everything in cash to avoid detection. I'm going to have a problem."

She handed him several wadded-up tens. "Here. That's all I have in the house. Let me order the release of the advance check on *Sander's Bay*. I can get it rushed through finance on Monday. Then, if you endorse it, I'll drop it in my account. Then I'll draw cash on it. I don't think they can trace that." She folded her arms and laughed for a second. "Sound like a real over-the-edge paranoid, don't I?"

"No. You sound practical. I'd better ditch the car, too. I'll come back on the subway. Look, Cath, if I don't come back, ah . . ." He looked to Dawn, who was manipulating the Braille writer on the distant couch. "Well . . . I suppose Dawn would have to go to the Ryans. They've got the money to take care of her."

"You'll be back. I think I know you. You're a survivor. But just in case Dawn and I have to bolt, let me give you this." She jotted a phone number on a slip of paper.

Ted glanced at it. "A 516 number? Long Island?"

She nodded. "My mother's. She has the remains of a farm at Northampton. She sold most of the acreage when my father died, but she kept the carriage house and turned it into a residence. She lives alone. It will be safe there. You could get there by train if you had to, and, well . . ." She shrugged. It was the best possibility of a safe house she could come up with. "If anything happens, we'll go there and wait to h—hear from you."

Ted looked at the number for a moment, then handed her back the sheet.

She looked to him, then to it. "I'd forgotten about that memory you have for stuff like names and numbers."

It was a moment later when Ted stood at the door. He'd kissed Dawn and explained everything to her. She'd taken the possibility that her father might be killed in the streets with an almost alarming, Buddhist calm.

Cathy stood a foot or so from him. She reached up and placed a hand on each side of his face, then pulled him down and kissed him gently on the lips. Her lips were cool, and yet there was something behind the coolness that Ted recognized instantly. He could only hope it would keep until everything was over.

"Please, be careful," she whispered.

He took her hands in his and squeezed them silently for a moment, then left.

Cathy locked the door behind him and looked across the wide expanse of loft to Dawn, who sat on the sofa, feverishly working with the Braille writer. The child would push a wisp of her hair back from her face every few seconds, move to the writer, then to the small cylinder on the table. Suddenly, Dawn stopped and raised her head.

"Miss Seward?" Her voice was thin, timid.

"Yes?"

"Oh. I wasn't sure where you were. I mean . . ."

Cathy crossed to the couch and sat next to the child, slipping an arm around the small shoulders. "I'm here,

Dawn. And I'll be here. Do you want anything to eat or to drink?"

Dawn shook her head. A sob suddenly erupted from deep inside her. Then another. She put her hands over her mouth and tried to stifle them. Cathy pulled her close and Dawn cried. Between the sobs, she spoke of Michael, of loving him and her mother. In her mind she had connected the deaths to the divorce, which she felt guilty about anyway. In front of Cathy sat a sobbing ten-year-old who was sure she was responsible for the murders of her mother and little brother.

It was twenty minutes later when Dawn, the last sob gone, lay cradled against Cathy. Cathy waited another ten minutes, until she was sure Dawn had drifted off to sleep. She gently lifted the child from the couch and carried her to the bedroom. She got her under the coverlet and made her as comfortable as possible, then left the bedroom, remembering to leave the door open.

She went to the kitchen and made a cup of coffee. She sipped the black, bitter coffee and noticed that her hand quivered ever so slightly. She took the cup to the living room and added about an ounce of the bourbon she never drank. Then Cathy returned to the kitchen and got the radio. She brought it into the living room and set it on the table. The hourly news carried stories of various rapes and murders—the normal fare of the city. The U.S. and the Soviets were screaming at one another about a fireball that had flashed across the Midwest. A falling piece of a Soviet skylab was what the U.S. spokesman had charged, something that should have been blown up in space. The Soviets claimed it was a close-approaching meteorite which had nothing to do with their space program or their orbiting laboratory *Salyut*. There was no mention of the Lawrence murders. Cathy sighed and turned the radio off.

She picked up the cylinder and started to look again at the small etchings that circumscribed the collar.

The sun was hovering close to the Hudson, and Ted could feel the chill wind bite through his coat as he cautiously left the loft and moved in the direction of the parking lot. In half an hour it would be dusk, and a protective darkness would settle over SoHo. For a second Ted debated waiting in a doorway until it was dark, then shook his head. The books he would need at New York Public Library were important, and the 42nd Street branch closed in less than an hour. He'd have to get the car in daylight.

He retrieved the car and drove west, intending to turn north on Sixth Avenue. He knew from his days as a cab driver that Sixth would get congested when he got up to Thirty-fourth Street. The rush of Christmas shoppers was just beginning.

He had turned north and started to make good progress through the timed lights on the wide, one-way street, when he glanced in the rear view mirror.

The gray Chrysler was there! It had just turned from a side street.

He accelerated, passing a cab and a bus, slipping to the right-hand lane.

The Chrysler slid in behind him.

Did they know about Cathy's? Should he go back? No. That would trap all of them.

He stepped on the accelerator. The Chrysler kept pace. Ahead of him, he could see the logjam of cars and buses that marked the southern approach to Herald Square. He'd have to lose the chase car before he got there. He came close to Thirtieth Street and spun the wheel to the right, scattering pedestrians as he made a sudden right turn. He sped across Fifth Avenue where he was stopped by a light. He couldn't see the Chrysler, as his vision was blocked by a truck. The light changed and he floored the gas pedal.

He crossed Madison, seeing that the truck behind him was blocking the street diagonally, trying to turn. It would give him a few more seconds. Ahead of him, the traffic light was still green, and he sped toward the intersection. His mind flashed ahead. He'd turn north on Park, swing through the Grand Central bypass, and lose the car on Park in the fifties. There were hundreds of parking garages in the neighborhood and he could park there and get to the library on foot quickly.

As he turned, he caught a flash of gray in the rear view mirror. Shit. The Chrysler had stayed with him. He accelerated to fifty, heading in the direction of Grand Central.

In the loft, Cathy sat on the couch, peering at the hieroglyphic etchings on the cylinder through a magnifying glass. Next to her was a pad, and each time she managed to interpret a convoluted shape on the polished surface she would approximate it on the pad. After a few minutes, she stopped and scratched her head. What she'd sketched on the pad looked like Arabic written by a drunk or a spastic. There was no sense to any of it. She moved back to the cylinder and managed to see that there appeared to be another line of the chicken scratches half concealed by the cap of the device. A single straight line on the body of the cylinder seemed to match up with another one on the body. Carefully inspecting the figure on the pad, she could see that these were the only two seemingly straight lines there. She rotated the barrel and adjusted the cap slightly until the two lines formed a single etched impression. She tugged the cap slightly and was surprised to find that it slipped out about a quarter of an inch.

The lights went out.

Startled, Cathy dropped the cylinder. It landed on the table cap first, driving the two parts together again. The lights in the loft went on again. Cathy could feel her pulse start to pound in her ears. Gingerly, she again picked up the cylinder and, making sure that the two parts of the device were aligned, gently tugged on the cap. Again, it snapped out some quarter of an inch.

The lights went out again.

She sat there with the cylinder in her hands for a long minute. Then, she pressed the two parts together again. The lights came on. She could hear the hum of the refrigerator in the kitchen restart with a gentle whine. Dear God. What was it? As she thought it, she knew. It was a weapon.

At the Consolidated Edison Plant on Fourteenth Street, recording devices noted the sudden drain of power and instantly increased output to compensate. As an alarm bell sounded in the control room of the generating plant, the power drain suddenly disappeared as quickly as it had come. The alarm bell ceased before the operating engineers could even look to their consoles to find the nature of the drain. It was less than two minutes later when the same kind of drain again registered on the recording devices, and this time the drain remained constant for more than a minute. Alarm bells clanged, and operators scurried from meter to meter in the plant. When the drain had lasted ninety seconds, all hell seemed to break loose. Power supply was falling as though there had been a break in a major feeder cable. Yet, in a lightning-fast inspection of the display board that visually outlined all of the major feeder lines in Manhattan, the engineers could find no red light indicating a snapped line or feeder cable.

All across the city, electrical devices that required constant power supply cycled into an off mode and awaited the automatic shift to auxiliary power. Everything north of the Battery and west of Lexington Avenue wavered for a few seconds and resumed operation. Everything else, east and south, stayed black.

That included all lights in the traffic system. Every traffic light in the most densely populated shopping area of the city winked out. Unknowingly, Cathy had caused a power blackout for more than a quarter of the city by the simple action of snapping open the cylinder.

Ted sped down Park Avenue, seeing the green light ahead of him. He was twenty feet from the intersection when the traffic light winked out. He could see the Chrysler only two or three cars behind him. He didn't have time to worry about the light. He darted out into the intersection, then spun the wheel to the left, in a tire-screeching turn onto Forty-second Street. He saw the bus only at the last second. The driver tried to swerve to the right, only to discover that Ted had left him no room. Ted's car sideswiped the bus, caromed out into the southbound lane, and hit a light pole.

Ted was slammed forward into the dash, smashing his head into the steering wheel. He slumped forward, unconscious.

CHAPTER TEN

Clifford Hurley ground out his cigarette in the large brass ashtray that decorated the corner of his highly polished mahogany desk. He glanced at his watch and unscrewed the top of a large thermos. He poured a cup of oily black coffee, took a sip, and looked at the red-bordered file in front of him for perhaps the fifth time in an hour. He knew it backward and forward. There was no sense in overpreparing.

He rose from the swivel chair and paced to the window. The flat rays of the December sun angled across the almost vacant Pentagon parking lot and the nearly empty Shirley Expressway. It was too early on a Sunday morning for there to be much traffic. Later, he thought, cars would fill Shirley, the Capital Beltway, and the other access roads. The Redskins were playing the Eagles at home, and that would account for perhaps twenty thousand cars. Hurley shrugged and took another sip of coffee. One of those cars should have been his, he thought. But interrupted plans and inconveniences went with the territory of being Director of the Foreign Intelligence Analysis Division. The long hours and the work he could talk about to no one outside the Defense Department were probably the reasons he had never married. The job demanded he stay silent, stay fit, stay alert. It was a jealous mistress that would not allow a woman in his life on any more than a fleeting, part-time level. It was ironic. For Hurley was a handsome, lean fifty-year-old, with jet black hair graying slightly at the temples, and dark blue, penetrating eyes. At six foot three, still trim and hard as when he was thirty, he could have had his pick of the women in the Pentagon.

But, he thought, none of them could have gotten him to the directorship. It was his skill and dedication that did that. It was the Sundays spent in the office preparing briefings for the Secretary, massaging intelligence together into meaningful trends and long-term plans, that made him a valuable resource to the Defense Department's intelligence-gathering operation. He felt proud that his field operatives, working in Russia, China, and the Third World, few in number compared to their CIA counterparts, fed back precise, accurate data that made his shoestring operation nearly as powerful as his rivals' at Langley. Actually, he thought, there was only one man in the Pentagon who rivaled him at all: Karl Weatherow. Their careers had paralleled each other since they had been field operatives with "Wild Bill" Donovan in the World War Two O.S.S. They had moved from CIA to Defense Department at the same time, been promoted at the same time. Their paths had crossed professionally for years, and it was natural that they should, with Weatherow directing the operation of the Internal Security Division. A rivalry had developed over the years. Who would get the fastest and most accurate information to the Secretary? Their track record was about even. And now Weatherow had called for a meeting . . . a Sunday morning meeting.

"Good morning. Cliff."

Hurley turned quickly from the window. "Oh, hello, Karl. I didn't hear . . ."

Weatherow, short, pudgy, and as frumpy as Hurley was natty, moved across the office and sat in an easy chair with a fat man's grace. Karl was jowly and his thick glasses made him look slightly owl-eyed. But Cliff Hurley knew that Karl's appearance was deceiving.

Behind the glasses were dark brown eyes that darted quickly from thing to thing, person to person. They didn't miss a detail, a nuance. They always looked for an advantage. They were the eyes of a ruthless intellect that thought nothing of betraying a field agent or sending one into a dangerous situation with erroneous information, knowing that the operative would get caught. Then, inevitably, the man would break after the professionals of the Hungarian AVO, or the East German Vopos, or the super professionals of the Soviet KGB finished a few days of ripping out fingernails, or crushing testicles, or shooting the poor devil full of drugs. Before the poor dupe died screaming, he would tell all he knew.

Hurley thought Weatherow could engineer such acts with dispatch and dispassion simply because it was his duty, and so his presence was slightly distasteful to the more emotional Hurley. He respected the man, but he didn't know if he'd ever be capable of liking him.

Karl unsnapped his briefcase and pulled a red-bordered file. "I'm sorry to have gotten you in on Sunday. But this one's thorny."

Hurley went back to his seat. "Shit, Karl. What's one Sunday." He smiled, revealing a row of straight teeth. "We've done a couple of months of Sundays what with one thing and another. I'm used to it. Coffee?"

Karl nodded. Hurley opened a deep bottom drawer and pulled out a stack of styrofoam cups, separated one from the top of the stack and poured a cup of steaming black coffee from the thermos. He passed it across the desk and Weatherow thanked him.

After the few minutes of coffee and cordiality were finished, Hurley lit a cigarette and sat back. "You mentioned Project Unicorn on the phone, so I pulled my file on it." He held up the folder that sat in front of him. "What's the flap?"

Weatherow sat forward and folded his hands, as if

in prayer. To Hurley he looked like a fat praying mantis. But he knew the man well enough not to underestimate him.

"Well, Cliff, as you know, Unicorn's been an operational file of mine since June of fifty. We worked with Air Force on security for as long as I can remember."

Cliff tilted his head to the side. "That's the Ogden site, right?"

Karl nodded, slowly. "Cliff, you fucking well know it is. I haven't got time or energy to feint and dodge with this one. It means too much to both of us."

Hurley raised a hand in mock supplication. "OK, OK. No diplomacy. I read the file. Now, what's the flap?"

"It was just over a month ago that we got a report from one of our field operatives in Boston. He said that he'd picked up a rumble that two men were about to expose some classified information to the Boston press. I didn't think much of it until the field agent indicated that the information dealt with Unicorn at Ogden. I ran a routine check on the men." He looked to the file in his lap. "One of the men was named Anthony Patrino. The other was an Andrew Rodgers. Both of them had been on the security detachment at Ogden during 1970-71. Both of them carried high clearances and were still bound by them. Before my man could get much further into the case, Patrino died in a fire in Springfield and Rodgers disappeared."

Hurley nodded. "Had they broken any information to the media?"

"If they had, we'd sure as shit know it. No. Nothing had surfaced. However, Walcott, my man in Boston, said that he thought they had something tangible to sell to the media. He thought it was a piece of hardware or classified orders."

Hurley's eyebrows raised. "Hardware?"

Karl nodded. "Perhaps a souvenir, lifted when the original five-man detachment secured Unicorn. The chances are that it sat in someone's attic for years before anyone attached meaning to it. At any rate, it was something tangible that could be used to expose Unicorn."

"Did your man find Rodgers? Was there anything there?"

"That's just it, Cliff. By the time Walcott tracked this guy Rodgers down . . . it was in a Scollay Square flophouse, Rodgers was dead less than an hour. It appears he was beaten to death by a wino. All Walcott could find on the body was a certified mail receipt for a package that he mailed to a man named Charlie Howard in Shore Park, New Jersey. Walcott was worried that the package might contain the information that Patrino and Rodgers had been gathering." Karl stopped and took a deep breath.

"And?" Hurley cocked his head to the side.

"And the next day it seems that Walcott went out a fifth-floor window."

"Pushed?"

"It seems like it. The hotel room was a shambles. Walcott was a good man. He'd been on my staff for eight years. He wouldn't have jumped or fallen. And anyone who was going to push him would have had to be one hell of a professional."

"Did you pick up on this guy in New Jersey, the one the mail went to?" Hurley said. There was a querulous tone to his voice.

"Yup. It seems that he's dead too. But we're not too sure about him. His real name was Lucas Morgan. He was in the same Unicorn security detachment with Patrino and Rodgers. But he'd been in and out of VA hospitals as a borderline paranoid schizophrenic for years. That was why he changed his name. If there was any contact between the two men in Boston and this guy Howard or Morgan, it might have been enough to set Morgan off in some paranoid fantasy. He simply might have suicided. I sent a detachment in the next day and they searched his room. They couldn't find anything."

"Had he gotten the package?"

"We think so. At least, the Post Office has his signature on the receipt. But there was nothing in the room. We think he passed it on. This is where things get really strange."

"How so?"

"Well, I'd had a surveillance team on Morgan from the time we found the receipt in Boston. I ran a routine check on all the people he contacted. One of them was a man named Lawrence, a college professor in New Jersey. It seems that Morgan was one of his students. Lawrence showed up at the funeral, and at Morgan's apartment."

"Perhaps he was a friend?"

Karl Weatherow smiled, sardonically, and passed a sheet of paper across to Hurley. Hurley looked at it for a long minute before looking back across the desk.

"Well, it's obvious he's not your man. Despite all of those security clearances when he was in the Army." He shook his head. "His wife and son?"

Karl nodded. "Yes. And two of my best agents."

"How? You didn't tell me about that."

"Head shots, both. We think minutes before the Lawrence woman and the boy. Same weapon." Karl paused to ensure that the words he was about to say would have the right impact. "It was a Graz Burya nine millimeter, Cliff. Does that tell you anything?"

Hurley folded his arms. "Standard issue for the KGB. So our counterparts in Moscow are after anything they can find about Unicorn. They come onto a lead in the same way your man in Boston . . . what was his name?"

"Walcott."

"Yes. Walcott was hit by the same operative who got the Rodgers fellow. He sniffed out the trail to Morgan and then to Lawrence. Why kill the agents and the woman and child though? It doesn't make sense."

"The house was torn apart. They were looking for the hardware. They believe Lawrence has it."

"Has he?"

"I don't know, Cliff."

Cliff Hurley knew he had the matter in hand. He leafed through the file on the desk. "Several questions arise. The first is, what level of complicity can we assume from Lawrence. The second is, who is the 'they' you spoke of?"

Weatherow extended his hands in a compliant gesture. "The first I can answer. Lawrence is clean. Oh, he's a maverick. His service record is dotted with reprimands from superiors. But there is also a smattering of commendations. The man has a first-rate mind, at least according to all his Army tests and efficiency ratings. He has a tour in Viet Nam behind him, and there he was a good intelligence officer. Past that, unless he's the best mole in the world, I don't see that he's in league with the leak."

Hurley nodded. A mole was an agent planted for years, one who would become a respected professional in a community, laboriously taking time to establish a cover. He would only be activated when his superiors decided he was needed. "How do you know he's not . . . a mole, I mean?"

"I don't know for certain. Besides, if he is a mole, would he kill his own wife and son as a cover? Unlikely. No, he's caught up in it in another way. It seems that Dr. Lawrence is a college professor and a commercial writer, and his books have nothing to do with the government."

Hurley gestured to Weatherow. "Perhaps he grabbed information from Morgan and got curious about what Morgan told him. The death of Morgan would have verified whatever he was told. Then, the death of his wife and son, was it? That would have put him on the run."

"Exactly."

Hurley shook his head. "Poor bastard. Doesn't know what's after him or why."

"That's the way I see it. The problem is that he's not really a part of it. However, he may have information that we can use. More than that, we're not sure how much he knows about Unicorn, or what Morgan told him. The local New Jersey police are after him as a suspect in the double murder."

"They can't be allowed to get him."

"Of course not. We have to get him first. At least we have to get to talk to him. See how much he really knows. What bothers me is that second question you posed. That's really why I called you last night."

"You want to know who 'they' might be?"

Weatherow nodded. "I think we'll have to work together on this one. It's too vital not to. Exposure of Unicorn would be a calamity."

Hurley folded his arms and peered across the desk. His eyes met Weatherow's with a cold, hard stare. "It would be worse than that, Karl." He paused and poured a cup of coffee from the thermos. "Do you know what Unicorn is . . . exactly, Karl?"

Weatherow cocked his head to the side. Hurley had hit him with an unexpected question. "All that the security documents reveal is that it was a Soviet secret weapon, developed in the fifties, decades ahead of its time. It had something to do with power generation and the creation of a power null, or drained area. It was rumored that it could black out anything. The background file says that after a team of American agents stole the hardware, they replaced it with other components and the machinery itself was shipped to Ogden and stored there."

"So far, so good. The Korean war threw a monkey wrench into all of it. The Soviets de-emphasized the research in a power-draining weapon and moved to support China in the conflict. Secrecy on Unicorn became vital, as exposure of the fact that we had stolen the machinery would have prevented the U.N. resolution that allowed U.N. troops to go into Korea. Luckily, the Soviets never found out about it. So the case was closed. At least, until recently.

"It seems that in the last six months there has been renewed activity on something that resembles a second generation of the Unicorn device. My people think it has something to do with a weapon that can be slipped into production before any more SALT concessions can be made by the Soviets. The new Unicorn project. The principles, as far as my operatives can tell, are the same. A piece of hardware that can black out power over a long distance; one that is portable enough to be carried by a small team. The design would be to install such devices near early-warning bases and missile silos. If the Soviets launched a first strike, they could engage the machines and foul up detection and retaliation. With the killings in Boston and New Jersey coming hard on the heels of one another, it would seem that the KGB has been ordered to sniff out any leaks on Unicorn, and plug them as fast as possible. In other words, they are making a push to see if we know anything about either the earlier Unicorn or the newer one. I'd guess from what happened in Boston, and the subsequent killings, that they know something. They would be in an all-out push to find out how much we know. It seems that there's a single operative on the trail. He'd be feeding back information as he got it. How much that agent would know or assume at this time would be the crucial element to us."

"Where's Lawrence now?"

"My people tailed him to Manhattan before he lost them in downtown traffic. They think he's somewhere in the SoHo area, and they've been chasing around, looking for more leads. The local police are looking for him, but they have orders to turn him over to us as soon as possible if he's apprehended. It shouldn't take too long to track him down. The airports and other mass transit facilities are covered. Lawrence would be traveling with his daughter, and the child is blind. It would make him conspicuous."

"What are you going to do with him when you get him, Karl?"

Weatherow smiled. "Drain him dry of all the information he has, and then arrange for an accident for both of them."

Hurley paused. It was Karl's style to do such things. He was fond of the maxim about dead men and no tales told. "Why?"

"Why what?"

"Why kill him?"

"Oh, for Christ's sake, Cliff! Are you getting soft? I told you about the KGB and the push for information on Unicorn. If we eliminate Lawrence, then substitute one of our men in his place, we feed the KGB all the wrong information and stop the chance of a leak. More than that, with Lawrence being a writer, he can't be allowed to live. He'd go out and write a book about it or something. No, he's got to be terminated."

Hurley shook his head. "There might be another way, Karl. It could stop your internal security leak and then help me with the KGB."

"Wha—"

Karl was interrupted by the phone. Both men stared at it for a minute. Calls to the office on Sunday were unusual, especially when neither man was supposed to be there. "Oh, I gave your number to my people. I forgot to tell you."

Hurley nodded, a bit miffed at the liberty Karl had taken. He picked up the phone and without saying anything handed it across the desk to Karl.

The conversation lasted only a few minutes and it was couched in opaque codes and side references indigenous to the intelligence community. When Karl hung up, there was a broad smile on his face. "We have him, Cliff. My people dragged him out of a car accident late yesterday afternoon. They didn't report earlier because they were too busy covering their tracks with the local police."

"Where do they have him?"

"A safe house. Site Bravo. It's in northern New Jersey."

"What about the girl, the blind daughter?"

"Nothing. She wasn't in the car with him. But that's no big thing. How far can a blind kid get alone in New York City? We'll get her sooner or later."

"Why don't you keep him alive, Karl? At least for a while?"

"Why would I want to do that?"

"It could help both of us. It could solve your internal problem with the Unicorn Project and my problem with identification of the KGB operatives in both Boston and New Jersey."

"How?"

Hurley explained.

CHAPTER ELEVEN

Ted stood above the world, like a god, staring down at the continents. Across each he could see a latticework of lines, intersecting each other like a vast, intricate spiderweb that pulsed and flowed with power. He drew closer, free of the earth, able to move and soar at will. He could not feel his body, nor anything around him. It did not seem to matter to him that he was standing on nothing, that there was no air to breathe, no sense of anything but the scene he studied.

Closer in, he could see the British Isles, alive with a network of lines and paths, surging with energy. He was sure he was the only one who could see it. With the speed of a thought he willed himself across the Atlantic, seeing the lines as luminescent traces across the water. Above North America, he again willed himself closer to earth. Below him lay cities, fields, highways, farms . . . all interlaced with glowing lines of force. They looked like a flattened and somewhat irregular geodesic dome seen from the air. Ted tried to remember what the importance of the lines was. In a second he had it. Ley lines . . . the lines of Alfred Watkins. There was a network of them all over the world. They were power, the raw power of the planet waiting to be harnessed. How could it be done? Who would do it? Who would even accept the concept?

He swooped west like a jet, following the thickest of the lines of force. It ran across the continent like a *highway, glowing, pulsating with a power that Ted was sure no one else could see. The broad east-west line swept across the great plains and headed to the foothills of the Rockies. Suddenly he could see another line; it glowed and pulsed with an azure light that hurt his eyes. It was a slash of raw power that swept north and south through the state of Utah. Like the cross hairs on a rifle scope, the two lines intersected—at Ogden.*

Ogden seemed to vibrate with energy, like Stonehenge and Avebury. Then the world exploded.

Suddenly Ted was falling . . . faster, ever faster.

In seconds he'd crash into the mountains.

And oh God, the light . . . the blinding blue light.

He screamed.

He could feel the coolness of the sheets on his back. His body seemed pinned down by a great weight. He tried to raise his head until a stab of pain forced him to stop. His forehead was on fire; a throbbing ache penetrated every inch of him. Slowly, he forced his eyes open.

The glare of the fluorescent light started another wave of pain surging outward from his head. He winced, but looked around.

It seemed to be a hospital room with a white ceiling, the kind that cushioned sound. He could feel restraints on both arms, and another around his chest.

Where the hell was he? And why the restraints?

He forced himself to remember the chase through traffic and the red light. There was something about a bus. Yes . . . the crash. His head had hit the steering wheel.

He tilted his head slowly to the right, taking care not to start another wave of pain. He could see a night stand next to the bed. In the distance, there were a desk and a few chairs. But he could see no window in the room. How long had he been in the hospital? He shook the question away. It really didn't matter. The fact that he was in a hospital at all was proof that whoever was chasing him had failed. If they had succeeded, Ted mused, he'd have been in a morgue or a coffin. And there was another bonus to being alive. It meant that the chances were that Cathy and Dawn were alive, too.

In an adjoining room, shrouded by darkness, the small, rotund form of Karl Weatherow stood squinting through the one-way mirror into Ted's room. Part of him felt sorry for the man; an innocent, swept inadvertently into the maelstrom of international intrigue. But Weatherow had seen many men die in three decades of his career, and he was sure many of them were bystanders also. It was a part of the deadly game of tactics that Karl played. Privately, he had little taste for such murders. But professionally Karl knew that it was sometimes absolutely necessary to a larger plan, as the sacrificing of a pawn might be in a game of chess. He folded his short, thick arms across his chest and peered more intensely at Ted through the glass.

No, the man was not a pawn. He was more important than that. A bizarre combination of circumstances had moved him to the middle of the board. He assumed the value of a bishop, or perhaps even a knight, in Weatherow's mind. Such valuable pieces had to be used to help mate the opponent. They were not to be sacrificed . . . until absolutely necessary.

He reached across to the wall and thumbed a small button. An opaque back plate slid silently across the side of the mirror in his observation room. He took a last look at the hastily assembled, though meticulously precise, dossier on Dr. Theodore Martin Lawrence. As he read, he formulated his tactics for the interview. He would *have* to be totally sincere to get the man's cooperation. And there was another factor: he couldn't let Lawrence know how desperately that cooperation was needed. There *had* been a quiet desperation in Hurley's briefing about the KGB operatives. The last time Weatherow had heard such a tone was when he and Cliff Hurley had manned adjacent evaluation desks at Langley and watched the Bay of Pigs operation dissolve into anarchy and failure. Lawrence had to be made to see all of it—without seeing it. Weatherow stopped outside the room for a second, gripped the small cassette recorder tightly in his left hand, and opened the door.

The man in the bed looked up at him. There was still some disorientation in his eyes, and a slight sense of pain registered on the thin, angular, bearded face.

"Good morning, Dr. Lawrence," Weatherow said comfortably. He smiled.

"Morning?" Ted asked, querulously.

"Yes. Morning. I'm afraid you've been unconscious for something over thirty-six hours. A mild concussion is that the doctors said. I'm told you hit the steering wheel of your car rather hard. It's surprising you didn't have a fracture. Your car, unfortunately, didn't fare as well. It was a total loss."

Ted started to reach up to probe the throbbing lump on his forehead, but the restraining straps stopped him. Weatherow allowed Ted a second to ponder their meaning before he approached the bed. He slid the small recorder onto the night stand where Ted could see it and wonder about it, then moved to undo the straps. "I'm afraid these were a necessity. You did a substantial amount of thrashing around for a while there. We were afraid you'd fall and hurt yourself."

Ted looked up, his face close to Weatherow. Karl could see the intensity in the eyes deepen. No, clearly not a pawn, he thought.

"We?"

"Excuse me, Doctor?"

"You said we. Is that the royal we? Or are you speaking for a group I'm not aware of? I don't know your name, and you seem to know mine. What's going on?"

Weatherow smiled tightly as he continued to undo

the straps with pudgy, though deft, fingers. "Forgive me. I intended to do that a minute ago. I'm Karl Weatherow." He flipped a small leather case out of his jacket pocket and held it a readable distance from Ted's nose. The card and picture identified him as the Director of the Defense Department Division of Internal Security.

Weatherow flipped the case closed and moved away from the bed. He stopped at the small dresser, turned and leaned against it. He looked down at the manila file he'd brought with him, and then looked to Ted, who'd managed, painfully, to get to a sitting position.

"Your full name is Theodore Martin Lawrence."

"You have the file," Ted said, half bewildered, half suspicious.

Weatherow nodded. The smile had evaporated from his face. "That's correct, Doctor. But security regulations being what they are, we have to insure that everything has been updated. Now, you were born in New York City—ah, correct me if any of these things is wrong. . . ."

He started to read through a dossier that included some of the more minute elements of Ted's life, both before and after his marriage to Lisa. It was a good beginning tactic that would make it crystal clear to Ted that the agency had all the information that they needed to track down Ted anywhere in the world. The data included credit card numbers, information on insurance policies, the comments good and bad from every Army commander Ted had ever served under. He went through all of Ted's security clearances as well as all his service assignments. He followed this with a good summation of Ted's stormy marriage to Lisa Ryan, and the tempestuous years at Paxton. In a few minutes, he looked up from the folder, his eyes fixed on Ted.

"Doctor, are you aware that the clearances you carried are still in force, and that you will be governed by them, as far as sensitive material is concerned, for another two years?"

Ted nodded. "Of course. Everyone with even the vaguest connection to Army Intelligence had to sign off on a twelve-year agreement when they got out of the service." Ted was sitting up now. He was starting to feel uncomfortable in the drafty hospital gown. But Weatherow could see that the man's eyes were alert, probing. He had obviously recovered from the head injury.

Weatherow moved to the night stand and snapped the tape recorder to "record." "If you don't mind, Doctor, we'll formalize the remaining time on that twelve-year agreement." He went through the formalities of the security inbriefing, cuing Ted to say things here and there. After a few minutes, he snapped the recorder off and popped out the cassette. He slipped it into his pocket and pulled out a small envelope. He tore off the top and reached out and poured the contents on the night stand. They were four small pieces of metal, mashed and mushroomed out of shape. It was obvious that they were slugs.

"Do you recognize those, Doctor?"

Ted looked at them for a minute before his eyes moved to Weatherow.

"Slugs, probably from a pistol."

"Exactly." Weatherow said. "Two of them killed your wife and son." He paused, waiting for the impact to sink in.

Ted looked back to the table and again to Weatherow. "And the other two?" Ted said, maintaining as much of the mask of a poker player as possible.

Weatherow could see from the strained calm on Ted's face that he had picked the right tactic. All he had to do was spin out the rest of the story and there'd be no trouble getting the man's cooperation.

"The other two killed two friends of mine; men I'd worked with for years. They died within minutes of your family, Doctor. All the bullets were fired from this." Karl slid the night stand drawer open and pulled out a pistol. He handed it, butt first, to Ted, who inspected it carefully. "It was not this gun, but another of the same make. Do you recognize it? The model, I mean"

Ted looked closely at the pistol for a long minute. Karl could see the man reaching back into memory, to Viet Nam. Ted reached up and handed the gun back.

"Soviet. I believe a Graz Burya."

"Exactly, Doctor. A nine millimeter automatic. It's the trademark of the KGB. This particular weapon was found in the room of another friend of mine, in Boston. He was trying to investigate the activities of one Andrew Rodgers. Does that name mean anything to you?"

Karl could see instantly that it did. All he had to wonder now was whether Ted would admit it or not.

"I've heard the name," Ted said carefully.

"The chances are that you heard it from Lucas Morgan . . . or perhaps you might have known him under the alias of Charles Howard. Is that correct?"

Ted nodded. Weatherow smiled, pleased. He had his man now.

"Did Morgan, or Howard, also mention a man named Anthony Patrino from Springfield?"

Again, Ted nodded.

"Patrino was killed in a fire. Rodgers had his skull fractured in a Scollay Square flophouse. My Boston operative was killed, as well as two men we had assigned to watch you. The last killings were of your wife and son. That's the picture, Doctor." Karl paused, letting Ted assimilate the information.

"Why my family, Weatherow? Why them?"

"You might be able to answer that better than I could, Doctor. The killer or killers were after something. Whoever killed Howard got there too late to find whatever he was looking for. The house was ransacked.

It was fortunate that you and your daughter weren't killed, too."

The two men looked at one another. Weatherow could see Ted gear up for the anticipated next question. He assumed Weatherow was going to ask where Dawn was. Weatherow had carefully led him into that position.

"I won't ask your daughter's whereabouts, Doctor. I'm sure you're expecting that I might. Rather, I hope that she is in a secure location. You must know that she is in extreme danger. By the way, the car that you eluded so cleverly in New York traffic was one that I sent to catch you. You see, you had no idea what you were dealing with."

"I still don't, Mr. Weatherow. I still don't. None of it makes sense."

"Have you ever heard of the Unicorn Project, Doctor?"

"No." Ted lied with assurance.

Weatherow explained succinctly and logically about the snatching of the advanced Soviet secret weapon in 1950, the recent Soviet reactivation of the project, and the deaths that were apparently attributed to that.

". . . now, are there any questions so far, Doctor?"

"Yes. Howard mentioned that the five men who put the whatever-it-was in the hangar all died in a year. He also mentioned that several other men who'd been on security there had died mysteriously. That doesn't jibe with a recent flurry of killings by the KGB. What it does fit is a government plan to keep secret what is in the hangar. Frankly, I'd never thought of a Soviet secret weapon. My thoughts were running to something more bizarre, given the way the thing was placed there and the security and the deaths since."

"Ah, the imagination of a fiction writer. Yes." Weatherow smiled. "What had you thought was there, Doctor?"

"Perhaps the wreckage of a UFO, Mr. Weatherow. Or perhaps something so alien, so inexplicable that the government would go to any lengths to . . . how do you put it? Terminate anyone who came close to inquiring about it."

Weatherow laughed. It was absurd. Exactly the kind of thing that he might have expected from a man whose imagination roamed into fantasy and fiction. "I trust, Doctor," he said as his laughter subsided, "that we have put your mind at ease about that. The hangar contains the Soviet secret weapon I mentioned. Nothing more and nothing less. There is no glistening ship out of science fiction. No little green men. The very real problem is that we think that a piece of apparatus from the Soviet weapon was removed from the hangar at the time that it was sealed. We think that we can trace it through the deaths of Patrino, Rodgers, and Howard. Then we think that whoever killed Howard, or Morgan, arrived too late to intercept the small mechanism. We think it arrived at your house, and the killers of your family and my operatives failed to find it. Have you gotten a package from him, Doctor?"

Weatherow watched Ted think for a second before answering. The pause told him that the college professor-writer had indeed gotten hold of something. He would have to adjust his tactics accordingly.

"No, Mr. Weatherow."

"Well, Doctor, in a way, it's immaterial. You see, as long as the KGB or its operatives *believe* that you have a clue to what is in the hangar, they will still pursue you and your daughter. They won't stop until you're dead and they have assured themselves that there is no information to be gained from either you or her."

"I can then assume, Mr. Weatherow, that my being here at all means that you don't intend that to happen?"

"Exactly, Doctor. But we have to have certain assurances from you in keeping with the security regulations still in force from the time of your discharge."

"You have them." Ted said. Weatherow could see that the professor-writer knew that he was mated. There was no way around it for him. The man was wanted for questioning by the local police in regard to the deaths of his wife and son. If he spilled anything to the media, he'd be slandered, discredited, and then prosecuted for a security violation by the government. Karl could see that Lawrence had gone through all of it in his mind. He was gaining respect for the man. "What do you propose?" Ted asked resignedly.

"Life returns to normal, Doctor. We will set up a perfect alibi for you on the morning of the murders. The local police will start to look in other places for the killer or killers, after we explain to them that you were out of state on some business for the government. You can return to your home with your daughter . . . or, if you have her in some safe place, you can keep her there. We will explain that she is staying with distant relatives until the trauma of her mother's and brother's deaths subside. You will return to normal and pick up the threads of your writing career. I understand that you no longer have your teaching position. We have a rather large force assigned to watch you, surreptitiously, of course."

"You're going to say that I've been on *government* business?"

Weatherow nodded.

"That will bring the KGB out in strength. I'm to be a target?"

"I prefer to say bait, Doctor. The idea is to intercept any move made against you, and I'm certain we can do that. It allows us to get the Soviet operative and get the information about the renewal of Unicorn that we need."

Ted shook his head. "That's not very reassuring, Mr. Weatherow. You didn't manage to stop any of the other killings. What makes you think you can stop an attempt on my life?"

"We weren't prepared for those. We will be for this, if it comes."

"I suppose I have no choice. But I have some other questions."

"Yes?" Weatherow said tentatively. He was not prepared for further inquiries.

"Are you absolutely sure of what's in that hangar?"

Weatherow folded his arms. "Absolutely, Doctor. I've seen the file on it. I give you my word."

"Another thing. What about the other deaths?"

"What other deaths?"

"The ones that took place from seventy on until now. They were the deaths that Patrino and Rodgers were looking into. They were the strange deaths of other airmen in various security details surrounding the hangar. And why secure the weapon on an Army base, and then assign Air Force personnel to it?"

"To my knowledge," Karl said with assurance, "there were no other deaths in connection with Unicorn than those I have mentioned to you. Though I promise you I'll look into the possibility, I also have to mention that your ex-student Lucas Morgan was a borderline paranoid schizophrenic. He had been in and out of VA hospitals for several years. I would not place too much credibility on what he said. By the way, Doctor, why did you go to his funeral and to his boarding house? Were you doing some amateur private investigation?"

Ted shook his head. "He was a student of mine and I felt obligated. Also, I'd hoped to find out more about what he'd told me in class; perhaps speak to some of the other mourners. Only there weren't any. I went to his rooming house to get back some books that I'd loaned him several weeks earlier."

"I see," Karl said, assessing the man's body language as he spoke. "Well then, I guess that is all there is to say. The doctors assure me that in a few days you'll be able to leave and start our, what shall we call it? Symbiosis?"

"Like the shark and the pilotfish?" Ted snapped.

"Perhaps, Doctor. It's a mutually advantageous marriage of convenience."

"Which are you, Weatherow? The shark or the pilotfish?"

Karl chuckled. "You decide, Doctor. You decide."

Weatherow picked up the tape recorder and strode out of the room into the antiseptically clean hospital corridor. It was the private and secure wing of one of the larger North Jersey VA hospitals. It was, in fact, the same place that had housed Lucas Morgan, Weatherow thought ironically. As he walked down the hall he pondered what Ted had told him. A UFO? How ludicrous. But more important, there were the other deaths. The other airmen. The file showed that there were no other dead. Could it be wrong? He wondered. He made a mental note to look again into the file and the computer backups on Unicorn. It would be a routine precaution.

CHAPTER TWELVE

In the five days that followed his meeting with Karl Weatherow, Ted did not once see the light of day. The secure location was everything it purported to be: absolutely anonymous, hidden, secure, and thoroughly mystifying. Meals were brought to his room, which, Ted found, had an adjoining bathroom, also without a window. On the third and fourth days a series of visits were made by men clothed like Weatherow and the men who brought the food. They were in dark business suits, neat, polite, meticulous, and laconic. There was absolutely nothing that Ted could have said to any of them that might have gained any information about where he was. The clothes that they brought were fashionable and expensive, though devoid of labels.

By the time he tried on the clothes Ted was starting to feel more or less recovered from the crash. The slashing pain that had marked the first day and had punctuated the conversation with Weatherow had diminished into an occasional twinge. The unnamed doctor who had examined Ted twice each day seemed pleased that his patient's recovery had been both speedy and complete. It was just before noon on the fifth day that Weatherow returned. Ted, clothed now in a white shirt, dark gray slacks, and loafers, watched the small, plump man come in. Weatherow smiled as he strode across the room and offered a hand to Ted. Ted could feel a surprising strength in the man's handshake. It seemed out of keeping with the plump, slightly ragged appearance that Weatherow created.

"Good morning, Doctor. Glad to see you've fully recovered." He smiled broadly.

"Thanks," Ted said, his eyes not leaving Weatherow's.

"I have good news, Doctor. You'll be leaving here today."

"That's good, Mr. Weatherow. But could you please tell me where 'here' is?"

"I beg your pardon? Oh, of course. The complex is rather secure, isn't it? We spent a great deal of time and energy designing it."

Weatherow revealed that the "safe house" was actually an underground complex attached to a Veterans Administration hospital in Warren County. It explained the absence of windows, and also the fact that Charlie Howard's landlady had been visited by men from the "VA hospital."

A car had been procured for Ted, and a round-the-clock surveillance team had been briefed and put "on station," as Weatherow termed it. Ted was given a small metal box, no larger than a pack of cigarettes. It was a hailing device, modified from one of the commercial brands of "pagers" on the market. Normally, the device would beep when the owner had an important call waiting at his or her answering service. The box that Weatherow gave to Ted had been designed to work in reverse. All of the men in the surveillance team had duplicates; if Ted pressed the small button on the side of his box, a signal would beep on their receivers. They'd arrive, Weatherow explained confidently, in a matter of seconds. Ted, sharing none of Weatherow's confidence, took the device and slipped it over his belt.

It was an hour later when Ted walked through a light fall of early December snow toward the parking lot of the hospital. The sky was leaden, and there was a raw wind blowing across the North Jersey mountains. Ted, in a new, unfamiliar topcoat, turned his collar against the cold wind. It was Saturday, Weatherow told him. Ted had been at the "safe house" exactly a week.

They walked across the parking lot and stopped at a small blue Chevy. Weatherow took a set of keys from his pocket and handed them to Ted. They were on the same ring as Ted's housekeys.

"You're very thorough, Weatherow."

"We try to be, Doctor. You'll find the registration and all the ownership papers in your name in the glove compartment. You bought the car a few months ago, and the odometer indicates that you've driven it about seven thousand miles."

He pointed off in the distance. At the far end of the parking lot, partially obscured by swirling snow blowing off the roof of the hospital, Ted could see a gray sedan. It looked to be a late model Olds, with a large CB antenna. "That's Ghost One, Doctor. There are two agents in it. We use three cars in the team; all of them are the same model and year. One of them will always be nearby."

Ted nodded. "That's comforting. How long—?"

". . . will all of this go on? A reasonable question. We don't really know. It could be a matter of a day or two. Perhaps a week. Certainly no more than two weeks. When all of it is over, you may keep the car, and the wardrobe. Call it a small gift from your government."

"You're assuming I'll live to drive it, Weatherow."

Weatherow smiled unconvincingly. "I'm certain you will, Doctor. In going over your file, I can see that you have a 'survivor' profile. The second anything seems to be awry, just hit the pager. My men will be there very quickly."

Weatherow gave Ted directions to the highway, which would put him on the fifty-mile drive home, and

Ted slowly drove out the front gate of the hospital, careful of the patchy ice. In ten minutes, he was moving at fifty-five on the main highway, with Ghost One a discreet distance behind.

Only a week. It was hard to believe, he thought. A week ago he'd come home to find Michael and Lisa dead. He'd . . . Suddenly he thought of Cathy and Dawn. He looked quickly at the mirror. The gray sedan was there, cruising two or three cars back. He'd have to find a way to get in touch with Cathy without alerting the chase car. He dredged the emergency number Cathy had given him from the musty corners of his memory, and resolved to get Cathy on the phone as soon as he could. Together, perhaps they could find a way to slip Ted out of the role of Weatherow's pawn. Ted's lifelong maverick approach to things made the role loathsome. He'd not buckled under the Army's oppressiveness, nor that of Oscar Small. And now he'd been forced into the role of resident target. There would have to be a way he and Cathy and Dawn could parlay the cylinder and the orders into something that could save all of their lives, while avoiding the ministrations of Weatherow and his agents. He was sure that Weatherow had not told him the whole truth about anything. It would be easy for the man to order an accident for Ted as soon as he located Dawn and Cathy. With all three of them dead and the cylinder back in his hands, Weatherow would be able to play his game of "chase and kill" with the KGB forever without fear of exposure.

He looked at his hands on the wheel and saw that they were white-knuckled, tense. He shook his head and leaned back against the seat, forcing his mind away from Weatherow. He forced himself to look at the scenery. The gray sky was starting to break into blue patches with small patches of scud clouds moving quickly before a freshening west wind. The rest of the day would be crisp and clear.

In front of him the road was totally open. Behind . . . He looked in the mirror and blinked. The chase car. It had changed lanes. He could see it accelerate up in the middle lane, roaring up to catch him . . . on a deserted stretch of road. Oh, Jesus, he thought. Was it all a set-up? Did Weatherow want him to die on the road? Was it a plan to flush out Dawn and Cathy? He looked in the mirror again. The gray Ghost was speeding ahead now. In seconds it would overtake him. He floored the accelerator. The small Chevy roared ahead, eluding the chase car that was about to overtake it. Behind Ted, Weatherow's driver also accelerated. In a second or two, Ted realized that he couldn't escape. The chase car had far too much horsepower for his small Chevy to elude. He let the car overtake him.

It screeched to a halt a few yards ahead and both front doors flew open. The driver, a tall and athletically lean young man, ran toward Ted's car, while the man in the right seat seemed to be on a radio. Ted tensed as the man reached the door.

"What happened?" he yelled.

Ted looked at him quizzically. "What do you mean?"

"I mean what happened? What did you see?"

Ted was totally confused. He'd been prepared to have the man draw a gun and empty it into him. He shook his head.

"Doctor, what made you push the button on the pager? We thought you saw . . ."

He paused and looked back down the road. Another chase car, the same make and model as the first, screeched to a halt on the roadside pebbles behind Ted's car. The two men waited to see what to do.

The driver of the first car looked back to Ted. "Doctor, when you hit that button, the shit hits the fan and people come running from hell and gone."

Ted suddenly realized what had happened. When he'd adjusted his position in the seat, the pager looped to his belt was pushed against the back of the seat. The pressure had apparently triggered the switch and activated the emergency signal. It had not been a setup. They were not out to kill him . . . at least not yet.

"I'm sorry," he said. "It must have triggered accidentally against the seat. I'll have to be more careful. I'm new to all of this." He reached back and moved the pager to a less vulnerable position against his side. The tall man nodded, repressing anger. He looked back to the car that had just arrived and waved them away. Obediently, the car's driver pulled out and moved up the road.

The man looked at Ted. "OK," he said perfunctorily. He strode off in the direction of the car and left Ted to his thoughts.

The event was disconcerting. True, Ted did not get gunned down. But that did not increase his belief in Weatherow. All it did was add a chill to the thought that out there somewhere was a skilled agent, or a team of them, waiting. He'd have to call Cathy at the first opportunity. He'd call from a pay phone and keep the conversation short. He ached to find out about how Dawn was managing. But he knew he'd have to be more than careful with the call. There was a good chance that Weatherow was monitoring all phone traffic that would be coming out of the Lawrence house. Ted would have to set up an alternate approach.

He had been driving east for more than half an hour when he swung off the interstate exit ramp and moved into the sparse flow of traffic on the southbound Garden State Parkway. He crossed the Raritan River bridge and swung the Chevy into the left lane as he approached the toll plaza. As he accelerated out of the plaza he moved to the express lane, flashing his turn signal at the last possible second. Perhaps taken by surprise, the gray chase car driver missed the fork and was forced to parallel Ted on the slower three-lane outer roadway. Turning his head to the right occasionally, Ted could see that Weatherow's man adjusted to the situation. It was what Ted wanted him to do. Ahead, he could see the exit that would take him into the rest stop. The peculiarity of this particular restaurant-gas station combination was that it could not be entered from the outer three-lane section of the road. Ted had often remarked to Lisa about the fact that it might have been a design screw-up. The chase car would have to drive south several miles before it could turn and drive back north to find the Chevy. It gave Ted a few minutes. That would be all he would need.

"Hello?" The voice was old and throaty. For a moment it surprised Ted, until he remembered that the number was that of Cathy's mother on Long Island.

"Mrs. Seward?"

"Speaking." There was a slight hitch in the old woman's voice. It was fear.

"This is Ted Lawrence."

"Oh . . . OH! Wait. Let me get Cathy."

Ted looked out the booth as he wasted precious seconds waiting for Cathy to get to the phone. The outdoor booth was in sight of the northbound lane of the Parkway. He wanted to have plenty of warning when Weatherow's car arrived.

"Ted. My God. Ted."

"Are you all right? Is Dawn?"

"Yes. We both are. We got out of my place when it got late and you didn't come back. What about you?"

"I can't tell you much now. I'm OK. I'm working for the government."

"You're what?"

"Never mind. I haven't got time to talk. Don't call me at home. I'll get to you. There can't be any connection between us and the . . . toys that you and Dawn have. Understand?"

"Of course. You're sure you're all right?" There was an urgency in her voice.

"I'm fine. Just keep Dawn and the . . . things we were looking at at your apartment totally under wraps."

He could see the gray car speeding in on the north-bound ramp. They must have turned off on one of the state trooper U-turn lanes. He only had a few seconds.

"Cathy?"

"Yes?" There was an edge of emotion in her voice. He could feel what it meant deep in his bones. Suddenly, he knew that what he felt was something he'd not felt in almost eight years. Something he thought he'd forgotten how to feel. The gray car screeched to a stop a few feet from the booth. The driver started to get out.

"Cathy . . . I love you.'" He hung up, swung open the booth, and smiled at the driver of the gray car. Again the man in the right seat was visible on the radio. He was obviously assuring all the other shadowing units that the quarry was safe and had not escaped. The driver's lean, blue-eyed face looked dour.

Ted's smile broadened. "Hi. Guess you didn't see my turn signal. Sorry." He turned and, without further comment, moved back to the Chevy and slid behind the wheel. In another twenty minutes, he was home.

CHAPTER THIRTEEN

He stood in the driveway, looking at the house, for a long minute after he got out of the car. It was the same as it had always been, and yet so much had changed. Three weeks from start to finish. No more. And his career had been shattered, his family butchered, his entire life turned upside down, all because of a strange story from a former mental patient, a story that had to be true . . . that couldn't be anything else. He could feel a raw northwest wind start to whip through the half-century-old maples in the back acreage. On a whim he started to walk out to the back.

The trees were bare and stark against the December sky. As the wind rose, they creaked in stubborn resistance. The early snow had melted and now was little more than an occasional crystal halo on a twisted branch. His feet shuffled through the fallen leaves, as he was sure Dawn's had done only a week earlier. Thank God she came out here, or she'd be dead too, he thought.

Pulling his coat around him, Ted sat on a log; one that he, Dawn, and Michael had shared for many hours in the summers. They'd come out to build campfires and roast hot dogs. Lisa had almost never joined them. She complained that Ted was simply reacting to his childhood in the steaming, hellish ghetto of the South Bronx. Perhaps she was right. He hadn't really seen grass and trees, except in parks, until he was a teenager. In those early years he'd vowed that he would never be hungry, never slip into the bottle as his father had, never abandon his fate to the "will of God," as his mother had. He'd vowed to claw his way up, to succeed. And that he had truly done. He'd mastered three fields, built a successful career as an academic, and started a second as a fiction writer. He'd married a rich man's daughter, fathered two children, and bought his comfortable middle-class house in the suburbs. Everything, with the possible exception of the marriage to Lisa, had been a success, until last week. Then it had come crashing down.

He got to his feet and started back to the house. He hated himself when he was depressed, and self-pity was not Ted Lawrence's forte. Not ever. None of it would bring back Michael or Lisa. None of the self-pity that threatened to wash over him could help Cathy or Dawn or himself. It wouldn't keep the vipers of the KGB from shadowing the shadowers and looking for an opening. Only cleverness and daring would do that. As he shuffled back Ted wondered how much of either he had. He was the target of professionals, hired killers—the kind that left no witnesses.

Ted cut through the sea of leaves and moved in the direction of the pillar mailbox near the road. It would obviously be jammed with mail, and he'd spotted the blue and white mail truck coming down the road. Ted hailed the mailman and took a handful of letters. Most of the delivery was junk mail; there was only one letter of real importance. It was from his publisher. The code numbers on the upper left corner of the envelope told him that the letter was from Cathy. He tore it open on the spot, then read the letter in confusion. It contained a check for the advance on his latest novel, called *A New Dawn*. Ted had never written such a novel. For a second he shook his head as he looked at the letter and the check for five thousand dollars. My God! The realization hit him. Cathy had gotten him the money, hoping that he'd be alive. If he hadn't, they'd have picked up the letter and returned it to the sender in five days. If the check had not been negotiated in thirty days, it would have been cancelled. He wondered if the money was from Cathy, personally, or from the publisher. It didn't really matter. The woman he'd so rashly told he'd loved, less than an hour ago, was saying in a letter that he might never have received that she supported him to the tune of five thousand dollars of her own money, or money wheedled from the publisher at the risk of her job. He shook his head and opened the mailbox.

It was empty.

It shouldn't have been.

He stared at it for a minute.

Weatherow!

The man had thought of everything. He'd had his agents take the mail, perhaps read and photocopy all of it. Weatherow had to be sure that Ted was holding something back. Otherwise there was no reason to do anything. Did the shadowy government man want to find Dawn? Did Weatherow suspect that Ted and Dawn had the artifact? He *had* to!

Ted walked through the yard and slowly up the front steps. He wiped his feet methodically on the welcome mat, then reached for the door. His hand stopped a few inches short of it. He was afraid to go into the house. He was right to be. What horror he had left there as he and Dawn fled: a shambles of overturned furniture; a sea of blood in the kitchen and hall.

After a few seconds, he reached for the knob, and found the door locked.

He fished in his pockets for the keys and unlocked the door.

The kitchen was spotless. There was no trace of . . . no trace. He found that the living room was much the same. All of the house had been gone over in the same way that Charlie Howard's room had been scoured. He scanned the kitchen, idly moving through it as though it were a place he had never lived, only one that he would be visiting for a few days. There was fresh food in the fridge; the date on a milk container was almost a week in the future. They must have shopped for him yesterday; business as usual. It made him angry. The mail was piled neatly on the kitchen table. On top was a single blank sheet of paper with a single typed line:

"NO SENSE LETTING THE MAIL PILE UP, DOCTOR."

It was simply signed with the letter "W." The thought of Weatherow collecting his mail for him, as well as everything else, was something that made Ted madder still. In the midst of the junk mail was a large, padded envelope addressed to him. It had been mailed a day before the nightmare had begun. The return address said that the sender was Mrs. Alice Hull. Ted pushed into his memory to find where the name connected. She was an older woman, a student in his parapsychology class. This must be her term project—the one she spoke of the night that Ted had made the mistake of listening to Charlie's story. He shucked off his coat, tossed it across a chair, and set the envelope down for a moment.

He took a rock-hard package of frankfurters from the freezer and, chiseling two away from the rest of the frozen mass, popped them into the microwave. The meal was makeshift; the franks and some bread, and a glass of milk, thanks to Weatherow. He sat at the table and opened Mrs. Hull's envelope. It was filled with carefully typed pages, lovingly sculpted into excellent prose, and dealt with the topic of his lecture on that fateful night. She had done a careful job of researching the work of Alfred Watkins. The bibliography included almost everything that the man had published in his lifetime. In the back of the paper was a huge set of appendices; maps with carefully drawn ley lines through England, France, the U.S. How? He stared at the maps. She'd started the leys that Watkins had plotted as crisscrossing the English and Welsh countryside and extended the lines out across the Atlantic. She'd carried out the lines until they moved like a random web made by a spider across the U.S. To Ted's mind, no one had ever plotted such a complex of leys, or straight lines, across the U.S. It was a valuable bit of research. Using the paper as a respite from the terror of the other thoughts that might have plagued him, Ted finished the meal and moved to the den. He read the paper several times, and admired the woman's thoroughness. He made marginal notes on the paper as was his custom and set it aside to return to her as soon as he managed to get back to Paxton. About all he'd do there now, he guessed, was clear his desk. Still, he had two more weeks of the fall semester to complete, unless they had suspended him in the interim week when he'd been with Weatherow. Or had the shadowy Defense Department director taken care of that, too?

After laying a fire in the den fireplace, Ted poured himself a brandy, and placed a yellow pad on his lap to make notes. The small metal pager was within reach on the end table.

He was going to need a plan; one separate from the ministrations of Weatherow and the marauding KGB. He sipped the brandy before he started to make notes. He placed the brandy glass on the end table next to the metal device that had caused so much furor.

Were they out there in the winter night? Were they watching the house? He was tempted by the first rush of the brandy to press the button just to see. He resisted. The last thing that he needed was a troop of agents storming in through the windows and doors to see if the KGB had succeeded or failed. Instead, he flipped on the small radio that sat on the far end of the coffee table, and tuned it to an FM station. They were playing a Bach concerto, and Ted let the music mingle with the brandy.

Charlie and the man from Boston, Andrew Rodgers, had served together guarding what Weatherow had called Unicorn. They didn't have a clue to what they were guarding. What purpose did the killings of the guards serve? Wouldn't the KGB be astute enough to realize that the guards were only small fish? Hadn't they done enough homework in intelligence to realize that enlisted men with fragments of rumors would avail them little?

Ted stopped and idly tapped the top of his felt-tip pen against the table top. No. That wasn't the way intelligence worked. There were no revelations, no magic set of secret papers that revealed everything. A spy or a group of spies simply hounded down the clues one at a time and later, when a mass of information was assembled, another team labored to make sense of what had been gathered. So there was a chance that the KGB *had* hunted down all of those men and killed them after extracting the pitiful bits of information that they carried.

But if the Russians were sure that the U.S. had their secret, albeit ancient, weapon project, why did they not simply shift their priorities and move to the development of something else—something newer? God only knew that there were hundreds of projects that Russia could have gone on with. And if the Russians had discovered this loss thirty years ago, why hadn't they moved in more forcefully then? Didn't Weatherow or his predecessors connect the deaths of the first airmen to a possible ploy on the part of the Russians? *And where in hell had the cylinder come from?* The only thing that Ted could think was that one of the original five airmen had picked it up as a souvenir and carried it with him. How did it find its way to Boston? What were the chances that Weatherow knew of the cylinder's existence, and moreover of the location of Cathy and Dawn?

The last thought made Ted put down the pen. He

got to his feet and moved to the corner hutch where one of the two phones sat. He took the handset from the cradle and unscrewed the mouthpiece. There was nothing inside that was out of the ordinary. He did the same with the earpiece. Again, nothing. He took a dime from his pocket and undid the plastic cover. He went over the phone almost microscopically. There was no bug that could be found. He went upstairs to the living room and did the same. Again, there was nothing. He did not let that reassure him. His background in physics, and the work he'd done in intelligence in Viet Nam, told him that a bug no longer needed to be an instrument placed inside the guts of a phone mechanism. It could be something as simple as a tap on the line far from the house, at the junction box. Or it could have been something as esoteric as a parabolic dish, aimed at any of the windows of the house. He couldn't risk trying to call Cathy at her mother's. He'd have to wait until Monday and call her at the office. He'd guard the conversation until he could see her and they could talk. Perhaps there was something more about the cylinder that Dawn and Cathy were able to figure out. If there was a clue there, it might spell survival for all three of them. He had no illusions about the fact that Weatherow considered Ted a use and discard piece on the checkerboard. Little more than a paper pawn.

He froze.

There was a sound near the window. Ted strained his ears; he heard the soft moan of the December wind, the creaking of the trees, the rustle of the leaves as the wind moved them.

What else had he heard? Slowly, he localized the sounds. Someone was moving through the leaves in the side yard, where they were thick and deep. Someone was coming closer to the house, nearer to the glass door separating the yard from the ground-floor den.

He sat motionless at the living room phone for several moments, a knot tightening in his stomach. All he could think of was that Weatherow had lost two agents to the same professional killer who murdered Michael and Lisa. And Ted had left the pager downstairs in the den.

Ted got to his feet and bolted to the stairs that led to the den. Maybe he could reach the pager first, but he was on the bottom step when he heard the glass doors of the den slide slowly open.

Raw terror gripped him. There was no way to get to the pager; he was trapped. His back hugged the wall of the downstairs corridor. The only chance was to make a break for the front door. He tensed his muscles.

Footsteps moved stealthily toward the fireplace, and Ted was sure that he had to make a break for it in seconds. Chances were that the intruder would have his back to the den door; that would give Ted the extra time he needed to reach the front door. He got ready to bolt.

"Dr. Lawrence?"

Ted stood dumbstruck. Should he answer?

"Dr. Lawrence?" The voice was louder, more insistent this time. There was something familiar about it. Oh, Jesus, Ted thought. He turned the corner.

The man was Weatherow's agent—the same one who'd sat in the right seat of the Ghost car. He stood, red-nosed from the cold wind, in the middle of the den.

Ted was sure that his shaking was visible. He knew that his anger was about to be.

"Why the hell don't you knock, or ring the bell? And what the hell do you want?"

The man shrugged. "The phone was busy, Doctor. We were just checking the place out. We like to know where you are in the house. We couldn't be sure that the phone hadn't been taken off the hook. I came to the window and saw the pager on the table over there." He gestured in the direction of the table, where the pager rested with the brandy glass and the yellow pad . . .

Another chill shot through Ted. The yellow pad had all of the rambling notes that he'd made about Unicorn, Cathy, Dawn . . . the cylinder.

He feigned nonchalance. "You gave me a fright, Mister . . . ah?"

"Fratianni, Doctor. Angelo Fratianni. Call me Frat. Everyone else does."

Ted smiled thinly. He moved slowly in the direction of the brandy glass, which he picked up in one hand as he retrieved the pad with the other. He couldn't be sure if his motions and words betrayed anything.

"Well, ah . . . Frat, I guess you're just doing your job."

The small, dark Italian man nodded and smiled, reaching a hand out to warm it over the log fire. "Trying to, Doctor. Trying to. I'll be going, then. Please remember to keep that pager within an arm's distance all the time. We don't want to be seen in the vicinity of the house unless we absolutely have to be. I'm sure you understand why?"

Ted nodded and gestured with the pad toward the hutch and the brandy bottle.

"Would you like a brandy, Frat? It's going to be a cold night out there."

The man shook his head. "Thank you, but no thanks. I go off duty in an hour and a half, and besides, I can't drink when I'm on watch."

The man slipped out the same way he came in, and Ted locked the glass door behind him. After locking it, he went to the garage and rummaged through a pile of scrap lumber. In a few minutes he came up with what he had searched for. It was a long, inch-thick strip of molding. He took it to the den and wedged it in the door track. Now, even if the door were picked or pried open, there would be no way that anyone could get in. He moved on to the garage and made sure to lock the two garage doors before putting out the light.

He poured himself another brandy and downed it immediately. He poured and sipped at a second. After a few minutes he noticed that the shaking seemed to abate somewhat. He turned up the volume on the FM station that had been playing softly in the background, in time to hear his name. It was only in a two-line story, a filler before the weather. The newscaster mentioned that Dr. Lawrence was no longer considered a suspect in the brutal Shore Park murders. The newsman, who sounded bored with his copy, said that the local police had been assured by the State Department that Dr. Lawrence had been in Europe on a mission of State Department-related business, and that there was no way that he could be considered a suspect in the case.

Ted turned the volume back down as the announcer moved to a commercial. Weatherow had been accurate and thorough. He had set up the perfect alibi for Ted. And, at the same time, he had done something else. He had managed to use the media to tell the KGB that Ted Lawrence was working for the U.S. government. It was an assurance to Ted's stalkers, who were waiting for the right time to kill him, that they were after the right target.

It was some fifteen minutes later that Ted Lawrence propped his head against the back of the sofa and drifted off to sleep.

CHAPTER FOURTEEN

He soared westward at incredible speed. Again the continent flashed below him. The great east-west line pulsated with a cold blue fire. Ahead lay the massive intersection. The north-south ley slashed across the one that his course paralleled. Then he was in the center of the swirling intermixture . . . or rather he was still above them, high above. And yet, he could feel the energy streams swirl together, huge torrents of water in a spring downpour.

He swooped down into the midst of it, into the cross hairs of unknown power. Lower, ever lower.

Flatland . . . the mountains in the distance. There was no one there, and the light was gone. In the distance there was suddenly something . . . a truck . . . several of them . . . bright lights . . .

He awoke at three in the morning, shaking all over, perspiration slipping down his back. It was the same dream, but there was more of it this time. There was something terrifying about it. Had he been looking at the end of his life? He couldn't be sure. As he calmed down and tried to ponder the question, something nagged at the back of his memory, something important. It scratched the back of his mind for release, with the irritation of a fingernail drawn slowly down a slate blackboard. What *was* it?

He sat up on the den couch and tried to unkink his

neck. Suddenly it struck him. The dream was like Alice Hull's paper. He reached over and grabbed the paper from the table, opening it to the large, lovingly constructed appendix that contained a map of the U.S. The lines of power he had traced in the dream, ley lines, of energy from deep in the earth, according to the man who'd first mapped them. But Alfred Watkins had never extended the lines to the United States. Mrs. Hull had done that.

Ted followed the lines with his finger. The east-west line was there, intersecting the second line with the precision of a rifle sight cross hair. The two lines intersected directly over Ogden, Utah—alarmingly close to the infamous hangar that housed Project Unicorn.

Ted stared at the map for a long minute. He could not remember when he first had the dream. Was it before Charlie had come to him with the bizarre story of the enigma in the hangar? Or had the dream come as a result of the madness and death that had followed? How did ley lines, that Watkins had plotted and Reich had claimed flowed with the immense energy of life itself, come to cross at Ogden? Was it a coincidence? Ted doubted it. But what was the significance? What might be the connection to Unicorn?

Was it a weapon that tapped the raw power of the earth?

The thought stopped him cold.

Consider a weapon that tapped into the planet itself, then transformed the ergs of planetary energy into some sort of a macabre weapons system. No wonder the Russians might kill a score of men to insure that the Americans did not have it. They would not have stopped killing at a million, if necessary. The American government, Ted thought, would do the same. But, just as obviously, this wonder weapon didn't work, or wasn't operational; otherwise the U.S. and Russia would have super aircraft. Unless the vehicles were seen as flying saucers . . . Ted shook his head and reached a hand up to massage a cramped muscle. He couldn't find the answer, and yet he could feel that there was one tantalizingly close, one that just eluded him.

He turned his thoughts over in his mind, as a child might rotate a small, interesting-looking stone. If the Russians had been working on a project that was a generation away from its time, they would have deadended it because technology was unable to actualize it. At least, that had been Weatherow's line. But if the cylinder and the enigma in the hangar were based on ley lines and drawing power from the earth, then almost no technology would be needed to realize it. After all, he thought to himself, how much technology did the ancient Britons have? The odds were that they made use of the power for psychic communication, healing, and a dozen other things, at least according to the writings of a handful of esoteric scholars. It had to be that the Russians were attacking the problem in the wrong way. If that was so, then the odds were that the Americans, master technocrats that they were, had been unable to decipher the purposes of the device. But then why waste lives stealing it? Why waste money replacing it with a non-working model? What intelligence told them to get the thing in the first place?

It was just past four in the morning when he shook his head and grunted in frustration. He didn't like the conclusions that he had come to. It was possible the thing in the hangar, the mystery-shrouded "Project Unicorn," was *not* something that the Russians had developed . . . He stopped in mid-thought, realizing that that would make everything that Weatherow had said a lie. There'd be no reason for KGB bloodhounds to pursue anyone to ferret out information on a dead issue. Then what was in the hangar? Why the murders? The secrecy? The whole question was like an equation for which there were too many unknowns and not enough givens.

He got to his feet and stretched his arms to the ceiling. His muscles groaned and his head throbbed for a second; a residue from the concussion. The embers of the fire were almost dead in the fireplace. Ted took a poker and stirred them randomly for a few seconds before trudging upstairs and taking a shower. After the fright he'd sustained from the visit of Frat earlier in the evening, he carried the small pager as a man would carry a fetish.

He let the needlespray shower beat on him until the water started to turn chilly. He'd emptied the tank. He stepped from the shower and toweled off, clearing the steam on the mirror so that he could see his reflection. There were deeply etched circles under his eyes, and laugh lines around them, that he didn't remember seeing before. But, generally, he'd worn the madness of the last weeks well, or so he was starting to think.

He moved into the darkened bedroom and paused, looking at the bed. He consciously tried to push aside the things that threatened to flood up in his memory. Lisa in the years before things turned sour. Michael snuggling up between them.

Standing nude before the bed, he threw back the coverlet and stopped for a second; though he couldn't hear anything, he felt a presence downstairs. A ball of ice formed immediately in his stomach. He dropped the coverlet and tiptoed back to the still-steamy bathroom to get the pager, then quietly moved out into the hall and strained his ears for sounds that might issue from the first floor.

There was a slight creak on the stairs. So someone *was* downstairs. Ted pressed the button on the pager. A tiny red pinpoint of light winked at him in the darkness.

He could feel his heart pounding like a piston, and he was surprised that whoever was on the stairs could not hear it. He tiptoed a few feet down the hall and slipped through the door to what had been Michael's room, leaving it slightly ajar. From there he would be able to see someone pass the splash of light from the bathroom. He slipped a few feet back into the darkness and waited. If he weren't so frightened he would have thought it was funny, something taken from a bizarre dream. Here he was, stark naked, and someone was prowling through the house. What could he do?

There was a slight shuffle on the top step. The ball of fear in his stomach tightened. Whoever it was had made the turn into the long center hall. He was heading for the bedroom. He would have to pass Ted.

Ted looked at the pager in his hand. It still winked a solitary red eye at him. Who was there in the hall, and where were his protectors? Or was the person in the hall one of the protectors, coming to tidy up Ted Lawrence with a bullet in the back of the head?

He waited.

Another shuffle.

He could almost hear the man breathing.

Suddenly, he was there, silhouetted by the light from the bathroom. He was a small man in an overcoat. He wore no hat, and Ted could clearly see a bright shock of red hair. He did not look like any of the men that Weatherow had sent, but Ted knew that he didn't have to. The man didn't seem armed as Ted peered at him through the crack in the door. At least there was no weapon visible. Who the hell was he, and how did he get past the guards? It didn't matter, Ted thought. Not now. Ted had another decision to make. Should he stay where he was, or attack?

The man took a step. He was almost out of the splash of light thrown by the bathroom overhead light. Ted decided to wait until the man was just past the door to Michael's room, then hit him in the back of the neck.

The man took another step. Ted tensed.

Everything went insane.

A thumping at the front door brought the man spinning suddenly, startled. The back door of the den and the garage door simultaneously slid open, their sounds making an explosive bang. Four armed men stormed up the stairs as Ted dove out of hiding and grabbed the red-haired man around the neck. The man clawed at Ted's arm, but Ted's desperate grip pulled him to the floor. In minutes, Weatherow's men had reached them and dragged Ted away from the choking intruder.

The man sat on the floor, stunned, while the tall, blond driver, whom Ted had eluded at the Parkway rest stop, went through the intruder's pockets. He found the man's wallet and went through the cards. He looked down and frowned as he spoke.

"You are Wallace Callaway?"

The man nodded as he rubbed his neck.

The tall, blond man, Chet Hammend by name, hunkered down on one knee and grabbed the man's tie. "I want an answer, not a nod, you son of a bitch. You're Wallace Callaway?'"

"Y-yes." The man's voice was a throaty whisper.

"Who retained you?"

"Wha—?"

Hammend tightened his grip on the tie. Callaway gulped. "R . . . Ryan. Mr. Ryan."

Ted's eyes widened. Lisa's parents? He wanted to interrupt but Hammend was doing a good enough job, it seemed. Again he tightened his viselike grip on the tie. Callaway's eyes widened, and the cords in his neck stood out taut.

"We have you for breaking and entering." He looked to Ted for a split second, then his ice gray eyes fixed back on the terrified Callaway. "We also have you for aggravated assault. Perhaps even attempted murder. It did seem that he was trying to kill you when *he* attacked *you?* Right, Dr. Lawrence?"

"Y—yes, it seemed that way," Ted said, his voice shaky.

Hammend pulled the man to his feet. "Now listen to me. You're indictable on three counts. Two of them are felonies. First, you'll lose this." He waved a salmon card in front of Callaway's eyes, which nearly bugged out of their sockets.

"I won't tell . . ." Callaway croaked.

"You're goddamned right you won't." Chet Hammend slammed Callaway into the wall. While he held him, he turned to two of his colleagues, who quietly and efficiently held the biggest pistols Ted had ever seen.

"Walker. Kelly. Take this son of a bitch out and shoot him. Dump the body in the inlet."

Callaway screamed. Hammend hit him in the face with the back of his hand. "Shut up."

One of the two men came forward and clicked the safety off his pistol. He shrugged and looked to his tall, muscular partner. "What the fuck, Chet. This guy's not stupid. He knows if he ever says a word, he's dead. He ain't worth a bullet. Let him go. Just keep the license. He can't work without it. If he keeps his mouth shut, we'll send it back to him."

Callaway was shaking and whimpering. A small curl of blood was starting to work its way down from the corner of his mouth. "I w-w-won't say a word. I was just doin' my job. Tha's all. Jus' my job."

The blond man pushed the mysterious Callaway in the direction of the stairs. "All right. You've bought your life, 'cause I'm in a good mood. Get the fuck out of here, and if I hear so much as a whisper about any of this, you'll be dead in twelve hours."

It was a minute later when Ted stood alone with Chet Hammend. It had been a good cop/bad cop routine. Ted had seen it a hundred times in Viet Nam. One interrogator wanted to kill the prisoner in the most hideous way imaginable. Another, more humanitarian, interrogator wanted to let the prisoner go. But Ted had never seen it carried out with such speed or terrifying efficiency. Chet looked to Ted.

"Better get some clothes on, Doctor. You'll get pneumonia."

Ted looked down at himself. He'd forgotten he was naked. He went into the bedroom and slipped into a robe, then came back out. Chet was examining the small, salmon-colored card that he'd gotten from Callaway's wallet.

"He was a private investigator?"

Chet nodded without looking up. "Yup. Worked for the Ryans. They were . . . ?"

"Lisa's parents. Dawn and Michael's grandparents. I guess they wanted to get information on their granddaughter."

"Yeah. Well, that fucker isn't going to work without his license for a while. He isn't going to say a word, either. Sorry about the commotion, Doctor."

"What if he were someone else?"

"Pardon?" Chet's ice gray eyes fixed Ted's.

"I said, what if he'd been the man you were looking for? What if I hadn't hit the button on the pager?"

Chet's eyes remained impassive for a second, then his face broke into a grin. "Sorry, Doctor. The pager didn't matter a hang. We saw him come in."

"You s—?"

"Of course. We also knew that he wasn't carrying a firearm. We had to let him get into the house. Otherwise, if he was our man, we'd have scared him off. When he hit the top of the stairs, we were ready to move. I was surprised that you hit him before we did. That was pretty alert of you. But then, you were a 'Nam vet, right?"

Ted nodded.

"Well, good night, Doctor."

Chet disappeared down the steps and out the door, into the December night. Ted stood in the hall for a long minute. There was no question that he wouldn't sleep. He began to think he might never sleep again.

CHAPTER FIFTEEN

Ted had managed to work his way through two scrambled eggs and three cups of coffee when the leaden Sunday morning sky started to streak with the faint, pink fingers of dawn. He cleaned up the kitchen and set to work. In happier times it had been his habit to write until dawn, then write a list of things to be done on the following day. With that finished he'd meditate for half an hour, then doze for another two, three at the most. He'd never needed much more sleep than that. Working on little sleep had been his stock in trade as he managed two full-time jobs, writing and teaching. So the missed night's sleep was not something monumental. However, he was disturbed that he didn't seem to be able to meditate. He was unable to reach a deep, satisfying state. After a few minutes he gave up, realizing that he was just going through the motions.

It was just past nine when he looked to the list and ticked off the first item. He went out to the car and drove a mile or so to get the Sunday papers. The Ghost car followed, and the pager was on his belt. He shook his head. He was adapting.

He made a list of all of the realtors in the area who seemed to carry houses in his range, and called three of them. It took an hour to firm up all the details of start-

199

ing a multiple-listed sale offering. He told all three realtors that he'd be moving out in a matter of weeks, and they could show the house using a key in a lock box. He moved to the next item on the list.

"Hello?"

Ira Kelton's voice was thick with sleep and, Ted suspected, with alcohol from a long Saturday night. In any event, Ted's agent was not used to late-night calls.

"Ira? It's Ted."

"Son of a bitch."

"That's what I like, Ira. An emotion-filled reunion."

"I'm sorry, Ted. Sorry. But the last I heard, the cops were hunting you, and . . . Jesus Christ. You know what I mean?"

"Yeah. They're still looking for the killer, Ira. But they got things straight with me."

"The paper said you were working for the government or something. You never told me any of that."

"You never asked. Look, Ira, I want you to do something for me. Arrange for a lunch with my editor at Halleck. There may be a new sale perking."

"First, why don't you ever tell me about these things? Second, why don't you call her yourself? You know Cathy Seward better than I do. And . . . oh shit. I'm sorry, Ted. I really am. I forgot about Lisa and the little boy. I apologize."

"It's OK, Ira. Just see if you can arrange a lunch for tomorrow or Tuesday. Tell her it's about the *New Dawn* project."

Ira agreed and Ted got him off the phone before the agent could ask too many more questions on what was assuredly a tapped line.

He moved down the list that now sat with a half a hundred other papers on his den coffee table. The phone rang.

"Dr. Lawrence?"

Ted did not recognize the voice. "Yes?" he said, cautiously.

"This is Martin Sandusky, of Warren, Tyler and Sandusky."

There was a slight pause in the man's voice, as if he expected Ted to recognize the name of the firm. Ted did, after a second. It was the firm that the Ryans had retained on Lisa's behalf in the divorce proceedings. Ted had not pegged the man's voice because another partner in the firm had been handling the case. But this was the senior partner, so the big guns had been brought in . . . for something. It didn't take long for Sandusky to get to the point. After a few minutes of condolences, he moved in.

"Dr. Lawrence, my clients are rather concerned about the health and welfare of their remaining grandchild, especially now that it has been publicized that you are abroad frequently in, ah . . . government work."

Thank God for Hurley. He'd kept his word and provided Ted with a legitimate alibi for his damning absence. But the newspapers, which picked up Hurley's statement immediately, were still trying to dig out more information. So Ted could understand how the Ryans were trying to use that against him still.

"What are you getting at, Mr. Sandusky?"

"Mr. and Mrs. Ryan would like to know their granddaughter's whereabouts. I'm certain you can understand their concern."

"I can assure you that Dawn Lawrence is in fine health, and being well cared for." Ted waited. He could feel Sandusky moving to a new, tougher plateau, like a mob enforcer getting ready to break a few legs.

"I'm afraid, though your assurances are sincere, my clients require substantially more than that. Not only has the child been through the loss of a mother and brother, but it has come to the Ryans' attention that you are no longer employed at the college—and your government employment is rather a mystery. They are concerned about your ability to create a good home for her. Quite simply, Doctor, they will take court action as soon as possible to assume guardianship of the child unless you cooperate in the matter and allow the child to see her grandparents."

"Speak to my attorney on Monday, Mr. Sandusky. I have nothing more to say."

"And who is your attorney, Doctor?"

"Speak to my attorney on Monday, Mr. Sandecker."

"Sandusky!"

"Speak to him tomorrow, please."

"Very well. Who represents you, Doctor?"

"I'm sure you'll figure that out. After all, you found I'd lost my job. Perhaps you should go to the same source."

Ted slammed the phone down. It was the last thing he needed now. His in-laws had had him convicted of murder in the press less than a week ago, and now they wanted Dawn . . . or did they?

Ted could feel a chill raise the hairs on his back. Could it be Weatherow? If it was, it was clever. He was a bloodless son of a bitch. And what could be done about it? Nothing. The call had been handled the right way. He had not revealed Dawn's whereabouts. He would not. Not ever.

He got up from the couch and stretched, then walked to the window.

Suddenly, there was a hiss, followed by a rumble. Ted's eye was caught by a flash of brightness in the sky. He looked up and then instinctively shielded his eyes. Something huge was flashing across the southern sky, crossing the line of the sun, and the sunlight prevented him from seeing the speeding object for a few seconds. It was a crimson fireball that streaked across the winter sky, leaving a trail of incandescent gases in its wake like a fiery finger. Ted's jaw hung slack as he watched it slash across the horizon. The whole event took less than five seconds.

It was the portent of something, Ted thought. It was like the priests and metaphysicians of the ancient world seeing and interpreting signs in the skies.

What did it mean?

CHAPTER SIXTEEN

Cathy had watched the clock in her loft apartment as more than an hour slipped by. She could feel a quiet terror. After the second and third hours had come and gone, Dawn woke up and, frightened for her father, started to cry. Cathy rushed to the bedroom and, fighting back her own tears, cradled the terrified little girl in her arms. By the time Dawn's sobs subsided, Cathy made the decision that she had been terrified to consider while she watched the hours pass in the living room.

Ted had to be dead. *They*—the ominous and brutal *they* who'd savagely murdered his wife and son—had gotten him, too. Cathy knew she was going to have to run. She thought that if it weren't so frightening, it might have been ironically funny. The brilliant young editor who had suddenly found herself in love with a dead man was going to have to join forces with a blind, orphaned, genius child. And together they would have to run for their lives from some terror that neither one of them could hope to identify.

Cathy explained as much of her plan as she dared to Dawn after she had calmed the little girl. She carefully omitted the part about Ted perhaps being dead. There was no point in shattering the child totally. In the early evening, they scurried around grabbing the things that they'd need at Cathy's mother's place. And, following a cryptic call to Anne Seward, Cathy bundled

Dawn into her ancient VW bug, and started the trek
to Northampton, Long Island.

During the two hours of the drive, all Cathy could
think about was that the settlers who named Long
Island had been correct. It was *long*. Between a hundred twelve and a hundred twenty miles, depending
whether you measured the north arm that went to
Greenpoint or the south arm to Montauk. For Cathy,
the total drive was just over a hundred miles. Northampton sat on the sandy southern arm of the island,
just twenty miles short of the Montauk lighthouse.

The town was old and quaint, devoid of the plastic
splash of East, South, and Westhampton, which attracted and fleeced jet-setting tourists in the summers.
"The North," as the town called itself, was quiet, old,
and more reminiscent of a Maine hamlet out of season than anything else. The setting attracted mostly
artists and writers in the summers. For this, the residents were thankful, though a bit envious of the cash
flow into their richer neighboring towns.

It was very late at night when Cathy's VW lights
swept across the old carriage house that Anne Seward
had redone into a cozy home. At sixty-two, Anne Seward was, in the view of the other residents of "The
North," feisty. Some called her irascible. Everyone respected her. She'd been a farmer's wife since she was
eighteen, and she'd watched her husband Andrew expand his small potato farm until it became the largest
in eastern Suffolk County. By the time he died, five
years earlier, the farm included more than three hundred fertile acres that yielded bumper crops every
season. When Andrew had died quietly of a coronary
in his sleep, Anne had refused to lie down and die with
him.

She'd parceled off the acreage and sold large tracts
to developers at premium prices, retaining the corner
twenty acres that contained the carriage house for herself. After razing the barn and outbuildings to lower

her tax base, she'd rebuilt the place and invested the balance of her working capital wisely. So, after a lifetime of toil, Anne Seward now earned her income not in the fields with her late husband and the farm hands, but on the phone with her broker. At sixty, she had run for and been elected to the town council, where she proposed that "The North" no longer be a recluse town, poorer than its flashier neighbors. She developed a plan for turning the town into the antique-revival center of Long Island. She managed to float a bond issue to refurbish the more time-ravaged Victorian homes and turn them into museums, shops, and small hotels. When she'd sold her land to developers it was with the legally guarded stipulation that the homes that they would build would be rustic in decor, fitting the flavor of the town. She'd pestered the county for road improvement and wrangled with the state for the extension of a highway that would facilitate commutation from the western portions of the island as well as New York City. In less than two years, Northampton was burgeoning with summer tourism and garnering more receipts than Westhampton, only a few miles away. There was a strong move on the part of the Northampton council to have Anne Seward run for mayor. She declined, saying that her place on the town council was all that she wanted.

When Cathy arrived, Anne greeted her cautiously, tactfully not questioning where the blind child had come from, or why the sudden, frightened call from her daughter had preceded the visit. The week that followed was one of tension and fear. Cathy explained everything to her mother: the episode with Ted and Charlie, the deaths, and Ted's disappearance. Anne's reactions made Cathy realize the strength that Anne had built in the years that she'd been a farmer's wife. The older woman took everything in stride, rearranging the house to accommodate a blind person, routining Dawn through all of the twists and turns of the unfamiliar carriage house, organizing the child's activities, and generally giving the little girl an incredible amount of love and support. It took Cathy only a few days to realize that Anne saw Dawn as the grandchild that she would never have. For Cathy, the realization was confusing, a strange blend of guilt for never having been the mother of that grandchild, grief for the man, perhaps now dead, who could have been the father of that grandchild, and a tremendous sense of anger at all of the events that had transpired so quickly.

One week later, the phone rang. It was exactly a week from the day that Ted had left and not returned to the SoHo loft. Anne answered and then called Cathy. Cathy could not remember the conversation very well. All that she could seem to pull from her otherwise excellent memory was the last phrase that Ted had uttered.

"I love you, Cathy," he said. Then, abruptly, before she could respond, he had hung up.

Cathy stared at the phone for a minute after she hung up. She didn't see her mother at the door. Anne was tall and lean, with stylishly short gray hair that had only recently defeated the deep, rich Nordic blonde that she'd been all her life. Her eyes were alarmingly green, set in a time-ravaged face.

"What happened?" she asked, seeing that Cathy was apparently in shock.

Cathy spun, surprised. "What?"

Anne crossed the kitchen to her daughter. "I said, what happened? Your color's gone. What did he say? Is he all right?"

Cathy nodded and slowly sat down at the kitchen table. Anne sat quietly at the round maple table next to her. "Is he all right?" There was a gentleness in her voice. She had known since Cathy had first mentioned Ted Lawrence's name that her daughter, her only child, was in love with this man.

Cathy nodded. "He said he was all right. He said to

keep everything secret about Dawn and that . . . thing we have. And he said," she paused for a second, "he said he loved me."

Anne looked to her daughter and smiled. Her eyes seemed to laugh, and yet there was an understanding in them that told her daughter she could feel the pain and the irony of all of it. "Hell of a time for it. Isn't it?"

Cathy nodded and started to laugh. Oddly, there seemed to be a slight thread of crying in the laughter. The two women embraced and Cathy's laughter slipped into sobs.

After a few seconds, she straightened and moved back to arm's distance, then rubbed the tear-scarred mascara with the back of her hand. "Oh, Mom. You'd think I was the one who was ten, rather than Dawn."

Anne spread her strong farmer's hands in a broad gesture.

"Everyone's allowed to be ten now and again. Especially when they're in love."

A few minutes later the two of them moved through the short hall that led from the kitchen to the large living room. The motif was colonial; hewn board floors and polished wing chairs blended with pine panels that stretched upward to the balcony that led off to the upstairs bedrooms. The austere elegance spoke of Anne Seward's personality; tough, businesslike, and yet, inside the walnut shell of a mask that she wore, there was a tenderness few ever saw. Cathy had always seen it, and Dawn was starting to make inroads in it.

The two women stopped and looked at the child who sat amid a pile of Braille books and papers on the couch. They had adopted her, or she them. It didn't matter to Cathy. In the week that Dawn had spent with Anne, the week that Cathy had spent in the city arranging for a payment to be sent to Ted and gathering theoretical texts in math and physics, her mother and Dawn had grown closer than Cathy might have ever suspected.

Dawn raised her head from the Braille book. "Hi." She had the alarming quality of looking right at Cathy when she spoke. Cathy reasoned that the child's hearing must be fantastic. "The call was from Daddy, wasn't it?"

The two women exchanged a look of surprise before Cathy spoke. "Yes. He's all right. But he wants you to stay here for a little longer."

Dawn smiled a sort of half smile. "I thought that. I'm glad, too. I like it here."

Both Anne and Cathy knew that there was an artificiality in Dawn's tone. Perhaps it was something that came from dealing with her mother, Lisa. Perhaps it was simply a matter of a child genius adopting a pattern of behavior that would not frighten away the adults who surrounded her. Still, the pert flipness was the glue that seemed to hold the little girl together after the shattering tragedy she'd experienced. And then there was her intellect.

She had spent the better part of the week ensconced on the couch with the small, mysterious cylinder. Anne had driven into Northampton and had denuded the small library of mathematics texts which she carefully read to Dawn, who deftly made notes with her Braille writer. Cathy had trekked to the New York Public library of mathematics texts, which she carefully read Braille books and tapes on Dawn's request. Most of them were mathematics and physics, and well past Cathy's grasp of scientific esoterica. Cathy had arrived from the city with the books and Dawn had told Anne that now she wouldn't have to waste her time reading regular texts any more.

The two women had watched as Dawn's skilled fingers had flown across the series of dots and impressions in the thick pages of the texts. She had moved from them to a Braille printer, and then to a small abacus that served as a calculator. She was dissecting the tiny engravings on the cylinder, a bit at a time.

Dawn chewed at her lower lip. "Will we see him soon?"

Cathy crossed to the couch while Anne went to the kitchen to prepare a late lunch.

"I hope so. He said everything was all right." Cathy looked at the calculations. "How are things coming?"

Dawn folded her arms and shook her head. "I don't really know. The books you brought are going to help, I think. But it's like putting a puzzle together without all of the pieces. If Dad were here he could help me with the math and some of the physics. But working this way I can only guess what some of the symbols mean. The first row of symbols I replaced with numbers. I was looking for a pattern. After some juggling," her fingers flew across some of the notes on the Braille writer, "I found one. But—"

"There's no pattern to the pattern?"

"Right. I tried starting with one, then doubling it several times in this first set of symbols. There appear to be nine or ten similar symbols before the set breaks off into something else. I end up with two hundred fifty-six, and no pattern. I tried it with two and I got five hundred twelve, and again no real pattern. Then I remembered something. I couldn't check it out until you got here with these." She patted the pile of Braille books. "I started with a base of three and doubled it nine times. The tiny symbol at the beginning of the sequence," she pointed to a small curlicue at the top of the cylinder, "might be a constant. If I use three as a base number, then the little symbol at the beginning becomes the first symbol plus the next number in an arithmetic chain. So we add four to three for a total. Then we add four to the next number that comes from doubling the first one. We keep that up through the nine numbers and the progression goes up to three hundred eighty-eight.

"I thought that it made some sense. I remembered my dad saying something about a series of constants like that. But I couldn't get a handle on it until I got these books. I found it."

Cathy looked down at the Braille, which made little sense to her, then back to Dawn. "What did you find?"

"Bode's Law."

"Who's? I'm sorry, Dawn, you'll have to take it slow with me."

"Oh, sure," the child said. Her blind blue eyes beamed with a fragment of success. "In the eighteenth century—" She ran a hand over a page of Braille to jog her memory. "—a man named Johann Bode said that if you start with three and double it nine times, then add four to the product of each doubling, then divide each of the nine products by ten, you'd come up with the approximate distances from the sun to each of the planets. The trouble is that I might simply be assigning values to the nine symbols that have nothing to do with them."

"You mean it could simply be a coincidence?"

Dawn nodded. "You see, I might be forcing it to be Bode's Law by starting with the number three. There are some other patterns in the etchings, but I'll have to go at them hit or miss until I find something. It really is a challenge."

"Yes, I guess it is." Cathy leaned across the couch and kissed Dawn on the forehead. "How about some lunch?"

The three devoured huge sandwiches and glasses of milk in the kitchen, after which Dawn, at the urging of Anne, took a break from her calculations and listened to some music in the living room. When Anne came back from the living room, Cathy could hear the first chords of a Brahms symphony on the stereo. Cathy helped her mother clear the dishes and then unzipped her briefcase and spread a file of papers on the round, polished table top.

Anne looked at the papers and shook her head. "Looks like you've been doing more during the week than putting books into production."

Cathy nodded and swept a tiny wisp of blonde hair from her forehead.

"I've got a friend in Boston who works for our distributor up there. Her name is Marge Wallace. I called her up on Monday, from the office, and asked her to ferret out what she could about this dead Bostonian Andrew Rodgers."

"What did she get you?"

"Well, it seems that Rodgers was unmarried and had no close family. What estate the man had is in probate, and that's being handled by a lawyer named Chandler. If I can get hold of Chandler, quietly, maybe I can get more information on the dead airmen. Maybe there's more information on the cylinder. You see, I don't know how Rodgers would have gotten it. Ted said he was certain that Rodgers had sent the package to Howard, or Morgan, or whatever his name was. If I can find how Rodgers came by it, there's a chance that I can start to establish a lead."

"How are you going to contact the lawyer?"

"I was going to call and say I was Rodgers's common law wife a while ago, and ask to see any papers. If I can swing that, maybe I can get some clues."

"When will you contact him?"

"I was thinking Monday. I'm sure a Boston lawyer wouldn't be in the office on the weekend."

Anne frowned. "He doesn't have to show you anything, you know."

"I know," Cathy said with a tone of frustration. "But I plan to wheedle him with a sad story about having a child by Rodgers. I'll ask how I might pursue survivor's rights. If Rodgers had any copies of any service documents, or any papers that might have survived that fire in Springfield, there's a chance maybe something will pop up. I don't know enough to know what Ted needs and I don't dare contact him. He'll have to get to me."

It was the middle of the next afternoon when Ted made contact, through a phone call from a more than slightly confused Ira Kelton, his agent.

"I'll be damned if I know why he's operating this way, Cathy. He knows you a lot better than I do. I told him that. Why all the formality all of a sudden?"

Cathy breathed deeply before she answered. "He's been through quite a shock, Ira. Perhaps he's just a little eccentric. Humor him. Call him and say I'll meet him for lunch at the Jefferson on Tuesday, say at one o'clock. OK?"

"Sure. I'll call him. Is there going to be another contract in this?"

"Maybe, Ira. Maybe. I can't say yet."

She finished the conversation and moved back into the living room, where Anne was talking to Dawn. She told them about Ted's second-handed contact and then looked at the cylinder that Dawn held.

"I'll have to get as much information to your dad as we have concerning that." She gestured in the direction of the cylinder, forgetting for an instant that Dawn could not see the gesture.

Dawn scratched her head. "I'm afraid that the math is past me, Cathy. That thing about Bode's Law looks like it's a dead end. The calibrations could be either different uses or power intensities. But at least we can make this thing perform."

The child snapped the top of the cylinder into position and tugged gently at the cap. It snapped outward some quarter of an inch and the lights in the living room went out. After a second she snapped it back to the original position that she had dubbed the "selector" setting. The upper position she called the "activate" setting.

"The power went out, didn't it?"

"Yes," said Cathy. "That was what I did back at

the apartment. Scared the living hell out of myself, too."

"It does more."

"It does what?" Cathy could feel herself stiffen slightly with fear. What the hell else *could* the damn thing do?

"It does more things than turn off the lights. Watch."

Dawn snapped the cap of the cylinder to the right, then gently eased it out to the "activate" position.

The whine started slowly, like the sound of a faraway turbine. In a few seconds, it rose in pitch and intensity until it was nearly a scream. Blessedly, Dawn replaced it before it reached ear-splitting proportions.

"I think that there are other functions, but I don't want to push this much further. You can tell Dad this when you see him. If this is some piece of a larger weapon, I wouldn't want to be on the other end of it. I think it might use sonics or magnetism. It's strange."

"It sure is," Cathy said and moved to sit on the couch.

"No. I don't mean the cylinder itself. Sure, that's strange because we don't have the rest of the thing to look at. If we could, I bet we'd figure it out fast. What I mean is sonics and magnetism."

"What's strange about those, dear?" asked Anne.

"Well." Dawn shook her head. "I don't think weapons back in the fifties had those kinds of things. If, like Dad said, this was part of a secret weapon, how come it was never used?"

Anne took the little girl's hand. "Dawn, in the First World War, they used poison gas. But after that, they decided it was too terrible to use ever again. So it was outlawed. In the Second World War, and the ones after that, one side didn't use it because they were afraid that the other side might, too. We've probably gots lots of things like that; germs, nuclear weapons. Things we just didn't dare use for fear the other side might use them on us."

"I think it's all pretty dumb, anyway. Why waste a lot of time and money and stuff on something you'd never use? It's silly."

Cathy and Anne started to agree when the front window was splashed in light. Anne and Cathy were rigid with sudden fear. Dawn, of course, couldn't see the object. But she could, as most blind people could, dimly perceive the flash of light.

"What is it? Is there something . . . ?"

Cathy was on her feet and running for the front door as she answered.

"Let me look."

She opened the door in time to be greeted by a blast of bitter December wind, blown from the nearby Atlantic. As she looked to the sky she gasped audibly, awestruck by the event.

At the zenith a fireball was speeding across the sky, flashing to the southwest. Behind it, a broad streak of churning gray smoke slashed a scar across the December azure sky.

CHAPTER SEVENTEEN

By Tuesday morning, Ted had gotten the house on a multiple listing and the prospects for getting a buyer were, according to the realtor, rather good. There had been three more calls from the attorney for the Ryans, and a call from George Davis, Ted's lawyer. Davis had indicated that the chances were that if the Ryans wanted to push a custody case to court, their chances of winning were more than good. Ted was a widower, with few assets except the house, and his writing income did not provide what George had called "adequate equity" for the proper care of Dawn. At least, George said, that would be the Ryans' argument.

He drove to the city through sparse traffic, carrying his pager on his hip and followed closely by the tall blond agent named Chet and the smaller Fratianni. The ubiquitous Ghost car parked in a midtown garage right behind Ted, and the agents moved up Madison Avenue about ten paces behind him. As Ted looked back to them, he could see that Fratianni was not looking at him; rather, the man's eyes scanned the traffic, both auto and pedestrian. If there was going to be a hit, he'd want to get a split second's edge on the situation. Chet's eyes remained riveted on Ted. The team worked with a frightening efficiency.

Cathy was waiting inside the restaurant foyer. She had just checked her coat. They saw each other at almost the same instant. Cathy smiled and strode in Ted's direction, hand extended. She was unsure of herself, attempting cordiality.

Ted slipped the hand around her back and leaned down to hug her. It was clearly a surprise to her. He could feel the tension in the small of her back. As his lips brushed her ear, he whispered, "I have company, so keep the talk quiet and intimate. They'll think we're lovers anyway."

His lips brushed hers gently. Ted could feel a slight tremble in her.

The maître d' ushered them to a quiet booth in the back. He had seen them there before and assumed that they would want a quiet place to work. At the epicenter of Publishers' Row restaurants, the Jefferson's staff was used to three-hour editorial lunches.

Ted watched as Chet and Fratianni slipped into a booth directly across the restaurant from them. Cathy glanced across to them before looking to Ted.

"Company."

"Yeah. I'm almost getting comfortable with them there."

He explained about the crash and the week spent in the secluded hospital; about the deal made with Weatherow. He paused as the waiter brought cocktails.

Cathy gently raised her glass and touched Ted's bourbon and water. "What do we drink to?"

Ted managed a sarcastic smile. "To staying alive?"

She reached across the table and took his hand. "How about to what you said on the phone?"

They sipped at their drinks. Cathy looked at him for a long minute before she spoke. "You know, I'm a little angry at you for the way you did that."

"Did what?" Ted said with a touch of mock surprise.

"Hung up before I could say anything."

Ted ran a hand through his hair. "Well, the chase car was coming up on the phone booth fast, and I had to get off the phone. I didn't want them getting to you and Dawn . . . and your mother."

She stared at him again in silence for a second. Her eyes seemed to draw the words from him. "Maybe . . . I was afraid you wouldn't say anything back?"

"Maybe I wouldn't have," she said.

Ted took another pull at the bourbon. "Oh," he said, with a strange air of finality.

"I love you," she whispered, leaning close to him Her blue eyes shone with vulnerability, tinged with a touch of fear. Her hand found his, and he could almost feel that fear in her grip. After a second, she looked away, still grasping his hand. "This is all insane," she whispered.

"I know." He leaned close. "But if I'm going to stay alive, I don't have any other choice. According to Weatherow . . ."

"Who?"

"Weatherow. He's the head of this Defense Department group. He was the first one who came into that hospital room they had me in." She glanced at his forehead as he spoke, looking at the remnants of the bruise that the steering wheel of his car had left. "According to him, the Russian KGB was chasing after the little thing that we were tinkering with in your living room."

"Why? Why kill Lisa and Michael for it?"

"For the same reasons, according to Weatherow, that they killed Patrino in Springfield, Andrew Rodgers in Boston, and a couple of Defense Department agents who were watching my house. It was something that would give them a clue as to what was in the hangar at Ogden."

"Did he tell you what was there?"

Ted looked at the two men who sat quietly across the restaurant. There was no way that they could hear him at that range and there would have been no time to plant a bug at the table. "He said Project Unicorn was something that the Soviets were developing decades ago. It was an advanced weapon system capable of draining off electrical power from anywhere on earth. He alluded to other applications, too. Anyway, the CIA or someone stole it from the Russians and started to examine it when the Korean War broke out. Apparently, the priority on the project dropped then. Secrecy became more important than exploitation. They hid it in the hangar. I'm told that there's been a recent push by the Russians to reexamine the principles and redevelop a new, more sophisticated version of the same weapon . . . for space, I guess. If they find that we have the older prototype, they'll escalate their work. The package that came to my house that morning Lisa and Michael died was one they'd been a step behind in Boston and Springfield and Shore Park. Dawn would have died, too, if she hadn't been in the backyard with the package when they came into the house. Weatherow seems to know that the package arrived, but I don't think he knows we have it."

"Have you considered . . . ?"

She paused as the waitress arrived and they quickly scanned the menu, then placed their orders.

Cathy waited until the waitress was well away from them before resuming. "Have you thought of simply giving the thing back to Weatherow?"

"I thought of it. But I know Weatherow's type too well. The only reason that I'm alive now is that I'm of some value to him as bait for the KGB. I worked with intelligence in Viet Nam. Life's cheap, especially a life that might cause a breach of security for them. I couldn't be sure that I wouldn't have an unfortunate accident immediately after it. All they'd have to say would be that I was despondent over the death of my wife and son, and they could set up a convenient suicide. Short of that, they could arrange for the New Jersey State police to pick me up for murder, by rescinding their cover story. The press would turn me into a berserk ex-college professor and an accused murderer. I could scream about Ogden all I wanted from my cell. There'd be no credibility. Then they'd get you and Dawn and probably your mother. No. The cylinder and the orders are the only aces in the hole we have."

Cathy shook her head. "I can't understand why the KGB would be hunting something that we stole from them more than thirty years ago. Especially when Dawn says the thing uses sonics and magnetism and all kinds of things that she didn't think were in weapons that long ago."

Ted blinked and put down his drink. "Run that by again. I think the bourbon is getting to me."

"I'm not kidding, Ted. It's really weird. When you rotate the settings on the cap of the thing, you activate the device. One setting shuts down electrical power for some distance. . . ."

"How—" Ted stopped himself, suddenly realizing that his voice was getting louder with surprise and excitement. He leaned in closer to her. "How does it manage to do that? I mean, did Dawn have any ideas?"

Cathy shook her head. "Not about how it works— only that it does. I found out about that after you left my place that day. I snapped the top of the thing to a new setting accidentally, and the power in the apartment went off. According to the radio and TV news, there was a minor power failure for a minute or two over a good part of southern Manhattan at the same time I did it. As for how it happened, you're the physicist. Dawn doesn't have enough information yet to know. She said no one really knew much about the way electricity worked. Is that true?"

Ted nodded and reached for his drink. "True enough. We can use it and generate it and apply some of the theoretical principles, but when we get down to an exact definition, I guess no one's really sure. But it would be impossible for something that small to do the job alone. It would have to be simply a trigger for something much larger—some sort of interrupter apparatus." He paused and downed the rest of his drink in a single swallow. "You said one setting did that. Was there anything else? I mean, the chances are that the ability to interrupt power is magnetic. It sounds like Dawn has that right. But on that kind of scale . . . I can't say just how. There was a rumor that Tesla once . . ."

"Who?"

"Oh. I'm sorry. Nikola Tesla. He was the man who invented alternating current. He was a Croatian who worked for Edison for a while, then split with him. They might have shared a Nobel Prize but Tesla refused to share the stage with Edison, whom he called a 'tinkerer.' Anyway, there was a rumor that Tesla developed and built a coil in Colorado. In essence, it was a rotary magnetic generator. When he activated it, it killed power for miles. There's not much written about it. Tesla kept everything in his head. But the size difference—"

"How big was it, this whatchamacallit of Tesla's?"

"Almost half a mile around. You see what I mean?"

Cathy gulped. "His machine took up half a mile, and the little thing we have is the size of a ball-point pen. Then . . . ?"

"It can't be the whole thing. It's just a trigger for something larger. There's no other answer. It has to be a remote control, but I didn't think that kind of miniaturization was available in the fifties."

Cathy chewed at her lower lip pensively. "Even if they, I mean the Russians, did develop this thing in the fifties and it was, say, decades ahead of its time, I don't understand why they didn't simply redevelop it as soon as possible and use it, in Hungary, or Viet Nam, or someplace. When Dawn bounced that question off my mother, she said it might have been like poison gas in the First World War. It was just too dangerous to use."

She stopped speaking for a moment and, brushing

a strand of hair from her face, looked across the width of the bustling restaurant to see Ted's bodyguards. "How much of what this man Weatherow said can you believe, Ted? I mean, given what Dawn has found out about the device. One of the settings on the cap of that thing starts it humming. In a couple of seconds the hum is deafening. Dawn had to snap it back to another position before all our hearing was lost or the windows of my mother's house were blown out. You're going to have to have more information about the thing, as well as about the men who are dead. It might give you—us an edge."

Ted gestured to the two men across from him. "I can't very well get any research done with them on my tail and my phone bugged."

Cathy nodded. "I know. That's why I called Andrew Rodgers's attorney yesterday."

Quickly and quietly, she laid out a plan that called for her to go to Boston and gather all the available information on the man whose death had preceded Charlie Howard's by just over a week.

Ted interrupted her. "No. I've put you as close to the middle of this thing as I dare. There's no reason for you to go up there and get yourself killed."

Cathy shook her head, her blonde hair again sweeping across her forehead. "Don't be noble. I set up a communication code with my mother. As soon as I get anything, I'll phone it to her, and she'll lay the code into a paper . . . like one of your student's term papers. She'll mail it off special delivery so that you can get it the next day. The key to the code will be to read the first word in the first line of the paper. Then read the second word of the second line. When you get diagonally to the bottom of the page, start at the upper right-hand corner and read diagonally to the left. Do the same with the second page and the third. If you're in trouble and there's anything I can do on the outside, call my mother. Call her Mary. That's her middle name, and no one ever uses it. When you get her on the phone, mention *Sander's Bay*. That will mean that we might have to run. If you mention Paxton State College, we'll know you got the information and everything's all right. Now . . ."

"How did you figure all of this out? And I still don't want you going to Boston."

Fratianni peered across the restaurant to Ted and Cathy. His eyes strained and his brow furrowed. Chet grew impatient.

"Are you getting anything?" the tall man asked.

"Shut up." Fratianni snapped. "I can't answer you, see through the waiters, and try to lip read all at the same time. I'm not a pro at this, remember? They're leaning in too close. There's no chance, not unless they lean back and the fucking waiters stop parading between us. I hate this shank's mare bugging. We should have had the place set up."

"We couldn't. We didn't know where he was going, remember?"

"Wait!" said Fratianni. "B-B-Boston. He said Boston. They're arguing about it. I . . . no. Shit, he turned away. That's all I got was Boston."

Chet smiled. "That might be enough."

Cathy folded her arms and glared at Ted. "I'm going and there's nothing you can do about it. I haven't got a shadow, and no one's trying to kill me. With freedom of action, the chances are that I can get a lot of information about Rodgers before . . ." It was the wrong thing to say, and she knew it. Her words trailed off.

"You were going to say 'before they get to you,' weren't you?"

"Okay. I was. But I'm not going to sit and let this Weatherow character dangle you on a hook in front of a shark. I'm not going to sit back and let you get butchered like Lisa and Michael and all those poor airmen. I just told you I love you. That won't mean anything if I don't fight to keep you alive. So I'm going."

Ted took a deep breath and looked across the table to her. She was strong and willful, and there wasn't a chance in the world that he was going to make her change her mind. Besides, he had to admit it to himself—the plan was good. She'd be able to get into Boston on the night flight, spend the balance of Wednesday with Rodgers's attorney and get back Thursday midday. The chances were that she could get up and back before Weatherow's men suspected a thing. Ted was wrong.

Fratianni nodded across the table to his colleague. "That's about the gist of it. Just Boston and an argument. I can't tell if he wanted her to go and she didn't want to, or the other way around." Fratianni's eyes met Chet's as the smaller man gestured with a salad fork. "Could just be a vacation?"

"Could be, but it's unlikely. This time of year you go to Miami for a vacation, not Boston. No. Our boy's spilling the beans about something. He knows more than he told Weatherow. Set up a team on her as soon as we get back to the car. This will be interesting."

The argument had spoiled the rest of the lunch, no matter what either Ted or Cathy pretended. He knew that his optimism was just whistling in the dark when it came to fooling Weatherow for long.

They paid the bill and left the restaurant on foot, strolling north on Madison. Cathy turned to him. "Where are we going?" she asked quietly.

"I'm assuming you're on vacation, or you wouldn't be able to make the trip this week. I don't know if those two back there"—he gestured in the direction of Fratianni and Chet, who had left the restaurant just seconds after them. Both men were staying close, so as not to lose them in the Christmas shopping mob that spilled across Madison Avenue from east and west —"know if you're headed to your office, or even if they know where the office is. Maybe we can lose them."

She didn't look at him as she spoke in hushed tones. "If they've bugged your phone, they have to know where my office is from Ira's call. From that they could easily get my home address. No. Let's wait for a chance to put me in a cab. If we walk over to Park, maybe we'll get a northbound empty cab. I drove my mother's car into the city and parked downtown. I'll lose them in traffic and have the cabbie take the long way to the garage. Then I can get to the airport"—she looked at him conspiratorially—"where I don't need a reservation for the Boston shuttle." She smiled. "See? I'm not a first-class editor for nothing."

"You read too many mysteries," he said, as he looped his arm in hers and they trotted across the street, moving in the direction of Park Avenue.

They moved at a comfortable speed through the crowds, fast enough to keep warm in the chill December afternoon, but not so fast as to alarm their tail.

"There's something you never told me about," he said.

"What's that?"

"The check. The one for five thousand on a non-existent book, *New Dawn*."

She smiled. "You needed money. If you were on the run, I took the chance that it would seem like a normal payment. Actually, my mother gave me the money when I explained things. Payroll set up the check. That part's legit."

"Your mother?"

"Yes. She said it could be a dowry if I wanted it that way."

They laughed and turned to hold one another.

Ted reached down and took her face in his hands. Her lips were warm and pliant, despite the biting cold. Her tongue flicked across his for the briefest instant before she pulled away. She held him at arm's length.

"Love on Madison Avenue? Or Fifty-sixth Street? Or whatever?" She threw her head back and laughed. Ted held her close, not caring what the two men who followed them thought or said or reported.

Chet and Fratianni held back a discreet distance, then picked up the pace as Ted and Cathy moved on toward Park Avenue. The crowds were thickening as they turned north on Park. They intended to move to a corner and catch a vacant cab as the light turned green. That would prevent the two behind them from getting a following cab, or so they hoped.

They stopped at the traffic-clogged corner of Fifty-seventh and Park. The crowds were six deep on the sidewalks as shoppers flowed across the crosstown artery to the posh shops and restaurants. As the light turned red, stopping the north-south flow, Ted could see a cab with his "vacant" sign on just a few feet away. He hoped that no one else would scoot past them and grab the cab. The light seemed to stay red for hours. He could see the "Don't Walk" signs starting to flash and he thought it was going to work. He would put her in the cab and head off in the opposite direction on foot. That would force the two men to split up or call for a back-up. In either event, the chances of Cathy eluding the tail were good.

It was seconds before the light turned when a tall older man in a tan topcoat moved from one of the shops in the direction of the cab at the curb. Ted could see that the man was going to get there first. He edged Cathy to the curb, trying not to betray the ruse to Fratianni and Chet too soon. He had to use every available second. The man was closer, only a few feet away now. There was no question that there was going to be a confrontation at the cab door. It was the last thing in the world that Ted wanted. Ted could not have known that he was about to get help from a totally unexpected source.

Ted was sure that he could block the man from the

door by stumbling into him. He took a step in the older man's direction, placing Cathy close to the cab door and himself between the older man and her.

Suddenly, a split second before the light turned green, everything seemed to freeze, as though it were caught by a stop action camera.

They could hear the hiss of it at first. It was loud and sinister. Then there was the trace of red light across the thin bank of high cirrus clouds. It was another fireball, arching across the sky, bigger and more frightening than the one that they had seen separately only a few days before. "Soviet Satellite Breaks Up," the media had screamed. The eight *Soyuz* space station link-ups had been in orbit for more than two years and the Soviets had planned to disassemble it and boost the orbit of each of the modules, but production delays and general problems in their scheduling had doomed the *Soyuz* to the fate of the older American Skylab. On the first few passes, she'd simply broken apart. Past that, there was no chance at predicting the area of impact. According to NASA, the east coast of the United States was going to be relatively safe. They had been wrong, twice now.

The view was terrifying, spectacular. The foot traffic on Fifty-seventh stopped dead in its tracks and peered as one, up at the midday fireworks display. For an instant, it seemed to Ted that the thing might land in Central Park. But the thin, fuzzy layer of cloud beneath the northeast to southwest track of the fiery wreckage told him that it was much higher than it appeared to be. The clouds were very high, perhaps at forty to fifty thousand feet. No. It wouldn't hit the park, or Manhattan, or anything close. He was sure of that.

The man in the tan topcoat was looking up and, for a few seconds, so were Chet and Fratianni. It was time enough.

Ted lunged for the door of the cab, swung it open,

and almost threw Cathy into the back seat. The light was already green and all he needed was a few more seconds. He looked at her fleetingly. "I love you."

He ducked out of the cab and slammed the door, as the traffic thinned just enough for the cabbie to press through and turn south onto Fifth Avenue.

Ted started quickly down the street, afraid to look back. He watched as the cab turned south on Fifth. No second cab followed closely. There wasn't one closer than five car lengths. He was sure that if one of the two men had followed, Cathy would have a better than even chance of losing him.

He slowed as he heard the sound of running behind him. It was Chet. The blond man was wide eyed, angry at having been duped by a moment's loss of concentration. Ted could see from the look on the man's face that there wasn't a chance in the world that he'd believe any cover story at all.

Chet came almost eye to eye with Ted. Ted looked past him for Fratianni. Had he gotten in another cab? Ted could feel a chill of fear slip up his spine.

"What the hell's going on, Doctor?"

"I beg your pardon? I didn't press the pager. I still have it on my belt."

"Cut the shit. Why did you drop her in the cab so fast?"

"Oh, you mean my editor. Well, we sort of got carried away. You know what I mean?" Ted smiled his best imitation of a "good ol' boy" smile. He knew it wasn't very convincing. "We lost track of the time and she completely forgot an editorial committee meeting that she had. It appears that it started ten or fifteen minutes ago. So I put her in a cab to her office. Didn't mean to rattle you." Ted looked up to the still-incandescent trail in the winter sky.

"Sure was spectacular, wasn't it? A close call, too. I'd say that had to have impacted less than a hundred miles from here. I bet the Russians will get their butts fried in the U.N. this afternoon."

Chet's eyes had not moved an inch from Ted's. He wasn't buying a word of it. Not a word. And both of them knew it.

Suddenly Ted smiled. He could see Fratianni running toward them. He hadn't managed to get in a chase cab. Cathy was clear. The small, dark man was breathing heavily as he slowed to a walk.

He shook his head to Chet. "No good. Too much traffic."

Cathy was terrified and yet exhilarated. She took the cab only three blocks south before she ordered the driver to pull over, tossed him a five, and lost herself in the shoppers. She moved through several of the large department stores jammed with holiday shoppers. She stayed with the flow until she was sure that no one was following.

She came back out onto Fifth Avenue and moved south a few more blocks before she spied a cab discharging a matronly woman at the curb. Cathy slipped in and gave the cab driver the address of the parking garage on the East Side where she'd left her mother's car. From there she could get to LaGuardia and the Boston shuttle. She didn't think that there was much of a chance that she could be spotted. She sat back in the cab and watched the shoppers moving along Fifth Avenue. As the cab passed Rockefeller Center she could see the Christmas decorations and the huge Norway spruce that had recently been lit.

She found herself wondering if she'd ever get Christmas shopping done. She caught herself thinking it and laughed. The cabbie glanced at her for a second, then looked back to the traffic-clogged street.

Ted walked slowly across Fifty-seventh with Chet and Fratianni on either side of him, matching his gait stride for stride. There was the chance that with the crowds, staying this close to him was necessary. But Ted was sure that was not the case. They were flustered, as flustered as professionals get. He made sure that he did not turn south on Fifth, which would trail the route Cathy's cab had taken. Rather he walked east, crossing Madison, Park, and Lexington.

"Where will you be heading now, Doctor?" Chet asked, his eyes never moving from the crowds ahead of him.

"Home. Looks like I closed the sale of another book. That is, if my agent can come to an agreement on the terms." Ted smiled politely.

Fratianni shook his head. "Sounds like a nice way to make a living, Doc. Writing those books and teaching all of those coeds?"

"It had advantages; teaching, I mean. I don't teach anymore. I write and act as a target for your boss. Neither of those pays all that much."

He lowered his head against the wind. It was the first time he'd thought about Paxton and the layoff. It seemed like years ago. He knew he'd have to go back and settle things, sick pay, and all the other administrivia. He'd loved teaching, and he'd been told he was good at it. There was a feeling of loss inside. It was one more that he could add to Lisa and Michael.

Suddenly Ted could feel the cold wind more intensely than before.

They returned to the midtown parking garage, and the chase car fell into line behind Ted as he headed for the Lincoln Tunnel.

Once they were on the road, Chet glanced across to Fratianni.

"He's lying through his teeth, Frat."

"Yeah," the small man said and reached for the radio. He looked to Chet before he pressed the talk button. "Boston, I make it. You?"

Chet nodded slowly. "Has to be. Get a team cranked up there. Have them start to trail her when she gets into Logan. Give them a description. The chances are that she'll be on a shuttle from LaGuardia. Weatherow will want to know every move she makes up there."

Fratianni pressed the button and started to transmit.

CHAPTER EIGHTEEN

Cathy had stopped shaking when the cab pulled up to the Kinney garage on Forty-first Street. She handed the cabbie a new ten and walked from the cab, not bothering to look back. Before she was inside the pick-up area of the large garage building, the cab driver had shrugged and pocketed the ten. As she saw the flicker of the yellow cab speed away from the corner of her eye, she stopped and moved back to the street. Traffic was normal: cabs, buses, passenger cars. A lot of passenger cars. She looked at her watch. It read a quarter of four. She thought for a minute.

Could she have been followed? No! She'd done that part right. Neither of the two men with Ted got near her before the cab turned the corner. She reasoned that if they traced her to her job, the chances were that they would find that she was on vacation and that would lead them to a stake-out of the apartment. When she didn't return, what would they think?

She laughed to herself, sarcastically. She was fast becoming a character in one of Ted Lawrence's mystery novels. It was all so unreal. And yet it was vivid and deadly.

A blast of cold wind whipped through the garage, which was open on both Forty-first and Fortieth streets. It hit her full force in the face and splayed her pixie hairdo out in stark relief. Suddenly, she knew.

Boston.

They would have to know about Boston. They would

233

have seen the relationship between her and Ted, known they were in cahoots. Where else would she go? It simply had to be Boston. They would have alerted someone there to watch her, or . . . She started to shake as she considered the possibilities. They'd have to assume, because of her fast escape, that she'd be getting to Boston in the fastest available way. That would mean the shuttle. And given the fact that they would have a rough physical description of her, the odds were that there would be men stationed at the airport, and assuredly there would be several at Logan International in Boston.

She turned and headed into the parking garage, fishing for the green parking stub. She handed it to the tall, bald black attendant. He smiled, displaying a stark gold incisor. Cathy tried not to react. For a split second, the man looked like Oliver J. Dragon.

What choice? She pondered the question, while she fought the fear for Ted, for Dawn, for her mother . . . for the whole affair. But, oddly, she realized that she and Ted might never have . . . if Lisa hadn't died. She forced the thought away, realizing the spider web of attendant guilt that it carried with it. It would be all that she could do to get to Boston now and pry as much information out of Rodgers's lawyer as she could.

There were two choices. The first was to change the mode of transportation. She could drive to Boston. No. She bit her lip. The trip was too long: five hours each way, longer if she drove all the way back to Long Island. Time was too precious.

The second choice was the only one left. She would go to the airport, but she would not match the description that the men following them would give.

The old Mercedes that her mother had lovingly cared for since just after her father's death screeched to a stop in front of her. The gold-toothed man got out; she paid him, got in, and slid the seat forward.

She drove west on Forty-first, then uptown on Sixth,

which was snarled with a blend of rush-hour commuters and Christmas shoppers. After parking the Mercedes in a garage on Fifty-fourth, she walked across to Fifth and strode in the front door of Bergdorf Goodman. She didn't dare use a national credit card; it could be traced too quickly. But store credit cards were another story, and there was one for Bergdorf's snugly nestled in her purse. She would completely redo the appearance that she had had at lunch. She smiled to herself, struck with a moment of gallows humor. She could buy almost anything she wanted to, and there was always the chance that Bergdorf's would never get paid; she might not live that long.

It was just over an hour later when she finished, leaving five salesmen and saleswomen frazzled in her wake. She stared at the pile of boxes in front of her and looked at herself in a full-length mirror. Her nearly flat walking shoes had been replaced with three-inch stiletto heels and the white dress from lunch had become an emerald green traveling suit. The black cloth coat had been discarded in favor of a new cream-colored Misty Harbor trench coat with a warm lining. The last, and by far the most expensive, purchase was a superb russet wig that flawlessly covered her blond shag cut. She added a pair of photogray sunglasses and stared at herself in the mirror again.

She didn't recognize herself. She snipped off all the tags, ordered the sales clerk to put all the discarded clothes in a shopping bag, and, without looking at the total on the sales slip, charged it on her credit card. Before she left the store, she picked up some make-up items and retreated to the ladies' room to slightly rework her face.

The traffic had thinned as she walked into the parking garage, and in a few minutes she was headed crosstown to the Queensborough bridge.

LaGuardia was jammed. In front of her, she could see a long trail of angry red brake lights creeping slowly off the Parkway exit ramp. She wove through the serpentine ramps and overpasses, moving slowly in the direction of Eastern shuttle terminal.

She passed parking area after parking area, whose neon blinkers indicated that they were full. It took more than forty minutes to find a parking space over a mile distant from the terminal in the long-term parking area. Carrying her suitcase and walking in the awkward stiletto heels made the long trek to the terminal slow and painful.

Once inside, Cathy slipped into the ladies' room and checked the wig and makeup. It still looked as good as it had in Bergdorf's. She headed out to the boarding ramp, in the midst of an undulating flow of passengers.

There . . . ahead . . . by the agents' counter. They were waiting. They weren't the two she'd seen at lunch, but they might as well have been. Both were tall and trim, in dark business suits and light topcoats. They stood, one to each side of the metal detector arch, and eyed passengers as they passed. Their eyes probed, analyzing, scrutinizing. Perhaps they were looking for a small blonde in a black cloth coat. As she slipped into the line that had built in front of the agents' counter, she knew that they were looking for her. They were far too intense for the normally bored airline security men.

She could feel her stomach start to tighten as she forced herself to avoid their eyes. There were seven people in the line in front of her, then six, then five.

Her feet were starting to scream for release from the damned stiletto-heeled shoes, and the backs of her legs throbbed with pain from the long trek in from the parking lot.

There were five people in front of her now, and her hands were swimming with perspiration inside the leather gloves. She remembered that as a child her hands perspired profusely and embarrassingly when she sat down to take a test in school. They soaked the papers and smeared the ink. It was her hands that told her she would not pass the test.

She was closer now, and the two men's eyes passed across the line, stopping briefly at her and then moving on. She could see the tall man on the left snap his head back in her direction. Their eyes met. His look was withering. He assessed, judged. She looked away.

Her stomach was suddenly churning like an egg-beater, and her head was swimming. She bit down hard on her lip, fighting not to faint.

The tall man's eyes were on her again. She could feel them burn into her like lasers.

Dear God. He knows. He has to know!

Nervously, she placed the small carry-on suitcase at her feet and started to fish through her purse for her wallet. She pulled off the gloves and dropped them into the purse, snapped open the clasp on the wallet and took out two twenties and a ten. She wasn't going to have the exact change that she had hoped to have so that she could get past the counter quickly. She slipped the purse back on her shoulder and picked up the suitcase again. It was heavy, and her right shoulder ached from lugging it.

There were four in front of her as she looked up again at the metal detector arch and the two men.

They'd moved.

They stood together in front of the arch, blocking the way for a minute.

The man whose eyes had burned into her looked at her again. She looked away and then back. He was leaning close to his colleague and speaking in a whisper. It was over. They'd seen through it. She knew it. They'd wait until she got to the front of the line, and whisk her away. Furtively, she looked around the terminal. Was there a place to run? A way to get lost in the crowd? Not really. Not now. She was too close.

There was only one passenger in front of her now. She was a few feet from the counter . . . from the men . . . from oblivion.

I'm sorry, Ted. I failed. I failed terribly!

The men moved. They strode quickly forward together. It was a practiced procedure. They came right up to either side of her. She bit her lip again.

"Would you come this way, please, Miss?"

It was the tall man who was speaking. Cathy looked up, wide eyed.

Dear God! Oh dear God!

They weren't speaking to her. They were speaking to the woman who stood directly in front of her.

The woman looked at them in surprise.

"What's this all about?"

The smaller of the two men smiled. "It'll only take a few minutes," he said as he flashed a set of credentials from a dark leather folder.

"I don't understand," the woman said, with a tone of anger starting to build in her voice. "Look, I have to catch this flight. I have to get to Boston."

"It'll only take a minute," the tall man said. She objected but they moved her quickly from the line and across the terminal. Cathy watched as they took her through a door that was marked SECURITY.

A small buzz passed through the back of the line. Cathy could hear the whispers. "Was she carrying drugs?" "Was she a criminal?"

"Yes? May I help you?"

Cathy stared after the woman for a second.

"Miss? May I help you?"

"Oh." Cathy looked at the agent. A man about forty. "Oh. Yes. What was all that about?"

The agent smiled and shook his head. "I really don't know. I think it was some routine police business. Where to?"

"Boston. One way." She passed the now soaked and

wadded bills across the desk as the agent punched the ticket information into the computer.

In a minute, she'd passed through the metal detector and was heading for the boarding ramp. She remembered the woman being whisked across the terminal and through the door. She'd been a petite blonde in a dark cloth coat, buying a ticket to Boston. *Jesus!* Thank you, Bergdorf's.

She tucked herself into a window seat near the front of the 727. The plane was filling rapidly. Once everyone was seated and the stewardess was going through her little welcoming speech, Cathy turned and looked around the cabin. There seemed to be nothing suspicious. But she reminded herself that she really didn't know what to look for.

She buckled her seat belt, reached down and slipped out of the torture instruments that she had on her feet. God, it felt good. She was just starting to sit back and relax when a man plopped down beside her.

He was pudgy and in his fifties. His vested brown suit was shiny and age-worn. He turned to her and flashed a broad, gap-toothed smile.

"Howdy."

"Hello," she said, trying to sound disinterested.

"Headed for Beantown too, huh?"

She nodded and looked out the window.

"Name's Howard Stiglee. That's with two 'e's. Glad to meetcha."

She turned back to him. "I'm Marsha . . . ah . . . Johnson." Again she turned to the window. Dear God, she had a talker. It was the last thing in the world that she needed.

The plane ramp had been pulled away, and the plane was slowly starting to taxi.

"Ya fly much, Miss Johnson?"

Christ! Don't let him get chummy.

She shook her head.

"I fly all the time. Business, ya know. I'm in plumbing supplies, and I troubleshoot for the company. Put in about twenty thousand air miles a year. The wife says I darn near live on these shuttle flights. Guess she's right."

Again, Cathy turned to him, nodded and looked out the window.

"There's really nothing to be frightened of. I always say you're safer in one of these birds than on the ground in your own car." He paused for a second, and she could feel that he was looking at her. "Bet you're going to meet a fella up there. Are you, Miss Johnson?"

Suddenly, she had an idea. She turned to him and looked at his eyes as she spoke. "I am. I'm going to a funeral. It was my fiancé. We were going to be married at Christmas. He was killed in an auto accident, yesterday, you see."

She looked back to the window. The runway was speeding past. They were almost airborne. "Oh. I see. I'm sorry," she heard him say.

He grew quiet. It had worked.

Cathy leaned back in the seat and closed her eyes. She was awakened by the announcement that the flight was in the Logan International traffic pattern. The walking, talking cliché who had introduced himself as Howard Stiglee was absorbed in a magazine. Her remark about going to a funeral seemed to have squelched his gregariousness. Cathy felt around with her toes on the carpeted floor until she managed to find her shoes. She pried her feet back into them and awaited the landing.

By the time that the plane had taxied to the ramp, almost all the passengers were standing in the aisle, waiting for the fore and aft hatches to be opened. Stiglee had gotten into the line, but Cathy kept her seat, in no hurry to spend more time standing in the uncomfortable heels.

A stewardess squeezed her way to the front of the line and started to open the forward hatch. She was apparently having trouble with it, from the impatient noises that the line of passengers was starting to make.

After a few minutes of audible grumbling from the line, Cathy could see the stewardess, slightly nonplussed, come to the line that waited at the front hatch.

"Excuse me, ladies and gentlemen. There seems to be a problem with our hatch-unlocking mechanism. I'm afraid you'll have to exit by the rear ramp. Thank you for your patience."

There was more grumbling, but the line that faced the front slowly turned and awaited the slow process of exiting through one door.

Cathy waited a few minutes, as she would be close to the end of the line in any event. When she got up and wriggled into her trench coat, she was next to last in line, followed only by a woman and a rambunctious five- or six-year-old boy. She worked her way slowly down the aisle. She didn't see the man in the last row until she was a few feet from him.

He was middle-aged, tall, lean, the picture of a successful businessman, and he was obviously content to wait until all the passengers were off before he got off. Or was he? His eyes moved from passenger to passenger as each passed his seat. He scrutinized, evaluated with quick-moving, catlike eyes that were dark, nearly black. Cathy felt her stomach start to quiver. It was the same look that she'd seen in the eyes of the men at La Guardia. But there was nothing she could do now except brass it out.

She was almost abreast of him now. She avoided his eyes, though she could feel them on her. Mentally, she went through the list of things that might have identified her. There was nothing, noth— The ring? The emerald ring that her mother had given her? She wore it on the ring finger of her right hand. But there could be no connection, no way that it could have been traced.

Her hands were starting to sweat. She pulled on her gloves and glanced at the man.

His eyes rose to meet hers. There was recognition in them, satisfaction. He had found what he'd been looking for. Cathy knew that he had seen fear in hers.

The man started to get to his feet. "Excuse me, Mi—"

Cathy strode past him, quickly ducked out the hatch, and made it down the steps as fast as the awkward shoes would allow.

The man lunged to the aisle and started to follow. He did not see the small boy skip ahead of his mother. Intent on Cathy, the man tripped over the child and landed in a heap in the aisle. The child started to wail, and the mother ran forward to comfort her child, yelling at the man for being so clumsy. By the time the man got to his feet and out the door, Cathy was out of sight.

Cathy moved quickly through the terminal, trying to keep from breaking into a desperate run. He would only be seconds behind. She took an escalator to the second level and walked to the far end of the terminal. How could they have known? Would he try to take her right in the airport, or would he follow? She assumed the latter. She dared not stop, and only allowed herself a backward look when she was close to the far end of the terminal. He wasn't in sight. She kept walking, but slowed her pace. She had to have time to think. If he was working for the people who were following Ted, he would want to see where in Boston she was headed. That would mean that he'd assume that she'd be met by someone or that she'd be getting a cab from the front of the terminal. She decided to do neither.

She followed the signs through the newly built connecting tunnel that linked the large Holiday Inn to the airport. Once in the nearly empty lobby, she headed for a bank of phone booths. It took her a minute to find the number she wanted.

"Hello?"

"Marge?"

"Yes. Who's this?"

"It's Cathy."

"Hi, Cathy. Talk about a surprise."

"I'm sorry to call this way, but I'm afraid I'm up a tree. Remember the lawyer you got me the information about?"

"Yeah, Chandler, I think. Timothy Chandler."

"Right. Well, I made an appointment to see him, tomorrow and I got in tonight, and—"

"You're here? In Boston?"

"That's right. I just got in. The problem is that the Holiday Inn screwed up my booking, and I'm stuck without a place to spend the night."

There was a pause before Marge spoke. "Stay here. If you're at Logan I can come down and pick you up. I'm only fifteen minutes away."

Cathy grimaced. "I'm sorry about all this, Marge. I don't want to impose. I—"

"Oh, shut up, Seward. Ken's away for three days and I'm here in the house with the two boys. It'll be great company. Give me fifteen minutes to get myself together, and another fifteen or twenty to get there. Where are you, exactly?"

"I'm—well, I will be in front of the main entrance of the Holiday Inn. That's on the far end of the airport complex. And I have long red hair."

"What? Boy, this will really be a day of surprises, Cath. I have one for you."

"What's that?"

"You'll see."

Cathy hung up and looked around the lobby. There were a few people moving through, but essentially the place was not crowded enough for her tastes, not if there was someone looking for her. Thirty-five minutes in the cold was not too much for her to bear. She grabbed the small suitcase, pulled on her gloves, turned up the collar of the trench coat, and headed out the front door.

She was under the portico of the Holiday Inn when she began to think that she'd made the wrong decision. The wind that swept across Logan from the bay was frigid. There was the smell of snow in the air, and she could feel the cold start to penetrate almost immediately.

Standing just out of the light under the portico, Cathy was almost frozen when the white Ford station wagon pulled up to the front entrance.

"Cathy?" A woman was calling and waving from the driver's window.

Cathy waved and walked to the right side of the wagon. She quickly opened the door and climbed inside and looked at Marge.

The surprise was evident even with Marge behind the wheel. Her friend was very pregnant.

They embraced, and after a second Cathy pulled back, feeling for an instant a twinge of guilt.

"Was this the surprise?"

Marge, auburn-haired and just into her thirties, smiled broadly. "Sure was."

"If you'd mentioned it on the phone, I'd have gotten a cab. I pulled you out on a cold night. Especially when you're . . . well, I'm sorry."

Marge waved away the comment. "Don't be silly. You're not just going to spend the night. You're going to pay your way. You can help me get them to bed." She pointed to the back of the station wagon. "This is Ken Junior, and Martin."

Ken Junior was a tow-headed boy of four or five, and his older brother and apparent partner in crime, Martin, seemed to be seven. Cathy and Marge had not really seen each other in the six years since Marge moved from New York to Boston. The only child she knew about was her first. In their few conversations since, no other children had been mentioned. And, it appeared in a month or so, there would be three small Wallaces.

Cathy shook her head as Marge pulled the car out into the airport traffic.

"I don't believe it. How soon?"

"About eight weeks. And don't worry about anything. Like I said, Ken's away on business. He's in Portland. He won't be back until the end of the week. I'd love the company. Can you stay longer than the night?"

Cathy shook her head. "No. I've got to see this lawyer, Chandler, tomorrow, and fly out as soon as possible. I wish I could. Maybe when things calm down a bit I can come back up for a few days."

Marge looked over at her for a second. "That's not your own hair, is it?"

Cathy smiled. "A wig."

"A what?"

The question had not come from Marge. Rather it was a whoop from Ken Junior in the back seat of the station wagon. The small boy reached forward and scooped the wig from Cathy's head. Cathy gasped, and Marge snapped her head back to the boys.

"You give that back right now. You hear? Right now."

Cathy was surprised to hear the tone of strength and anger in Marge's voice.

Ken sheepishly apologized and handed the now limp russet wig back to Cathy.

The small suburb of Rosedale was new and situated at the north end of the city. It had been created in a huge urban renewal project in the last five years. A deserted factory area had been torn down through a federal grant, and the land had been opened to the developers of a large condominium community.

The Wallaces had a double condo with a good view of the northern suburbs and a backyard with a jungle gym for the boys. Cathy was ushered in amid a flurry of excitement by the boys, who seemed utterly tireless. After about fifteen minutes of peppering her with questions about New York, Martin and Ken were cut off by their mother and ordered to get ready for bed.

It was close to two in the morning when Marge and Cathy finished talking over old times and Cathy fell gratefully into a bed in the guest room. She would need all of the energy she could muster for her encounter with Timothy Chandler, Esq., in the morning.

The tall, lean middle-aged man pounded his fist into his palm and sat in one of the orange plastic waiting room seats at Logan. He had checked the cab dispatcher and the row of cars at the main access ramp for more than an hour. She had slipped out, and he was furious. He sat for a long moment before he looked around for a phone booth. Spying one in the corner of the large waiting room, he got to his feet and went to it, only to find that there was no directory. He searched for another for several minutes until he found one with an intact directory.

Inside the booth, he leafed through the white pages. C . . . Ch . . . Cha . . . Chandler, Timothy, Atty. He smiled. He'd found what he wanted. He took a pad and a pen from his inside coat pocket and copied down the number and the address. Everything would be fine . . . tomorrow.

Cathy awoke to the sounds of Marge's two sons. Martin and Ken were whooping and squealing, and Cathy didn't know what their excitement was about until she pulled on a robe and went to the window.

The snow had started during the night, and the storm was still smashing sheets of snowflakes against the condominium complex. By the time Cathy dressed and grabbed a quick cup of coffee with Marge, the small clock radio in the kitchen was warning that the storm would intensify by late afternoon. The greater Boston metropolitan area was bracing for more than a foot of snow. Cathy knew she'd have to move quickly. Her appointment with Chandler was at eleven, and by then God only knew what kind of transportation snarls would have developed because of the snowstorm.

An hour later Cathy watched from the window of an MTA trolley as it lurched its way along Commonwealth Avenue. Despite the snow, the Boston University campus was bustling with students moving from building to building. Cathy could see a young man of perhaps twenty, playfully tossing a snowball at a coed. The girl chased him in mock anger. Cathy wondered how long it had been since she'd done something like that. But she didn't have time to dwell on the thought. Three stops past the university she got off the trolley and, carefully walking on the icy street, she approached the small professional building that housed the office of Timothy Chandler.

The waiting room told Cathy that Chandler was not the most prestigious of Boston attorneys. It was small and apparently furnished from a Sears catalogue. Chandler had a single secretary-receptionist, who Cathy suspected doubled as a steno and several other things. The woman, who appeared to be in her fifties, looked up as Cathy came into the empty waiting room.

"May I help you?"

Cathy smiled. "Yes." Cathy paused for a second, fighting to remember the name she'd used in her call from New York. "I'm Cathy Morrison. I have an appointment with Mr. Chandler."

Chandler was small and trim with a moustache and a cool, articulate demeanor. He listened to her story about being Rodgers's live-in girlfriend when "Andy" had been in the Air Force. She'd mentioned that they'd lived near where he was stationed at Ogden. She spun out a story of her pregnancy and his desertion, of the rigors of raising a child alone.

"But early on, before I got pregnant, Andy had filled out papers with the Air Force. They had something to do with my becoming a dependent. The Air Force told me they didn't have a record of them, and that if I was going to file a claim, I'd have to have something in writing. When I finally traced Andy here to Boston, I found that he had just died."

Cathy looked directly into Chandler's eyes and pretended quiet desperation. "You see, Mr. Chandler, if I can find anything in his papers that said he was going to declare me a dependent, the Air Force will pay me survivor's benefits. After raising Jonathon, that's my son's name, for almost ten years alone, I think I deserve those benefits."

Chandler balked. "I don't know, Miss Morrison. Normally, we'd let a claimant have access to personal papers only if they had a direct claim on the estate of the deceased. That's not your situation, as I see it. Your claim will be on the government. But you want to use the late Mr. Rodgers's service papers to gather evidence in the case. I don't know if I can let you go through the papers until the last of the probate is finished."

She offered him whatever fee was customary, and he still hesitated. Cathy played her hole card. She started to cry.

He gave in.

He pressed the switch on the intercom and told his secretary to bring in the file. Cathy's eyes widened as she saw the size of the file. It appeared that Andrew Rodgers had a double ream of personal papers.

It took her almost half an hour to find what she wanted. It was a large, battered manila envelope filled with service records and more. She found what Rodgers had been working on when he'd died. He'd made copies of every shred of information that he and Anthony

Patrino, the man from Springfield, had been gathering about Ogden. Knowing she'd be unable to get any of the papers out of the office, she went through them carefully, looking for patterns, searching for the single piece of information that might have gotten Rodgers killed. She made notes on a small pad, listing all of the names of all of the airmen and officers who appeared on the recorded sets of orders. She jotted down the code numbers and names as well as duplicating all the small marginal notes that Rodgers had made before he died. Suddenly, something struck her. On the page in front of her a single name had been underlined. WILFRED THAYER.

She'd seen the name before. She leafed through the other sets of orders and found that the name appeared no less than seven times on different sets of orders dating back to the first set that had been issued in June 1950.

Who the hell was Wilfred Thayer? And why did he have a different serial number every time? And a different rank? Thayer appeared as a major in 1950 and as an airman first class in 1958. Not wanting to press her luck in pushing Chandler for more time with the files, Cathy made the last of her notes and left as quickly as possible.

Outside the snow had slackened, but the sky was still lead gray and threatening. Cathy half ran, half skidded across the ice-covered street and caught an MTA trolley. She'd take it all the way downtown and then get a cab to the airport.

He was furious. The rented car had been stuck on Commonwealth for more than an hour. The sheet ice on the road had caused a dozen fender-bender accidents, clogging traffic on Commonwealth and slowing progress to a crawl. He'd intended to stake out the lawyer's office all day, waiting for her to arrive. Now it was well past noon, and he'd have to go in and feel the lawyer out. It was not something that he relished. The fewer people he came in contact with, the better the chances of keeping his cover intact. It was nearly one o'clock when he got to the small professional building. He parked the car on a small side street just off of Commonwealth and headed into Chandler's office.

"May I help you?" the secretary asked as he came into the waiting room.

He approached the desk and took a small leather folder from his pocket. He opened it and held it in front of her face. "Yes. I'd like to see Mr. Chandler. The matter is urgent. Unfortunately, I haven't had time to call in advance."

"Well . . ." She squinted at the leather folder and the cards it contained. "Ah, Mr. Thayer, let me see if Mr. Chandler can see you. I can't guarantee anything. He's rather busy today."

She got up and went through the only other door in the office. Thayer looked down at her desk. Between the small phone-intercom console and the typewriter he could see a folder. His eyes widened as he saw the name on it. "RODGERS, ANDREW."

He reached over the folder and grabbed the desk calendar. The last appointment listed in the careful hand of the secretary had been at eleven. The name had been Morrison. Next to the name was a brief note. "re: Rodgers."

Shit. He was too late. She'd come and gone. And the file. What had she gotten from the file? What had she told Chandler? He shook his head. There was only one thing left to do.

He reached inside his topcoat pocket and eased the Graz Burya automatic from the soft holster. He screwed on the custom-made silencer and pumped a round into the chamber.

"Oh, my goodness!"

The secretary was standing in the doorway, her eyes wide and staring at the pistol. Thayer raised his right hand, steadying it with the palm of his left.

The Graz Burya spat twice. The secretary was dead before she hit the ground.

Chandler was getting up from his desk as Thayer strode across the secretary's body and into the inner office. He said nothing, simply raised the pistol and fired another two rounds. The impact caught Chandler in the forehead. The back of his head dissolved, splattering the wall behind the desk with skull fragments and brain tissue. Thayer calmly turned and again walked over the inert form of the secretary.

He took the folder from the desk and, after wiping the pistol clean, dropped it on the floor next to the body of the secretary. He set the office door to lock and walked out of the complex, moving quickly to his car.

The airport. She'd be headed to the airport. If he was lucky, he'd catch her there.

Cathy watched the university slip past the window. It was still crowded with students, several of whom got on as the trolley stopped. One was a young black man in a parka. He carried a radio propped on his shoulder. Rock music blared from it.

It was fifteen minutes later when the rock station interrupted its musical program for a news and weather roundup. Logan was running three to four hours late on all flights, the newscaster said. And then there was a news bulletin.

Timothy Chandler had been murdered along with his secretary.

Cathy sat stunned, listening to the words. She strained to hear more, but the man carrying the radio changed the station.

Dear God! It would have been only minutes after I . . .

She started to shake. It was the man from the airport. It would have to be. But how would he know about the lawyer? It didn't matter how, she thought. He'd be after her now. She had to think.

The airport. Logan was backed up with outgoing flights. He—whoever he was—would be looking for her in the crowds, carefully watching the New York shuttle line.

A few minutes later the trolley came to a stop and Cathy got off. She hailed a cab. The Boston Sanitation Department was starting to catch up with the snowfall. The roads had been salted and scraped, in close to the inner city. A cab would make much better time than it might have several hours earlier.

She told the cabbie to take her to the train station.

An hour and a half later, Cathy was on a fast Turbo-liner, headed for New York. She'd called her mother, who was already coding the information for Ted.

At the airport, Thayer waited through the afternoon. The change in Cathy's plan had saved her life.

Karl Weatherow swung the large executive chair around to face the computer terminal on the corner of the desk. It was a convenience that he allowed himself because of the need for fast information. He'd spent two months in a crash course absorbing the volumes of access codes and commands that were required to release the stores of defense information stored in the leviathan computer complexes of the CIA at Langley and the Defense Department in the Pentagon. The *other* deaths, Lawrence had said. The remark had piqued Weatherow's curiosity as well as his sense of caution. There had been no mention of other deaths in his conversation with Cliff Hurley. Was it a detail that Hurley had forgotten to mention?

Weatherow's pudgy fingers played over the keys, sending the computer on an electronic search of the files of those connected to Project Unicorn. The small visual scanner in front of him flickered to life as the computer displayed the first page of what looked to be a multi-page report. By the time the computer moved to the third page of names, Weatherow was on the phone asking for a hard printout of the list. Meanwhile, he asked the computer other questions. In a few minutes, the answers were starting to get frustrating and redundant.

"List Unicorn personnel currently deceased."

The screen again flickered. INSUFFICIENT DATA. CONSULT CODE 444.

Weatherow cursed to himself as he thumbed through the manual to the right of the small console. The code required that he enumerate the nature of the deaths. The chances were that the only ones listed would be those that either the CIA or the Defense Department had a special interest in; perhaps those that were service connected. He typed the code and the required information into the machine and waited. Of the three hundred or so Unicorn-connected personnel, it appeared that there were only seven deaths that were service connected. Two died in an air crash in 1951. Another had been killed in a jeep accident a year after that, and the four remaining men died in various accidents in the years that followed.

He returned to the machine and queried about the non-service-connected deaths. The answer didn't surprise him.

INSUFFICIENT DATA.

There would have been no reason for either department to keep records of ex-servicemen who'd fallen from ladders or walked in front of trucks or had heart attacks. So it was a dead end. Seven deaths out of three hundred servicemen over a thirty-year period was not something to get paranoid about. It was obvious that Lawrence didn't have his facts straight, or that he'd been listening to the paranoid ravings of the man called Morgan.

He was distracted from the screen by the arrival of a secretary who plopped the sheaf of computer paper on his desk. He nodded and looked down to it. The three hundred names were listed by the years of their assignment. There was only one name that triggered even a glimmer of recognition for him. It was Thayer, Wilfred Thayer. The glimmer faded as Weatherow realized that he could not place a connection properly in his mind. Still, the name gnawed at the more remote portions of his memory. No. He couldn't dredge it up. He placed the name in a mental holding file for future access.

He turned back to the terminal and was about to turn it off when he saw that a message was winking at him from the screen.

ADDITIONAL DATA ACCESS CODE ARC497.

Weatherow leafed through the code manual, looking for the name of the file and department that would have secreted the information. There was none. He went through it a second time. Nothing. He punched in ARC 497 and waited. The answer was cryptic. LIMITED ACCESS MATERIAL PLEASE ENTER CODE UN-LOCK NUMBERS.

He stared at the screen for a long minute. ARC497 had not been assigned to anyone. It was, in effect, an empty and secret code bin containing information relative to the non-service-connected deaths of Unicorn personnel. But without an "unlock" code being punched into the machine there was no way to get the information. And there was no way to acquire the unlock code unless you already knew it. It was Catch-22.

Who had put the information there? Why? Were

there other deaths? Lawrence's remark from the hospital room started to become an itch that Weatherow couldn't scratch.

Weatherow reached for the phone. "Get me Cliff Hurley, please."

CHAPTER NINETEEN

It was an impossible three days for Ted. Sandusky, the Ryans' lawyer, had moved swiftly. He had called several times, informing Ted of the status of the custody case that the Ryan family was starting to develop. It was harassment, pure and simple. After the third call, Ted stopped taking his calls at all. He had too many other things on his mind. He'd not heard from Cathy since he put her in the cab; he knew that there was no safe way they would be able to get in touch as long as Weatherow's watchdogs were so close to him.

Part of his time had been spent dealing with realtors and assessing the three tentative offers that had been made on the house. The highest offer was still a bit below his asking price. Still, he had all but decided to take it. There was too much memory in the house; too much pain. He'd stood in the kitchen and watched the blood-red sun rise from the ocean overcast. By the time the sun was filtering through the trees on the front lawn, he'd decided. He called the agent, who was overjoyed at the commission he'd make on the sale.

After he got off the phone, he made some coffee and went through a list of condominiums he'd winnowed from the listings of the same realtor. He'd narrowed the choice to two, predicating his decisions on enough size to accommodate Dawn's needs, and proximity to the specialized school for the blind to which she commuted. He was conscious of avoiding one chore, a clearly distasteful one. He knew he was going to have to go to Paxton State College to settle things there, and he had no stomach for it. Dear God, how he loved teaching and hated the fact that it had been taken from him. He knew that the odds of getting another teaching post were slim. To go back to the place and go through his papers would be a grim post-mortem on a once-promising teaching career. Still, he knew there was no way to avoid going in and doing the housekeeping. There were student grades to submit, and piles of papers and books to be removed from his small cubby-hole of an office. Then he'd have to go to personnel to cash in the annuity and retirement funds and transfer medical and hospitalization plans to a personal account. It would take the better part of the day. But there was another reason for the trip.

The sprawling campus of Paxton State College was so familiar to Ted that he was sure that he'd be able to slip Weatherow's men long enough to make a call to Cathy. Perhaps he might even get a chance to talk to Dawn. In his mind he could still see her sitting in the living room, clutching the damned package to her chest. And he could see Cathy's face as she stood on a Manhattan street corner waiting to slip into a cab. He ached to see her; to see them both.

He stretched, groaned, and sipped the last of a mug of hot black coffee. He pulled on the parka he'd tossed over the back of a kitchen chair and grabbed the small pager, his constant companion now. He was headed for the door when the front door bell rang.

The postman handed him the special delivery package and asked for a signature. Ted took it back into the house and ripped it open. He slipped into a chair at the kitchen table and looked at the enclosed typed sheets. The composition was gibberish, constructed as a cover for the code that Cathy's mother had devised. Ted covered one diagonal side of the page with the straight edge of the bottom of the envelope. He started to make a mental note of the message, as any attempt to make a written record of it would be foolhardy.

It took him only a few minutes to decode the message.

LAWYER KILLED AFTER I LEFT. WHO KNEW? YOUR SPOOK FRIEND? THE ONLY CLUE IS THE NAME THAYER, WILFRED. APPEARS SEVERAL TIMES OVER THIRTY YEAR SPAN. IS HE THEIRS OR OURS? REMEMBER PHONE CODE. I HAVE AN ESCAPE PLAN. I LOVE YOU.

Ted fixed the name in his memory. Was it the cover name for some master KGB spy? He had no way of knowing. And what was the escape plan? He felt a sudden chill. His Irish mother would have said it was the feeling of someone walking across his grave. But for him at the moment it was not so much a fear of death for himself. It was Cathy and Dawn. They were corks in a stormy sea as much as he was. The fear melted away like a multi-colored candle melting into a pool of wax. In its place came a sense of guilt. There was no reason for it. All of the things that happened might have taken place even if he hadn't listened to Charlie's cryptic story. The guilt that started to bubble from him was for the first call to Cathy. Her eagerness to help and the intense feelings that they'd started to share in the last weeks only served to heighten the sting of the guilt.

He got to his feet and walked downstairs to the den. He touched the paper to the flame of a lighter and watched it curl into an ashen snake before he dropped it into the fireplace. As he watched the last flames flicker across the ash he pushed away the guilt. It would, for a time, be like the many terrifying things he'd pushed from his memory when he was in Viet

Nam. It was not permanent; just a convenience, a survival mechanism.

He left the house and strode into the driveway, stopping next to the car. He squinted up for a moment into the brilliant morning sunlight. Westerly winds had brushed the overcast out to sea, and overhead the sky was a deep cobalt blue. He watched a jet contrail slide across the zenith and move out across the Atlantic, then he climbed into the car.

He backed carefully and slowly from the driveway, wary of the piles of slushy ice that were just beginning to melt from the light snow of the previous day. He moved down the side street slowly, and with an eye to his mirror. He had gone less than a hundred yards when he saw the chase car pull onto the road and accelerate behind him. He shook his head, sensing the irony of all of it. They had become as much a part of his life as the pager. It was a three-way symbiosis, each needing the other, for different reasons.

The access road that led to the Parkway was nearly deserted in the mid-morning and Ted drove at the speed limit to the Parkway entrance. He could see in the mirror that the chase car on station about a hundred yards behind him had been stopped by a red light, while a large black sedan had slipped through the light, accelerating all the time. He thought nothing of it. The men in the chase car would be able to see him slip onto the Parkway ramp. They'd catch up in no time when they got to the open stretches of the superhighway.

The northbound side of the Parkway was almost as deserted as the access road had been. It wouldn't see heavy traffic until the homebound side of the rush hour clogged it with commuters heading to the bedroom communities of the shore area. He moved through the Shore Park toll plaza, tossing a quarter into the exact change bin. A green light with a mute "THANK YOU" printed on it flashed on, and Ted ran the car up through the gears until he was at about sixty. A glance in the mirror told him that the chase car had still not caught up. He laughed to himself sardonically. Had they gotten a ticket? A flat? In a strange way, he would have been happy to see them get either. However, after a few seconds prudence got the better of him, and he slowed to fifty and moved to the right lane.

His eyes flicked to the mirror. There was another car in the distance. In an instant, he could see that it wasn't the chase car. It appeared to be the large black sedan that had run the light that had slowed Weatherow's men. The driver was accelerating in the middle lane, ranging up to pass.

Ted looked back to the road in front of him.

In a minute, he realized something was wrong. The large black car had tucked itself in behind Ted, following closely. *Why doesn't he pass?*

He could see in the mirror that the car was a Cadillac Coupe de Ville, perhaps five years old. Was it the other chase car? Had the first one gone off duty? He slowed to forty-five, then to forty. The Caddy stayed with him, laying back some twenty or thirty yards. Ted could feel his hands grow cold, and he was sure that his knuckles were white under the thin leather driving gloves. Something was very wrong. *The chase cars were all gray!*

He drove the gas pedal to the floor. The little Chevy leapt ahead, accelerating to sixty. The Caddy kept pace. Then, suddenly, it roared out into the center lane and made a move to pass.

Ted came off the gas and tapped the brakes. The Caddy would fly past and everything would be fine.

It didn't.

The huge black car slid up to Ted's until it was moving parallel to the Chevy.

The driver of the Caddy was a man, but that was all

Ted could make out through the darkened polarized windows. Suddenly the right front passenger window slipped down, obviously controlled from the panel on the driver's side.

The Caddy's driver looked to his right and raised his right hand.

A gun!

Ted jammed his foot down on the brakes as the explosion of the pistol shot roared in his ears. He fished for the pager on his belt and stabbed at the button, then spun the wheel to the left and pushed the gas pedal to the floor.

The small engine of the Chevy screamed and the little car flashed past the Caddy, which shifted to the middle lane and roared up to keep pace. This time the driver's window slipped down, and again Ted was looking at a pistol being aimed by the driver. He braked and skidded to the rear as the second shot slashed across the front of his hood.

Dear God, where are they?

Weatherow, where the fuck are they?

Ted reached down and slammed the automatic transmission stick to the position marked with a numeral 2. The engine screamed, this time with an agonizingly high pitch. He prayed that the tiny four-cylinder engine held together. The speedometer read sixty when he slammed the engine back into drive. Again he shot ahead of the Cadillac on the driver's side. His idea was to head for the next exit ramp, which was less than two miles away. It would take him into crowded streets and Christmas shoppers. The Caddy wouldn't be able to get off a shot there. But he had to reach it first.

He slipped into the middle lane as the Caddy again roared up. Then he swerved to the right as he saw his pursuer extend an arm out the driver's window and try to bring the huge pistol to bear.

A shot smashed through the rear window and whizzed

by Ted's right ear, puncturing the windshield and creating a round sunburst of tiny cracks in the safety glass. Ted swerved to the left lane as another shot was fired.

How many did he have? How many were in the clip?

A quick burst of five shots followed. The last one ripped into the Chevy's right front tire, exploding the tread.

Ted swerved to the right and then to the left, trying to get the Chevy under control.

The driver of the Caddy again ranged up on the right as Ted swerved from the left lane into the middle. Ted understood immediately what the man was going to do. He was going to wait until Ted's car was inert on the side of the road, then come and finish him at his leisure.

"NO!" Ted roared to himself. He was tired of being a target, tired of all of it. The Caddy was almost parallel to his right side when he spun the wheel to the right and the Chevy veered into the Caddy. With a sickening crunch of sheared and crushed metal, the smaller car slammed into the front end of the Caddy's driver's side. The larger car lurched to the right and Ted bore in again. The second impact must have severed the steering linkage on the Cadillac. It spun crazily off the right side of the road and roared up the side of the sloping embankment like a roller coaster car taking a sudden bump.

Ted tried to keep control of the Chevy as a sea of sparks erupted from the naked wheel that now gouged into the roadway. The tire was gone completely.

Only yards ahead of him, the Caddy still swung up the embankment. Inertia fought centrifugal force. The Caddy tilted onto its driver's side, then toppled on its roof. It made a complete roll and landed upright.

Coming to a stop only yards behind the crippled Caddy, Ted could see a curl of smoke start to slip up from the hood. He released his seat belt and opened his door. He staggered toward the Cadillac like a drunk, barely able to make one foot follow the other.

The Caddy's driver was slumped forward over the wheel. Ted ran for the driver's door as flames started to lick up through the hood openings. The driver was starting to move as Ted tore at the battered door. It wouldn't open. Putting all his strength on the door he pulled and pulled again.

Fire started to eat its way back toward the passenger compartment. The driver's head lolled to the side; he opened his eyes and stared at Ted, dazed, confused. He was an older man, a small man whose glasses had been knocked askew by the crash. He didn't have the look of a professional KGB assassin. He had the look of a college professor . . . a college president. *Mother of God!*

Oscar Small!

Ted wrenched the door open and, grabbing Small under the arms, pulled the man from the front seat. He dragged him a few feet away and then dropped him. He ran the few steps back to the car. The heat from the fire was starting to grow. Ted could feel it on his face. It would only be minutes before the gas tank went.

He looked in the front seat, then on the floor. He found the gun, a Graz Burya, on the floor and jammed it in his parka, then retreated from the car. Then he half carried, half dragged Oscar Small out of range of the potential explosion.

Small was conscious but in obvious pain. Ted reached down and pulled his old educational adversary up to a sitting position by his tie. He screamed into the man's face.

"Why? Why my family, you son of a bitch? Why kill them? Why try to kill me? Who are you working for?"

Small's mouth hung open. His eyes were wide and the pupils were constricted to pinpoints. The man started to make sounds, gurgling sounds. His right hand clawed for his left arm and chest. In seconds, his face was a grotesque mask of pain.

He was starting a coronary.

"Why? Who are you working for? Tell me!"

Small's words came out in hot, quick gasps as he clutched his chest.

"D-d-din kill them. Din't do it. Nnnooo. Th-they made me do this. Made me. Had to. Pho-photos . . . they had the photos. Would have ruined me. Did this for neg-neg-tives. Blackmail. They made me. *They . . . THEY!*"

Small was slipping deeper into the first stages of a coronary. Holding him, Ted felt as though the man were sand slipping through his fingertips. He had to get more information. He pulled the gray, pain-contorted face of the college president close to his until they were almost nose to nose.

"Who are they? Who are you talking about? Who is the KGB operative? Tell me and I'll get the negatives back for you. I promise. Tell me." Ted wasn't sure if he could do anything about the negatives at all. But there was no time to worry about moralistic niceties. The man was dying in his arms and would never live to retrieve the negatives of whatever photos he was afraid of.

Small's eyes were glassy. He squinted, trying to make sense of what Ted was saying. For a second, he looked like a deaf man trying to make sense of a whisper. "N-n-noo KGB. No. KGB. American. I work before. He's had photos for over a year. He for-ced me to term-term-nate Howard . . . too. Got to help me. Get photos . . . negatives b-back. Hate this. No more sanctions, please God. Help me. Oh God, help me . . . It hurts." The last was a shriek of pain.

Ted was screaming in his face. "Who? Who's your control?"

Small's eyes were starting to roll back up in his head. His lips tried to form the word for a long time. It came in a signal burst, half a word, half an agonized scream. "Thayer. Thayer . . . TH—"

He stopped in mid-word and went limp in Ted's arms.

Something burst in Ted's brain. Thayer! The name Cathy had dragged from the lawyer's files in Boston. But Small had said he wasn't working for the KGB. He was an American. Who was he really working for? Was Small delirious or was Weatherow lying in his story to Ted? Another term flashed into Ted's mind. It was more chilling than the first. Sanction. Small had said *sanction*. It was the intelligence community term for the systematic killing of everyone surrounding any project. The rumor was that one had followed the JFK assassination in Dallas. That had taken more than forty lives . . . God only knew how many more. Was the killing of the men in Boston and Andrew Rodgers's lawyer part of a sanction? Ted remembered that Weatherow had said nothing about other possible deaths with connections to the Unicorn Project. Was it a lie? Or did Weatherow simply not know about it? There was one thing for certain; the sanction was absolute and sweeping. The chances were that it had lasted thirty years. Perhaps Thayer was in charge of the project . . . whoever Thayer was.

No matter what the answers to all of the questions were, Ted would now have to fear for his life even more. Thayer, whoever he was, could consider Small's death a lucky gift. The clear next step, if Ted's memory of his Saigon intelligence work was accurate, would be to kill him, too. Then they'd go for Cathy and Dawn. If it was going to come, it would come soon. He would have to get a call through to Cathy. She was going to have to run with Dawn, whether he survived or not.

The roar of a car engine and the squeal of brakes turned Ted's head from the now-unconscious Oscar Small. It was the chase car slamming on its brakes and spraying pebbles up from the service lane. As the gray car came to a lurching halt, the doors flew open and two men, their guns drawn, ran in Ted's direction. Though the car was the same model, the men were not the same two who had shadowed him from the house. Ted grabbed Small's Soviet automatic from the coat pocket into which he'd jammed it. Still on one knee, he turned to face them and, supporting the butt of the heavy pistol with his left hand, he cocked back the bolt with his right and leveled the sights at his pursuers.

Seeing the gun, the two men lurched to a stop and lowered their drawn weapons.

One of the men took a step forward. Ted swung the weapon into line with the man's head.

"Lawrence?" The man's tone was something between supplication and fear. "Lawrence, for Christ's sake. We're Ghost Two." The man pointed to the inert, crumpled form of Small. "That guy blew out a tire on Ghost One. Put them out of action. They got us on the radio and we played catch-up with you two."

Ted stared at the man's eyes for a long second before he slowly lowered the gun. He tossed it at the feet of the man who stood only a few feet away.

The man picked it up and released the clip. He looked up at Ted.

"It's empty."

Ted nodded. "I knew that. You didn't."

In the distance, they could hear the warble of a police siren. The man beckoned to Ted. "Get in our car, Doctor. We have someone coming to get yours. We've got to get out of here."

They left Oscar Small's body and climbed into the chase car. They were several miles down the road when the gas tank blew on Small's car, creating a strange, ironic funeral pyre for the college president.

He convinced them to take him to the college and they agreed grudgingly, then made a number of coded reports on their radio, to Weatherow, Ted suspected. When they got to the campus the driver stayed with the car, while his partner, the man who had spoken to Ted on the road, accompanied Ted. They walked through the labyrinth of underground tunnels that connected almost all of the buildings of the modernistic campus. Ted had always thought that they were a convenience, allowing him to move from building to building without having to go outside. But today they would serve a different purpose. They would buy him some time. Or so he hoped. But as he and his companion moved through them, it was clear that, short of slugging the man, there was no way he was going to elude him.

Ted trudged up the stairs to the second floor office area, and the man came into his office with him and sat in the corner.

His desk was a sea of pink phone messages. He looked down at them and decided to take a chance.

He sifted through the messages, making his shadow in the corner think that he was assessing them into a priority order. He finally picked one and grabbed the phone. He dialed the college operator.

"Operator, this is Dr. Lawrence. I'm calling a student back. Could you get me an outside line?" He waited while she did, and when he could hear the dial tone, he quickly dialed the number. The voice that answered was that of an older woman.

"Hello?"

"Hi, Mary. This is Ted Lawrence. Can we get together and talk about *Sander's Bay?*"

There was a pause at the other end of the line. Then

the older woman's voice responded. "I understand. I'll pass the message on."

The line went dead, though Ted faked some small talk before he hung up. Then he made a few legitimate calls to give credibility to the vital first one.

He went through the rest of the errands with the certainty that Cathy and Dawn had been warned to flee.

CHAPTER TWENTY

"Did your people have anything on this man Small?" Clifford Hurley asked as he poked at the topmost log in the huge Georgetown fireplace. The vast library was well appointed, in a style that Karl Weatherow could only characterize as austere elegance. The walls were paneled with a deep mahogany, and the ceiling beams were hewn oak. The colonial furniture was uncomfortable and spartan. A small couch with too-thin cushions; a set of fanback chairs and a coffee table cut from a tree trunk sat in a semicircle in front of the large fireplace, which Hurley absently tended. A roll top desk, polished to a mirror finish, sat in the corner of the room, and the far wall was dominated by floor-to-ceiling built-in bookcases. The books were neatly arranged; Weatherow was sure that they were perfectly on line, and probably indexed by subject and author.

Hurley placed the poker back in the holder and crossed to a small cabinet that hid a well-stocked bar. Weatherow was surprised. He'd not even noticed the cabinet when he'd been ushered into the library. Or perhaps he'd overlooked it as he tried to discover why the room made him uncomfortable. It took him only a few minutes to realize that the room was the very epitome of Hurley's meticulous perfectionism. Weatherow had to respect it, but it annoyed him, nevertheless.

Hurley came to the couch and handed the small, portly man a glass of Courvoisier. "I mean, was there a file on him, or anything that might have given you a hint?"

Weatherow nodded and smiled as he took the glass. He sniffed the bouquet before he answered. "We didn't have a thing on him, Cliff. He was totally clean. He'd been in World War Two in the Navy . . . saw some action in the Pacific. He got his education on the G.I. Bill and got into college administration. Past that, we didn't have a damn thing on him until this afternoon."

"Well, neither did we. I got the follow-up just a few minutes before you got here." He picked up the red-bordered top secret folder from the coffee table. He leafed through it and then looked at Weatherow. "He was a mole, Karl."

Weatherow's eyebrows went up a full half inch. A mole! A sleeper agent. Someone planted in a country years before and only activated when they were totally above suspicion. Weatherow shook his head. "I'm sorry, Cliff. I can't buy that. A mole would be the finest of professionals, and would be in a much more anonymous position. Small was an amateur. His methods were absurd. There were a hundred possible ways Small might have gotten Lawrence. The one he chose was flat-out stupid. It was an act of desperation. It was—"

Hurley silenced Weatherow with an upraised hand. "I'm sorry, Karl. Perhaps mole isn't the right term, exactly. He'd been recruited several years ago. True, he was an amateur, but he was acting in the capacity of a mole."

"What did they have on him? It would have to have been blackmail."

"Exactly," Hurley said. He paused to sip his brandy before he continued.

"They had these." He reached into the folder and removed a set of slightly grainy eight by ten glossy prints. They were taken with a telephoto lens. The first two of the five shots showed a man who was apparently Oscar Small unlocking the door of a motel room. Next to him was a young girl. She looked to be a barely nubile teenager. The last three shots had been taken through a slightly open window and, though the quality of the photos was poor, it was clearly a tangle of arms, legs, and torsos. It would have been enough, by far, to ruin Small as the president of a college.

Weatherow tossed them on the table. "That proves that someone was blackmailing him. It doesn't say he was a mole."

Hurley leaned forward. "Karl, you're the one who told me that the pistol Lawrence recovered was a Graz Burya. What else do we need?"

"There's something about it all that's too pat. Why a Graz Burya? Why would a KGB operative give an amateur a pistol that was a virtual signature of the KGB?"

"Karl, I've a small confession to make."

"Oh?" Weatherow was surprised. "Do I put on my cassock and alb to hear it, or is it going to be informal?"

"Let's call it informal. I put a team on monitoring your reporting frequencies. My thinking was that you only had so many operatives that you could spare to cover Lawrence and . . ."

"And you just couldn't resist helping an old friend? That, Clifford my slimy friend, smells about as fragrant as a heaping pile of fresh lizard shit. If there was a chance to get in and get credit with the Secretary for the operation, you'd find it. And you did."

Hurley smiled sheepishly. "All right. I won't say that wasn't in my mind. You know me too well. At any rate, things worked to our advantage. When my people intercepted the message about Lawrence's girlfriend, Cathy Seward, slipping you in Manhattan, I sent a team to La Guardia. I assumed, as you did, that if Lawrence had something more than he said, she'd head to Boston. She was pretty clever, really. That disguise of hers worked well. My two men at the gate grabbed the wrong woman. As soon as they realized that, they radioed Boston.

"When the flight landed, my two people who were watching all the flights saw a woman tear-assing off the ramp."

"So you intercepted her?"

"No. One of the two men I had there saw someone else come off the flight. It was a man, moving very quickly through the terminal, almost as fast as she was. He assumed that the man was going after her. He wasn't sure if the guy was working for you or someone else. So the team split up. One trailed her, and the other trailed him.

"Well, to make a long story short, her shadow, who- ever he was, lost her, but so did our man."

"Cliff, I don't see how any of this connects to Small."

"Patience, Karl. Patience." Hurley held up his glass. "Another?"

Weatherow shook his head. Hurley got up from the sofa and crossed to the liquor cabinet, where he filled his glass with amber brandy. "It's really good. Are you sure, Karl?"

"Quite sure," Weatherow said.

Hurley came back to the couch and sat down on the edge. "You see, I assumed that the only reason this Seward woman might go up there would be to get information on Andrew Rodgers. As he had no mean- ingful family, the chances were that she'd try to get information about him from the lawyer who was pro- bating the estate. Sure as hell, that was where she showed up, the following day. I put someone on her when she left, and left a team at the lawyer's. The man who'd chased her in the airport turned up at the office less than a half hour after she left."

"He wasn't mine. We never got near her at La Guardia. Who was he?"

"I'm getting to that. Miss Seward slipped her tail, but the man who was shadowing her then went on from the lawyer's office to the airport. My people stayed with him and it looked to them like he was waiting for her."

"So what happened?"

"She never showed. We also don't know if she got anything from the lawyer that might have helped us. Luckily, the man who was waiting at the airport solved our problem for us."

"You took him?"

"Yes. Fairly quietly. The team took him to a safe house and started to interrogate."

"Did they get anything?"

Hurley smiled broadly and took an envelope from the file. "They got a lot. But it took the better part of four days. Knowing that they wouldn't break him any other way, especially after three and a half days of trying, they gave him a shot of Pentathol this morning. They got a name from him."

Hurley passed the envelope to Weatherow. Karl undid the seal and pulled an intelligence file from it. The picture was of a tall, lean, dark man in his fifties. The name listed was Colonel Vasili Broskovich. He was a high-ranking intelligence operative known to be assigned to the U.S.

Weatherow whistled through his teeth. "Son of a bitch. They really put the big timers on this. You're lucky you broke him at all. He's quite a catch."

"Under Pentathol he mentioned Small, but that wasn't until this afternoon, at about the same time as the attempt on Lawrence's life. So there was no way I could pass the information on."

Weatherow smiled sarcastically. "We'll settle whether there was time later. You could have told me about the man three days ago. Remember what I said about lizard shit."

Hurley nodded penitently.

"It turns out that Broskovich had these prints in the hotel he was staying at in Boston. We retrieved them after he mentioned them. We never did get the negatives, though. I guess that doesn't matter, with this man Small dead. The most important thing, though, is that Broskovich killed the lawyer and the secretary in the lawyer's office. He confessed that he retrieved a vital file relative to Unicorn. He said that he passed it on to Moscow."

"Jesus H. Christ." Weatherow sat bolt upright on the couch. "I think I'll have that other brandy, Cliff. If the offer's still open."

Hurley went to the bar cabinet and this time brought the bottle back to the coffee table. He poured a glass for Weatherow and the pudgy man downed it, this time not pausing to sniff the bouquet. He inhaled and sighed deeply. "So the shit has hit the fan?"

"I'm afraid it has, Karl."

"Have you told the Secretary?"

Hurley nodded. "The decision was to destroy Unicorn."

"That seems reasonable. Especially if we don't know what was in that lawyer's file. I'll get a team on it. Is there a time frame?"

"There is, Karl. But you won't have to put a team on it."

"Why not? Domestic Security should—"

"Excuse me, Karl. I think this is the lizard shit you mentioned. The President ordered the Secretary to destroy the hardware in the hangar. The Secretary then directed my branch to do it."

"Well played, Cliff. I hate to say it, but you won the round."

Weatherow saluted him with the brandy glass, then got slowly to his feet and paced before the crackling fire. He extended his hands and savored the warmth on them. "You know," he said, as he kept his back to his colleague and career adversary of more than thirty years, "I'm amazed I've been able to keep pace with you all these years, Cliff."

Hurley laughed. "Don't play humble with me, Karl.

You're one of the best in the business, and we both know it. If the Seward woman hadn't gotten through your screen at the airport, you would have gotten Broskovich."

Weatherow turned back from the fire, which now warmed his ample rump.

"Yes. And I'd have had to call you in for the identification. You have all the information on the KGB operatives. So, the best I could have done was a tie, as far as points with the Secretary was concerned."

Hurley spread his hands in an expansive, generous gesture. "You said it yourself a minute ago. We've managed to stay neck and neck for years because of things like that."

The two men stood facing each other for a long minute in silence. They respected one another, despite their differences. But Weatherow had a fetish about loose ends. And there were several now that he couldn't rest until he resolved. "Cliff? Where do they have Broskovich now?"

Hurley's eyes bored into Weatherow for a second before he averted his glance. "They don't, Karl. He's dead. When he came out of the pentathol he managed to get hold of a water glass. He smashed it and cut his throat."

"Did he kill Howard and the Lawrences, or did Small?"

"He sent Small to finish Howard, but he moved in on the Lawrences when it looked like Howard had managed to get something off in the mail to Lawrence. We think that Broskovich had traced the small piece of hardware from Boston, where he'd been too late to get it. It looked as though he was just a step behind all the time. Yet he seemed certain that Lawrence had gotten something in the mail. As far as the pistol was concerned, the same one that killed the Lawrences and your two men killed Andrew Rodgers's lawyer in Boston. A second Graz Burya was the one that Lawrence found in Small's car. We think that Broskovich had first given it to Small a while back when he started to blackmail him."

Weatherow rubbed his palms together thoughtfully. "It's still wrong, Cliff. First, why would our late Russian friend bother to kill Lawrence or send Small to do it? And second, why leave not one but two Graz Buryas lying around? It would tell us just who he was."

"No. It was meant to throw us. He left it for the same reason that he killed the Lawrences and for the same reason that he gave Small a gun of the same model. We were supposed to think that Small was a long-time mole and the man who had killed all the airmen as well as the Lawrences, Howard, and your men. It was the perfect dodge. If Lawrence hadn't killed Small, your men would have, or Broskovich would have done it himself and made it look like suicide. Then, he'd have exposed the pictures and the whole thing would be wrapped up in a bundle. The KGB would have all the information on Unicorn, and we would have blamed the entire incident on Small."

Weatherow pondered for a second, then shook his head. "How did Broskovich find Howard and what was he after?"

"There you've got me. I can figure out part of it but not the other part. Broskovich confessed to killing Rodgers and Patrino. Before Rodgers died, Broskovich must have extracted information. Rodgers must have told him that he'd sent vital Unicorn information to Howard. Then Broskovich gets to Howard, and before *he* dies, Howard confesses to sending the information to Lawrence. Broskovich kills your two men and the Lawrence woman and the child, and finds that there was no information sent; at least none that he can find in the house. He assumes Lawrence has it. And there we are."

"And so Dr. Lawrence sends his girlfriend to Boston to follow up on something, after he's played dumb with me. He was lying. He has to have some insurance policy. That had to be what Broskovich was after. Lawrence isn't as stupid as I thought he was."

"Well, whatever it is, you're going to have to squeeze it out of him, Karl. It will be a part of Unicorn that is going to have to be destroyed. Also, it might be a duplicate of what the Russians were sent by Broskovich."

"It can't be that. If it was, why should the Seward woman have gone to Boston? No, Broskovich was after something else when he went to the Lawrence house. It was something that Charlie Howard told him he'd sent. It was vital enough to kill the Lawrences for and start this whole parade."

"It'll be something that we have to get back. Honestly, Karl. There's no lizard shit in this. If there is anything at all, and I think, as you do, that there is, you'll have to get up there and get it back from him. It will have to be destroyed with the rest of Unicorn. The President and the Secretary ordered that all of the project be destroyed, and that's what I aim to do. I'm sending a team to Ogden late tonight. Everything would tie together in a neat bundle if you could retrieve whatever it is by then.

"And there's another suggestion. Knowing you, I'd expect you'd thought of it, too?"

"You mean Lawrence?"

Hurley nodded, his eyes boring into Weatherow's. "Him, and the girl, and, I suspect, the daughter. I'm sure that whatever it is we're looking for, it's hidden where the girl is. It's going to be a job of tying up the loose ends. Miss Seward could simply disappear, I suppose. As for Lawrence and the daughter, I think an accident would have to be arranged. Unless, of course, you can think of another way to wrap up the matter?"

Weatherow came back to the couch and sat down with a grunt. He leaned back, breathed deeply, and exhaled with a sigh. It was not a job he relished, this killing of women and children without reason. Still, it was what he accepted when he took on a career with intelligence. There was no question that Hurley was right. They were going to have to die, all of them. And whatever Lawrence was sitting on as an insurance policy was going to have to be ferreted out first.

"I think I'd better handle this personally, Cliff. Don't you?"

Hurley nodded.

It was a few minutes later when Weatherow left.

Hurley moved to the fire and jabbed the bottom log in the burning stack into brilliant, crackling life.

CHAPTER TWENTY-ONE

Chet Hammend was just finishing the second of two circuits of the Lawrence property. He was going through the motions now. He didn't see that there would be another attempt on Lawrence. The pressure was off. He moved carefully through the wooded back acre and a half, wary not to stumble over any of the fallen branches, a full moon illuminating his path through the woods. He thought he was lucky to be alive; so was Fratianni, at least as lucky as Lawrence had been. The man in the Cadillac, the one who'd been president of the college, could as easily have blown his head off as knocked out a tire. They had skidded to a stop on the median of the access road and radioed the other chase car. By the time the tire was changed, their partners had radioed that it was all over. They'd gotten the man they'd wanted, even recovered a Graz Burya. It might have been a big flag that emblazoned KGB. And then they had gotten a second radio message, one that had been coded. All it had said was, "Tighten fence." Chet had trouble making sense of it, at least until he remembered the way his boss had always liked to operate.

It was too bad, he thought. Lawrence wasn't a bad guy. He was quick and bright. He'd really saved his own life on the road, and he had been in the process of beating hell out of that private dick when Chet had arrived in the hall that night. Yeah. It was too bad. But there was only one meaning that Chet could figure for the "Tighten fence" message as he traversed the grounds, and that was totally in keeping with the personality of the director, Karl Weatherow. Lawrence would be terminated. They'd probably have to set it up as an accident. Maybe the house would burn and the professor would be found in it. Maybe there'd be an accident on the local highway. In any event, it was the part of the job that Chet Hammend liked the least. Still, he knew that the chances were that Weatherow was going to have him devise a way to carry out what had to be done. It could come in a matter of hours or days. Chet would have to be prepared. There would be contingencies to figure, and Lawrence would have to be mollified until the last moment. He'd done it before and so he could rely on experience. Just shut off the emotions and get on with the job. Still, he didn't have to like it.

He was moving through a small stand of birch when he stopped. Had he heard something? He craned his neck to listen for a sound. A branch snapped. Chet slipped the Magnum from its holster and cradled it in his right hand. He crouched and waited, listening for another sound, a footfall, a snapped twig, a rustle in the leaves.

"Chet?" The voice was a whisper a few yards away. It was Frat.

"Jesus Christ. Don't do that, Frat. I damn near killed you. What the hell is it?"

"We got a radio message."

The smaller man, who had also been in a crouch when he'd seen his partner drop into one, came up to his feet and moved through the brush. "It's Weatherow. He's coming up. Should arrive in an hour. They said his helicopter will be at the local airport, and I'm supposed to meet him."

"What about Lawrence?" Chet asked, returning the Magnum to its shoulder holster.

"Still tighten fence, as far as I know. Keep him in the house. He can't leave for anything. Oh, and Weatherow said for us to stay in the house with him." Frat shook his head, ominously. "Something's jumping."

"Yeah," Chet said, as he started to move back in the direction of the house with Frat. "Maybe the old man wants to waste Lawrence himself."

They walked back to the driveway and called the other surveillance car to remain on station, circling the block five times an hour and reporting in every ten minutes. Frat would take the calls in the car that was parked in the driveway, and Chet would move into the house with Lawrence. Weatherow would be there soon enough, and Chet would feel a weight lift from him. The old man could make the decisions.

Ted sat in the living room. He kicked off his shoes and was sipping a bourbon. He tried to look relaxed, but there was a great deal going on in his mind and he hoped that Chet Hammend could not see it. He looked across to Hammend. "Are you sure you won't have a drink, ah . . . Chet?"

"No thanks, Professor." Hammend's eyes never left Ted as the man spoke. They were the eyes of a professional poker player. How many of them had he seen in Viet Nam? Dozens, at least. The very fact that there was no reaction in Hammend said that the man was on guard; even more than he had been after the attack by Small. Were they setting up the last elements of the sanction? And who was Thayer? Small had said he was not a Soviet, and yet that didn't have to be true. If he was one of the best that the KGB could muster, the chances would be that the man would have been more American than Ted.

Ted eyed the distance from his chair to Chet's. It was a good twelve feet, and there was a coffee table between them. He would have to disarm and quiet Chet before he could give an alarm, and then manage to take on the three others outside. He sighed to himself. The odds were too great. There would be no reason for them to hesitate in killing him. Not now. Not if Small had been right about Thayer and the sanction. If he was going to get out, he was going to have to use another method.

He downed the drink and got to his feet, slowly. Chet's eyes followed his every move, and Ted knew it. He started for the kitchen and then stopped at the door to the long hall. "I'm making some supper, Mr. Hammend. Nothing fancy. A sandwich, perhaps. Would you or any of the others care to join me?"

Chet shook his head. "No thanks, Professor. I'm not hungry at all. And the rest of them will eat . . ." He paused for the barest fraction of a second.

When we've finished with you, Ted thought. *Dear God. When you're dead, Lawrence. That's when we'll eat.*

Chet shifted a fraction on the couch. ". . . as soon as we go off duty," he said uncomfortably. He had betrayed something, and it looked as if he knew it. What was more, Ted knew that Chet knew, etc. Ted turned to the kitchen. Chet's voice behind him stopped him.

"Professor?"

"Yes?" Ted ducked his head back into the living room and came eye to eye with the young agent on the couch.

"Mr. Weatherow called on the radio. He'll be arriving soon. He wants to talk with you."

Ted nodded and moved out to the kitchen. He didn't know whether to feel elated or depressed. Did Weatherow want to give him a thank you before he was done away with? Or was there another motive? All he could do was wait.

It was less than two hours later when Karl Weatherow arrived.

Weatherow shucked his topcoat and moved into the living room. Fratianni followed him. He wasted no time in getting to the point. As the man spoke, Ted could see a mix of anger and frustration in his face.

"All right, Doctor. You lied to me and got away with it. It was clever of you. But I'm telling you right now that there's only one way you'll get out of all of this alive, and that is to tell me the truth right now."

"Mr. Weatherow, I'm prepared to tell you all the truth you can stand."

"What came in the mail that day? The day your wife and son were killed."

"A package."

"From Howard?"

"You must know that, Weatherow. Why ask?"

"I don't know what was in it."

Ted ran his hands up through his hair and looked across the living room to the small, spectacled man. "A set of orders was in it. They were the orders that assigned Howard to the Unicorn Project. Later, at his apartment, I found a duplicate set hidden behind a picture."

"What else? There had to be more. The orders weren't enough. There had to be something really important for an agent to come in and kill for. What was it?"

Ted told him about the cylinder. He would try to buy his life with it. Weatherow cocked his head to the side as he listened.

"How did your daughter survive?"

"She was out in the back with the package; out in the woods. Small must have come in and killed Lisa and Michael, then torn the place apart looking for what he'd seen put in the mailbox. It wasn't there. It was out back with Dawn. She heard the car in the driveway and came back only minutes after Small had left. She found Lisa and her brother. When I got back, she was here, in the living room, in shock, with the package in her arms." He pointed to the corner of the room, seeing Dawn terrified and blood-covered in his mind's eye. "I found her that way. We took the package and ran. We had no way of knowing that whoever had been here wasn't going to come back for Dawn and me."

"And so you linked up with Miss Seward?"

Ted blinked. Did Weatherow know it all? And if he did, what did it matter now? Ted had managed to warn Cathy. Was Weatherow going to hunt her down after killing him?

"Yes. That's right."

"Why did you send her to Boston?"

Ted didn't react. It was clear that Weatherow knew everything.

"She went to get as much information as possible on Andrew Rodgers. He was the one who sent the package to Charlie Howard, or Lucas Morgan, or whatever the hell his name was. She found the name of the attorney and went to see if there was any information about the man, any more orders or evidence."

"What did you intend to do with it?"

"I intended to buy back our lives from you, Weatherow. That's what I intended. It was clear that I would know too much when all of this was over to be allowed to stay alive. What had you planned? An accident? A suicide? Perhaps I was going to hang myself with my necktie like all those airmen had done."

"That's very astute of you, Doctor. Also very clever. I have to admit that I wanted to terminate you as soon as we had you, and one of my colleagues persuaded me to wait. I'm glad I did."

"Until now, Mr. Weatherow?"

"Until now, Doctor. Tell me more about this cylinder."

Ted explained as much as he could remember from the luncheon meeting with Cathy. The cylinder had something to do with draining power, and there was a chance that it had been something that had been taken from Unicorn at the time the weapon was secreted in the hangar. He assumed that it had been passed from person to person from that time to this. Of course, he said, there was always the chance that the cylinder had been taken by someone as a souvenir and stored in an attic until recently, when Rodgers and his newspaper reporter friend, Anthony Patrino, had ferreted it out as a part of the case that they were trying to build about the murders of airmen.

"I thought, for a time this afternoon, that I'd be allowed to live after I'd gotten Small for you. But Small wasn't the one you were looking for. Was he, Weatherow?"

Weatherow smiled. It was clear that he admired Ted's mind.

"You're right, Doctor. The man we were after was the one who was pulling the strings for Small. He was blackmailing him. Pictures from a motel, if you know what I mean. He was a KGB agent in Boston, named Broskovich. We got him at the airport."

"Then he was the one who killed the lawyer?"

Weatherow pulled off his glasses and his eyes riveted Ted's.

"How did you know the lawyer was dead, Doctor?"

Ted did his best to smile convincingly. "I have my methods, Mr. Weatherow, just as you do. How does Broskovich relate to the man called Thayer? And how did all that connect up to the sanction?"

Weatherow's eyes did not move but Ted could see the man's mind working.

"Where did you pick up those terms, Doctor? If I may ask?"

"Small told me he was working for a man named Thayer. He said that the man was an American, not a Russian. Of course, the chances are that that could simply have been a lie that Broskovich told Small and the poor fool bought. But the Russians would not have been able to mount anything like a sanction, certainly not one that would last for over thirty years. And why would they want to, in the first place? Why kill all the airmen? It wouldn't profit them. It would have been far better to plant a long-term agent in the detachment guarding the hangar. Or perhaps buy a guard, or blackmail one. You see, Weatherow, the story you told me back in that hospital room really doesn't make any sense. The methods don't indicate a KGB plot at all. They indicate an American plot, and the only assumption I can make is that you're behind it. You have to be Thayer."

Weatherow eyed Ted for a moment, then sighed. He really did respect the man. It was a pity that he had not been recruited into the Defense Department or the CIA at the time of his discharge from the service. Killing him would be a great waste of brain power. "What else do you know about the elusive man named Thayer, Doctor?"

"Only that his first name was Wilfred, and that a man with that name appears more than a dozen times over the thirty-year span that the Ogden hangar has been guarded. Oddly enough, he was one of the first five men who moved the Air Force flatbed into the hangar and after that he supposedly, from what Howard told me, died. He became a missing person: drove to work one day and simply never got there. What I suspect happened was that he arranged for the deaths of the other four and then simply dropped from sight. He came back on the case whenever it started to look like someone was getting too curious about what was in the hangar. The device that you're so interested in was what fouled things up. Thayer, or perhaps you, Mr. Weatherow, had to surface in a more violent and persistent way than his normal methods dictated. But he was the operative in charge of the sanction, perhaps taking orders from someone above, perhaps working on his own. You're best qualified for that, Weatherow. You have authority, and complete freedom of mobility."

In Weatherow's memory, a small pinpoint of light

flashed. It was the same glimmer that he had noted when he'd been looking at the computer runs in his office earlier. Thayer. Thayer. Suddenly, he remembered. *My God,* he thought.

"I'm sorry to disappoint you, Doctor. But I'm not the mysterious Thayer. However, I'm beginning to think I know who might be . . . if any of the things you've told me are true."

"Who is it?" Ted asked with an edge of tension in his voice.

"I'm afraid I'm not in a position to speculate with you. As we say in my business, you really don't have a need to know."

Ted, who had been leaning against the kitchen sink, folded his arms and laughed sarcastically. "You are an unbelievable son of a bitch, Weatherow. Some maniac or agent who works for your people kills twenty people, my wife and son among them. You're probably planning on killing me and my daughter and Cathy. Every one of us is totally innocent of anything more than occasionally cheating on our taxes. And we don't have a need to know. You are un-fucking-believable. Do you know that?"

Weatherow took a small UHF set from his inside coat pocket. He thumbed the switch. "Frat? Come into the kitchen. I'll need your help."

A tiny voice on the small receiver responded. "Yes, sir."

Then Weatherow called to Chet, who'd been waiting in the living room. In a few minutes, after both men had arrived, Weatherow took a small leather case from his suit pocket and placed it gingerly on the kitchen table.

"Doctor?" he said with a sadness in his voice. "I'm afraid I'm going to have to ask you where the device is; currently, I mean."

Ted's eyes narrowed. He knew what was coming and there was little he could do about it. Chet and Frat were superb professionals, he was sure. They would be experts at getting any shred of information they could from him in the most efficient way possible. If they muscled him, Ted assumed that he could hold out for several hours before they managed to get the location of Anne Seward's farm and whatever else they wanted. "I think you already know that I am not prepared to tell you that, Mr. Weatherow."

Weatherow frowned. "Unfortunate, Doctor. But I was prepared for that contingency." He looked at the black leather case on the table. Then he reached down and unzipped the Velcro binding. He took out a small hypodermic needle and attached it to a syringe. When he was satisfied that the seal was tight, he removed a small vial of a clear substance and started carefully to draw off an amount into the syringe. He looked to Ted as he finished. "You see, Doctor, I anticipated your unwillingness to cooperate. This is a special mixture of scopalomine derivatives and a small amount of sodium pentathol."

Ted stared at the menacing needle. It was something he had not anticipated and he swore to himself for not considering it as one of Weatherow's options. With it, they could get all of the information that they wanted from him in a matter of minutes. Then they could give him a second, stronger dose and, when he was comatose, drop him in the ocean. The headlines would read "Despondent College Professor Commits Suicide."

"It's fatal, I presume?" he said.

Frat and Chet moved to each side of Ted as Weatherow answered.

"No, Doctor. In fact, we need only give you a small dose to get the answers we want." The portly Weatherow took a step toward Ted and, as if on cue, Frat and Chet moved to take each of his arms. Frat locked Ted's left arm in a police grip, levering his elbow against the sink. Chet held the other arm in a viselike hammerlock, with Chet's hand pinioned against his shoulder blade. Weatherow readied the hypo by squeezing a few drops from the tip of the needle.

Suddenly the back door bell rang. Ted craned his neck to see if there was a car in the driveway as Weatherow secreted the hypo in its case and answered the door.

The man at the door carried a case of liquor over his shoulder. Behind him, another carried a second case.

"Mr. Lawrence?" he asked, looking at Weatherow.

Weatherow started to answer but Ted called from the kitchen, "I'm Lawrence."

Chet and Frat released their hold.

The man with the whiskey carton slipped in the door past Weatherow and, taking the heavy carton from his shoulder, thumped it down on the kitchen table. The man who followed him also deposited a carton of liquor next to the first one. He took a yellow slip from his pocket and glanced at it before he spoke to Ted. "This is the liquor you ordered; or I guess it was your wife who ordered it. She said to get it here right away." He gestured to the man who had followed him in, to go back to the car and get something else. "He's just got to get the beer and the ice, Mr. Lawrence. Would you sign this?"

He handed Ted the receipt. As Ted looked at it he noticed that the order was placed by Mrs. Cathy Lawrence. What the hell was she doing? he wondered.

Ted signed the receipt and handed the yellow sheet back to the delivery man. The second man came back into the kitchen with two cases of beer and a carton filled with plastic bags of ice. They left and Weatherow eyed the packages on the table. "Were you planning a party, Doctor?"

Ted shook his head as he watched Frat and Chet again move menacingly close. Before they could get near him, the doorbell rang again. This time it was a caterer. Four men brought in steaming trays of food.

Ted guessed that there was enough food for twenty or thirty people. Again, the food had been ordered by someone calling herself Mrs. Cathy Lawrence. In the hour that followed bedlam reigned. No less than twenty cars arrived, clogging the driveway and the long, narrow access road. All of them came for a party that they had been invited to at Ted's. Some of them were colleagues from Paxton. Most of the members of Ted's department arrived, saying that they had gotten phone invitations to drop by. On top of them came some students from Ted's classes, and a large number of strangers whom Ted could not recognize at all.

The kitchen and living room were jammed with people looking for food and liquor. Ted served drinks while he watched Weatherow, whom he'd introduced as a writer friend, get cornered by two middle-aged women from one of Ted's classes who pestered him with questions about the kinds of books he wrote.

Weatherow flushed and smiled. "Mysteries, mostly. Spy stories," he said, eyeing Ted in the distance. Chet and Frat had managed to take up positions by the door that led to the living room. Ted was sure that the other chase car was outside at the end of the driveway, its two agents waiting for directions from their chief, who could not break free for a moment to give them instructions on the small UHF set he carried in his pocket.

The doorbell rang again. Ted answered it and saw four more strangers standing in the back doorway. They were two couples. The women were two small brunettes in their twenties. Their escorts looked like young businessmen, perhaps in their early thirties. The taller of the two men, perhaps Ted's height, smiled and stepped forward. "Is this where the party is?" he asked.

Ted smiled. "Yes. Where did you hear about it?"

The man smiled back. "Oh, we were at the Purple Plum. You know, the disco in Shore Park. Well, we got a phone message that a guy named Lawrence had invited people from every nightclub and bar in Shore Park to drop by for a drink. So we came."

Ted grinned, managing to look authentic. "Well, come on in. You're in the right place." He took their coats and got them to the bedroom, with Frat shadowing his move down the hall. He kept his distance, simply making sure that Ted did not manage to get out a window or a door.

The next hour was pure insanity.

Twenty-five or thirty more people arrived, jamming the Lawrence house with almost fifty freeloaders looking for food and liquor. In the midst of their influx, yet another delivery truck brought ten pizzas and cases of soda, again ordered on the phone by Cathy, and paid for on a credit card number.

Weatherow managed to work his way through the crowd toward Ted.

"Just what the hell are you doing, Lawrence? What's this all about?"

Ted turned to him and smiled in the chaotic kitchen. "Having a party. Sure is fun, isn't it, Weatherow?"

Weatherow grimaced. "The party can't go on forever. You know that."

The doorbell rang and Ted moved to answer it.

It was Cathy. She slipped in the door and pulled Ted to the side of the kitchen.

He moved close to her. "What the hell are you doing here? How . . . ?"

Unexpectedly, she reached up and pulled his head down and kissed him. Her mouth was warm and pliant against his. When she pulled away she was breathless for a second. Ted could see a shine to her eyes that seemed part fear, part excitement. She managed a smile. "Like the party, darling?"

He leaned close to her. His voice was a throaty whisper. "You shouldn't have come. Weatherow is standing over there in the corner, and a couple of his hired guns are in the house. There are two more cruising outside."

She pulled up close to him. "I know about the ones outside. The car circles the block once every twelve minutes. I clocked it. My car is just across the street, next to what looked like another government car. I'm getting you out of here. The party was the best diversion I could muster." Her eyes darted to her watch. "In exactly eight minutes, when that government car is on the far side of the block, all the power will fail here and for about a mile around."

"But . . . ?"

"Damnit, Ted, shut up and listen. Dawn is in my car. She'll trigger her little . . . toy in exactly eight minutes. The inside of the house will be chaos. We can slip out and get to the car. Then we'll run like hell; at least we will when Dawn turns the device back off. Don't be mad at me. It was the only way I could manage to do things."

"Have you planned where we're going?" Ted asked, his voice just above a whisper.

She shook her head. "No. But if we have the device, perhaps that will be a lever, maybe a way we can stop them from coming after us."

Ted shook his head with finality. There was no way on earth that they would be deterred from following. And they had time and speed and communications on their side. The idea came to him suddenly. They could not run. That would only play into Weatherow's hands, or the sinister clutches of Thayer, whoever that strange shadow figure was. Ted looked at his watch. There were two minutes to go. He would have to insure that Frat and Chet did not follow them. But that wouldn't be hard, not if they had Weatherow with them.

The phone rang. Ted snatched the handset from the wall phone near the kitchen door. "Hello?"

"Let me speak to Weatherow." The voice was steady, intense.

"Wait a minute." Ted waved the handset in the air and attracted Weatherow's attention with it. The portly Director of Internal Security elbowed his way through the crowd and got to the phone. He eyed Cathy for a second before turning away from her and Ted to concentrate on the caller.

There was less than a minute to go until Dawn would black out the area. Ted could see a bulge in the back of Weatherow's jacket. It would be a holster, and the odds were that a pistol would be in it. All Ted could hope was that the pistol was loaded.

Weatherow was speaking animatedly into the phone as Ted edged close to him. Cathy looked to her watch and then to Ted. She couldn't be sure what he was going to do. Ted grabbed his parka from the back of the chair next to Weatherow and his hand fished for the pager. He found it with his fingertips and pushed the button.

The lights went out.

Ted's hand lashed out and clawed at the holster in Weatherow's jacket. Weatherow tried to turn but could not before Ted had the pistol. He cocked the hammer back on the revolver and let his fingertips feel the fronts of the chambers. Yes, the noses of the slugs were there. He'd been lucky. People were starting to stumble into one another in the kitchen and Ted suspected in the rest of the house. He jammed the barrel of the pistol into the fat man's gut.

"We're getting out, and you're coming with us. I'll kill you if I have to. I believe you know that."

In a matter of seconds, the three of them were in the car-choked driveway.

"Where's Dawn?" Ted yelled to Cathy.

"In my bug. She'll keep the power out until we get there."

Ted turned Weatherow toward the backyard. "This way. Cathy, bring up the rear."

"But—" she started to say. He cut her off.

"Listen, I'll take him to his chase car. It should be stalled just on the other side of the block. The agents will be coming in from it on a dead run. I pushed the button on the pager before the lights went out. If they couldn't get the car to start, then they're coming on foot. As we get to the back woods, swing away to the right. Follow the path; it'll curl back to the street. Get to your car. Wait one minute and turn the power back on. I'll bring the chase car and him." He gestured to Weatherow. "We'll pick both of you up."

Cathy nodded. Ted could see plumes of her breath in the moonlight. They moved to the edge of the woods and Cathy bore off to the right. Ted pushed Weatherow ahead of him through the long stand of trees that would lead to the other side of the block. Suddenly Ted grabbed Weatherow and stopped. Ahead of them in the woods he could hear the crunch of dead sticks and the shuffling of leaves. The two agents from the now-dead chase car were crashing through the woods to the house. Ted pushed Weatherow to the ground and crouched down next to him, placing the gun to Karl's head. "Quiet," he whispered.

The two agents crashed past them, some twenty yards to the right. When he was sure that they were far enough in the distance, Ted got Weatherow to his feet and they moved out of the woods and into the street.

The gray sedan was only fifty feet from the spot where they emerged.

Ted ordered Weatherow into the driver's seat. The fat man looked across to Ted as he swung into the passenger side. "It's impossible, Lawrence. The keys aren't here. It's standing procedure for an agent to take them, whenever he gets out of the car."

With the gun trained on Weatherow, Ted fished under the glove compartment until he found the small magnetic case that he sought. He thumbed it open and handed the spare ignition key to Weatherow. "It's also procedure to keep the spare inside the car. I saw Chet check for it when they drove me back from the college today." He handed Karl the ignition key. "As soon as the power cuts back in, drive to the front of . . ." As Ted said the words, lights in the neighborhood surged to life as fast as they had gone out.

Taking Ted's directions, Weatherow eased the car around the block and stopped near the long access road to the Lawrence house. Ted bellowed to Cathy, who was at the wheel of the VW, and she, with Dawn in tow, ran for the gray car. As soon as the two of them were in the back seat, Ted ordered Weatherow to head for the main highway.

"It's stupid, Lawrence. Where do you think you can go?"

"We're going to get a plane, Weatherow. You're going to get one for us. Then we're going to take a flight to Ogden. Hill Air Force Base is close, I think. We're going to fly there and get into the hangar and see what's there. I'm betting four lives, yours included, that it's not a vintage Soviet secret weapon."

Weatherow shook his head as he drove. "It's too late, Lawrence. Unicorn's been ordered destroyed. The order came in this afternoon. One of my colleagues is en route to do the job, now."

Ted held the pistol menacingly close to Weatherow's right ear. "Then he's probably your man. He's got to be Thayer. Or whoever sent him is." Ted picked up the mike from the car's complex radio rig. "Call someone and have him stopped. Then get a plane for us, one that can accommodate all of us. Then we go right to the damned hangar and see what's there. Understand?"

Weatherow shook his head, stubbornly. "There's no way in the world they'll let us through to it, Lawrence. No way."

Ted nudged Weatherow's ear with the pistol. "Find a way. Or, so help me, I'll blow your head off."

"Daddy?" Dawn's voice was small and frightened in the back seat. "Daddy? I'm frightened."

Ted reached his free hand back and stroked her face, still keeping the gun leveled on Weatherow. "It's OK. Honey, we're all frightened. It's not a bad thing to be frightened."

He handed Weatherow the mike. "Get working."

It only took a few minutes for Weatherow to get the radio-to-phone patch set up. The voice that came from the speaker was faint, and the transmission was broken with static. "Foreign Intelligence Analysis Division. Baker speaking."

Weatherow held the mike close to his mouth and did his best to speak clearly. He steered the car with the other hand, heading it south, per Ted's instructions. Their goal was McGuire Air Force Base.

"Baker? This is Chapstick four zero niner. This is an unsecured radio patch. However, I have a flash red priority radio message to be transmitted. Do you copy?"

"I copy, Chapstick. It's irregular but we've already heard from Ghost location."

So they knew that Weatherow had been taken by Ted, Cathy, and Dawn. They would play the game, giving him everything he asked, knowing that Ted had a gun at his head.

Weatherow thumbed the button. "First request follows. I require a jet aircraft which can handle at least half a dozen passengers. I'll also need a full crew. Make those arrangements at McGuire Air Force Base, immediately."

There was a pause on the radio. "Chapstick, what is the destination of this flight?"

Weatherow started to answer and Ted cut him off. "Don't tell him."

"I have to. They'll have to know how much range to

fuel for. There are flight plans and clearances to take care of. None of this is very simple."

Ted nodded.

"Baker? This is Chapstick. Destination is Hill Air Force Base, near Ogden, Utah. I'll need a car there, and there is no chance of intercept. Is that clear, Baker?"

"Roger, Chapstick."

Weatherow looked to Ted and then pressed the mike button again.

"Baker, I also need an abort order on the Unicorn destruct mission. Do you copy?"

"Ah . . . I copy, Chapstick. Hold one."

The seconds stretched almost to a minute. Ted was getting nervous. "What's going on?" he asked.

"He has to verify all the codes that were assigned to the destruct order by the Secretary. When he does that, he can stop the mission."

The speaker crackled to life in a few more seconds. "Chapstick?"

"Roger," Weatherow said crisply.

"We have nothing like a destruct order on that operation. Are you sure your information is correct?"

"Yes, Baker." What followed was a string of codes that Weatherow yelled into the mike. Again there was a pause, and the speaker hissed with static.

"Chapstick? We still have no destruct order on the project. There is no authorization at any level."

Weatherow shook his head. "Baker? There has to be. It would have been ordered by the Secretary yesterday or the day before. Foreign Intelligence Analysis Division is operational on it. Check it again. And get in touch with Clifford Hurley to confirm it."

"Ted?" Cathy's voice from the back seat was tinged with fear. "There's a car following us. It sped up until it was about a hundred yards behind. Then it slowed to match our speed. It's been there for a few minutes, now."

Ted's eyes moved to Weatherow. "Back them off."

The speaker squealed before Weatherow had a chance to use the mike. "Chapstick, this is Baker. Hurley is not available and the Secretary confirms that no such destruct came from him."

"Where's Hurley, Baker?"

"We don't know, Chapstick. He is not at his home and not in the office. We have not been able to locate him."

The reply struck Weatherow like lightning. Sweet God, it was true. Hurley was Thayer. "Baker, get me a computer access and a console operator. You stay on the line. I'm going to switch frequencies for a second. Stay with me."

Weatherow looked to Ted. "Shift that dial to one one five point six." Ted did. Weatherow pressed the mike switch. "Chet? Is that you shadowing?"

There was a pause and then an answer. "Roger, sir."

"Well, back off a mile or so. You're making this man with my gun nervous."

"Roger."

Dutifully, the car that had matched their speed drifted back into the nearly deserted stretches. Ted knew that they would not be far. But having them further away gave them more breathing room.

Ted switched back to the original frequency, and Weatherow linked up with his computer console operator. "This is Chapstick. Get me the last known location and status of Vasili Broskovich. KGB. Do you copy?"

There was a new voice on the phone. Ted could only assume that it was the man at the computer console. "Roger, Chapstick. Working."

"What are you doing?" Ted asked.

"Checking. It's something I don't want to check, Lawrence. But if there is no order to destroy Unicorn, then Hurley is out there on his own hook. If that's the case, then . . ."

"Then he's Thayer, isn't he, Weatherow? You said in the kitchen you had a hunch who it might be. But you were still ready to kill me just to tidy things up. Right?"

"Not right. I didn't plan to kill you. I would have if ordered to do so. I was sure you were holding out. I had to find out. I . . ." The speaker interrupted Weatherow.

"Chapstick. Last known data was gathered forty-eight hours ago. Broskovich, Vasili. Rank, colonel. Status of assignment: North American branch, KGB. Last known location, Riga, Latvia, two days ago. Do you require anything further?"

"Yes. Locate Clifford Hurley. The Secretary will clear it."

The car had pulled from the Parkway and was weaving its way through the local roads of Burlington County, headed in the direction of McGuire Air Force Base, when another message came in. "Chapstick."

"Roger."

"Hurley took a jet and a crew along with a quantity of explosives. The destination on his flight from Andrews Air Force Base was Hill Air Force Base. His departure time was just under an hour ago."

"Roger. Stand by." Weatherow breathed deeply. He glanced at Ted and then back to the road. "You were right, Lawrence. It appears that Clifford Hurley might have been the man that you call Thayer."

"Then he was the one who killed all the airmen, my family, and your agents, too. Broskovich was never in the country. Hurley, as Thayer, has been at all of this for almost thirty years. Can you tell me why?"

Weatherow slammed a hand itno the steering wheel. "No, Lawrence. I can't."

"Well, I think I can," Ted said. "He was guarding something more important than a Soviet project. He became a fanatic about it, slipped a cog; perhaps it was the pressure of the job. Perhaps it was something more frightening."

"What?" Weatherow asked.

"Something awesome . . . something terrifying. The thing in the hangar, the thing that he now has to destroy before anyone can see it, Weatherow."

"Well, what the hell is it, Lawrence? You seem to have all the answers."

"I don't know, exactly. But it's for sure that Dawn couldn't knock out power with that small device without the technology being more advanced even than this decade. I think there's something alien in that hangar, and I think it powered itself on lines of force from the planet itself. To do that would have been enough to terrify anyone in 1950. It would terrify people now. That's why Hurley has to destroy it."

Weatherow shook his head as he headed for the main gate of the air base.

"So what is it, Doctor? A flying saucer? Little green men?"

"It might be, Weatherow. In any event, we'll see, won't we?"

CHAPTER TWENTY-TWO

The small jet sped westward at almost the speed of sound. It was all madness, Weatherow thought. He was flying west to stop an old friend from destroying something that had been kept secret for more than three decades; something that a great many people had died to keep secret. With him was an armed college professor, a literary editor, and a child. But beyond that was the fear. Hurley had lied to him, and the chances were that Hurley had lied to others. It was the why of it that frightened Weatherow. Who was his old friend really working for? Why? And what would have commanded his loyalty in so persistent and long-lasting a way? What the hell was really in the hangar? Weatherow had to respect Lawrence's intellect. There was a chance that the man was right, that there was something in the hangar other than a Soviet weapon. And all three of them, the professor and his daughter and his girlfriend, were running for their lives. They had to know that. Somehow, the revelation of what was in the hangar had to be so stupendous that Lawrence would have thought it could help to save his life. Even the little girl took it all seriously. She'd said when they took off that if there were aircraft following them she could flip a switch on the small device she carried and drop all air traffic out of the air. The jet engines, especially those in the plane in which they were flying, would flame out, and the crew would not be able to ignite them, the child had said. Weatherow believed her.

They'd been in the air for more than three hours when Ted could start to feel his ears pop. They were starting to descend into the Hill Air Force Base traffic pattern. The co-pilot came back from the cockpit and looked to Weatherow. There was concern on the man's face as he hunched down and spoke in quiet tones.

"It will be an instrument landing. Hill's socked in with a snowstorm."

Weatherow peered out the window into the night sky, then back to the Air Force officer. "When did Hurley land?"

"They cleared him through the pattern about forty minutes ago. He checked out a staff car and left the base. That's all they know."

"Did you manage to get Ogden on the horn?"

"Yes, sir. They claim not to have any Air Force Security Service personnel there, and they won't answer any questions on the radio without direct presidential clearance."

Weatherow nodded. "They're just doing their job. I can't blame them for that. Arrange for a car to meet us, Colonel. I'll want to get to the supply base at Ogden as soon as possible."

The colonel went back to the cockpit, and Weatherow looked glumly out the window.

The Hill Air Force Base duty officer, a young captain, waited for them at the bottom of the steps. He shuffled on one foot and then the other to keep warm. The worst of the snow was over, and all the runways had been cleared and were operational. But behind the storm that had dumped more than a foot of snow on the Rockies came the cold and the wind. With the wind chill, the effective temperature was ten below zero, and the captain had been waiting for more than twenty minutes in the teeth of that wind. He wasn't prepared for what got off the plane: a Defense Department VIP, a civilian male, a female, and a small child.

The trio did not look like kidnappers. They were not PLO maniacs, nor some other group of wild-eyed extremists. They simply looked like a family, the father of which was directing a major Defense Department official at the point of a gun. The captain's orders were to let them have exactly what they wanted; not to interfere, or attempt anything as foolish as a rescue. He ushered them into a sedan and watched as Karl Weatherow, with Ted Lawrence next to him, drove from the base. He shook his head.

The trip from Hill Air Force Base to the small Army supply base at Ogden took some forty minutes. They were a half hour into the ride when Cathy spotted a car following them. It was the same pattern she'd seen in New Jersey. The chase car sped to catch up and then took up station. Ted warned Weatherow but the agent simply shook his head.

"There's nothing I can do about that one, Lawrence. We're just going to have to live with it. It's one of the most secure installations in the country, and there's no way those Air Force Security types back there are going to be deterred." Ted shrugged and peered through the windshield. Through the blowing snow, he could see the ghostly halos of perimeter lights. They were approaching the post.

The officer at the gate passed them through without delay and the Air Force team at the hangar perimeter did the same. Obviously both had been alerted to the situation. Once through the outer fence, the staff car lurched through foot-deep snow, heading in the direction of the hangar. Suddenly, a blue flash erupted from a power line just to their left.

The perimeter lights winked out. A transformer had blown under the weight of the wind-driven ice and snow. The only means of illumination now were the headlights of the sedan and those of the two Air Force security jeeps that trailed it at a distance, as it followed the tracks of Hurley's car, which had passed through only a few minutes before.

Weatherow took a hand from the wheel and looked at his watch. He shook his head. "He's still almost twenty minutes ahead of us, Lawrence. I really don't know if we can get to him in time. Not now, not before he blows the hangar."

Ted turned to him. "We're going to have to, Weatherow. What kind of explosive charges was he carrying?"

"I'm not sure. Ordnance back at the Pentagon wasn't sure either. The chances are that it was C-four."

"C-what?" Cathy asked.

"C-four. Plastic explosive. Each of the issue satchels weighs something over ten pounds. The explosive is pretty potent. Three or four satchels of the stuff would be enough to blow the hangar sky high."

"How would he place the explosives?" Ted asked.

"How the hell should I know?" Weatherow snapped.

"You worked with this lunatic all these years, didn't you? You should know how he'd operate with explosives," Ted snapped back.

"I can only guess. He'd have to use at least one satchel to blow one of the armor plates off the side of the hangar. Once inside, the chances are that he'd place the satchels in a triangle around the target. Then he'd set the timers and get out. The armor plate cladding on the outside of the building would act to shape the explosion and force it back inward. That would utterly destroy what was on the inside."

"How do they go off?" Dawn asked from the back seat in a small voice.

"How do they what?" Weatherow asked.

"I mean, what sets the charges off?"

"Normally, they are set off by a small, battery-powered timer. Once it's set and activated, the battery energizes a blasting cap, and that sets off the charge. Why?"

Dawn showed Cathy the cylinder that she'd held

tightly in her hand for hours. "Daddy? If this timer thing works on electricity, I think I can stop it with this. But if I do, it will knock out the car electrical systems the way it did back home. That would mean that you'd have to get there on foot."

Ted peered through the windshield. They had passed through the open gate of the third perimeter fence. The dark form of the hangar was only a hundred or so yards in the distance. "I can see it. We're close," he said.

"Should I, Daddy?"

Ted nodded. "Yeah, honey. Do it."

Dawn was about to turn the top of the device to the setting that she remembered so well when a huge flash of light blinded them all. Weatherow swerved the sedan to the left in time for the car to be rocked by the blast. Though stunned and slammed against the side of the car, Ted managed to keep hold of the pistol. As the car skidded to a stop he saw that Weatherow had slumped forward over the steering wheel. He reached over and pulled the man's head from the wheel. There was a small gash on the man's forehead. The blow had apparently knocked him unconscious. Ted looked into the back seat. Cathy had cradled Dawn in her arms when the concussion had hit them and, aside from being shaken up, both of them seemed to be all right.

"Dawn? Is the thing still working? I mean, can you still stop the batteries?"

Dawn fingered the settings on the device for a second before she looked in the direction of her father's voice. "Yes. I think it's still all right. Do you want me to turn it on?"

Ted opened the car door and started to get out into the snow. "Do it . . . right now," he yelled above the sound of the wind. "We've got to stop him before he sets the charges inside." He checked the pistol, looked toward the hangar, and then looked to Dawn, Cathy, and the inert form of Weatherow. The man was starting to moan and stir. Obviously, the injury wasn't too serious. "Stay here, both of you. Get on the floor of the back seat, just in case something goes wrong." Before Cathy could respond, Ted was trotting off through the snow in the direction of the hangar.

He had only gone a few yards when the headlights of the jeeps and the sedan winked out, as Dawn snapped the device to its power-draining setting. In the distance he could make out the shape of a car not far from the corner of the hangar that had been breached by the first explosion. Hurley, or Thayer, or whoever the man was, was a shadow figure silhouetted by the flames that licked hungrily at the hangar insulation and cables that had been blown outward into the snow.

Ted was running hard now, making the best headway he could in the deepening snow. The wind lashed through his light parka and ice started to coat his chin.

He was less than fifty yards from the corner of the hangar when another explosion tossed him into the snow. He was groggy and disoriented when he got to his feet. He screamed curses into the wind-blown snow when he thought he had been too late. Ahead, a pillar of fire blossomed in red and orange in the night sky. The fire intersecting with the snow created an eerie, glowing effect.

Ted took a few steps in the direction of the hangar. The hangar! It was still there. Thayer had not managed to blow it. Rather, his car had blown up; perhaps it was the gas tank of the car, exploding from the heat of the first blast. There was still a chance.

Ted started to dash for the hangar. He veered to the right. He slowed, then sped up again. Once more he veered to one side. The blast had somehow gotten to his middle ear. His balance was off. He staggered on toward the looming shape of the hangar until a bullet whizzed past his ear. He dropped to the snow, and propping his hand up at the wrist, he squeezed off two shots in the direction of the shattered end of the hangar lit by the ball of fire that had been Hurley's, or Thayer's, car.

There were no other shots. Ted pushed himself to his feet and staggered toward the cover created by the looming wall of the large hangar. He reached it and pressed himself against the welded armor plate, then moved cautiously in the direction of the open end. The man inside would not know that the timers on the charges would not work. He would set them and then try to fight his way back out. At least, that was what Ted thought. Then, Ted thought, he'd have him, the man who'd killed Lisa and little Mike; the man responsible for the deaths of all the airmen.

He was only twenty yards from the shattered corner of the hangar when he saw a figure dart out of the ripped metal opening.

Ted raised the pistol. "Stop!" he screamed into the roaring blast of wind. The man stopped and wheeled, his gun already leveled in Ted's direction.

Ted fired as the other man did. The man's bullet ricocheted from the metal hangar, and Ted's slammed into the pyre of the car. Ted was about to fire again when the figure ducked back inside the hangar.

Ted edged toward the burning car, protecting his frozen face from the sudden heat with an upraised hand.

Suddenly Ted could hear something above the wind and the crackling of the fire. It was the sound of people running in the snow. He spun in the direction of the footsteps and aimed the pistol. He could make out three figures after a second. Two were adults and the third was a child. Weatherow, Cathy, and Dawn.

In the flickering flames of the car, Ted could also see others running toward the hangar. They appeared to be airmen, armed with rifles. Weatherow and Cathy were winded when they managed to flatten themselves against the hangar wall. Dawn seemed tired, but was clearly not as out of shape as the adults. Ted trained the pistol in the direction of the hangar opening and then turned to look at them.

"I told you to stay in the car."

Weatherow, his hand pressed against his forehead, obviously in pain from the blow of hitting the steering wheel of the car, took a step in Ted's direction.

"It was the girl, Lawrence. Something about the cylinder." He looked in the direction of the hangar entrance. "He's in there, isn't he?"

Ted glanced back at the jagged rip in the hangar and nodded. "Yes. He took a shot at me and then dove inside. I imagine he's trying to set the charges. He can't know that the batteries won't work." He looked to Dawn. "What's wrong with the device, honey?"

Dawn held the cylinder tight in her fist. She shook her head and the red stocking cap that she wore whipped back and forth, punctuating the gesture. "I don't know, Daddy. It's just wrong. It tingles a tiny bit in my hand. I was worried about those explosives that the man had in the hangar. I was frightened that this might not work, and they might explode."

Ted shook his head. "He won't blow the place up while he's in it. Just keep the setting on the device the way it is. I'm going in after him."

Weatherow took a step forward. "No. Give me the gun. I'll go in. He's one of my people, Doctor. I'm responsible. If you kill him, it's murder. If I do, it's . . . well, execution. Besides, we want him alive, if we can get him. We have to know more about what all this is about. Give me the gun." His hand reached out for it.

Ted shook his head and trained the pistol on Weatherow. "Sorry. He killed my son and my wife. This is my job. Besides, I have to see what's in there. And if I give you this," he gestured with the gun, "there's a chance that I never will. So stay here. I'm going in."

Weatherow waved back in the direction of the men who were running in formation and rapidly closing on the hangar. "Don't be stupid, Doctor. I could have all of you killed by those men. But I'm not going to. Give me the gun."

Ted looked at the armed airmen who were spreading out in a cordon around the hangar. In the distance there were still more converging on the site. Weatherow was right, and Ted knew it. He had come to the end of the adventure. There were just no more cards to play. He reversed the pistol in his hand and handed it to Weatherow, who reached for it. Ted clung to the gun for a second before passing it over. "Weatherow. I'm younger and stronger than you. Perhaps a bit faster. Let me dive in through that opening and try to flush this man out to where you can talk to him, or, if you have to, get a shot off."

Weatherow paused a second, took the pistol, and nodded.

Leaving Cathy and Dawn at the wall of the hangar, they maneuvered to either side of the gash. Weatherow nodded to Ted, and Ted ducked low and dove inside. He hit the concrete floor with a thud and scrambled on hands and knees toward the dark, inner wall. He squinted and stifled a cough. He had stirred up a cloud from the nearly three-inch-thick dust coat that had accumulated. He couldn't see a thing. He listened for movement, but there was none.

As his eyes got used to the dark he could see the shape of a truck in the distance. The odds were that the man he and Weatherow sought was hiding behind it, or perhaps under it. Ted got to his hands and knees. "You!" he yelled and dove to the right. Two bullets from a silenced pistol spattered the concrete where he had been crouching. With the two shots outside, that had been four. How many rounds were in the gun? And how much extra ammunition did the man carry? Ted had no way of knowing. "You!" he bellowed again as he rolled to the right. This time there was no fire. The adversary had guessed that Ted was trying to draw fire. That would mean that he was low on ammunition.

There was a sudden noise behind Ted and he craned his neck to see what it was. Weatherow had dived through the aperture in the hangar wall. Ted could barely see in the dust cloud that the fat man had rolled to the opposite side.

"Cliff?" he called out. "It's Karl. Come out. We have to talk."

There was no answer, but for a second Ted thought there was someone moving at the rear of the truck.

"Cliff?" Weatherow again called. "The charges can't go off. There's no way you're going to pull this off. So come out, and let's talk."

Again there was no answer.

Suddenly there was a sound near the truck. It sounded like something between a moan and a gurgle. Then there was the sickening thump of a body falling to the floor.

Ted and Weatherow advanced cautiously in the dusty darkness to the side of the truck. Keeping Ted behind him, Weatherow wheeled around the side and crouched into a firing position.

Beside the flatbed of the truck was the crumpled form of Clifford Hurley.

Weatherow moved cautiously. He approached the body and nudged it with his foot. After passing the gun to Ted, he turned the face-down form up. Hurley's face was set in a grotesque death mask. His lips were purple and there was a slight trickle of blood coming from his mouth. Weatherow looked up to Ted.

"Cyanide. He took an L capsule. He was dead in seconds." He looked back down at the form of his dead friend. His voice was just above a whisper. "Why Cliff? Why all of this?"

"I think I know," Ted said. "Dear God, I think I know."

He looked to the flatbed, which was rusted with age. It still bore the U.S. Air Force markings. Both cab doors were still open. He took a step in the direction of the flatbed, then coughed as his step raised a cloud of acrid dust from the concrete floor. Suddenly Ted stopped. There were voices calling from the jagged tear in the hangar. Airmen were pouring in, feeling their way in the dark.

"Find the other charges. Pull the timers and the detonator mechanisms. Don't worry. They'll be harmless." It was less than a minute later when an Air Force lieutenant shuffled across the dust-covered floor. He reported that his men had found and disarmed three satchel charges assembled in a triangle around the truck. They had been in exactly the places that Weatherow had predicted.

"Ted?" The voice was Cathy's, coming from the tear in the hangar corner. She and Dawn had climbed through the opening, and were moving through the now almost opaque cloud of dust.

"I'm here," Ted yelled. "Follow my voice."

Weatherow looked toward the two shrouded forms moving in the direction of the truck. "Have the little girl turn off the device," he called to them. "The explosives are disarmed, and that way we can get some light in here."

Dawn clicked the top of the pen-like device to its original position, and in seconds the flashlights of airmen were cutting through the dust.

"On the truck," Ted yelled. "Play the lights across the truck."

Obediently, more than a dozen flashlights hit the truck.

The battered tarp had rotted away, over the years, and fallen from the secret cargo. It was oval, and burnished to reflect light. It carried not the slightest trace of tarnish. Several stubby antennae projected from various places. It looked to Ted like a sophisticated satellite. But suddenly he remembered.

There were no satellites in 1950!

Sweet Jesus!

Across the hull of the oval-shaped craft were a series of strange markings that Ted recognized immediately as being similar to the ones on the device that Dawn carried. They were sweeps and curls, whorls and loops, resembling no language on earth.

No language on earth!

Ted realized it a second ahead of the others. No wonder, he thought. No wonder why Hurley would kill a million airmen if he had to. The glistening form on the back of the flatbed had to be the best-kept secret in the history of the species. To reveal it would have been to set loose the greatest wave of culture shock in the history of the planet.

Ted jumped up on the flatbed and examined the craft. He looked back to Weatherow. "Get up here, Weatherow. Look at this. This is your Soviet secret weapon."

Weatherow climbed to the top of the flatbed and shone a flashlight on the craft. As they walked gingerly around it, they could see the damage. It appeared that the side of the craft had been smashed flat, perhaps by a crash, perhaps by gunfire. There were too many perhapses to even consider. They were peering into the wreckage of a UFO. It had finally happened. The government had managed to get hold of one thirty years in the past and then, terrified of the public reaction, stuffed it in a hangar.

Weatherow leaned in close to the craft, playing his light across what seemed to be a transluscent domed hatch. "Lawrence. Look!"

Ted let his light join Weatherow's. There on the inside of the ship was a dark roundish mass, a form clearly not mechanical. Weatherow, his eyes wide, looked to Ted. "We have to open it."

Ted shook his head. "No. We'd need a team of experts, exobiologists . . . experts on alien life. No, we can't. Whatever is in there is long dead."

On the floor of the hangar Dawn screamed, and the sound of her shrill cry reverberated through the huge hangar. Ted leapt to the floor and ran to her.

"What is it? Are you all right?"

Cathy, stunned by the cry, was holding Dawn to her breast. Dawn was clutching the cylinder at arm's length and grimacing.

"Hot. It's getting hot," she moaned.

Weatherow jumped to the ground and ran to Ted. "What—?"

"Drop it. Dawn! Drop the thing," he yelled. She did, and the clatter of the small cylinder was muffled as it hit the dust of the hangar floor. As Dawn stumbled backward, still half held by Cathy, Ted could see that beneath the dust there was a slight blue glow. The object was starting to pulse with light. In another few seconds, it started to emit a low hum. The hum grew louder. In seconds, it was an ear-splitting scream. They turned and, hands covering their ears, Ted, Cathy, Dawn, and the airmen, with Weatherow bringing up the rear, started to dash to the split in the wall. In the teeth of the gathering blizzard, they dashed back in the direction of the cars. They didn't make it. They were only a few hundred yards from the hangar when they all fell to the snow, covering their ears from the incredible sound. Ted held Cathy on one side of him and did his best to cradle Dawn on the other. Dawn was screaming, her lips moving, but Ted could hear nothing but the ear-splitting wail from the small device on the hangar floor.

It came across the sky, trailing blue fire and turning the night into day. Ted saw it and the sight paralyzed him. It was like the fireball he'd seen in the street and the one he'd seen at home. It moved with incredible speed and headed directly toward them.

The screaming sound from the hangar stopped.

So did the fireball—right over the hangar.

The light was like nothing any of them had ever seen. It lasted for more than a minute, turning the frozen snow into instant rivulets as the ice melted from the hangar. Now the stillness of the night was broken by the sounds of rushing water. The light grew stronger, more brilliant, and the stunned onlookers covered their eyes—but the light reached through hands that tried to block it out.

Dawn pulled from Ted and got to her feet. She turned in the direction of the hangar. It was turning to blue fire itself.

"Get down, Dawn. Get down!" Ted screamed.

Dawn shook her head and slowly lifted her arm and pointed toward the fireball.

"Daddy, the light . . . the light . . ."

Dawn Lawrence, blind from birth, could see. She pointed in amazement to the hangar, completely enveloped in light. It shimmered for a second—then vanished. The flatbed was gone, as was the strange alien craft, the cylinder, the entire hangar. All that remained was the concrete foundation, in a pool of ice water.

CHAPTER TWENTY-THREE

They never did fully explain it. Weatherow could not find supporting orders for the sealing up of the alien craft. Though Ted was sure that Weatherow did not try too hard. Hurley's death was listed as accidental, and the airmen on the scene were sworn to secrecy. Weatherow made it clear what would happen to them if word of the happenings at the hangar ever leaked out.

Ted and Cathy were also sworn to secrecy. Both of them had no desire to say anything about the incident. Dawn's eyesight seemed to be permanently restored. No one could explain it. But no one bothered to try. It was what primitive man would have called a gift of the gods.

Ted's secret theory was that the UFO somehow connected up to ley lines, and might have used the electromagnetic energy of the earth for fuel. But, with the craft and the cylinder gone, there would be no way he could begin to prove it.

Ted and Cathy were married in March, and Anne Seward finally got her grandchild, the one that she was sure that Cathy would never have.

It was a beautiful dawn, and the view of the sea was magnificent from the hotel balcony. Ted rose quietly and went to the balcony. The pale yellow sun was slicing through clouds that were touched with gold and crimson. He stood, nude, watching it and feeling the cool breeze on his chest.

Behind him, Cathy stirred.

"Ted?" Her voice was sleepy.

"Hmmm?"

"You're being an exhibitionist, love."

Ted stepped back from the balcony. He'd totally forgotten that he was nude. He turned to her and slipped back into bed. He propped himself on an elbow and looked down at her. "See what you do to me? When I'm around you, I forget where I am and whether I'm dressed or not."

She reached up and kissed him. After a few seconds, she pulled away.

"You know? I've been thinking. We signed those papers that said we'd never say or write anything about what happened at the hangar. Right?"

Ted nodded.

"But it's such a fantastic story—it would make a wonderful novel. You could write it—"

Ted reached down and put a hand over her mouth.

PLAYBOY PRESS
PAPERBACKS
SCIENCE FICTION

A SUPERB SELECTION
OF THE BEST IN
SCIENCE FICTION
FOR YOUR READING PLEASURE